D0168053

MAGNETO™
THE CHAOS ENGINE
BOOK 2

Author STEVEN A. ROMAN made his professional writing debut in 1993 with the publication of his comic book horror series *Lorelei*. Outside the comics industry, Roman was a contributor to the prose anthologies *Untold Tales of Spider-Man* and *The Ultimate Hulk*, and was the editor of the ibooks, inc. novels *Heavy Metal: F.A.K.K.²*, *Moebius' Arzach*, *The Alien Factor* (by X-Men co-creator Stan Lee), and, yes, even *Britney Spears is a Three-Headed Alien*. Currently, he's working on Book 3 of *The Chaos Engine*, planning a summer 2002 re-launch of *Lorelei*, and scripting *Anteca*, a techno/horror series created by artist Juda Tverski. He lives in Queens, New York.

Illustrator MARK BUCKINGHAM is presently the artist on Marvel's *Peter Parker: Spider-Man*. Before that, in the years since he became a comic book artist, he juggled his time among DC Comics' *Titans* and almost every book in the Vertigo line, and Marvel's *Dr. Strange*, *Amazing Spider-Man*, *Star Trek Unlimited*, and *Generation X*. He is also renowned for his experimental artwork for Eclipse Comics' *Miracleman*. "Bucky," as he is often known, is honorary chairman of the Comic Creators Guild, and co-organizer of the United Kingdom's National Comics Awards. He lives with his wife, Gail, and three cats in the Victorian seaside town of Clevedon, England.

X-MEN®

MAGNETO™

THE CHAOS ENGINE

BOOK 2

STEVEN A. ROMAN

ILLUSTRATIONS BY MARK BUCKINGHAM

BP BOOKS, INC.

DISTRIBUTED BY SIMON & SCHUSTER, INC

An Original Publication of BP Books, Inc.

A BP Books, Inc. Book

Distributed by Simon & Schuster, Inc.
1230 Avenue of the Americas, New York, NY 10020

BP Books, Inc.
24 West 25th Street
New York, NY 10010

The ibooks World Wide Web Site Address is:
http://www.ibooksinc.com

ISBN 0-7434-0023-2
First ibooks, inc. printing January 2002
10 9 8 7 6 5 4 3 2 1

Edited by Dwight Jon Zimmerman

Special thanks to Chris Claremont
and Bobbie Chase for their editorial assistance

Cover art by Bob Larkin
Cover design by Mike Rivilis

Printed in the U.S.A.

For
Patrick J. Moylan and Dr. James "Doc" Collins
two high school English teachers
who showed me the magic of the printed word

A NOTE FROM THE AUTHOR

Given the time that's elapsed between the publication of the first trade paperback edition of *X-Men/Doctor Doom: The Chaos Engine, Book 1* and this volume, and the major changes that the X-Men have undergone in their comic book titles during the past year, it should be noted that this story arc takes place between the events of *X-Men* #99 and #100.

Your comments about *X-Men/Magneto: The Chaos Engine*, Book 2 are welcomed. Please contact author Steven A. Roman at starwarpco@aol.com

MAGNETO™

THE CHAOS ENGINE

BOOK 2

No man chooses evil because it is evil; he only mistakes it for happiness, the good he seeks.

Mary Wollstonecraft Godwin
A Vindication on the Rights of Man

Flashback

"WHAT I wouldn't give fer a cold beer right about now."

Teetering on unsteady legs, the man known only as "Logan"—though what few friends he possessed more often referred to him by the colorful codename "Wolverine"—licked his dry lips, the metallic taste of fresh blood mingling with salt-tinged sweat on his tongue. Exhaling sharply, he drew himself up to his full height of 5' 3" and gazed around the battlefield on which he stood.

The grounds of Washington, D.C.'s John F. Kennedy Center for the Performing Arts had definitely seen better days—but, then again, so had the building itself, even before it had been renamed to honor the tyrant currently residing in the White House. The formerly gleaming marble façade was now pitted and blackened by heavy weapons' fire and a variety of powerful forcebeam projectors. The south wall lay in a crumbled heap, the unfortunate recipient of angry blows delivered by the fists of a woman named Rogue—a teammate of his—as she created an escape route for the patrons of the arts who had gathered at the Center this evening. As Logan watched now, a dozen or so opulently-dressed people streamed through the hole, running in a blind panic to escape the war zone behind them, apparently unaware that the path of their

I

flight was taking them through yet another. The sounds of gun-shots and energy bolts echoed inside the building as armed guards rushed to protect the so-called "Emperor of the World" from a band of super-powered revolutionaries led by a charismatic man named Erik Magnus Lensherr—or, as he was more widely known, Magneto, Master of Magnetism. A man who had dedicated himself to one goal: the subjugation of mankind by him and others of his kind—the species *Homo sapiens superior*. Genetically-gifted indi-viduals whose unique abilities made them both admired and feared by a world that still found it difficult to accept them.

"Mutants," as they had become known to the general public.

Like Lensherr.

Like Logan.

The fact that Logan had been forced to help this revolution in order to stop a greater evil, to give aid to someone he regarded as a bitter enemy, left a knot in his belly. But he knew he'd learn to live with it, as he had come to grudgingly accept a great many other unpleasant moments he'd been part of over the years.

Near Logan, on what had once been a well-manicured lawn that faced the Potomac River, were the unconscious bodies of a trio of lower-tier costumed villains named The White Rabbit (a blond-haired woman dressed like the character in *Alice in Wonder-land*), Diablo (a rail-thin sorcerer with a glass jaw), and Deadly Nightshade (a bikini-clad refugee from a "blaxploitation" film fes-tival). Arriving first on the scene, they had made the mistake of trying to stop Logan and his fellow revolutionaries when the attack began, rather than withdrawing and sparing themselves the pain-ful beating that had left them scattered about like tenpins.

His attention was drawn to the far side of the lawn, to the man who had led the trio, before breaking away to directly confront the scrappy Canadian intruder. A man Logan knew all too well . . . and hated with every fiber of his being.

At 6' 6", Victor Creed—a bloodthirsty, mutant sociopath who preferred going by the name Sabretooth—stood more than a foot taller than Logan, and outweighed him by at least one hundred pounds. Under normal circumstances, this sort of match-up would have appeared decidedly one-sided, with the bear-like Sabretooth having the advantage over his smaller enemy. And that didn't even take into account his metal-encased skeleton, coated with adamantium, the strongest man-made metal on the planet, or an accelerated healing factor that allowed him to recover quickly from any kind of wound he might suffer.

Or the two dozen well-armed men and women who comprised part of the Emperor's worldwide security force, their rifles and energy weapons all aimed at the smaller man.

But Logan had advantages of his own, not the least of which were the half-dozen, foot-long adamantium spikes that protruded from the backs of his hands, just above the knuckles. And, like his adversary, Logan possessed a metal-hardened skeleton and a special healing factor that restored him to full health, even after receiving potentially fatal injuries. Combined with an all-consuming anger, Logan could be an unstoppable engine of destruction once he started handing out punishment to his enemies . . . as those few lucky enough to have survived an encounter with him could attest to.

Unfortunately for Logan, Sabretooth was one of those fortunate handful, despite the diminutive Canadian's best efforts to rectify that problem over the decades. Today's confrontation would be the latest round in their on-going battle . . . at least in theory.

What made this particular life-and-death struggle so unusual was that, although the snarling, blond-haired, orange-and-brown-garbed figure before him was clearly Sabretooth, it wasn't the *real* one . . . or, at least, not the one Logan knew so well. This was a doppleganger, an alternate version of his oldest foe, one who seemed unaware of their long-standing feud; either that, or Sabretooth—and the rest of the world, apparently—had been brainwashed to a degree Logan couldn't even begin to fathom.

A crazy idea, perhaps, but when one considered that an honest-to-God madman had apparently done exactly that, it didn't seem quite so bizarre a notion. . . .

* * *

Less than a week had passed since Wolverine and his fellow X-Men—a group of superpowered men and women dedicated to protecting the world from all manner of threats, including those posed by mutants like themselves—had returned from a mission beyond the boundaries of Time and Space, to discover that Earth had fallen under the rule of a man named Victor von Doom—or "Doctor Doom," as he had started calling himself years ago, when he first began trying to take control of the planet.

The self-proclaimed monarch of a small central European country called Latveria, von Doom had long been a proverbial thorn in humanity's side, his attempts at world domination often resulting in dozens, if not hundreds, of lives lost and billions of dollars in property damage. And yet, no matter how grand his schemes, no matter how momentarily successful he might be, von Doom always lost in the end. Whether it was at the hands of the X-Men, or one of the other super hero groups that called the New York area their home, Doctor Doom had never had a clear victory over his enemies.

But those days were past, it now appeared. In the period of just a single month—the time in which the X-Men had been fighting in a parallel dimension to put an end to the dictatorial rule of a woman named Opul Lun Sat-yr-nin—von Doom had somehow, in some way, finally succeeded in doing what no other power-hungry villain had ever been able to do: create a world-spanning empire, and make every man, woman, and child—both human and mutant—his willing subjects.

That included some of the people who had been important parts of Logan's life, like Carol Danvers, one of his oldest friends, who had worked with him in the Intelligence community. She had died recently, when von Doom's forces had captured the X-Men for questioning. Logan had been unable to do anything to save her, and the guilt he felt for failing her still gnawed at his soul. And then there was Ororo Munroe, the weather-controlling mutant called Storm. Before the nefarious Doctor had seized control, she had been a member of the X-Men; now, she was Empress of the realm, von Doom's devoted wife.

Given the opportunity, Logan would have relished the chance to teach von Doom the price for messing with the people closest to him. And yet, he knew there were more important issues to address. There was still the matter of discovering how von Doom had managed to take control of the planet, and then finding a way to reverse the process. Taking a piece of the "Emperor's" hide would have to wait until things were back to normal.

But that was all right. The time for retribution would come—Logan was certain of it. And he could be a patient man ... when he wanted. Until the opportunity presented itself, though, he was more than willing to take out his anger for von Doom on whoever was handy ...

"Ready to give up, runt?" Sabretooth asked. He smiled, revealing twin rows of sharpened teeth that gleamed like miniature daggers in the glow of the security floodlights under which he stood. "Ya look a little run-down."

It was true, though Logan would be the last to admit it, especially in front of an adversary. Experience had taught him long ago that showing any weakness in a fight could be fatal. He was bruised and bloodied—even a mutant healing factor took time to work—and the yellow-and-blue costume he'd been wearing had been reduced to tatters that flapped and twisted in the light breeze coming off the Potomac.

"What's wrong, Creed?" he shot back. "You gettin' tired already?"

"Yeah. Tired of kickin' yer sorry butt," Sabretooth replied. "My foot's gettin' sore."

Logan clenched his fists, and raised his lance-like claws. "Got a cure fer that right here, bub." He smiled, though there was no warmth in it. "Might sting a bit."

Above the battlefield thunder rumbled, and black stormclouds began to take form, obscuring a night sky that only moments before had been filled with stars. The light breeze that had been drifting across the area now became a stiff wind.

Must be Ororo's doin', Logan thought, feeling the hair on his arms and chest tingle with the static electricity that was building in the air. *Gonna be a pretty big blow, too.*

He snapped his head to one side, flinging away drops of sweat that had obscured his vision, then turned back to glare at Sabretooth. The wild-maned killer had eased into a combat-ready stance, but hadn't moved from his original position.

"Well, punk?" Logan bellowed. "Whattaya waitin' for?"

"Just fer you t'say the magic words, runt," Creed answered.

Logan slid his claws against one another, creating a sound not unlike that of fingernails being drawn across a blackboard. The security guards moaned loudly, hands pressed to their ears, trying to block the sound. It didn't appear to work.

"Come get some," Logan growled through clenched teeth.

"Those're the ones!" Sabretooth hissed. Then he charged.

Logan slipped on a patch of his own blood as Sabretooth rushed to meet his challenge. Sparks flew as metal-coated bio-weapons clashed.

"That the best you got?" Wolverine hissed, ignoring the pain that ripped through his body after the animalistic sociopath had raked his claws across Logan's abdomen.

"*Wait* for it, runt," Sabretooth growled. "It gets *better.*"

And then, with an ear-to-ear grin splitting his haggard face, he unexpectedly broke off the attack and jumped back.

Before Wolverine could go on the offensive—or even question his foe's motives for a sudden withdrawal—a fusillade of armor-piercing bullets tore into his back, his neck, his legs. Sabretooth's military support, it appeared, had finally decided to join in.

The rounds rattled around inside him, glancing off the super-strong metal that protected his bones—but not his organs. Logan staggered about in blinding pain, unable to see, unable to stand.

Then something slammed into his chest—hard. He couldn't

breathe, couldn't speak. Blood spurted from his wounds, coating his eyes, filling his mouth.

Blinking his eyes rapidly, wiping the heels of his hands across his face to wipe away the arterial spray, Logan finally succeeded in clearing his vision—just in time for him to see Sabretooth plunge adamantium-tipped claws into his chest. Sharpened metal raked across his heart.

Logan howled.

"What's the problem, midget?" the wild-maned sociopath asked as his victim thrashed about, unable to pull free. "Need t'get somethin' off yer chest?" He grinned. "Well, spit it out—I'm all ears."

And that's when the transformation happened.

There had always been a darker side to Wolverine—a savage, bestial part that he always fought to control; often winning the battle, but sometimes giving into it wholeheartedly. In Norse legends, it's referred to as a "berserker rage": a situation when a Teutonic warrior, inspired by the god Odin, momentarily lost his sanity in the heat of battle and gave into an unquenchable desire for bloodshed, for destruction. Possessed by such drive, the warrior would feel no fear or pain. Logan was all too familiar with the sensation—it was what gave him the advantage in a fight, and made him so deadly an opponent to his enemies . . . and sometimes even his friends.

"His friends." Even now, Logan still found it hard to believe that he could regard *anyone* as a friend, let alone a group of do-gooding men and women like the X-Men. And yet, it was among the X-Men that he had at last found acceptance—of his mutant powers, of his acid-tinged personality, of his savage nature. If not for people like the X-Men's leader, Professor Charles Xavier, Logan might have given into the darker, bestial urgings that made him so dangerous. But with the help of Xavier and his students—especially Jean Grey, the redheaded beauty who had once stolen his heart—he had been able to rediscover the man who still existed within the hard-edged warrior. To face the monsters that lurked in his psyche, and defeat them. To avoid taking that last, fatal step into the depths of madness.

But now, he gave into the madness, even welcomed it.

With a roar that took even Sabretooth by surprise, Logan raised his arms and swept them in front of his body, raking his claws across Creed's face and throat. Sabretooth cried out in pain and staggered back, loosening his grip on Wolverine, who dropped to the ground and immediately rolled to his feet. Logan sprang forward, giving his opponent no time to recover. He slashed back and forth, time and again, at Creed, cutting deep swatches from his legs, arms, and body, then reopening the wounds when the larger man's healing factor started closing them. There was no logic to the assault, no plan of attack considered—this was simply a case of a smaller animal trying to bring down a larger one.

Around them, the security force froze, as though uncertain of what to do now. Some members looked on in horror, some in admiration of the two opponents, while others, sickened by the savageness of the battle, moved away to disgorge whatever meal they'd had earlier in the evening. A few turned and ran, joining the throngs of attendees who were fleeing the area.

Wolverine continued pressing forward, claws moving so swiftly that they only registered as a flash of white to the naked eye before striking their targets. Sabretooth tried to fight back, but it appeared that the severity of the pain he had experienced at the outset of the attack, coupled with the surprise he'd shown when his victim had somehow summoned the strength to continue fighting, had cost him any chance of duplicating the smaller man's mindless rage. The best he could hope to do was put some distance between himself and Wolverine, and allow his body a few moments to heal before starting the next round.

But then Creed stumbled over the prone form of the White Rabbit, lost his balance, and fell to the ground.

It would prove to be the deciding factor in this struggle.

With a triumphant roar, Wolverine pounced, landing on Creed's chest as the larger mutant started to regain his feet, driving him back down onto the neatly-trimmed grass. Adamantium-sheathed claws flashed in the moonlight, then swept downward, slicing across Sabretooth's throat—one of the few areas on Creed's body not protected by metal-encased bones. A geyser of blood erupted from the carotid artery and jugular veins, coating Wolverine's arms and face, coloring his gleaming metal bio-weapons a deep crimson.

The fatal blow had been delivered—one that not even an advanced healing factor could repair in time to save Creed, considering it had already been overtaxed by Wolverine's continuous assault.

Stepping back from his prey, Wolverine cracked a malicious smile and licked the blood from his lips, savoring the taste of the kill.

And as Sabretooth watched his life pour out onto the ground, Wolverine raised his head ... and howled in victory.

It was a bloodchilling sound that made the remaining soldiers gathered around the combatants turn on their heels and start racing after their teammates.

Then the storm broke, and rain began to fall.

It came down hard, big drops that fell like miniature missiles to impact on Logan's skin; in less than a minute he was soaked, the blood of his kill washed away to pool at his feet before being absorbed by the thirsty grass. Slowly, a genuine smile came to his lips, and Logan closed his eyes, then sheathed his claws; the bio-weapons slid back under the skin of his forearms with a gentle *snikt*. He tilted his head back, allowing the water to douse the fire that burned in his soul, to ease the tension that had knotted his muscles.

To calm the beast, and return it to the cage from which he had released it, deep in the recesses of his mind.

He inhaled deeply, momentarily reveling in the tangy scent of the air—the mixture of a storm-tossed sky laced with ozone as lightning flashed high above, and the sweet, cloying odor of damp earth as the water worked its way into the ground. But then the stench of death filled his nostrils, a reminder of the carnage around him, and he opened his eyes.

Sabretooth still lay at his feet, lifeless eyes staring at the blackened sky. Raindrops splattered against the widened pupils, then streamed down the sides of his face to collect on the grass under his head.

Logan grunted, still not quite ready to believe Creed was dead, but the evidence was right there in front of him. But it was a hollow victory for the feral X-Man—this wasn't *his* Creed, his lifelong enemy, no matter how much he had sounded, and acted, and smelled like the genuine article. This was just some poseur dreamed up by Doctor Doom.

Or was it?

Logan shrugged. He was too tired to figure it out, too angry to really give a damn. All he wanted to do right now was get his hands on von Doom and force him to put things right. After that, he'd down a few beers and contemplate his victory over Sabretooth; maybe he'd even like the answer he finally came up with when he was done.

The sounds of the battle between von Doom's troops and Magneto's forces were beginning to diminish, the echoes of weapons' fire replaced by the moaning of the injured and dying, and the wailing of survivors for those lost in the fight. Logan glanced through the hole in the south wall of the Performing Arts Center and sniffed the air, but could detect none of the scents that would tell him whether Magneto or any of the X-Men were still inside the building.

They'd moved on, then, probably in pursuit of von Doom.

Logan jogged around to the front of the Center. Out on New Hampshire Avenue, fires were burning, created by limousines and troop transports that had exploded. Emergency vehicles were just arriving on the scene. Firemen moved quickly to control the blazes, while paramedics saw to the injuries of soldiers and policemen— and the dozens of innocent bystanders caught in the middle of the war zone. He pushed his way past the few humans and mutants still clashing in front of the arts center's main entrance, and made his way to the street, then paused to sniff the air.

"Where the flamin' hell did everybody go?" he wondered aloud.

And then an all-too-familiar scent filled his nostrils. A particular mix of pheromones and perfume—Wings—that could belong to only one person.

"Jeanie," Logan muttered.

Ignoring his still-healing injuries, he set off at a full run, heading toward Constitution Avenue to the east and, further along it, the White House.

The Present

SO THIS *is how the world ends,* thought Betsy Braddock. *Not from nuclear warfare, or an asteroid strike, or even from a world-devourer like Galactus dropping by because he felt a bit peckish—but from a* wish. *A simple wish, and a scientific Aladdin's lamp to make it come true . . .*

The Earth was literally coming apart at the seams—or at least that was how it appeared to the lavender-tressed telepath who was usually known in super heroic circles by the more colorful code-name "Psylocke." Dressed in a glamorous, black evening gown and opera gloves that had never been designed for combat conditions, she was standing in a sub-chamber of the White House, amid the rubble created during a clash between opposing bands of super-powered mutants—one, a group of villainous renegades called the Acolytes; the other, the heroic X-Men, to which Betsy belonged. Nearby lay the unmoving bodies of her teammates: Cyclops, Phoenix, Rogue, and Nightcrawler, all rendered unconscious by their enemies before they had a chance to defend themselves. On the far side of the chamber, the only other conscious X-Man—the always deadly Wolverine, who had arrived only moments ago—was engaged in battle with the green-garbed speedster called Quicksilver. Moving almost too fast for the eye to follow, the swift-footed mutant easily evaded Wolverine's claws as they sliced through the air near his chest. It was clear to Betsy—and, more than likely, to Quicksilver as well—that the feral Canadian scrapper was doing his best to gut his enemy and bring a decisive end to their fight.

Momentarily transfixed by the savage ballet that was being performed in front of her, Betsy shook her head to clear her thoughts. What was she doing, just standing around while her friends had fallen around her?

She turned from the conflict, her attention brought back to the blindingly brilliant wall of light that had suddenly formed in the center of the room. Beyond that wall, she knew, was the device responsible for the madness unfolding around her. A device that—though small in size—contained enough power to transform an entire planet and its population into anything its owner desired. A device that, she had learned only a short time ago, threatened to tear asunder not only the Earth, not just the dimensional plane in which the world existed, but the length and breadth of the omniverse—an infinite number of parallel realities, each stacked one upon the other, separated by only the thinnest of celestial energy curtains.

A device called the Cosmic Cube.

But the Cube was not a living entity capable of restructuring reality on its own . . . at least, not to Betsy's knowledge. Rather, it was a tool whose energies were directed by whoever happened to be holding it. A paintbrush in the hands of an artist, as it were, if such an artist possessed the sort of vision and creative dedication needed to transform a simple canvas into an awe-inspiring masterpiece.

Of course, the quality of the final product would depend on who the artist was, and what their perceptions of beauty might be . . .

At the moment, that particular artist was a man known more for his acts of terrorism than his appreciation for the fine arts. A man who, like Betsy, was gifted with extraordinary powers, but whose all-consuming goal in life was nothing less than the total subjugation of humanity at the hands of mutantkind. A man by the name of Erik Magnus Lensherr, who, more often than not, preferred being addressed by his far more impressive—and fear-inducing—codename: Magneto. The self-proclaimed "Master of Magnetism."

Just moments before, Betsy and her fellow X-Men had failed to stop Lensherr from taking possession of the Cube; failed in their mission to put an end to the threat posed by the device before it resulted in the destruction of all realities.

And now the entire world was going to pay the price for their mistakes.

The energy wall surged forward, consuming everything in its path as it flowed across the chamber. Betsy could only stare help-lessly as each of her friends were taken, absorbed by the power of the Cube to be reshaped, recreated, by whatever dark urges lurked within the mind of Erik Lensherr, driving him ever onward to at-tain his perverted dream of world domination.

Though it was difficult to see him clearly through the cosmically-charged barrier, Betsy could just make out the distinc-tive form of Magneto as he sat upon an elaborate throne, his hands wrapped around the Cube.

The throne, however, was not a construct of Lensherr's mind, but of the mind of another power-hungry villain—the infamous Victor von Doom, dictator of the small European nation of Lat-veria, and the bane of almost every hero and heroine on the planet. It was his twisted genius that had created this latest version of the Cube, his mad desire to rule the world that had provided the Cube with the raw psychic material it required to fashion a suitable approximation of von Doom's dream. Unfortunately for the super-villain-cum-Emperor, creating such a world had come at a terrible cost . . .

The wave moved closer. Betsy took a step back—knowing such a reaction was pointless, since there was nowhere on Earth she could go to escape the chaos forces bearing down on her—and gasped as a gauntleted hand closed around her ankle. She looked down to find von Doom staring back at her.

He was a disturbing sight to behold, this man who had, only a short time ago, held the power of a god in his hands. His body was withering away inside the gleaming, silver-hued battle armor that was obviously keeping him alive. The degree of physical decay he was suffering was plain to see just by looking at his face—the skin was wrinkled, waxy, and paper-thin; blue-tinged veins pulsed frantically, just below the surface. The villain had been aged at an alarming rate by the Cube, drained of his life-force by the device in order to maintain the reality he had created—a "perfect" world in which von Doom had defeated every one of his enemies, and taken Betsy's fellow X-Man, Storm, as his bride. For a time, his plan had worked: for the past ten years (or so it had seemed to Betsy, and everyone else in the world) he had reigned supreme as Emperor, his long sought-after dream at last made reality by a device no bigger than a Jack-in-the-Box.

The dream, however, had come to an abrupt end when the X-Men had returned from a mission in another dimension and set out to put things right. At least, they had *tried* to put things right, and would have, if not for the untimely intervention of Magneto and his followers.

As she gazed down at von Doom, it was immediately clear to Betsy, just by watching how he labored for every breath, how he struggled to raise himself up on one elbow, that the strain placed on his body by the Cube—not to mention the abuse he had suffered at the hands of Magneto when the mutant overlord forcibly took possession of the device—was too much for the man once known as "Doctor Doom"; he was almost at death's door. But in spite of his failing health, the anger, the sheer hatred he obviously felt toward those who had robbed him of his victory seemed to give him strength. Tightening his grip on her ankle, he glared up at the Asian telepath.

"Doom never concedes defeat, girl," the prematurely old man said, eyes burning with rage. "Not while he still has one last hand to play." He pressed a hidden stud on his armor's chestplate.

The air around the villain and Betsy crackled with electricity. Her nostrils filled with the smell of burning ozone, and her skin began tingling as a powerful current ran through her.

A transportation device? she thought with some surprise. *But where could Doom be taking us? And why* me?

Before she had a chance to voice those questions, however, the room and everything in it—her colleagues, her enemies, the Cosmic Cube itself—faded into darkness.

And then, her ankle still held fast in von Doom's grip, Betsy was yanked into infinity.

1

SUPREME GUARDIAN, we *must* destroy the crystal!"

Sitting on her throne in the highest level of the Starlight Citadel—a city-sized collection of soaring metal towers and minarets that floated at the exact center of all Time and Space—Roma, the Supreme Guardian of the Omniverse, closed her eyes and tried to ignore the impassioned—and increasingly loud—pleas of her lieutenant, Opul Luna Saturnyne.

She wasn't having much luck.

"*Enough,* Saturnyne," she finally said, fatigue evident in her voice. "Your point has been made—emphatically so."

"I apologize, Supreme Guardian," replied Saturnyne, speaking at a more tolerable volume. "I don't mean to belabor the obvious, but under the circumstances . . . "

Letting her voice trail off, the white-haired, white-gowned woman gestured across the throne room toward a large crystalline globe that floated a foot above the highly polished marble floor. This was a scrying glass—a device Roma used to monitor the countless dimensions that fell under her protection. At the moment, the glass was dark, but not because it had been deactivated; quite the opposite, in fact. Humming softly, the cosmic viewer had been running nonstop for the past ninety-six hours (Earth time), tuned to events on the dimensional plane numerically designated as "616" by Roma's father, Merlyn, the former Supreme Guardian who had created the citadel millennia ago.

Unfortunately, there was nothing to see. For reasons unknown to either Roma or Saturnyne, something was preventing them from gazing upon the dimension that was home to an unusually high number of superpowered beings. Men and women like the members of the uncanny X-Men had spent the past month aiding the Supreme Guardian end the reign of terror perpetrated on the inhabitants of Earth 794 by the mad dictator Opul Lun Sat-yr-nin, an alternate reality version of Roma's second-in-command. The very same group of heroic mutants who had unhesitatingly volunteered to return to their home dimension in order to learn the source of the interference.

But it wasn't just the poor reception on her scrying glass that troubled Roma. There was the crystal, too.

Twelve inches high, six inches wide, it should have looked like an ordinary sliver of quartz—one among hundreds of similar pieces that jutted up from a podium-like structure that stood near Roma's throne—and normally would have, were it not for the disturbing imperfection that had formed just below its surface only days ago: a black spot that continued to grow with each passing hour.

A black spot that only hinted at the chaos that had been unleashed upon the inhabitants of Dimension 616.

There was nothing ordinary about *any* of the other crystals, for that matter. Each contained the life-force of an entire dimension—a creation of Merlyn's father, back when the omniverse was still young. Why her grandfather had done this Roma had never been able to discover; his son, Merlyn, liked to have his secrets, and there were some—far too many, in her opinion—that the technomage refused to pass on to his daughter, even after he had turned his duties over to her. And yet, despite Merlyn's always infuriating silences about his reality-affecting schemes, it hadn't taken long—a century at most—for Roma to truly understand the power contained within the crystals . . . and what might happen if one were broken.

Such a tragedy had only happened twice in her lifetime, and both occasions were set in motion by unforeseen circumstances. The first came about when her father had made a poorly chosen move in "The Game," the cosmic chess match Merlyn often played when he was in the mood to manipulate the lives of mortals. Sometimes, Roma was his opposing player; more often than not, he chose to play alone, as he did so in that particular instance, when Merlyn had focused his attentions on the Skrull Empire of Dimension 4872. As with most of their counterparts in other continuums, the Skrulls were a warlike race, constantly expanding the boundaries of their territory by conquering other worlds and enslaving their inhabitants. *Unlike* their counterparts, though, these Skrulls were more highly developed on an intellectual level, their scientists working round-the-clock on the development of new and more powerful munitions that would aid the war effort.

One of these weapons was called the World Ripper.

Not a terribly original name for a weapon of mass destruction—in any dimension, the reptilian Skrulls had never been known for possessing a flair for the dramatic—but it was an accurate name, nonetheless . . . if it worked according to specifications. Truth be told, the scientists hadn't been certain the device would ever work, since testing it would have required tapping into the Skrull homeworld's molten core; a successful activation of the Ripper would have essentially turned the core into the most powerful bomb ever created and atomized the planet. Nevertheless, the technicians completed their work on the weapon, silently praying to S'lgurt, their god of war, that they would never have to learn first-hand if they'd done their work properly.

But then Merlyn moved one of his pawns—a green-and-white-garbed warrior named Mar-Vell, who belonged to the race called the Kree, the Skrulls' oldest enemy—further across the game board, influencing the alien captain's decision to infiltrate the research and development laboratories where the World Ripper was housed. A battle between the Kree soldier and a Skrull battalion soon erupted. So heated was the exchange of blaster fire that no one—not even Merlyn—was aware of the weapon's activation by a stray bolt that hit its firing mechanism . . . until it was too late.

The resulting explosion not only shredded the Skrull home-world, but the force of the blast tore apart the protective barrier separating Dimension 4872 from its neighboring realities. A ragged hole was created in time and space, causing the formation of a vacuum that began to suck in large sections of Dimensions 4871 and 4873, thus destabilizing their barriers, as well.

All too aware that this collapse of realities might become an unstoppable domino effect that would ultimately destroy the omniverse, Merlyn wordlessly removed the crystal containing 4872's life-force from the podium—then smashed it on the floor.

And somewhere within the depths of time and space, a continuum died.

Billions of sentient creatures were wiped from existence within the space of a heartbeat. Merlyn spent the next two decades in a state of depression so deep it seemed as though he might never recover. Yet recover he did, and was soon hard at work on his next plot, acting as though nothing had happened. Watching her father return to his old form, Roma was never certain if his ennui had been caused by the realization that he had just destroyed an entire dimensional plane . . . or because he never got to see his intended plan—whatever that might have been—come to fruition.

The second catastrophe took place shortly before Roma became Supreme Guardian, when events on the Earth of Dimension 238 had gone horribly wrong. Surprisingly enough, Merlyn was not the cause of the trouble . . . this time. His attentions were focused elsewhere.

As Omniversal Majestrix, Saturnyne had been—and still was, to this day—the one to maintain order throughout all dimensional planes, answering only to her superior; in this instance, Merlyn.

Traveling to Earth 238, she was assigned the task of helping the planet reach its evolutionary potential—to give the inhabitants of this world "The Push."

A less than awe-inspiring title, this Push—one would almost believe the Skrulls had a hand in assigning it its name—and yet, the procedure itself could affect entire populations. It was rarely used, though, since a Push carried out incorrectly might cause the inhabitants to go mad from the strain of having their consciousnesses expanded so rapidly. Nonetheless, there *had* been times when forcing a world to "grow up" virtually overnight became necessary for the good of the omniverse.

And so it was with Earth 238.

The "Earth series""—as the multitude of similar-yet-different planets became known—had always been Merlyn's pride and joy, for the people of these alternate realities had always shown great promise as they constantly strove to attain enlightenment and peace. His 50,000-year program for the omniverse—the details of which had never been given to Roma—depended on all variations of the Earth achieving this goal by the year 2000, and almost all had managed to make significant headway along this path . . . with the exception of 238. It was the most primitive version of all the planets, with its focus on greed and war, its repression of basic human rights, and blatant misuses of power. With such a staggering amount of negative energy flowing through that dimension, the progress of the other Earths was being retarded. The master plan was in jeopardy of failing.

But Merlyn had a solution: Saturnyne and her team would go to 238 and pour drumfuls of a special life-enhancing fluid into the drinking water. When the populace sat down in the morning for their first cup of coffee, first glass of water, first bottle of formula, every man, woman, and child in this nation would automatically leap up a few rungs on the evolutionary ladder. Within a year, the DDC would have done the same with every other city around the world, and 238 would have at last been able to join its counterparts at the dawn of a new Golden Age.

Unfortunately, it hadn't taken long for matters to spiral out of control, almost from the outset.

It all started with a man named Jim Jaspers—Sir James Jaspers, to be precise. A member of Parliament, a man of great influence, a powerful, psycho-kinetic mutant . . . and a lunatic. It was he who initially turned the world against its super hero population. Earth 238 was his plaything, and he didn't care much for people who tried to spoil his fun.

Yet even with all the troubles caused by Jaspers, the DDC partly succeeded in their goal. Earth 238 was on its way to enlightenment.

And then Jaspers pulled the plug on the operation by using his powers to turn the world inside-out.

It was called a reality storm. As Saturnyne looked on in horror, the laws of physics were rewritten around them. Men burst into flame. Women turned into pillars of salt. Children melted into puddles of goo. Gravity ceased to function. The streets and buildings of London twisted into the sort of landscape one usually found in a Salvador Dali painting. And within the calm eye of the storm sat "Mad Jim" himself, calmly watching his universe tear itself apart.

It was all too much for Saturnyne. Gathering her few remaining colleagues around her, she ordered the Avant Guard to teleport them all back to the Starlight Citadel.

Arriving at the citadel, Saturnyne was immediately placed under arrest by the Supreme Omniversal Tribunal. The Majestrix was charged with negligence on a cosmic scale: the Tribunal insisted that she had been the cause of the trouble; that, under her command, The Push had gone wrong, and her only (cowardly) solution had been to cut her losses and escape before Earth 238 came apart at the seams.

It was a short trial, to be truthful—Saturnyne never had a chance to mount a proper defense. It took but a moment for her enemies to come to a decision about the fate of Earth 238.

With the simple turn of a crystal key, the dimension was eliminated, and whether the Tribunal's judgment was brought about by a deep-rooted sense of duty to protect the other continuums before the "reality-cancer" spread, or simply to destroy any evidence that might have aided in Saturnyne's acquittal, was never made clear. Not that it mattered in the end—the inhabitants of 238 were still very much dead . . .

And now, as she gazed at the darkened scrying glass, Roma knew she was faced with the possibility of having to condemn yet another reality to extinction. The difference this time was that her final decision would shatter the lives of people she knew personally—mortals, true, but ones unlike the majority of the beings on their world. Hated by most, misunderstood by all, feared because of their incredible abilities, the X-Men had never shirked responsibility, never refused to come to the aid of even those who so often sought to destroy them. Mortal they might be, but they possessed the kind of spiritual dedication to a dream of universal peace that was normally only found in more highly developed races. Even a celestial being like Roma could not help but admire their resolve, given the magnitude of the dangers they faced every day. To destroy such enlightened creatures was unthinkable . . . at least in her opinion.

For the first time since becoming Supreme Guardian, Roma wished that someone else would have to pass judgment on the inhabitants of Dimension 616.

"I, too, hope you will not be forced to make a decision you will come to regret, Your Majesty," said a deep male voice.

Roma started, her pale green eyes snapping open. Looking up, her gaze settled on a man seated a few feet in front of her. It was difficult to determine his age, since his head was completely bare, but there was a distinguished air about him that made him seem far older than his years—although, to an immortal like Roma, he was more like a child when measured against her own age, which could be counted in centuries. His expression as dark as the conservative business suit he wore, the telepathic mutant called

Professor Charles Xavier, leader of the X-Men, sat—back ramrod-straight, hands folded across his lap—in the antigravity unit-propelled device in which he traveled: a hi-tech version of the sort of wheelchair to which he had been confined since losing the use of his legs, many years ago.

"I assure you, Your Majesty," Xavier continued, "although the outlook seems bleak at the moment, my X-Men will yet prevail."

Roma frowned. "I do not appreciate prying minds, Charles Xavier. My thoughts are my own, to be shared with no one else."

"I understand your anger, Your Majesty," Xavier replied politely, "but I would *never* presume to scan your thoughts without permission. However, in point of fact, you were broadcasting your concerns with such intensity that I could not *help* but detect them."

"I . . . see." Roma's lips twisted into a brief half-smile as she brushed aside a strand of dark hair that had settled across her high forehead. "Then, in the future, I shall endeavor to 'keep my thoughts to myself,' as you humans say." The smile quickly faded. "I admire the resolve you show for your students, Charles Xavier, but even you must admit that they have failed in their mission. In truth, they have exacerbated the situation through their attempted—though well-intentioned—intervention." She gestured toward the scrying glass. "You have seen the evidence for yourself: Not only were they unsuccessful in reversing the effects of the anomaly created on Earth 616, but your world has undergone yet *another* change, further weakening that universe's dimensional barriers." She turned to face him, eyes full of life but devoid of emotion. "My father toyed with the fates and futures of worlds and peoples. Thousands of realities. Billions upon countless billions of sentient beings . . ." Her voice trailed off. "I played his games because he compelled me to do so . . . but the gameplay must now come at an end."

Slowly, Roma shook her head. "I am sorry, Charles Xavier—not just for you, or your students, or even the people of your world, but for the untold billions of souls I must eliminate in order to save billions more. I *must* destroy the crystal, rather than allow the anomaly to spread to other dimensions."

Behind the Professor, Saturnyne suddenly cocked her head to one side, and placed a hand to the tiny receiver/transmitter that dangled from the lobe of her right ear. A finely-shaped eyebrow rose in a quizzical fashion. "Is that so?" she muttered to the person at the other end of the transmission. "All right, then—stand by." She looked up to find Roma and Xavier gazing at her.

"You have an update on the situation, Saturnyne?" Roma asked. There was an unmistakable tone of hope in her voice.

"Indeed, Supreme Guardian," Her Whyness replied. "I've just been informed by the DDC that their sensors have detected a signal being transmitted from Earth 616. *A transportation beam.*"

"A traveler," Roma whispered, her eyes widening slightly. "Tell them to intercept the beam. I would speak with this being."

"At once, Supreme Guardian," Saturnyne said.

As the Majestrix conveyed Roma's order to the Dimensional Development Court, the raven-tressed Guardian turned toward the professor. "Now, Charles Xavier," she said, "we may at last have the answers we seek to the madness that plays out before us."

Xavier nodded. "Indeed, Your Majesty. Answers . . . and perhaps a solution to our problem. . . ."

I haven't the slightest *idea what I'm doing here,* Betsy thought as she and von Doom shifted across realities, moving away from their home dimension and the transmutational curtain of energy generated by the Cosmic Cube that had enveloped their world. *I'm certain, though, I'll learn* why *Doom wanted me to accompany him . . . eventually. Just as I'm* also *certain I won't like the answer a single bit . . .*

Looking around, Betsy stared in awe as time and space flowed around her like a surging river, giving her quick glimpses of the true length and breadth of the omniverse. In one reality, she saw the costumed adventurer Spider-Man as a member of the legendary Fantastic Four—or, rather, Fantastic Five, to be precise; in another, her fellow X-Men were engaged in a battle royal with the Hulk and members of Earth's mightiest heroes, the Avengers, at the base of Niagara Falls. So many different versions of her own planet, most of them varying only by the slightest of degrees: the Confederacy winning the War Between the States in America; a World War II-era test detonation of the atomic bomb at Los Alamos, New Mexico, that—as the scientists on the Manhattan Project had feared might happen—ignited the world's atmosphere, turning the Earth into a massive cinder hanging in space; a reality in which ninety-nine percent of the super hero population had been exterminated, and the major cities were controlled by their killers: giant robots called Sentinels; a certain type of butterfly accidentally stepped on at the dawn of mankind. Openly gawping at the sights, sounds, and colors flowing around her, Betsy couldn't help but be reminded of the penultimate moment of the film *2001: A Space Odyssey*, when astronaut Dave Bowman rushed along a special effects corridor to find himself within the world of the mysterious, alien-constructed Monolith. Not one of her favorite movies—Stanley Kubrick was always a little too "out there" for her tastes, though she *had* enjoyed seeing Tom Cruise's bare bottom in *Eyes Wide Shut*—but it was the first thing that popped into her mind as she struggled to take in the spectacle of everything whipping past her.

The flow of the images began to accelerate, the windows to the various realities opening and closing so quickly that Betsy could no longer tell what she was looking at—it all became one blur leading into the next leading into the next, moving faster and faster until she felt her mind starting to close down from the visual overload—

And then it all disappeared, and Betsy suddenly found herself sprawled across a white-tiled floor. She panicked for a moment when she was inexplicably plunged into darkness; then she realized it was caused by her voluminous, lavender-hued hair falling in front of her eyes.

Wonderful, she thought dryly. *Abducted to who-knows-where by one of the deadliest villains in human history, cut off from my friends and teammates, and I'm frightened by a curtain of "bedroom hair." Well done, Betsy . . .*

Brushing her hair aside, she looked up to get her bearings. She was in a large, white-colored room; how large was impossible to say—the walls, floor, and ceiling were all curved and evenly lit, blending together to create an illusion of a chamber that seemed to stretch off toward infinity. If, that is, it really was an illusion, or even an actual room; for all she knew, she and von Doom could have materialized within the heart of the Cosmic Cube.

Betsy started, an unwelcomed chill suddenly working its way up her spine. Could *that* have been what von Doom meant when he said he still had one last hand to play? Could he have been that *mad* to think he could regain control of the Cube from the inside?

Well, yes, he could, she knew all too well. After all, hadn't he elected to continue using the reality-changing device that he had created, fully aware of its defective assembly—that, because of a miscalculation by one of his technicians (or so he had said), the Cube now relied on the power of its possessor's life-force to maintain the vision of the world they so desired? Of course he had, even though his aging process had been accelerated at an alarming rate, even though each moment he selfishly held onto the Cube brought him that much closer to death. And what had been his ultimate wish for the Cube to carry out just before he died? To destroy the world, so that no one else would be able to rule it.

Mad enough to wrest control of the Cube from within? There was never a doubt in Betsy's mind. She was more surprised by the notion that he might actually be able to pull it off . . . if, indeed, that's where they had landed.

Not to say his madness wasn't catching, Betsy had to admit. It wasn't all that long ago—ten or fifteen minutes at most, by her reckoning—that she had been willing to take von Doom's place; to take possession of the Cube and maintain the reality he'd created, in exchange for the chance to bring Warren back to life.

"Warren ..." Betsy whispered. She closed her eyes, fighting back the tears that now burned so hotly behind the lids.

Warren Worthington III had been *her* world: best friend, confidante, lover. A founding member of the X-Men, Warren had started out in life as the quintessential playboy—rich, handsome, and quite full of himself—but he had taken to the role of costumed adventurer like he'd been born to it. When he wasn't busy saving the universe, or trying to spread Charles Xavier's message of peace and understanding between man and mutant, he dined in the finest restaurants, drove the fastest cars, traveled everywhere he went in style. Between battling super-villains and living the high life, it was a wonder he'd ever found time to sit still for a moment.

But then he had met Betsy—a British telepath whose big brother, Brian, happened to be England's premiere super hero, Captain Britain, no less—and his life had changed. Hers, too. For Betsy, merely being around Warren made her feel as though her chaotic life at last had some sense of stability. She drew strength from him, and he from her. They'd started out as teammates—kindred souls facing constant peril from an intolerant world—but soon had become so much more. There had never been a man in her life like him.

And yet, her love for Warren was never to last. Dashed to pieces with the impact of his body on the grounds of The Mall in Washington, D.C., all because of a misguided, stupidly heroic attempt to protect von Doom—*Emperor* von Doom, Betsy angrily reminded herself—from an attack by Magneto. The mutant overlord had blasted Warren with a powerful bolt of magnetic energy, then moved on to refocus his attentions on his intended target. Warren had died in her arms, in the middle of a battlefield, and she'd been grateful that he'd never seen the futility of his efforts, for the man he'd tried to save had been nothing more than an android stand-in for the real monarch. A pretend emperor, through which a pathetic creature huddled in a sub-basement of the White House could vicariously live his life. A handsome, department store dummy that took the place of a withered, angry old man who ultimately sought to destroy the world, rather than see his dream come to an end.

Nevertheless, her thoughts in chaos, consumed by grief, Betsy had been more than willing to sacrifice herself if it meant that Warren might live one more day. She had foolishly agreed to von Doom's proposal, had even gone so far as to reach for the Cube. If it hadn't been for the timely arrival of the X-Men . . .

A loud groan from behind caught her attention. She glanced over her shoulder to find von Doom lying face-up on the floor, his metal-encased hand still gripping her ankle. A bit too tightly, Betsy realized—her foot had gone numb.

She pulled back on her leg to get von Doom's attention, then pointed to her restrained ankle. "Do you mind?"

The old man stared blankly at her for a moment, as though he didn't recognize her, then followed her gaze down to her foot. "Ah," he said, and opened his hand.

Sitting up, Betsy reached down to restore the circulation to her leg. She winced as the first pins-and-needles sensation of a properly working bloodstream raced through her foot.

Struggling to a sitting position, von Doom looked around, his rheumy eyes widening with surprise. "This is not my castle," he said with more than a trace of indignation. "What is the meaning of this?" He pounded his gauntleted fists against the floor; the room echoed with the hollow sounds of his feeble protestations.

"Who dares meddle in the affairs of Doom?" he demanded.

As if in response, a doorway suddenly appeared a few feet away, and a phalanx of Union Jack-garbed men and women poured into the room. Wordlessly, they formed a rough semicircle around the two travelers.

"The Captain Britain Corps?" Betsy said in astonishment.

The guards by the door stepped aside to admit a willowy, elfin-faced woman dressed in flowing white robes, her waist-length black hair pulled back in a severe ponytail. She came to an abrupt halt as she spotted her lavender-tressed "guest," and a shapely eyebrow rose in mild surprise.

"Elisabeth Braddock," she said evenly.

"Hello, Roma," Betsy replied, a smile slowly coming to her lips. "You have *no* idea how glad I am to see you. . . ."

2

FROM BEHIND Roma stepped another woman, wearing a white gown that accentuated her curves as much as Roma's attire hid hers. White hair cascading over the right side of her face in a Veronica Lake fashion, she peered at Betsy with her one visible eye; the pupil seemed to burn with cold, blue fire.

Betsy's smile quickly faded. "Saturnyne."

The Omniversal Majestrix haughtily looked down her nose at the X-Man. It was the sort of disgusted, look-at-that-grotesque-little-bug stare that suddenly made Betsy extremely self-conscious of her appearance, with her rumpled evening dress and disheveled hair. *I must look a* sight, she thought grimly.

"*The sister,*" Her Whyness said with a sneer. "Given the circumstances, I should have *known* you'd somehow be involved in the thick of things." Saturnyne practically spat out the words, which came as no surprise to Betsy. There was no great love lost between the two women, considering all the trouble the former had caused Brian/Captain Britain over the years (at least, in Betsy's mind), and Lady Braddock had never been shy about reminding Saturnyne of that fact . . . as often as possible. The thin layer of civility projected by tyrant and telepath whenever they met tended to transform lively parties into tension-filled evenings. Simply

33

having them in a room together caused the temperature to drop.

This occasion was no different, though neither woman was foolish enough to start an altercation with the Supreme Guardian of the Omniverse standing right in front of them.

"May I enter, Your Majesty?" asked a familiar—and most welcome—male voice.

Roma motioned for the guards to move from the doorway, and Charles Xavier glided into the room, his hoverchair humming softly.

"Professor!" Betsy exclaimed, and leapt to her feet. She stepped over to join him—hobbling a bit on her tingling foot, the blood flow not yet fully restored to her insensate toes—and clasped his hands in hers. "I didn't know you were here. When Jean and Scott briefed me on the details of their mission, it must have slipped their minds."

A flicker of hope shone in Xavier's eyes. "You've seen them, then." He looked to Roma. "There is *still* a chance, Your Majesty, that my students might succeed. All they need is time."

"Time the omniverse can ill afford, Charles Xavier," the Guardian replied. "As much as I respect the sacrifices that your X-Men have often been willing to make in the cause of justice, despite the fact that they did not hesitate to place their lives in my hands, my foremost duty is to the protection of the omniverse. I allowed your students an opportunity to set things aright, and they have failed. Now—"

"I implore you to wait just a little while longer, Your Majesty," the Professor insisted. "Now that Psylocke has joined us, we can use her knowledge of events within the anomaly to formulate a new plan of attack." His steely gaze locked on the Guardian's dark eyes. "Need I remind Your Majesty that you gave your *word* to my students that they would have one standard Earth week in which to stop this terrible threat, yet only four days have elapsed. Would you now go back on it, before learning the nature of this destructive force that threatens us all? Would you deny them the chance to set things right in the time that remains?"

34

Roma's eyes flashed with unbridled anger. "You play a dangerous game, Charles Xavier, with one who has learned everything there is to know of games from her father, the greatest player of all. The word of Roma has ever been her bond, but the daughter of Merlyn was not raised without the understanding that there is a time and a place when a bond can be broken. Know this: To preserve the safety of all creation, I would be willing to do *whatever* is necessary." She paused, the anger draining from her face. "But I hope it will not have to come to that unfortunate conclusion. For now, I would be willing to listen to any alternate plan you may devise after you have spoken with Elisabeth—but be quick about it."

A nauseating weight suddenly settled in the pit of Betsy's stomach. Until now, she'd been under the impression that, given Xavier's presence, other members of the X-Men might also be on board the citadel. But to realize that the success or failure of this mission—more than that, the safety of the universe itself—might depend on her alone . . .

"Who's your friend, Psylocke?" Saturnyne asked, gesturing toward von Doom. "Some half-dead geriatric paramour you picked up along the way while you were fleeing your Earth?"

"What insolence!" the old man snapped. "You *dare* speak of your betters in such disrespectful tones, woman?" He struggled to his feet. "Though Doom is well known for his benevolence towards the most *ignorant* of creatures, not even *he* should have to tolerate such an affront." At last standing erect, the monarch raised a gauntleted hand and pointed it, palm forward, at the Majestrix.

But nothing happened.

"Sorry to disappoint you, *Grandfather,*" Saturnyne commented dryly, "but the Starlight Citadel exists in a state of temporal grace. Any weapons your armor may possess won't function here."

The former emperor raised an eyebrow, clearly intrigued. "Indeed." Slowly, he lowered his arm, and a sly grin illuminated his sharp features. "But do not delude yourself into thinking such measures will protect you for long, woman. Doom has ever been resourceful—he *will* find a way to instruct you in proper etiquette . . . and soon."

Saturnyne sniffed. "I shall count the—" She halted, eyes narrowing with suspicion. "*Who* did you say you are?"

The armored tyrant drew himself up to his full height, head held high. "I am Doom the First, you cretin—the Lion of Latveria, and rightful ruler of the planet Earth."

The Majestrix turned to Betsy. "Does he mean to say that he's *your* Doom? The one from Earth 616?" She snorted. "Impossible."

"He *is* Doom," Betsy replied. "His rapid aging is a side effect of using a defective Cosmic Cube."

"Cosmic . . . ?" Saturnyne glanced at Roma, who looked surprised by this news—and terribly worried. "M'lady . . ."

"Yes, Saturnyne," Roma said. "At last we know the source of the anomaly." Her brow furrowed. "And yet, never in the history of the omniverse has such a device caused the amount of damage we have witnessed." She turned to Betsy. "You said this Cube was defective—how so?"

"Tell them nothing, mutant!" von Doom ordered. "The true genius of Doom's work cannot be comprehended by lesser beings such as yourself." A thoughtful, condescending smile cracked his withered features. "However, hearing your explanation might, indeed, prove interesting—though purely for entertainment value, of course, since it would irrefutably prove your lack of understanding."

Betsy snarled in disgust. "I've had all I can stand of you, 'Your Highness.' Without your weapons, without the Cube, you're no threat to anyone. And as for comprehending the 'true genius' of your work, if that included having Magneto backhand you onto the floor of your chamber so that he could take possession of the Cube, then you're absolutely right—I *do* fail to see the 'wonder' of it all."

Von Doom sneered. "Bah," he muttered, then fell silent.

Betsy turned back to Roma. "To be quite honest, I haven't the slightest notion what's wrong with it. Doom mentioned a miscalculation of some sort that was made during the Cube's creation, but beyond that . . ." She shrugged. "I *can* tell you *he* doesn't know, either." She cast a heated glance at the old man. "At least, that's what he *claims.*" A disturbing light suddenly shone in her eyes. "I'd be more than willing to find out the truth for you, though."

"Elisabeth . . ." Xavier said, his tone low and warning.

Without taking her eyes off von Doom, Betsy said, "Don't lecture *me* on the abuses of power, Professor. You don't know what this monster did while he held the Cube—no idea of the lives he ruined, the misery he caused, the . . . the . . ." She bit her bottom lip as she turned to face him. "The people he allowed to die . . ." she whispered.

Xavier's eyes opened wide in surprise. "The X-Men . . . ?"

"I . . . I don't know for certain," Betsy admitted. "Before we teleported, they'd been captured by the Acolytes, and the Cube was in the hands of Magneto." She ignored the Professor's shocked expression. "But . . . Warren . . . Warren . . ." She drew in a deep breath to steady herself, slowly released it through her nostrils. "Warren was . . . killed—" she waved a hand at von Doom "—trying to protect this filth."

Xavier said nothing in reply. He just sat quietly, eyes closed, gripping the edges of his seat until his knuckles turned white.

Betsy knew it wasn't the first time the Professor had received such disturbing news. In his years as founder and leader of the X-Men, he had watched far too many of his students die "on the job," as it were. Like firemen or police officers, they faced risks each day of their lives, never knowing if their latest mission would turn out to be their last.

Warren, however, was special. Like Jean, and Scott Summers, and Hank McCoy, and Bobby Drake, he'd been one of Xavier's first—and still greatest—successes. Those original five members were not just part of a team, they were the closest the Professor had to a family.

"Elisabeth . . . I'm sorry," Xavier said at last. "I know how close you and Warren had become over the past year." He opened his eyes, and Betsy saw the fires of determination that burned deep inside them. "But we shall have to put aside our grief for the time being. Although Roma has managed to entrap the man responsible for our predicament, we still lack the *means* by which he twisted our universe to suit his purposes. The Cosmic Cube is our focus now. And with someone as powerful as Erik in control of such a device, with his desire to live in a world run by mutants blinding him to the dangers involved in operating the Cube—not just to himself, but to everyone in our universe—there's no telling *what* further damage he might cause."

"Which brings us back to my original argument, m'lady," Saturnyne said to Roma. "If that destructive little box continues moving from one owner to another, each use of its power restructuring 616 to suit the whims of whichever costume-draped buffoon happens to be holding it at the time, then it's *imperative* that you remove that continuum from existence before the reality-cancer spreads."

"Fascinating," von Doom commented. "Then, Xavier's costumed whelps *were* telling the truth."

"Of *course* they were, von Doom," the Professor replied. "Unlike *you,* my students feel no need for subterfuge. What Saturnyne has said is accurate: Our universe is quickly unraveling, and your Cosmic Cube is the cause of it."

"And now you're going to tell us how to counteract its effects," Betsy said. "You didn't actually believe for a moment that I swallowed your story about not knowing what's wrong with the Cube, did you? The great and powerful Doctor Doom, a man who *claims* he's the intellectual superior of Reed Richards of the Fantastic Four—" she ignored the warning growl that issued from the monarch's throat "—at a loss to explain the flaw in his most fantastic creation? Don't make me laugh, von Doom." She took a step toward him, teeth bared. "Now, tell us what to do to repair it, or—"

"Or *what,* mutant?" von Doom asked. He smiled malevolently. "Your tiresome hero's code of ethics prevents you from forcing me to provide whatever information you think I might possess—though, I assure you, I have none to give."

Betsy glared at him, reining in her growing desire to use her martial arts skills to shatter every bone in his body—without allowing him to lose consciousness. "What you say is true, Doctor," she finally said. "Most members of the super hero community *would* be loathe to sink to your level, to pay such utter disregard to basic human rights that they'd be willing to blacken their souls by crawling into the dark corners of your mind and tearing out the knowledge they seek." A disturbing smile slowly twisted her beautiful features. "However, I fancy that none of them are former members of Britain's S.T.R.I.K.E. Psi Division, trained to extract information by *any means necessary.*" Her lavender eyes flashed brightly. "But *I* am."

Von Doom suddenly cried out in great pain and clutched the sides of his head.

Tell me what I need to know, Doctor, Betsy ordered through the telepathic link she had created. *Tell me* quick . . . *before I burn out every synapse in your twisted little mind.*

ELISABETH—STOP! roared a voice in her head.

Betsy staggered back as though she'd been slapped across the face, her link with von Doom shattered by the sheer force of Xavier's mental command. The Latverian monarch groaned and sank to his knees; he was kept from striking the floor only by the timely assistance of two members of the Corps. One was a woman with a shock of white hair erupting from the top of her mask, whom Betsy instantly recognized as Linda McQuillan—the Captain U.K. of Earth 794, the world to which the X-Men had been summoned by Roma, in the days before von Doom's reign of terror in their home dimension had started. Their task had been to aid Linda against Opul Lun Sat-yr-nin, a goal which the team ultimately achieved. Betsy had wanted to assist them, if only as a way to thank Linda for all the help she'd provided Brian over the years as he became acclimated to his role as Britain's foremost protector, but the Professor had ordered her to stay behind so that his school, the Xavier Institute for Higher Learning in Westchester County, New York, would not be without a telepath in residence . . . in case of any trouble.

Linda's teammate was a bear of a man, his bare chest and arms covered with a matting of hair that curled around the edges of his white gauntlets and the stylized "X" formed across his pectorals and over his shoulders by the arms of the Union Jack. The bottom half of his face was exposed beneath the mask he wore, although it was hard to tell at a distance, considering his jawline was hidden beneath a thick, brown beard and mustache. Though she didn't know him all that well, Betsy knew he was Captain England from another of the multitudes of Earth; it was difficult to keep them all straight. He clearly required no assistance in handling the weight of von Doom's armor, yet he politely allowed Linda to help him lower the tyrant to the floor.

Xavier ordered his hoverchair forward, placing himself between his student and her victim. "I empathize with your situation, Elisabeth—your anger, your sense of loss—but such actions will *not* be tolerated, for *any* reason." His eyes narrowed. "Do not place me in a position where I would be forced to *shut down* your powers— and you *know* I am quite capable of doing that."

Eyes closed, Betsy slowly massaged her temples, head still aching from the psychic blast. "My TK powers, perhaps, but not the abilities I acquired from the Crimson Dawn." She opened her eyes, and immediately saw the stern look on her mentor's face. "Not that that was meant as a *challenge,* Professor," she added coolly. "Merely a statement of fact."

Xavier frowned, then turned his chair toward von Doom. The tyrant lay on the floor of the chamber, wheezing hoarsely with each breath. Wisps of snow-white hair were plastered across his deeply creased face, soaked in sweat that had beaded across his forehead and poured down in rivulets to the collar of his armor. Beside him knelt Captain U.K., gloved fingertips lightly touching the carotid artery in his neck.

"What's his condition?" Xavier asked.

"Not good," said the Captain. "His pulse is erratic, breathing is shallow. From what I've been overhearing, his body was already starting to break down as a result of the Cube's influence." She cast a withering glare at Betsy. "That mental attack only made things worse. He needs immediate medical attention."

"Take him to the infirmary on Level 492," Roma commanded. "Have the physicians stabilize his cellular and psychic damage, and then post guards outside his door. Severely aged though this one may be, the Victor von Doom of *any* reality is neither a man to be trusted, nor left to his own devices. He is *not* to leave the infirmary without a direct order from myself or the Majestrix."

"Understood, Supreme Guardian," both Captains responded.

"Then, go. I shall speak with him once he has sufficiently recovered." Roma waved a delicate hand at them. They and their charge vanished in a burst of light, presumably teleported to the medical center by the Guardian's immeasurable power.

"M'lady," Saturnyne said. "The crystal . . ."

Roma gazed at her lieutenant for a moment, then slowly nodded; she suddenly looked extremely fatigued to Betsy. "Yes, Saturnyne. I have not forgotten." She turned to Betsy. "Elisabeth, I ask that once you and the Professor have drawn up your 'new plan of attack,' as it were, you both join me in the throne room. But do not take too long in doing so. Clichéd though the saying may be, time truly *is* of the utmost importance . . . and it is running out for your world." She paused. "For all of us."

"I understand, Roma," Betsy said solemnly.

"Thank you, Your Majesty," Xavier said. He turned a heated gaze toward his former headmistress. *We shall discuss your reckless behavior another time, Elisabeth,* he warned her telepathically. *For now, though, take some time to rest. We have a great deal of work ahead of us.*

Yes, Professor, Betsy thought sullenly. Head bowed, she watched Xavier follow Roma from the room. The coterie of Captain

Britains fell in step behind them, and soon Betsy was left alone with her thoughts . . . and Saturnyne.

"So . . . did you learn anything?" Her Whyness asked.

"Not much," Betsy admitted. "Nothing helpful to our problem, at least . . . Doom really *doesn't* know what's wrong with the Cube. But I *did* find out why he brought me along." She slowly shook her head in bemusement. "A crazy idea, really."

"And that would be . . . ?" Saturnyne prompted.

"Well, his transmat beam was aimed at his castle in upstate New York. He was planning to use the time platform he keeps there to send me back to prevent Magneto from getting his hands on the Cube."

Saturnyne grunted, her perfect teeth gnashing loudly. "Oh, you *fools* and your notions of time travel!" she bellowed. "When will the people of your dimension come to realize that, when you try to affect past events, you don't change your present, you only create a divergent timeline. You have *no* idea how mind-numbingly *tiresome* it becomes policing every new reality that's created because someone tried to go back and prevent John F. Kennedy's assassination, or because they wanted to warn the captain of the *Titanic* to watch out for icebergs." Saturnyne paused, then glanced sideways at the Asian mutant. "Do you have *any* understanding of what I was just saying, Braddock?"

"I'm not an *imbecile,* you bleached-blond cow, despite what Doom might say to the contrary," Betsy sniped playfully. She smiled broadly. "I saw *Back to the Future 2.* I know what you're talking about."

The Majestrix sighed. "You're as frustratingly obtuse as your brother, Elisabeth."

Betsy turned her nose up at her chic adversary, imitating Saturnyne's haughty attitude. "Sticks and stones, old girl. You're really just angry because having me around reminds you of all the times Brian refused to sleep with you . . . which, if memory serves me right, was about as numerous as the ways in which you *threw* yourself at him."

Saturnyne frowned. "You *are* aware that I absolutely loathe you."

"And I, you. With every fiber of my being." Betsy smiled.

The Majestrix nodded. "All right. Just so we're clear on that point." She gazed at Betsy's disheveled appearance, and wrinkled her nose. "Well, the best thing to do now is make you look *somewhat* more presentable for your meeting with m'lady in the 'morning.' Sleep would be a good start; I'll escort you to one of the chambers formally occupied by a member of your group. After that . . ." Saturnyne shrugged and smiled beatifically. "Well, let's just say I'll keep you in my prayers tonight." She gestured toward the doorway. "Follow me." Without waiting for a response, Saturnyne turned on her heel and strode past her, into the adjoining corridor.

Delicately grasping the folds of her evening gown between her index fingers and thumbs, Betsy politely curtsied. "Why, *thank* you, Your Whyness," she said happily.

Your Whyness. Not for the first time, she wondered about the origins of that ridiculous-sounding title. She *had* asked about it, though, and why it applied equally to a man as much as a woman—it's just that no one seemed willing to give her an answer. Saturnyne had simply turned up her nose on the last occasion the question had been put to her and walked away—one of those cases, Betsy had assumed, where, if you had to ask, you simply weren't part of the right social circles. And Brian had been no help whatsoever because he'd never given it a moment's thought; but then, that was Brian—he'd never really been one for details. However, based upon her dealings with the Majestrix, the sole conclusion Betsy had been able to reach was that the title must be given to only the most conceited members of Roma's staff—if so, Saturnyne was more than qualified for the position. Betsy shrugged. Titles had never impressed her, but it probably looked quite impressive on a résumé . . .

"Are you coming, Braddock?" Saturnyne called back from the

hallway. "Some of us *do* have more important things to do, you know."

"Egotistical cow," Betsy muttered, and grinned.

Holding her head high, determined to look every bit the manor-born English lady that she was, Betsy set off, ready and eager to engage in another battle of wits with her guide. It was childish behavior, she knew, but she always enjoyed seeing the bright shade of red that painted Saturnyne's cheeks when the right buttons were pushed. . . .

One hundred levels below the women, in the medical wing of the citadel, the former emperor of Earth 616 and his guards materialized to find a battery of physicians awaiting their arrival. The infirmary was roughly the length and width of an aircraft hanger, with rows of empty beds stretching off in all directions as far as the eye could see. Captain U.K. had been here only once before, when she and Brian Braddock were recuperating from injuries received during the chaos created by "Mad" Jim Jaspers, in the days following the annihilation of Dimension 238. She wrinkled her nose in disgust—the place still smelt heavily of antiseptics and pine-scented cleaning solutions.

"Who's in charge?" she asked the men, women, and various creatures assembled before her.

"I imagine that would be *me,* young lady," answered a smallish, wide-eyed man wearing green surgical scrubs and gray, checkered pants, his voice tinged with an unmistakable Scottish burr. "I'm the Chief Physician." He gestured toward a diagnostic table. "If you'd be so kind as to place the patient on the bed, we can start treatment immediately."

Scooping von Doom into his arms, Captain England carried the tyrant to the bed and placed him on the soft mattress. The weight of the despot's body immediately activated sensors in the table that began monitoring von Doom's vital signs. The doctor watched the readouts for a few moments, then pinched his lower lip between thumb and index finger and nodded slowly.

"Yeessss . . ." he muttered. "Very interesting." He turned to a tall, balding, stern-faced man who was watching him with a measure of disdain—it seemed that, even at the center of time and space, such a concept as the "disgruntled employee" was not an unfamiliar one. "Doctor Stanton, we have a man here suffering from severe mental trauma. Be a good chap and run down to the Psionics Wing—tell them we need a Level Two empath to help ease the man's pain."

"And what would you like me to do for the *patient?*" Stanton asked cuttingly.

The Chief Physician slowly smiled. "Still working on our sense of humor, I see, Doctor. Well, keep at it—I know you'll be successful one of these days." He waved his hands at his colleague, shooing him away. "Now, off with you, and don't come back until you have an empath by the hand . . . or tentacle."

Lips pulled back in a sneer, Stanton turned and stomped off toward the exit.

"A good chap, that Stanton," the doctor said once he had left the room. "A bit on the unapproachable side, though. Terrible bedside manner."

"He's a troublemaker, that one," commented Captain England. "I can tell right off. Best keep your eye on that one, Doctor—he's got a bit o' the devil in 'im."

"Oh, I shall," the Chief Physician replied. "Thank you, Captain."

Lightly grasping an elbow on each Captain, the doctor gently moved them away from the patient. As he did so, a half-dozen nurses—some human, some not, but all attired in full surgical gear—moved in and started removing von Doom's armor, while the other physicians began administering the first stages of treatment.

"Now then, if you don't mind," the doctor explained, "I think it would be best for all concerned if you were to step into the observation lounge, where you'll have an unobstructed view of your prisoner—I assume this man *is* a prisoner, given the nature of his escort?" Captain U.K. nodded in acknowledgment. "Yes, an unobstructed view of your prisoner without—"

"Getting underfoot?" asked the Union Jack-clad heroine.

The doctor smiled broadly. "Precisely."

The captain nodded. "The observation lounge."

"Two-and-a-half levels up, one level sideways," said the doctor. "We'll see you in a bit, then." He reached up to his head as though to politely tip a hat, realized he wasn't wearing one, and slowly lowered his hand.

Chuckling softly at the strange behavior of the little man, Captain U.K. cast a bemused glance at Captain England, then turned and led her teammate from the infirmary.

Almost immediately, a soft, chiming alarm began sounding.

"Doctor, I think you may want to look at this . . ." burbled one of the nurses, an octopoidal creature with thick tentacles and a rheumy eye the color of runny egg yolk.

Turning his attention back to the matter at hand, the Chief Physician walked back to join his team. "Yes, Nurse, what is it?"

The caregiver gestured toward the monitors displaying von Doom's vital signs. The doctor's eyes widened in surprise as he stared at one in particular.

"That can't be right . . ." he murmured, then stood silently for a few moments, pulling at his bottom lip and watching the stream of data that flowed across the monitors. "This man *is* human, isn't he?"

"All evidence—genetic, psychological, chronal, dimensional—indicates that he is," replied a fresh-faced, blond-haired physician. "Except . . ."

"Except we shouldn't then be seeing what we are seeing," interjected the doctor. "Yes . . ." He grimaced, scratched the top of his head, and sighed. Then, hands clasped behind his back, he turned to face his troops. "It seems as though we have been presented with a riddle, doctors . . . and I'm quite certain our esteemed Supreme Guardian, Roma, will not be gladdened by our answers . . ." He slowly shook his head. "No, she won't be pleased at all . . ."

Dr. Henry P. Stanton was *not* a happy man.

As he stomped through the corridors of the medical center, heading for the Psionics Wing, his mind swirled with dark thoughts—about his life, about his work, about the pompous attitude of that grinning jackass called the Chief Physician. Not for the first time, he grumbled over the decision that had led to the comical little Scotsman being appointed to that lofty position, and Stanton being left standing by the side of the road (metaphorically speaking, of course), wondering how he could have lost a job that was supposed to have been his from the start. At least, that had been his understanding when Merlyn recruited him, taking him away from a lucrative medical practice on Earth 1629.

It had been shortly after the events of the "Jaspers' Warp" incident, when Merlyn had appeared in Stanton's Los Angeles office to make his offer. After dealing with Henry's volatile receptionist, Helene—for Merlyn had tried to barge in without an appointment—and then making a suitable display of the powers he possessed in order to prove he was for real and not some lunatic wandering in off the street, the Guardian of the Omniverse began interviewing his job candidate. *Why* he wanted Stanton in particular was never made clear; as the doctor later found out, Merlyn never bothered to tell *anyone,* including his daughter, the details of any of his plans. That didn't mean Henry didn't have his own ideas about the selection process, of course. Always willing to fall back on his overinflated ego, he eventually came to the conclusion that he had been picked because he was just too good a physician to ignore, even among the millions of other Henry P. Stantons in the omniverse.

Whatever his reasons, the technomage had made it quite clear that Stanton was his choice for the position—once he'd been properly trained in treating the illnesses and injuries of the myriad races that visited the citadel. No surprise there—after all, what good was a Chief Physician to his patients, or his staff, if he knew nothing of their physiology? And so Stanton willingly, eagerly, abandoned his practice and plunged into his studies, determined to answer this higher calling.

But then one day, seemingly out of nowhere, that infuriatingly smug little man had appeared, and Stanton saw the prize quickly slipping from his fingers.

It had all been Roma's doing, of course. Apparently dissatisfied with her father's candidate, she had found one of her own, and called him in from whatever godforsaken corner of the omniverse in which he'd been living. The bothersome gnat had even managed to charm Merlyn with his encyclopedic memory and smug wit in record time.

So what if he could rattle off the symptoms and treatments for a hundred different ailments that were commonly—and not so commonly—found in a handful of dimensional planes? Given enough time, Stanton would have been able to do the same. Who cared if he had a superior bedside manner? Patients were supposed to be healed, not coddled. Where was the logic in talking to the staff as though they were his friends? Nurses and orderlies, medical interns and administrative workers—they weren't peers, they were subordinates, and should be treated as such.

Stanton should have seen it coming, should have taken steps to prevent the Fates from abandoning him in his hour of need. But he was so absolutely certain that he was the only sentient being for the job that he hadn't even considered the possibility that Roma might take advantage of her closeness with her father to turn him against the physician.

It could have been avoided. Perhaps if he hadn't insulted her, calling her a "child" in the heat of an argument over the treatment of a visiting Z'Nox dignitary from Dimension 8158 who'd mysteriously fallen ill, he wouldn't have fallen so far out of favor, and caused her to go looking elsewhere for a suitable applicant. Come to think of it, the doctor had to admit to himself, labeling her a "naive little girl" on one occasion because she obviously didn't understand the intricacies of medicine probably hadn't done anything to help his case. But, so what if he'd momentarily forgotten that she was older than he by *centuries*—physically, she looked barely mature enough to have graduated college yet. Besides, neither of those unfortunate incidents would have come to pass if she hadn't tried to second-guess his diagnoses—"I don't tell *you* how to run the universe," he'd commented sharply during the second contretemps. "Don't presume you can tell *me* how to practice medicine."

She'd reacted as though he'd slapped her across the face, and stormed out of his office. Given the power she possessed, he was lucky that she hadn't wiped him out of existence right there on the spot; instead, she'd settled for knocking him down a peg or three, and denying him the chance of becoming Chief Physician.

Stanton had never gotten over that snub. After all, was being truthful about Roma's lack of medical training any reason to cheat him out of a job? Of course not. However, as the doctor had quickly come to learn, despite their immortality and seemingly limitless wisdom, despite their mastery over the forces of time and space, despite the power they held over every living creature throughout the omniverse, both father and daughter tended to let their emotions get in the way of important decisions.

Damned unprofessional, in Stanton's opinion—not that anyone ever asked for it.

And now, here he was, running errands for that blasted Highlands jackanapes—a menial task that an orderly could have carried out. His vast medical talents going to waste, while the Guardian's pet caregiver grabbed all the glory for himself.

This nonsense—this indignity—had to end. There had to be *some* way to prove his worth, to show how wrong Merlyn and his spiteful little whelp had been in slighting him. Some method that could be used to hurt them as much as he had been hurt.

Admit it, Doctor, he told himself. *You're just looking for a way to get back at Roma and her favorite clown. You don't want an apology from them—you want* revenge.

Or retribution; either one was good. Such thoughts were certainly foremost in his mind while he made his rounds each day. How many hours had he spent replaying the same scenes over and over again in his dreams? The Chief Physician misdiagnosing a patient, and Stanton coming to the rescue at the penultimate moment, before death could claim its latest victim. Roma apologizing for her behavior and awarding him his rightful position, while that Scottish buffoon was run out of the citadel in disgrace.

The doctor sighed. If only there really *was* a means by which he could find the sort of justice he'd only been able to have in his dreams. At least, there were no means to be found on the citadel; he'd searched long and hard, to no avail. Perhaps he just needed to look elsewhere.

Stanton smiled mirthlessly. Daydream though it might be, he'd still give just about anything to see the look on the Guardian's youthful face if the opportunity to make it a reality ever presented itself. . . .

"I feel like bloody hell," Betsy muttered as she and Saturnyne walked along one of the countless beige-colored corridors that ran throughout the citadel. "It's like my mind is racing a hundred kilometers an hour, but my body can't get past the starting gate."

"It's called 'universe lag,' " Saturnyne explained, coming to a halt before one of the many doors lining the corridor. She waved a hand in front of an electric eye, and the door irised open with a soft hiss of air. "A few hours of rest, though, and you'll be back to your old, insufferably-annoying self."

Since her head was aching so, Betsy decided to ignore the playful jibe and stepped into the room, Her Whyness close behind. The chamber was roughly the size of a loft in a New York commercial building, its walls colored a mellowing cream shade, the lighting globes scattered about the spacious area dimmed to a pleasant softness. To the right of the door, at the end of a short corridor, stood a bathroom, complete with shower; to the left were the living quarters proper, complete with chairs, couch, writing desk, oval-shaped bed, and a large, wall-mounted viewscreen that received the over one hundred and seventy-nine billion (and still growing) television channels that were broadcast throughout the omniverse. On the far side of the room, running the length of the suite, was an enormous observation window that allowed a staggering view of the powerful, multi-hued energies that comprised all of time and space as they swirled around the citadel.

But it wasn't a front row seat to the wonders of Creation that caught Betsy's attention as she looked around the room.

"Ororo stayed here," she said softly, and smiled.

Saturnyne cast a sideways glance at her.

"I can sense the remnants of her thoughts," the lavender-tressed telepath explained. "Like a lingering trace of perfume in the air." Catching sight of the Majestrix's suspicious expression, she gently patted her verbal sparring partner on the arm. "Don't worry, Saturnyne, I have no interest in scanning *your* mind to gather information. With all the clutter in there, I'd be afraid of stumbling over some unpleasant memory and stubbing my toes." She smiled. "Metaphorically speaking, of course."

Her Whyness snorted.

Betsy closed her eyes as she stepped into the room, allowing the essence of her teammate to drift into her mind. It was a pleasant sensation, sending an invigorating chill up her spine. "I've never known anyone so at peace with everyone—with every *thing*—in the world like Ororo. Her thoughts, her feelings, her outlook on life—it's all so . . . refreshing."

"Then you should have no trouble sleeping," Saturnyne commented sarcastically. "With all that love and happiness permeating the air, I'm certain you'll soon be dreaming of cherubs and puppy dogs."

Betsy gazed evenly at the Majestrix. "Don't you ever grow tired of making snide comments all the time?"

"I only make them when the opportunity presents itself," Saturnyne replied haughtily. She smiled frostily. "It just so happens that practically every word that tumbles from your mouth makes for such a delicious set-up line." She snorted. "I imagine your boyfriend considers that one of your more endearing ..."

A melancholy expression darkened Betsy's features; she suddenly looked twice her age.

"... qualities ..." As Saturnyne's voice trailed off, it was obvious from her shocked expression that even the Majestrix realized she had gone too far with her caustic remarks. "E-Elisabeth ... I'm sorry," she said haltingly. "I-I didn't mean to ..."

Slowly, Betsy reached out to take Saturnyne's right hand, then gently clasped it in both of hers. "Saturnyne, I know we've had our differences of opinion over the years—it's to be expected, I imagine, when a sister tries to protect her brother from what she perceives to be the 'wrong sort of woman.' " A wisp of a smile came to her lips as she saw the Majestrix wince as though lightly slapped. "But I also know that, beneath that cool, professional, infuriatingly superior attitude you constantly throw in everyone's faces is a caring, loving woman."

"Not according to your brother ..." Her Whyness muttered.

"I truly *do* hope that, one day, you'll find someone special," Betsy continued. "Someone you can share your hopes, your dreams, your love with, as I did with Warren. And when you do, don't *ever* let a minute pass without letting them know how wonderful it feels to have them in your life ... because you never know how little time you may have together, in the end."

For what must have been the first time in years, the Omniversal Majestrix suddenly seemed to be at a loss for words. Her one visible eye widened in surprise, she stared at Betsy for a few moments; her lips moved, but she appeared to be unable to form any words.

"Umm ... I'd ... I'd best be going," she finally stammered.

Betsy nodded and released Saturnyne's hand. Then she headed across the chamber toward the bed, pausing only long enough to slip out of her opera-length gloves and once-elegant gown before climbing under the covers.

"Good night, Elisabeth," Saturnyne said as she walked to the doorway. She paused for a reply, but received none, and the door irised shut behind her.

Alone in the dark, Betsy pulled the gown close to her and buried her face in the material, inhaling the few traces of Warren's cologne that still clung to it. She'd been able to maintain a cool façade in front of everyone—well, except for that momentary display of anger toward von Doom, of course—but only through the greatest of efforts. It was expected of her, she knew—wasn't she the mighty *Psylocke,* telepathic femme fatale who was as deadly as she was beautiful? Who never allowed personal matters to cloud her judgment?

Absolute rubbish, of course, but it wouldn't have done any good to allow the weight of her grief to overwhelm her in front of a roomful of people and force her to go running to Professor Xavier for support. No—now that she had some understanding of the severity of the situation, she had to concentrate on helping Charles; he needed her to focus on the mission that lay ahead. So, for the time being, she would "keep a stiff upper lip," as the old saying went . . . at least in public. Warren would have been proud of her.

Warren . . .

Betsy squeezed her eyes tightly shut, and the tears that had been building for the better part of an hour at last found release.

And as she drifted off to a troubled sleep, Betsy couldn't help but wonder what sort of horrific punishments her *other* friends might even now be suffering at the hands of their oldest enemy. . . .

3

SCOTT, I-I'M not sure I can take much more of this."

Glancing at her husband, Jean Grey nervously chewed on her bottom lip. Smiling warmly, Scott Summers reached over and brushed away a strand of bright red hair that had draped itself across her left cheek.

"It'll be all right, hon," he said assuringly. "We've been through tougher situations; we'll get through this one, too."

Jean tried to flash a confident smile, but could only succeed in twisting her lips into a rough, sickly approximation. She glanced past Scott, to the huddled shapes in the darkness around them; the creatures barked and growled and gesticulated wildly at one another and the handsome couple. Jean could only understand some of the hand gestures that were being made; the blinding glare of the spotlights that shone on Scott and her made it difficult to clearly see much of anything beyond ten or twelve feet.

Her gaze drifted to the man who sat before the Summers. He was not a particularly impressive figure physically—with his gaunt features, receding hairline, and sallow skin tone—but Jean knew all too well that he possessed an intellect almost second to none. He was agile enough to be three steps ahead of her in an open confrontation, despite her own prodigious mental abilities; wily enough to twist her own words against her; powerful enough to leave her beaten and bloodied if she faltered for even a moment on the field of battle.

"Deep breaths, Red," Scott whispered in her ear. "Stay focused, and everything will turn out fine."

Jean nodded, not really agreeing with her husband, but unwilling to allow her fears to overwhelm her in such a perilous situation. From the corner of her eye she spotted one of the creatures pointing toward something next to it. And then, from the darkness, a blood-red eye began to glow ominously . . .

"Welcome back to *Viewpoints*," Archer Finckley said to the television camera trained on him; his voice was rough and somewhat nasal, and he delivered each word with the force of a roundhouse punch. "For those of you just joining us, our guests tonight are Scott Summers and Jean Grey, directors of the Erik Lensherr Institute for the Genetically Gifted, an academy for special children named after a *very* special man."

The red light above a second camera winked on, and Jean caught a glimpse of herself and Scott on a nearby monitor. They made an attractive couple—he with his strong jawline, toned physique, and dark, slightly-ruffled hair, she with her supermodel looks, bright green eyes, and flaming red tresses—which was the main reason they'd been included in *People* magazine's "Fifty Most Beautiful People" two years running. But they were more than mere window-dressing; together, they ran one of the most successful schools for young mutants in the world, with a student enrollment recently topping five thousand. And it was because of that commendable success—plus the fact that the school, on the eve of its fortieth anniversary, was about to open "satellite" branches in other countries—that they had been invited by renowned journalist Archer Finckley to appear on his program—the most watched talk show currently on the air. Scott had jumped at the chance, always eager to spread the good word about the institute and its founder. Jean had reluctantly agreed to join him; few and far between though they had been, television interviews made her nervous, and this one, she was certain, would prove to be no exception.

They had dressed conservatively for their appearance on *Viewpoints*: Scott in a dark, double-breasted business suit, charcoal-gray shirt, and solid red tie, his eyes perpetually covered by a pair of sunglasses, its lenses carved from ruby quartz—the only substance on Earth strong enough to contain the powerful force beams that continually threatened to erupt from his eyes; Jean in a black, knee-length dress that complemented her hair, which had been pulled back into a ponytail in the hope that it would make her look more like a serious-minded headmistress and less like a giggling pin-up from the pages of *Sports Illustrated*'s Swimsuit Edition. The choice of clothing had been at her insistence, given that their everyday attire consisted of formfitting red-and-purple-hued work clothes based on the costume design of the school's founder—a man named Erik Magnus Lensherr, who was known to everyone on the planet by a far more colorful nom de guerre: Magneto.

The self-proclaimed "Master of Magnetism" and leader of the *Homo sapiens superior* rights movement. A loving father and devoted husband. A Nobel Prize-winning peacemaker.

And the man who just happened to be master of the world.

Jean and Scott had not been among the first of his followers—they hadn't even been born yet when Lensherr had begun fighting for equal rights for mutants in the 1960s—but once their own powers had started to manifest, it hadn't taken long for them to join his cause. Here was a man who had led a march on Washington, D.C. in 1967, culminating in his famous "Children of the Atom" speech at the base of the Washington Monument; who had been given an audience with President Richard Nixon in 1971 to protest the use of mutants as advance troops ("cannon fodder," Lensherr had called them) during the Vietnam War; who, in 1980, single-handedly overthrew the government of the island-nation of Genosha, where mutants were treated worse than animals—beaten, starved, used for sport. A man who had been feared by a vast number of enemies, true, but a man whose message had been heard. Meeting him had been the moment of a lifetime for Jean and Scott—one they would have remembered the rest of their lives. But Lensherr had gone even further than simply shaking their hands; he invited them into the fold, asked them to help him in his ongoing campaign, and they had jumped at the chance, their heads full of youthful idealism.

And yet, the struggle had never ended, despite Lensherr's numerous successes. In most parts of the world, the United States included, mutants were still treated as second-class citizens. By the time Jean and Scott had become acolytes, their kind was still living in secrecy, always dreading what might happen should they accidentally reveal their abilities in public. And as for non-powered *Homo sapiens*, the very mention of the word "mutant" brought forth mental images of Sissy Spacek's bloody night of psychokinetic terror at the climax of the film *Carrie*, complete with exploding cars, burning schools, and buckets of pig blood.

As the past forty years had shown, it was *never* a good time to be a member of *Homo superior*.

But then, five years ago, everything changed. One morning, the people of the world awoke from a particularly pleasant, shared dream—in which the nations of the world had come together under one rule, and man and mutant lived in harmony—to discover there was no more hatred, or prejudice, or fear. It was as though those feelings had been expunged from their minds—a cleansing of negative energies, as it were. Some called it a miracle; others thought it the result of a harmonic convergence, though the planets of the solar system had been nowhere near alignment; a few even thought it might be an early sign of The Rapture, that moment when God summons to Heaven all the truly devout just before the arrival of the End Times. Whatever the supposition, however, somehow, in the depths of their subconscious, they all knew they had one man to thank for this incredible event.

And Erik Magnus Lensherr had never been the type to let an opportunity slip through his fingers . . .

Finckley turned to Jean. She felt her throat tighten

automatically. "Now, before we went to commercial, Jean, you were about to give us some background on your mentor and his world-renowned school."

Jean politely cleared her throat, trying her best to ignore the eye of the camera that stared unblinkingly at her, putting her on display for the people of the world—all six billion plus. "Well, Archer, I'm sure just about *everyone* knows the story by now, but...all right. The institute was originally founded in 1985 by Erik Lensherr, a Polish immigrant whose parents had died in World War II, during the Holocaust; the Lensherrs had been prisoners in the Auschwitz concentration camp, and Erik had been the only one to survive. By the time the Allies finally liberated the camp in 1945, Erik had fallen in love with a woman named Magda, who'd also been a prisoner; together, they left Poland, hoping to put behind them the nightmarish experiences they'd endured, and traveled to America."

A frown creased Jean's flawless features. "Unfortunately, once they reached the streets of New York, they were confronted by the same sort of foolish intolerance they had fled in Europe." She slowly smiled, starting to feel more at ease as she continued with the story. "But, after surviving the horrors of the Nazi death camps, Erik and Magda weren't about to let something as petty and annoying as mere prejudice keep them from turning their dreams of a fresh start into reality—especially now that they had a new member of the family with them: a baby daughter named Anya, who'd been born during the voyage across the Atlantic.

"But Erik had an even more difficult time than most, considering the unfavorable factors he was faced with when he arrived on our shore: he was a mutant, true, but, even worse in the eyes of others, he was an immigrant, a Pole, and a Jew. No one cared if he and his family had escaped extermination; here, he was just another unwanted outsider, trying to take away someone else's job. He was harassed at every menial job he could find, beaten, kicked—he was even stabbed once. Putting food on the table became a daily struggle, and then, when Anya almost died of pneumonia..." She shook her head sadly. "The strain of it all came close to destroying him."

"Obviously, it didn't," Finckley noted wryly.

"No, he wasn't broken—he *persevered,*" Scott said, a triumphant tone in his voice. "And once Anya was well again, he vowed that the hatred in this country that was being directed toward him— the same kind of hatred that had nearly killed him in Auschwitz— had to end. *Something* had to be done to change people's minds before our nation turned into another Nazi Germany." The rugged headmaster frowned. "At that time, though, he didn't know how that could be accomplished. All he had was his family to keep him strong—his family, and his dreams."

"And yet, he *did* ultimately find a way—his greatest dream has been a reality for the past five years," Finckley stated. "Mutants no longer have to live in secret, as was the case when the institute first opened its doors; they now live in the open, as equals of mankind. In fact, we humans have willingly embraced your peo- ple—*'Homo superior,'* as Lensherr has called your race—with open arms ever since 'The Morning of Unity,' as it's come to be known." He turned back to Jean. "So, with that in mind, in an enlightened society such as we now have, do you find it's still necessary to *have* such a place as the institute, which is solely devoted to work- ing with gen-active children—or even to open other branches— when there are school programs already in place around the world that have also been set up to help them come to terms with their powers? What makes *yours* so special?"

"Well, Archer," Jean replied, "I think you should remember that, if it hadn't been for the Lensherr Institute, those very programs you mentioned would never have been created in the *first* place. I hate to sound like a walking promotional brochure, but the Len- sherr Institute has always been at the forefront of gen-active train- ing—we have the best facilities, the best faculty, and the friendliest environment. And, since most of our staff have powers of their own, we have a better understanding than non-gen-actives of how chaotic life can seem during the stages of early development." She smiled. "You could say that ours is *still* the ruler by which all other schools are measured." She leaned forward, her voice dropping in volume just enough to make Finckley—and the audience, hopefully—"prick up their ears," as the saying went, and pay more attention to her words. "You see, Archer, despite the 'enlightened society' we live in, kids are still kids, and children can be very cruel with their comments, even if they're meant to be in jest." Her smile faded, lips drawing together in a thin line. "I can't tell you how many times I'd been called a 'gene-joke' by the time I got into college."

"I imagine it made growing up all that more difficult," Finckley commented.

Jean's right eyebrow arched dramatically. "Archer, if you think having your first period is a traumatic experience for a young woman, try waking up in the middle of the night to find you're floating three feet above the bed, and every object in the room is orbiting you like you're the sun." She snorted. "No, growing up wasn't difficult—it was sheer hell."

Finckley nodded, trying to look sympathetic, and failing miserably.

"That's why the work we do at the institute is so important," Jean continued. "We help the students through those tough times, and encourage them to celebrate their differences from *Homo sapiens*. Our race has made great contributions to the world, and it's always been important—not just for Scott and myself, but the entire staff—to constantly remind our young men and women that they're the ones who are going to be shaping the world in the future, and they're the ones who are expected to carry on the legacy of Erik Lensherr when the rest of us are sitting around, playing mah jong, down at the retirement home." She smiled, eyes sparkling. "And *that,* getting back to your original question, is what makes our school so special."

Finckley flashed a brief smile, clearly pleased with her answer. *Thank God for* that, Jean thought. "Now, getting back to the *formation* of the school," he said. "Did the idea for that come around the same time Lensherr decided to reach out to help people like himself, or was that a by-product of his work in the mutants' rights movement?"

It was Scott who answered. " 'Mutant' is such an outdated term, Archer. We prefer to think of ourselves as 'genetically gifted.' 'Children of the Atom,' as it were." He smiled. "Actually, the word 'mutant' didn't really come into vogue until the late 1950s, when Hollywood filmmakers latched onto it and turned it into a buzz-word." He sighed dramatically. "We're *still* trying to live down the 'Metaluna Mutant' from *This Island Earth*."

Jean laughed softly—it was a joke Scott often used during in-terviews—and glanced toward their host. Finckley merely smiled tightly and nodded; obviously, he'd heard it before, and didn't find it all that amusing. The laughter quickly died in her throat.

"Ummm . . . getting back to the point . . ." she continued, break-ing the awkward silence. "When Erik first began exhibiting his powers of magnetism—just after puberty—he'd never heard of the word 'mutant'; there were so few of them at the time, no one knew exactly *what* they should be called—" she grimaced "—other than 'freaks' or 'monsters.' What he *did* know was that he was different, but he saw it as a blessing, not a curse. And once he learned there were others in the world like him—once he knew that he wasn't alone any more—it gave him back the sense of hope for the future he thought had been beaten out of him by his captors during the war."

"So, what would you consider to be the ultimate turning point in your mentor's life?" Finckley asked. "What was it that made him the man he is today?"

Scott . . . ? Jean telepathically said to her husband, cueing him to jump in with an answer as she reached for a mug of water near her chair. The image of a ventriloquist taking a drink while still speaking through a dummy briefly flashed through her mind, and she had to fight down the laugh that threatened to bubble up through her lips.

"Well, in the early 1960s, with the civil rights movement in full swing," Scott explained, "Erik *found* the 'something' he'd been looking for. While watching the evening news one night in 1963, he saw a replay of Martin Luther King's 'I Have a Dream' speech on the steps of the Lincoln Memorial, and his eyes were suddenly opened. There, right in front of him, was proof positive of the power that one man with a dream could possess." A brief smile flickered at the edges of Scott's lips. "Erik says he wept that night because he was so moved by Dr. King's words—each and every syllable struck a chord deep within his soul. And having felt the power of that message, he wanted the same opportunities for him-self—for his family. So, with Magda's support, he dedicated his life to his own dream: of the genetically gifted co-existing peacefully with man, no longer afraid to hide their special talents, but rather accepted by society as equals."

"And he thought he could best do that job wearing tights and a cape and calling himself 'Magneto'?" Finckley asked incredu-lously.

Scott chuckled softly and shrugged. "Well, you never know *where* inspiration is going to come from. You see, one day back in the late 1950s, Erik had taken Magda to the movies, and he saw how enthusiastically the audience responded to newsreels of Cap-tain America and Bucky in action during the war—the image stuck in his mind. That, combined with the success of a comic book featuring another 'mystery man'—as super heroes were called in those days—who wore tights and a cape, made him realize that, perhaps, the best way to get people's attention was to be as—"

"In-their-face?" Finckley interjected.

Scott smiled. "I *was* going to say 'as flamboyant as possible,' but, yes, 'in-their-face' is just as good." He shrugged. "Whatever you want to call it, it worked—Erik got their attention."

"In spades, some would say," Finckley replied. "He wasn't ex-actly greeted with open arms by the public when he made his first appearance, was he?"

Scott's easy smile dissipated, and he nodded morosely. "Unfor-tunately, it's human nature, Archer—people *always* react poorly at first to anything different; anything they don't understand."

"Anything that could be potentially *dangerous,*" Finckley added. "Not knowing what to make of a magnetically-powered mu—'genetically gifted' person showing up out of the blue—"

"As I said, an unfortunate example of *human* nature," Scott quickly interjected.

"—and the fact that superpowered beings hadn't been seen since the close of World War II—"

"—which he felt would only help create the kind of impact he wanted to make—"

"—in addition to Lensherr's less than . . . tolerant reaction to the jeers of a lunchtime crowd in the middle of Times Square on the first day he wore his costume—"

"—a crowd that tried to silence his message—"

"—and the way in which he lashed out with his powers against the police officers arriving on the scene—"

"—who had their *guns drawn* when they approached—"

"—then I think you can understand how 'Magneto' originally wound up being classified as a criminal by law enforcement agencies around the globe," Finckley concluded.

"And Dr. King and Malcolm X and Ghandi were all considered dangerous troublemakers by *their* enemies, too." Scott waved a hand at his host, dismissing Finckley's argument. "It's all a matter of perspective, Archer—perspective, and the petty fears of those unwilling to really *listen* to the message. But, as you and everyone watching this program well know, Erik overcame those obstacles and gained the respect of the world's leaders—*they* listened, and *they* understood." He leaned forward, jabbing the end of an index finger against Finckley's desk to emphasize his point. "The bottom line is that, without Erik Lensherr, this world would *never* have achieved the level of peace we enjoy today."

Finckley shrugged. "Well, there's no denying that, despite his initial setbacks, Lensherr *has* accomplished quite a lot since he first went public forty years ago—"

"Archer, the man has eliminated hatred and intolerance across the planet—in our lifetime!" Scott shot back. "There are no more wars, no more deaths, no more senseless shows of force caused by petty differences. But, even more, he's helped change the very shape of the world—there are forests growing where there once were deserts; freedom where there'd been oppression; lawfulness where there'd been chaos. Most importantly, through his efforts, both *Homo sapiens* and *Homo superior* have learned to co-exist, without fear, without mistrust, working together to better the Earth—not just for generations to come, but for *right now.*" Slowly, he smiled and shook his head. "After all that—after the life of every man, woman, and child on this planet had been changed forever by the power of one man's dream—is it any *wonder* we made him our emperor?"

His point made, Scott fell silent and slowly moved back in his seat, then looked to Jean. Beaming with pride, she reached out and patted his arm in a congratulatory manner; after all, it wasn't every day that Archer Finckley was beaten at his own game.

Finckley grunted, clearly conceding the argument. "I think it's time we took some calls," he mumbled, quickly changing the subject. He glared at his stage manager, who stood to one side of the camera that was trained on the sour-faced host. Above the camera, a TelePrompTer flashed the location of the first person calling the station. "Hello, Saskatoon. You're on the air . . ."

"Well, *there's* two hours of my life I'll never get back . . ." Jean muttered one hour later, relieved to have finally escaped the hot studio lights and even hotter glare of their host.

All in all, it hadn't turned out to be anywhere close to the traumatic event she'd been expecting, since she and Scott had continued to hold up their end of the interview, even managing to sneak in a plug or two for interested parents to get more information by either calling the institute's toll-free number (1-800-GEN-PRIDE) or by logging on to its Internet Web site (www.childrenoftheatom.com); and, much to her surprise, Finckley had concluded the show with an open invitation for them to come back another evening. A gracious move, and one Scott was sure to follow-up on, but one that Jean felt she could, hopefully, decline. Let her run the school and have Ororo or Rogue make the next appearance, she figured; they've always been better at this Public Relations stuff, anyway.

Right now, though, the only thing Jean was interested in was a warm bath, some scented candles, and a cup of jasmine tea to soothe her frazzled nerves. And a massage—*definitely* a massage. If there was one thing that had convinced her that marrying Scott Summers was a good idea, it was the fact he had *great* hands, and an incredible knack for loosening up the tightest knots.

But all of that would have to wait, much to Jean's growing annoyance. Standing outside the side entrance of WSLP-TV, from which *Viewpoints* was broadcast, she and Scott huddled under a gold-trimmed, maroon-colored awning, trying to stay dry. Just beyond the protective canopy, rain was falling in a heavy, perpendicular downpour, turning the intersection of Tenth Avenue and Fifty-seventh Street in Manhattan into the closest approximation Jean had ever seen to the canals of Venice, Italy. All four street corners had disappeared beneath a small lake caused by backed-up sewer drains, and the streams it created stretched toward every point on the compass. Walking anywhere was completely out of the question, since the rushing waters looked more than capable of grabbing a careless pedestrian in an undercurrent and sweeping them into the Hudson River, which flowed just a few blocks to the west.

And there wasn't a taxi cab to be seen—an unfortunate, though quite typical, situation for New Yorkers to find themselves in on a dark and stormy night.

"I thought Ororo guaranteed a clear evening," Jean said, watching a bolt of lightning rip across the darkened sky; the resounding boom of its thunder two seconds later rattled windows and set off what seemed to be every car alarm in the neighborhood. She sighed. "Well, *that'll* teach me to trust a weather goddess. Wouldn't surprise me if she caused it in the first place so she could water her plants properly." She glanced at Scott, and jerked a thumb toward the downpour. "What do you think—should we chance it?"

Scott, however, seemed to be in his own little world. He laughed heartily and turned to face his wife. "Did you see what happened back there, honey?" he asked, motioning toward the studio. "I walked right into the lion's den, and I'm still alive to talk about it!"

Jean smiled. "I know. I was there, remember?" She pointed a warning finger at him. "But don't let it go to your head, 'Slim.' You caught Finckley on a bad night—even without scanning his thoughts, I could tell he was trying his best not to say anything derogatory about Erik; it'd be like badmouthing the Pope. And *being* that overly cautious threw him off his game." Jean's eyes went wide. "Believe me, hon, if you ever saw the replay of the show where he tore Strom Thurman apart over budget cuts to the National Endowment for the Arts, you'd realize just how *lucky* you were in there." She shook her head. "No, if Finckley had been running on all cylinders, he would've found a way to chew your butt right off." Leaning back, she peered around her husband, and smiled. "Well, maybe he *did* get a little piece of it . . ."

An eyebrow rose above the ruby quartz lenses of Scott's sunglasses. "Is that so?"

Jean nodded, still staring at her husband's posterior. "Mm-hmm. Must've happened when you got a little heated over him questioning the need for the Children of the Atom Museum that's opening in Paris next week—you *did* come off as a little too fawning over Erik." She shrugged. "But it's hardly noticeable."

"*You* can see it," Scott noted.

Grinning broadly, Jean turned to look at him in the eye. "Honey, I'm your *wife*. There isn't an inch of that butt I'm not familiar with—who *else* would know what to look for?" Her eyes narrowed. "And if there's an answer to that question other than 'my mom,' I don't want to hear it."

Scott grunted and folded his arms across his chest. "I notice he didn't chew any of *yours* off," he said with mock indignation.

"That's because I'm the *cute one,*" Jean replied, green eyes sparkling with mirth. "You think people would still respect the great Archer Finckley tomorrow morning if he'd been seen knoshing on a redheaded school marm tonight?" She patted her hips. "Besides, my butt's so small, it'd only be an appetizer for him." She glanced at Scott. "It *is* small, isn't it?"

"Of course, it is," he quickly replied. As Scott had learned early in life, there were certain questions that arose in any given relationship—it made no difference whether it was human or mutant—that, when lobbed like grenades by the female half of the couple, had to be expertly defused with fast, straightforward, and *always* positive answers; there were no alternatives if the participants wished to remain happy together. And in *this* particular relationship, with the love of his life *literally* able to read his mind, Scott knew how easily he could be caught in a lie—and how dangerous would be the repercussions.

Truly, hell hath no fury like a telepath/telekinetic who can hurl a roomful of furniture at you when she's provoked, *and*, at the same time, give you a migraine headache while you're busy trying to dodge the chest-of-drawers.

"Speaking of appetizers . . ." he said, changing the subject.

Jean laughed, all too aware of his ploy. "My husband—the master of the segue."

"Speaking of appetizers . . ." Scott continued, clearly choosing to ignore her comment, ". . . I'm starving. How about you?"

Jean's stomach responded on her behalf, rumbling ominously. The redheaded telepath laughed. In point of fact, she hadn't had anything to eat that day, beyond a buttered, cinnamon/raisin bagel and a large espresso in the morning; her nervousness over the impending interview had made her too nauseated to contemplate eating anything else . . . well, except for that handful of Hershey's Kisses she'd found in the bottom right-hand desk drawer in her office. A girl's gotta have her chocolate fix, she'd told herself, even if she's about to get her head handed to her, and soon the ink blotter had been covered with discarded silver wrappings. But now, looking back on her time in the studio, Jean was amazed that her stomach hadn't voiced its protest earlier. Now, *there* would have been something for Finckley to seize on!

"I'll take that for a 'yes,' " Scott said, nodding toward Jean's outspoken digestive cavity. "Well, there's an all-night diner on the corner of Fifty-sixth that's open; I've eaten there with Hank a few times."

"That's fine," Jean said, raising her voice to be heard above the rumble of thunder. "Now, all we have to worry about is *getting* there."

Scott stared past her, at the rain that seemed to sizzle as it struck the pavement around them. "Okay, so, what do you want to do?"

Jean stared thoughtfully at the canopy. "Well, you could always use your power-beams to snap the awning posts, and we could try carrying it . . ." She caught his look of disapproval. "Just a thought. What do *you* propose?"

Scott smiled and shrugged out of his jacket, then handed it to his wife just as another crack of thunder shook the blackened sky directly above them. "Run for it?"

Jean grinned broadly and draped the coat over her head like a hood. "Sounds like a plan."

And then, laughing and screaming with joy, they raced out into the storm, trying to dodge between the raindrops.

An ocean away, another member of the "genetically gifted" was just as pleased with how the *Viewpoints* interview had gone . . . though he might have used his fearsome powers to turn the narrow-minded little human inside out for daring to question the awe-inspiring accomplishments of the master of the world. Even so, he had to admit that Jean and Scott had handled their parts admirably, reminding the home audience time and again of the wondrous Golden Age in which they all lived—and the man who had made it possible.

With a wave of his hand, Erik Lensherr turned off the wall-mounted flatscreen television that hung in his salon. "Excellent," he murmured. "The reprogramming of Summers and his wife has gone even better than I could have imagined—one would almost believe they had *never* been tainted by the influence of Charles Xavier. . ."

Rising from the couch on which he'd been sitting, Lensherr stepped across the room and drew back the red velvet curtains that hung in front of the windows. Outside, the streets and buildings of Paris still blazed brightly in the wee hours of the morning, the sprawling, Old World metropolis truly living up to its reputation as "The City of Lights." Along the banks of the Seine, couples— human and mutant, some intermixed—walked hand-in-hand, enjoying the warm summer air and each other's company. Silhouetted against the bright, full moon, a man and woman, powerful wings sprouting from between their shoulder blades, gracefully danced through the air around the Eiffel Tower.

Lensherr smiled. Here was Paris as he had always wanted it to be: the cornerstone of modern civilization; the gateway to a new era in history. A shining example of *Homo sapiens* and *Homo superior* living harmoniously—under his rule, of course.

It had been a shame to have destroyed it in the first place— more von Doom's fault than his, of course. Back when that Latverian imbecile had controlled the world—was it only hours ago? It felt like years—his lackeys had cornered the mutant overlord in the capital, where he and some of his followers had been making plans to overthrow the armored dictator. The resulting battle cost Lensherr his most devoted acolytes, and was brought to a swift, and bloody, conclusion only when he used his magnetic powers to pull a spy satellite from its orbit and bring it crashing down on the city, obliterating millions of innocent lives and centuries of irreplaceable art and architecture.

Or had he?

As Lensherr had discovered—with help from, of all people, his oldest enemies, the insufferable X-Men—none of the events had taken place; or, rather, none of it had taken place in the *real* world, the one in which von Doom was merely the monarch of a Latveria, and not the omniscient ruler of the Earth, and Magneto was lord of the island-nation of Genosha. No, it had all occurred in a fantasy realm—a construct formed from the dreams and ambitions of Victor von Doom, made real by the use of a Cosmic Cube. And in this topsy-turvy reality, Magneto had become Emperor von Doom's plaything: memories altered, allies scattered around the globe, constantly on the run from Imperial forces. A genetically superior mouse set loose in a danger-filled maze solely for the amusement of its owner.

The realization had galled the mutant overlord—to think that a *human* should dare to abuse someone who was his evolutionary better!

The abuse had ended, though, in Washington, D.C., when Lensherr's gauntleted fist smashed against the right cheek of his rival, savagely disconnecting von Doom from his power source. Lensherr hadn't stopped to think about how or why his enemy had been transformed into a feeble old man incapable of defending himself— he was only interested in taking his pound of flesh from the lowly human who had wronged the great Magneto.

But then he had heard the siren call of the Cube, whispering softly in his mind, enticing him with dreams of power, with worlds for the making, and von Doom was all but forgotten. With the X-Men incapacitated and the mighty "emperor" sprawled across the floor, wheezing for air like some dying animal, there had been no one to stop the mutant overlord from taking possession of the most powerful reality-generator in the universe and . . . correcting the situation.

In the space of a few moments, the Cube restructured the world to suit Magneto's tastes, removing all traces of von Doom's authority, restoring Paris to its former glory, and replacing the despot's police state with images from his own dreams: of a world ruled by *Homo superior*; of he as its master; of the X-Men, their wills reshaped, becoming his unquestioning servants. All of it had come to pass, in some fashion; he couldn't fathom why the Cube hadn't followed his instructions to the letter, as it appeared to have done for von Doom, but he was learning to live with the differences. So *Homo superior* was not the dominant race, but had come to live peacefully with humanity—at least he was still master. And if Scott Summers and Jean Grey wished to spout drivel detailing his fictitious accomplishments—though he had no idea where *those* had come from (the depths of his subconscious, perhaps?)—then, by all means, let them; it only added further detailing to the fantasy and proved beyond a shadow of a doubt how completely the X-Men were under his thrall. No, not everything he'd desired had been laid at his feet, but when he stepped back and took full view of what his dreams had made possible, only one word came to mind to describe it:

"Perfection," Lensherr said. "Absolute perfection . . ."

"Are you talking to yourself again, Erik?" asked a feminine voice from behind him.

Lensherr turned, his deeply lined face practically glowing with joy as he gazed at the woman standing before him. She was beautiful, as she always had been, as she always would be. Tall and lithe, in her mid-forties, but looking ten years younger, Magdalena Lensherr stood in the doorway, hands resting lightly on her hips, one eyebrow raised questioningly. At her husband's silent invitation to join him, she walked across the salon, taking care to avoid the documents, communiqués, faxes, and requests to which the master of the world was expected to respond—at his leisure, of course—that he had allowed to accumulate. Her dark brown, curly hair, normally worn in a short, stylish bob, was a mess—the result of what has commonly come to be known as "bed hair"—and she delicately placed a hand over her mouth to stifle the yawn that was building; she failed. The floor-length, blue satin negligée that hugged her figure made subtle, sweeping sounds as it brushed against her legs.

In his mind, he knew she wasn't real—nothing more than a simulacrum of the woman he had once loved and lost, decades before, culled from memories he had thought long faded. A dream-figure, given life by the power of the Cube. And yet, in his heart . . .

In his heart, she was everything he remembered: the light brown eyes that always seemed to shine with joy; the bubbling laugh that sent a pleasant thrill up his spine; the sway of her hips when she walked; the touch of her skin; the way she tilted her head to one side when she smiled.

Yes, in the "real" world, Magda had been lost to him on the night Magneto was born; the night their daughter, Anya, had died in a fire, and Lensherr had slain the humans who had kept him from rescuing her. Magda had run from him then, terrified of the monster her husband had become; and he, too consumed by grief and hatred, had allowed her to go, choosing instead to focus his anger on punishing all mankind for the actions of a few, prejudiced fools.

But here, in *this* world, Magda had never left him, and Anya had grown to become a beautiful woman. In *his* world, Erik Magnus Lensherr had never suffered such tragic losses; instead, he had found the man buried deep within the blackened soul of the archvillain Magneto. Had rediscovered the joy of being a father and husband.

Had learned what it meant to *love* again.

"I apologize, my dear," he said with a smile, "but speaking aloud is a habit I find increasingly difficult to break." He shrugged. "I imagine it comes from those occasions when, as the saying goes, I was the only person with whom I could have an intelligent conversation."

Magda looked at him sternly, but he knew there was no real heat in her gaze. "A fine thing to say to the woman who supported your efforts for so long."

"For which I have always been grateful," Lensherr replied graciously. He placed his hands on her hips and drew her into a deep kiss. The scent of sandalwood in her hair and dewberry soap on her skin was intoxicating.

When they at last parted, Magda reached up to gently stroke

his cheek. "I accept your apology," she said softly.

Lensherr chuckled. "Now, my dear, you see why I was honored with the Nobel Prize, for Magneto has always been able to find a peaceful solution to any potential conflict."

"Unfortunately," Magda said playfully, "he's never been able to stop referring to himself in the third person."

The mutant overlord raised an eyebrow in amusement. "You *did* know what you were getting into when you married me, dear lady."

His wife nodded. "Including all your little eccentricities—yes, I know."

Lensherr's eyes widened in mock surprise. "I thought you found those 'little eccentricities' attractive."

"*Charming,*" Magda said. "I *never* said they were attractive."

"I stand corrected," he replied humbly, and smiled.

Magda reached up to playfully tousle his snow-white hair. "Come to bed, Erik. The sun will be up soon enough, and you wouldn't want to miss the chance to see your oldest daughter when she returns from her trip to America because you overslept." She paused, and her smile slowly faded, then, as she stared deeply into his gray eyes.

"What is it?" Lensherr asked.

A troubled look darkened Magda's features, and she gently placed her hands along the sides of his face. "You look so tired, Erik. Are you all right?"

Lensherr put his hands atop hers, and smiled reassuringly. "I'm fine, Magda—really. I imagine it has to do with these late hours I've been keeping; they can be quite debilitating." His eyes sparkled with mischief. "In fact, if I'm not careful, I'm liable to nod off to sleep at any moment."

And with that, his eyes snapped shut, and his chin dropped onto his chest. Then he began snoring lightly.

An instant later, he opened his eyes, to find Magda glaring at him, arms folded across her chest.

"I don't find that the *least* bit amusing, Erik," she said curtly.

"A small joke, my love," he replied with a smile. He bent forward to kiss her lightly on the forehead. "But now, please don't let me keep you up any longer. I will be along in a little while."

It was obvious that Magda understood she was being politely—but firmly—dismissed; the annoyed frown that bowed her lips couldn't be missed. "All right, Erik . . . but do not wait *too* long, all right?" A playful light came into her eyes. "You know how I hate to sleep alone."

The master of the world nodded, a wolfish grin creeping its way across his rugged features. With a peck on the cheek, Magda turned and left her husband, swaying her hips *just so* as she walked, making it quite clear that he'd be a fool to remain cloistered in a drawing room for even a moment longer when a beautiful woman awaited his "charming eccentricities" on the next floor.

Lensherr sighed contentedly and glanced at the gold-trimmed mirror that hung above the salon's fireplace. Magda had been right—he *did* look tired; older even than his true age. And considering the fact that he had been alive long enough to be able to provide first-hand accounts of the Nazi atrocities during World War II, that was saying quite a lot.

But still, he had managed to stave off any signs of aging for years: he didn't suffer from arthritis, or osteoporosis, or rheumatism; still had all his hair and teeth; still possessed the healthy constitution of a man one-third his age—all, more than likely, were benefits of his genetic "gifts."

And yet, despite his genetic superiority, he was slowly dying.

It had something to do with the Cube—of that he was certain. Something that was causing him to age rapidly, as von Doom had while the device was in his possession. But what? And how could he stop the process before it killed him? He'd tried "wishing" it away by using the Cube, but that hadn't worked, and he'd quickly dismissed the idea that von Doom might have created some sort of "fail-safe" mechanism that would turn the Cube's power against its owner; a man capable of constructing a reality-generator never would have allowed its protective systems to backfire on him. There *had* to be a way to fight it, though; now that Lensherr had achieved his life's dream, he wasn't about to let it fade away with the exhalation of his last breath.

The mutant overlord strode across the salon, stopping before a painting hung in an elegant, gold-leaf frame—an original Matisse, given to him by millionaire industrialist Anthony Stark on the thirtieth anniversary of the "Children of the Atom" speech. With a touch of a hidden button, the frame swung out from the wall, revealing a safe constructed from adamantium—the hardest-known metal on Earth. Small in design, yet impervious to any explosive, the safe's most unusual design was that it had no door—no means of entry . . . for anyone but Magneto.

A slight gesture from his hand, and the metal rippled, then flowed in two directions, creating a gap—one that shone with the brilliance of the Cosmic Cube contained within. Lensherr had dis-covered, through experimentation, that he did not have to hold the device all the time in order to make it work; he merely had to be within close range of it. And by sealing it away in a block of damage-resistant metal, he had made certain that only he would have access to it, for he knew that, despite the wonders of the "enlightened society" he had created, he still had enemies. Not on Earth, of course—the Cube had given him the power to neutralize all the so-called "super heroes" who originally existed simply by making them forget they had ever possessed superpowers, or had ever worn a costume outside of a Halloween party.

But Charles Xavier was still out there, somewhere; he, and the remaining slack-jawed sycophants he called "students" who hadn't journeyed to Earth with the X-team that had ultimately been forced into aiding Magneto and his acolytes in their attack on von Doom. He had learned that much from Jean Grey, when she had used her telepathic abilities to repair the damage done to the mu-tant overlord's memories by the armored tyrant. And knowing Charles as well as he did, it was only a matter of time before his former friend elected to send a second team after the Cube, to put an end to some alleged threat to the "omniverse," about which Grey and Summers had been constantly prattling.

Well, *let* them come, Lensherr decided. They would find Magneto ready. This was *his* world now. And fantasy-construct though its origins might be, it was still real, still vibrant, still the sum of everything he had ever desired, and no one—human *or* mutant—was going to deprive him of his dreams . . . even if he had to die for them. . . .

4

HE WAS dying, and there was nothing she could do to prevent it.

Betsy knelt on the grassy expanse of The Mall in Washington, D.C., her thoughts in turmoil, her body growing numb. A steady rain was falling, drenching her clothes and hair, but she was unaware of it. Around her, people were shouting, screaming, running in panic, but she couldn't hear any of it. Her attention was focused solely on the man lying in front of her, his body broken, his beautiful white wings fluttering limply.

Warren coughed hollowly, phlegm rattling in lungs hard-pressed to draw in air. Kneeling down, Betsy gently raised his head and cradled it in her lap. She slowly stroked his blond hair with a gloved hand . . . and tried her best to ignore the smell of burnt flesh that assailed her nostrils.

"Warren, I'm going to find a doctor, or a paramedic," she said. "I'll be right back, okay? Just please, *please* hang on."

She started to rise, but Warren grasped her hand and pulled her back down. "No . . . don't go . . ." he said, slowly shaking his head. His voice was growing fainter.

Betsy opened her mouth to say something—some words of encouragement, or even anger, telling him he had no right to give up, not when they still had a whole lifetime ahead of them to explore—but in her heart, she knew it was too late.

Too late for anything more than good-bys.

So did Warren. Tenderly, he reached up to stroke her cheek. "You really *are* . . . the most beautiful woman . . . in the world . . . you know . . ."

Betsy took his hand and brushed her lips against his fingers. "Warren, I . . ." she began, then fell silent, unable to speak. A tear dropped from the corner of her left eye, to splash on Warren's cheek.

"Don't leave me . . ." she sobbed.

Warren smiled. "Love you, Betts . . ." he whispered.

And then he was gone.

Betsy awoke to the sound of screams ringing in her ears. It took a moment to realize they were hers.

The screams subsided, giving way to ragged sobs as she buried her face in her pillow, tears staining the satin casing. Eventually, this, too, passed, and she slowly sat up in the bed, body trembling from the effort. She felt drained, unable to think clearly. Looking back on it, sleep had originally seemed like a good idea—an escape from the unsettling memories that she'd fought to keep buried in the back of her mind since arriving at the citadel; a momentary respite from the grief that threatened to overwhelm her if she didn't maintain control over her emotions.

But there had been no escape, no solace, from the images that played and replayed on the projection screen of her subconscious: Magneto using his fearsome powers to tear apart the limousine containing Emperor von Doom and his wife, Ororo; Warren, ruggedly handsome, wings bright against the storm-tossed sky, swooping down to protect the tyrant; the blinding crackle of magnetic energy as it erupted from the mutant overlord's hands, enveloping Warren; his limp body dropping to the ground, landing with a sickening, bone-crushing impact on the grass as she raced

to join him; the smile that had won her heart twisting into a pain-racked grimace as he drew his last breath. No, sleep hadn't been an escape—it had been a chamber of horrors.

Betsy swept lavender-hued tresses back from her eyes, her gaze immediately falling upon the velvet evening gown. A wisp of a smile played at the corners of her mouth as she gently ran her fingertips over the material. It had been a gift from Warren—one among many she'd received during their time together—for her "Big Night": a solo singing performance at the Von Doom Center for the Performing Arts, part of a celebration held in honor of the Emperor's tenth anniversary in power. He'd convinced her to wear it in place of the red "lucky dress" she'd often worn at his New York nightclub, the Starlight Room, by explaining that if she was going to make an impression on the Emperor she should at least do it in a gown befitting the occasion. He'd been right, of course, but, as eye-catching as the dress was, it had been her singing that really caught the attention of von Doom—his, and that of the hundreds of attendees at the gala that night.

But then, Magneto and his followers had attacked, and Warren had gone to von Doom's aid, and—

Betsy bit her bottom lip to stifle another sob—hard enough to draw blood—and angrily threw back the sheets, forcing herself to step from the bed before she could allow herself to collapse into another crying jag.

"Lights—fifty percent," she said hoarsely, throat raw from the screams that had awakened her. The citadel's computer responded instantly, and the room filled with dimmed lighting—bright enough to see by, yet low enough that it didn't cause her to wince as her eyes became accustomed to it.

Now that she was awake, Betsy decided that the only thing to do was to get ready for the day ahead; by keeping active, by focusing on the mission, she'd at least be able to escape the memories that haunted her. She hoped.

She stalked across the suite to the bathroom, the lights automatically snapping on as she stepped over the threshold. The lavatory was similar to that found in any home or apartment, its floor and walls tiled—the alternating blue and white pieces of ceramic forming intricate Celtic symbols—its facilities consisting of a toilet, sink, and shower.

Betsy looked at herself in the mirror above the sink, and grimaced. Her eyes were bloodshot and puffy. Her lower lip was swollen where she'd bitten it. Her hair was tangled, wispy strands floating around her hair like cobwebs caught in a slight breeze. And at some point during the night, her mascara had gotten smeared from all the tears she'd shed. All in all, she looked more like a bloody purple-haired raccoon than a glamorous super heroine.

"Oh, *pants*," she muttered. She waved a hand under the tap, activating the hot water, and cupped her hands in the flow so she could splash her face and wash away the ruined makeup. But then, gazing at herself once more, a slow smile came to her lips.

She remembered being awakened one morning by the gentle prodding of Warren as he poked her in the shoulder, asking if she were awake in that playful, wolfish tone he affected whenever he was feeling particularly amorous. But, considering the celebrating they'd done the night before—in honor of a recent victory over Kuragari, the self-proclaimed "Shogun of the Shadows," who had tried to make Betsy one of his followers—and the night of passion it had ultimately led to, every muscle in her body ached. It was hard to try and put even two coherent sentences together with her brain so addled. Nevertheless, she had rolled over in bed to point out that not everyone had the stamina of a man who could fly cross-country under his own power, only to see him draw back in horror, yelping sharply like an injured dog.

For a world-renowned playboy, one would almost think he'd never seen a woman with her makeup in disarray; not that she'd remembered to take it off, of course, given the heat of the moment. But then, he'd smiled, and commented that he'd never slept with a raccoon-woman before, and . . .

And this time, Betsy couldn't stop the tears that ran hotly down her cheeks. Her knees buckled, and she slipped down to the tiled floor. As her sobs mixed with the sound of running water, she wondered when the ache in her heart would finally subside.

It was going to be a bad day.

Charles Xavier knew it—the weight in the pit of his stomach told him so. The last time he'd felt that weight was only a few months ago, when he and Piotr Nikolievitch Rasputin—the Russian-born, armored X-Man whose codename was "Colossus"—had been trapped in the realm of a nightmarish creature called the Synraith. True to form, his stomach had been right: it *had* been a bad day.

A *very* bad day.

And so, the Professor now sat on the edge of his bed, buttoning his starched, white dress shirt while he listened to the gurgling of his abdomen, staring out at the forces of Creation that endlessly roiled beyond his windows, wishing the new day wouldn't come . . . yet knowing it was unavoidable.

He'd slept poorly, his dreams peppered with images of Warren in happier times, and what might be happening to his other students with Magneto in possession of a Cosmic Cube: Scott's force beams raised to such an intensity that his body could no longer contain the energy; Jean's mental powers turned against her, driving her insane; Nightcrawler's teleportational powers run amuck, until the strain ultimately tore him apart; Gambit's kinetic energy making him avoid touching anything or anyone, for fear of causing them to explode; Rogue's "power-leeching" ability gone wild, her slightest contact instantly killing whomever she was near. And as for Wolverine . . .

Well, Logan had already undergone painful torture at Magneto's hands once before, when the mutant overlord used his powers to seize control of the adamantium that coated the feral X-Man's skeleton—*and draw out every ounce of it through Logan's pores*. If it hadn't been for Wolverine's mutant healing factor, the process would have killed him. But Magneto would be well aware of that, and find some way to compensate for that ability—perhaps by killing Logan, only to resurrect him time and again, never allowing him the peace of oblivion.

As Xavier knew so well, Erik Lensherr was a man with an *extremely* vivid imagination . . .

But the fate of his "advance team" was not the only thing on Xavier's mind. What also troubled him was the unknown—specifically, what might have happened to the other members of the X-Men, the ones left on Earth 616 while he and his hand-picked group had gone to aid Roma against Opul Lun Sat-yr-nin. Psylocke's arrival on the citadel made it clear that she and Warren—Archangel—had been "restructured" to reflect the changes made to the world under Doctor Doom's rule, but what had become of Colossus and Shadowcat? Iceman and the Beast? Storm and Marrow? The members of Generation X? And where would *they* fit into the schemes of Erik Magnus Lensherr?

Xavier felt the threads of his life unraveling. For so long, he had fought the good fight, striving constantly to find a way to bring peace between mutants and humans; sacrificing any chance of having a normal life, a normal relationship, as he focused all his energies on that dream; putting at risk people who trusted him with their lives, who believed in his cause even though they were despised for what they were; watching as friends, even family members died around him. But now, apparently, it had all been for nothing—the lives lost, the battles won, the selfless dedication. Once Magneto had placed his hands on the Cube, Charles Xavier lost his chance to realize his own dream, lost the opportunity to create a world of equality, based not on the genetic composition of an individual, but on their strength of character, their willingness to use their talents—whether superhuman or not—to usher the races into a new Golden Age.

But now, though, there would only be *Homo superior* in control, with mankind looked upon as something akin to offal; a reversal of the situation before then, true, but Xavier had always believed in a peaceful solution to the problem. He *never* would have resorted to forcibly changing the world to get his way.

Would he?

Here, then, was the real question that puzzled—and deeply dis-turbed—the world's greatest telepath as he considered it. When he figuratively stepped back to look at the "big picture," was he both-ered by what Magneto was doing with the Cube . . . or jealous that Erik had succeeded where he had failed . . . ?

A soft chiming sound interrupted his thoughts; he had never been so grateful for an interruption.

"Come!" he called out.

The door to his suite irised open, and Psylocke stepped inside. She was dressed in her X-Man uniform: a dark-blue, high-necked, one-piece outfit that resembled a swimsuit, with matching thigh-high stockings and gloves that ran from her upper arms to her wrists; a red belt was cinched around her waist, its buckle a stylized "X." The Professor realized that, since she hadn't been wearing it when she came aboard, Elisabeth must have used the citadel's matter replicators to create it. Her hair was drawn back in a severe ponytail, allowing the lights of the room to accentuate her Asian features . . . and the blood-red, J-shaped tattoo that ran down the left side of her face, from her temple to just below her cheekbone—a side effect of her acquisition of the mystical powers of the Crimson Dawn. Equally as red as the tattoo were her eyes; it appeared he hadn't been the only person unable to sleep.

"I hope I'm not disturbing you, Professor," Psylocke said qui-etly.

Xavier smiled warmly as he tucked his shirt into his dark trou-sers. "Not at all, Elisabeth. I was just getting ready for the day." He reached for his tie. "Do you feel up to talking?"

Psylocke nodded. "Yes, but . . . first, I'd like to apologize for my earlier behavior. You were right: I *shouldn't* have attacked Doom like that. It was wrong, and pig-headed, and unquestionably stu-pid."

"Unquestionably," Xavier said. His smile widened. "Apology accepted."

That seemed to relax her. "Thank you."

The Professor nodded and completed the Windsor knot in his tie, then shrugged into his dark blazer. He cast a quick glance at his hoverchair, broadcasting a mental command to its computer system. The machine floated forward from its place by the observation windows, the top half of the chair quietly swinging open on well-oiled hinges to reveal the padded leather seat within. As the device pulled alongside the bed, Xavier grabbed hold of its sides and hauled himself into the seat.

"Now, then," he said to Psylocke as he settled in, "why don't you fill me in on the situation . . ."

He hadn't liked what he'd heard.

Psylocke had told him everything—well, at least as much as she knew from the brief contact she had had with Jean Grey's mind, when the redheaded X-Man linked with Elisabeth in an effort to restore the latter's memories, which had been "rewritten" by the Cube to reflect the changes in von Doom's world. She knew of the team's mission to find and correct the anomaly that threatened to unravel the omniverse; of their alliance with Magneto (a particularly upsetting revelation for the Professor); of the events leading up to Warren's death, though that took some effort to get through. She described her confrontation with von Doom in his hidden chamber beneath the White House, where the armored dictator had admitted to the flaw in the Cube's construction and the drain it now placed on its owner's life-force in order to maintain his chosen reality. And then, hesitantly, she talked about his offer to resurrect Archangel in exchange for her promise to take possession of the Cube under his command, so that he could continue ruling the planet without the fear (her word, obviously) of having his remaining life-force taken away.

She wouldn't say if she had agreed to his terms.

Instead, she related the final moments, when Magneto and his acolytes had burst onto the scene, just as the X-Men were on the brink of victory, handily defeating the heroic mutants and claiming the Cube for their leader. Then, von Doom's hand had clamped around her ankle, and—

"—here we are," Psylocke concluded.

"Indeed," Xavier murmured.

She watched him in silence for a few moments, obviously waiting for him to say something further. When he didn't—mainly because his brain was still processing the information she'd provided—she softly cleared her throat. "Any suggestions as to what we should do next?" she asked.

"Not at the moment," Xavier admitted. "And you're certain von Doom has no cure for this reality-cancer he's created?"

Her lavender eyes sparkled with mischief. "I could always go down to the infirmary and ask him again."

"No, that's quite all right," the Professor replied. His voice was laced with just enough of a warning tone to let Psylocke know she was treading on dangerous ground.

The conversation once more lapsed into silence.

"You know," Psylocke remarked quietly, "on my way over to talk to you, I was thinking about all the times Warren and I spent together; all the fun we used to have." A melancholy smile slowly tugged at the corners of her mouth.

"Warren mentioned a few of those occasions in passing," Xavier said. He smiled warmly as he saw his student blush. "Nothing risqué, however—he was always too much the gentleman for 'locker room talk.' "

Psylocke nodded. "Always. Even in the most uncomfortable of situations." She gazed past the Professor, as though looking through a window, into the past. "I remember that one night, when I was singing down at the Den of the Night Wolf in the Village, while Warren was stuck entertaining Doom's little toady, Sebastian Shaw—"

Xavier raised an inquisitive eyebrow. " 'Entertaining'?"

"Oh, you know what I mean, Professor—show him the sights,

take him to a Broadway show, introduce him to a celebrity or three . . . " Psylocke paused. "Oh, that's right. You weren't there for that." She shrugged. "I'm certain you would have enjoyed it, though." A bright smile lit her exotic features. "You should have seen the look on Shaw's face when Warren brought him to the club, and I sat on his lap and sang 'I Want to be Loved by You.' " She chuckled softly. "I thought the poor dear was going to have a stroke, his face had turned such a ghastly shade of red."

Xavier nodded, but said nothing. From what he knew of Elisabeth's background, however, she had never been a nightclub singer in New York's Greenwich Village; in fact, she had never even been to the United States before joining the X-Men a few years ago. He *was* aware of her time as a much-sought-after fashion model—when her name had often been spoken in the same breath with such notables as Naomi Campbell, Claudia Schiffer, and Mary Jane Watson—and her short and thoroughly unenjoyable time as a Psi Division member of S.T.R.I.K.E., the British spy agency equivalent of America's S.H.I.E.L.D., not to mention her first brush with super heroics, when she had filled in for her brother, Brian, as Captain Britain—a well-intentioned but nearly fatal action that had cost her the eyesight of her original body at the hands of the superpowered assassin Slaymaster.

But a career as a cabaret singer? Never.

And as for Warren having to "entertain" Sebastian Shaw for an evening? Preposterous. The man was the notorious Black King of the equally infamous Hellfire Club, a hedonistic organization that believed in the pursuit of pleasure above all other endeavors in life. An organization that had caused more than its fair share of trouble for the X-Men over the years, from subtle psychic manipulation to outright blatant attempts at killing Xavier and his students, including Warren. Like Magneto, the upper echelon of the club were mutants bent on world domination, though Shaw and his cronies preferred pulling puppet strings from the shadows rather than do anything that would draw attention to themselves.

No, Warren spending time with Shaw would never have happened in the real world—it must be a fabricated memory; a remnant of the Cosmic Cube's influence.

But why, then, did Psylocke fail to see that as well? There had been no hesitation in her voice, no sign of confusion as she'd told her story, so clearly she must regard the event as part of her life experiences.

Xavier frowned. If, indeed, Jean had restored Elisabeth to her proper self, why should she now be casually speaking of such an evening as though it had been real? Could von Doom still be controlling her mind without her knowledge, even though he'd been separated from the Cube? Or could she be allied with the tyrant, as part of the agreement he'd offered, but about which she refused to discuss further?

A far more troubling question, though, now crept into his thoughts: Could Psylocke truly be relied upon to complete the mission? Knowing the amount of grief she must be bottling up inside over Warren's death in order to concentrate on the work ahead, combined with whatever promises she *might* have made to von Doom, her ultimate goal might not be to deactivate the Cube, but to *use it herself.* As much as the Professor hated to admit it, Elisabeth *had* had her moments over the past few years when she'd been working under her own secret agendas, sometimes to the detriment of her fellow X-Men.

Could she be doing the same right now?

Xavier's lips set in a thin, firm line. He could ask her straight out, but he knew she'd deny having any ulterior motives; she'd probably act surprised at his question, say her duties as an X-Man took precedent over her private life, that she'd never even considered using the Cube for personal gain, whether or not that involved the possible restoration of her lover, and how could he ever think that she would? And unlike Elisabeth, the Professor was unwilling to claw his way into her mind in order to find out the truth.

His shoulders sagged. There was only one thing to do, then, to ensure the success of the mission . . .

"I think, perhaps," he said slowly, "it's time we spoke with Roma."

Psylocke's eyes lit up. "You have a plan?"

Xavier nodded. "I'll tell you on the way."

Quickly rising from the bed, Psylocke smiled at her mentor and headed for the door, clearly eager for them to be on their way.

Behind her, the Professor grimaced; the weight in the pit of his stomach seemed to be growing heavier with each passing moment. He sighed softly, and slowly shook his head. Only fully awake for the better part of two hours, and it was *already* turning out to be a *very* bad day. . . .

Interlude II

ITHIN THE confines of Dimension 616, however, matters were much worse . . . at least in the opinion of one particular inhabitant.

"*No! This is unacceptable!*" roared The Controller. He lashed out with a gloved fist, scattering the contents of his desktop: report folders, paperweights, pens, pencils, computer disks, music CDs, and other personal items went flying onto the floor. He slapped the palms of his hands against the dark green ink blotter on which the articles had been resting and shot to his feet. The backs of his legs collided with the edge of his leather-backed chair, sending it hurtling into the dingy gray wall behind him, and the room echoed with the sound of wood striking metal. "I will *not* allow my carefully-laid plans to be upset by the saccharine-sweet dreams of a . . . a *sub-human!* Not when I am so close to success!"

He stepped out from behind the desk, fists clenched, and stomped over to a nearby window. Beyond the protection of the three-inch-thick glass lay the airless landscape of the moon. The satellite's pitted and scarred surface was barely visible past the glow of the perimeter lighting that ringed the edges of this secret base of operations, here on what was known as the planetoid's "dark" side. It had been constructed years before, away from the prying eyes of Earth's super heroic population, as the first step toward stellar domination; a launch point for a planned invasion of other worlds. And, although that proposed attack never got beyond the early stages of development, the Controller had never been the type to admit defeat. So, rather than abandon the base, he had turned its resources toward a simpler—though no less lofty—goal: ruling the Earth.

Yes, he had to admit to himself, it was true that he had made similar overtures in the past, and most of those attempts had been quickly disrupted by men and women garbed in outlandish costumes, the retina-damaging colors of which were usually found only in a child's box of crayons. It was also true that there were countless others who shared the same goal as he—for their own purposes, of course. Von Doom and Magneto, for example, could be counted among those hapless dreamers, who sought to impose their sense of order upon the world, only to wind up tasting the bitter ashes of defeat, their dreams ground to dust under the boot heels of the Fantastic Four, or the Avengers . . . or the X-Men.

But the Controller was different—at least in his own opinion. He was not one of those bumbling cretins like the Master or Count Nefaria or the Mandarin, who only focused on the game at hand, and not the big picture. It was that sort of tunnel vision that resulted in them always being outmaneuvered by lesser intellects who, unlike their villainous counterparts, were able to think quickly on their feet. No, the Controller saw himself as a chess master, sweeping his pieces across the board with unrivaled skill, always three or four moves ahead of his opponents, always thinking of how those moves might aid him in his next match. His enemies might think he was on the verge of being checkmated each time he found himself in conflict with them, but the Controller always had a pawn or two that he kept on reserve, to be used only at the last possible moment to grasp victory from what seemed to be certain defeat.

Von Doom had been one of those pawns, allowed to make use of the Cube only so long as such use fit within the scope of the

Controller's plans. Of course, he had been completely unaware of it, and the Controller had been denied the chance to bring it to his attention. No matter; the gamesman would make up for that lost opportunity—of that, he was quite certain. Soon enough, it would be the illustrious "master of magnetism," the great peace-maker, who would know what it was like to face him across the field of battle . . .

On the other side of his desk, the Controller's assistant, Leonard, stood rigidly at attention, eyes fixed on a point on the far wall. His uniform was not as crisp it had once been, the armpits now stained with sweat, the toes of one jackboot coated with ink from a pen that had shattered during the Controller's tirade. It was obvious he was doing his best to remain calm, to show no emotion in front of his leader, but the glimmer of terror that shone in his eyes, the slight tremors that threatened to buckle his knees, could not be missed.

It pleased The Controller; at least *one* lowly creature in this metamorphosing universe still knew its place. "I allowed that gypsy pig von Doom the opportunity to play out his trifling fantasies while I studied the effects of his Cosmic Cube. Once that had been accomplished—once I learned that that armored cretin had somehow managed to create a version of the Cube more powerful than anything the scientists of A.I.M. had ever devised—I knew it must be mine. For what use to me are a gypsy's pathetic dreams of empire, when the stars themselves are for the taking? *That* is why mine should be the hand that holds the Cube—for only *I* understand the nature of its incredible powers! Only *I* have the limitless vision to make use of its full potential!"

His feral snarl appeared even more disturbing in the room's low lighting. "But then, just as I was finalizing my plans to strike, those *verdammt* X-Men and that *Juden* dog Lensherr robbed me of the chance to take possession of the Cube. And *look* at what those genetic inferiors have done with it!" He grabbed a remote control unit from the pile of items scattered on the floor and pressed a button, activating the wall-sized monitor across the room. The screen filled with static, then slowly cleared to reveal a view of Earth from space, provided by one of a series of cameras that his followers had placed on the "bright" side of the moon. Adjusting the controls, he replaced the full view of the planet with a collection of smaller images: aerial shots of its major cities. Another flick of the remote, and one of the cameras zoomed in on Paris. The sun was shining brightly, the streets were busy, and all seemed right with the world—because one man had *made* it so.

"The power of a *god* in his hands, and he *wastes* it creating a harmonious society, when he *should* be crushing his enemies, or building an *empire.*" The Controller sneered. "So much for the great dreams of *Homo superior.*" He cast an even glance at his assistant. "Do you not agree, Leonard?"

"Yes, Controller!" Leonard replied immediately. "As you have often said, such lack of vision is to be expected from members of an inferior race."

The Controller nodded, pleased with the response. "Indeed. And Magneto is *truly* an inferior, for he clearly has no understanding of the power he possesses. I doubt he is even aware that the effects of the Cube have spread beyond the confines of the Earth." With a grunt, he switched off the viewscreen, then glanced at a clock that was mounted on another wall. "The gas should have dissipated by now. Come with me—we have much to do before this day is over."

He stalked across the room, heading for the door, and Leonard hurriedly moved to open it for him. Not bothering to acknowledge his assistant's action, the Controller pushed past him . . . and stepped into a slaughterhouse.

The command center of the base was littered with the bodies of technicians and soldiers. Blood and gore stained everything, coating the floor, the walls, even the ceiling in some spots. Some of the staff—their skin liquefied so thoroughly that the floor was slick with the remains—were piled around the bottom of the door to the Controller's office; it seemed they'd tried to break down the door before the end, to no avail. Others had died where they sat, or where they'd collapsed onto the floor. And although he could not see the balance of the hundred or so members of his staff, scattered as they were throughout the base, the Controller knew that every corridor, every laboratory, every sleeping quarter would look the same.

The gas that had been released just minutes earlier was an extra security measure personally installed by the Controller years ago; no one on his staff, including Leonard, had been aware of the canisters hidden inside the air ducts. But with a press of a button, the commander had made them *all* aware of their existence ... and what they contained. In seconds, every square foot of the base—excluding the Controller's office, of course—was flooded with a combination of lethal chemicals that dissolved flesh and bone, yet left machinery unaffected. So well-protected was the Controller's office that neither he nor his aide had heard the pitiful screams for mercy that strained to be heard through the sound-proofed walls and door.

Looking back at those moments, the Controller felt disappointed. It seemed that in designing his base *too* well, he had robbed himself of a small pleasure.

He glanced around the nerve center of his base, ignoring the grotesque sight stretched out before him. "Even here, a quarter of a billion miles from Lensherr's peaceful little world, the Cube's energies have taken their toll." He frowned. "The work of years, wiped out in a surge of cosmic forces. Had it not been for my prior experience with—and mastery over—the power of similar devices, everything within my office might have also been transformed into tools of that magnetically-charged freak—" he gazed at his assistant "—including *you,* my sweat-stained lapdog."

"I am honored, Controller," Leonard replied.

His leader grunted. "Do not seek to flatter your master, lackey— your life means nothing to me. I may have spared you from the mutant's taint, but that doesn't mean I would not hesitate to sacrifice your worthless soul in an instant if the situation required it ... as it did with these others." He dramatically waved an arm around the room, gesturing to the bodies. "They were not as fortunate as you, changed as they were by the Cube to become 'productive members' of *his* new society. Once that happened, they were of no further use to the cause—or me—since there was too great a risk that they might inform their new master of my whereabouts. And with all things that lose their value, they were easily discarded." He chuckled softly at his own joke. "But even had these dolts *not* been transformed, they would have met the same end for not informing me of the energy wave before it struck." He glared at his assistant. "Remember this sight well, boy— *this* is the price of failure."

Leonard's Adam's apple bobbed up and down furiously for a few moments. "Y-yes, C-controller," he finally stammered.

The Controller grunted and moved over to study the computer screens at one of the monitoring stations. To get a better view, he roughly pushed aside the corpse of a man slumped there. The top of its head was missing, skin, hair, and bone all eaten away by the gas.

"Come here, Leonard," the Controller said. The blond-haired young man leapt to obey, trying not to look down at the gelatinized flesh that pooled about the floor. His superior pointed to a series of readouts displayed on one screen. "You see this? The Cube's power has not faded one iota, even though the energy wave it created has moved beyond our solar system." His eyes widened in mild surprise. "There are now signs of life on Mars—" he glanced at another readout "—and an atmosphere on the Jovian moon Europa." His eyes glinted with desire. "Fascinating. A single release of energy, and worlds are being recreated right before my eyes. And with no indication that the wave will dissipate at any time soon, who knows *what* will happen as it spreads across the stars . . . ?" He turned to Leonard. "The Cube *must* be mine. It *will* be mine."

"What would you have me do, Controller?" Leonard asked.

The Controller clasped his hands behind his back and walked away from the console, head bowed in concentration. He came to a stop before one of the vast observation windows, and stared out at the depths of space.

The stars themselves for the taking . . .

"We go to Earth," he said, his back still to his assistant. "Together. This mission is far too important to trust to a mere boy." He caught sight of Leonard's expression in the reflection on the three-inch-thick glass: the youth was clearly angered by the comment, but wisely kept his mouth shut. "And when the time comes, *I* shall be the one who pries the Cosmic Cube from that sub-human's lifeless hands—no one else. Is that understood?"

"Of course, Controller," Leonard replied quickly.

The Controller sighed—was he ever that toadying in his youth? He shook his head sharply. No, of course not. If he *had* been, he never would have been selected for the honor bestowed upon him by his own, dark master so many years before; never would have had his eyes opened by a cause he could finally believe in, or been given the means to carry forth its inspiring message of bringing order to a chaotic world; never would have had his long-repressed dreams of becoming someone *important* made a reality.

In the old days, someone as ineffectual as Leonard would have been placed on the front lines of the battlefield—the sooner he died, the sooner he would cease being a liability to the cause. But today, with so few qualified people available . . .

Turning from the window, he strode toward another console; this one was connected to a raised platform large enough to accommodate two people. It was a teleport device, often used in the past by the Controller to evade his enemies, whether heroic or villainous, whenever his latest plan for world domination started to fray at the edges. Although the Controller would deny it, the teleporter had been activated quite a bit during the past few years.

He gestured to his assistant, then set about activating the device. "Get onto the platform while I enter the coordinates."

Leonard did as he was told, stepping gingerly over the bodies of friends and co-workers—with whom he had built what they'd all thought would be lasting relationships—as he made his way to the teleporter. He *just* managed to avoid falling as he slipped in a puddle of gore that had formed around the half-dissolved corpse of what had once been a very pretty young woman named Kate Ashbrook. She had been a twenty-three-year-old computer hacker Leonard had dated for a short time; her identification tag was still pinned to her uniform. Her eyes had melted inside their sockets; the gaping holes in her skull seemed to stare accusingly at him. Why should *he* be allowed to live? What made *him* so special?

Unable to come up with an answer, Leonard turned quickly and walked away. When he finally reached the platform, he found the Controller gazing heatedly at him.

"I have no patience for weak men who quake with fear in the presence of death," the gamesman said, his voice low and tinged with menace. "Are *you* a weak man, Leonard?"

"N-no, C-controller," Leonard replied. "I-it's just that I've never seen this much blood before . . . you know, outside of the movies and TV shows."

The Controller shook his head sadly. "That is what is wrong with your generation, Leonard—your minds have been poisoned by fantasies. There are no 'commercial breaks' in combat, no computer-generated 'special effects'—only death and destruction. Back in my homeland, the *battlefield* was all the entertainment I craved: to smell the sweet, coppery tang of blood in the air; to feel the pulse of your enemy slowing as he died by your hand; to hear the screams of the dying as their bodies were torn apart by bullet and mortar and bayonet; to know that *you* will live another day, while those lying broken and bloodied around you have become nothing more than carrion for the vultures. *That* is far more awe-inspiring than a bunch of flickering images cast on a screen, *because it is real.*" He poked a gloved finger into the chest of his assistant. "You, too, will learn to appreciate such things, Leonard—if you live long enough."

"Yes, sir," Leonard muttered.

The Controller nodded. "Excellent. Now, we go." He pressed a button on his belt.

As the hum of the teleporter filled his ears, Leonard took one last look around the command center, then closed his eyes, trying to block out the image of the twisted, melted bodies that lay at his feet, trying to ignore the smell of death that clung to his clothing, that filled his nostrils.

But then he forced his eyes to open, forced himself to acknowledge the carnage displayed before him. He had chosen to serve the Controller, as had his unfortunate peers. What had happened to them was to be expected, since they had failed in the service of their master.

He would not.

5

HAVE YOU *gone completely mad? What kind of plan is* that?"
Walking alongside Xavier's hoverchair as she and the Professor made their way down one of the seemingly endless corridors in the Starlight Citadel, Betsy threw her hands in the air in utter exasperation. "It's *insane*, Professor!"

"*No*, Elisabeth," Xavier replied. "It's the best possible plan . . . under the circumstances."

Betsy shook her head. "I'm sorry, Professor, but placing yourself in harm's way by accompanying me to Earth is *not* the best possible plan. In case you've forgotten, Magneto and you haven't exactly seen eye-to-eye in decades . . . except on those rare occasions when the two of you share a common enemy—like the Sentinels, or The Brood, or a roomful of Congressmen discussing the Mutant Registration Act."

"I understand your concern, Elisabeth," Xavier countered, "but we're running out of precious time. By speaking with Erik directly, I may be able to make him come to his senses before it's too late." He paused. "I know it's a longshot, but with the other X-Men incapacitated—"

"What about the Captain Britain Corps?" Betsy interjected.

"Why can't *they* come with me? After all, my brother is a member—they should be *eager* to help one of their own."

The Professor shook his head. "I already discussed that possibility with Roma. She refuses to place any of her people at risk, now that the reality-cancer has started to spread throughout our universe. She doesn't want to risk the chance of 'infecting' either the citadel or another dimension with the Cube's taint."

Betsy sucked on her bottom lip for a few moments, brow furrowed in concentration. "The Technet, perhaps? With the proper incentive, those disgusting little mercenaries could be quite an asset, especially Gatecrasher's 'porting abilities; she could take me straight *to* Magneto. I could grab the Cube from him and have everything set right in time for brunch." She frowned. "Oh, but they answer directly to Saturnyne, don't they? And *she'd* never allow them to accept any offer from *us.*"

"Not to mention she's quite adamant that the only solution to the problem is to destroy our dimension. I also seriously doubt their teleportational powers are greater than Roma's; if *she* couldn't place Scott and the others at the heart of the anomaly before, due to the interference created by the Cube's energies, it's unlikely the Technet would have any better luck." Xavier flashed a wry smile. "And *that,* my dear Miss Braddock, brings us full-circle—"

"To a plan that relies far too much on you being able to reason with a man who has dedicated his life to making *Homo superior* the dominant lifeform on the planet . . . and who, now more than ever, has the power to *annihilate* anyone who dares to oppose him." Betsy grimaced and rubbed her throat, remembering the moment back in Washington when she'd tried to attack von Doom while he held the Cube—only to suddenly find herself floating miles above the Earth. She would have died from lack of oxygen within seconds if the tyrant had been in the mood to end her life, and not merely teach her a lesson for her foolish action. She swallowed, hard. "I'm sorry, Professor, but I *can't* let you take that sort of risk."

"It is not *your* decision to make, Psylocke," Xavier replied sternly. "In case *you* have forgotten, I have faced my *own* share of dangers as the founder of this group, from the N'gari to the unleashed fury of the Dark Phoenix, long before you were ever invited to join us." He tapped the armrests of his hoverchair. "Just because I need to travel about in *this,* do not think for a moment that I am helpless."

" 'Helpless?' *You,* Professor?" Betsy smiled. "Of all the words that come to mind that I could possibly use to describe you, I'd find it *very* hard to include *that* one." She traced the edge of one armrest with the tips of her fingers. "I'm not questioning your ability in the field . . ." She paused, catching sight of his bemused look. "All right, perhaps I *am.* Despite your incredible telepathic powers, even *you* would have to admit that your handicap *does* add a complication or two to the mission. But I'm *more* concerned about the danger you'd be putting yourself in by walking into the lion's den—we *both* face the possibility that we could be killed long before we even get close to Magneto. I'd just like to better your chances for survival." Betsy closed her eyes, tight enough to create flashes of color in the darkness; she imagined she could see Warren's face among the multi-hued lights that burst like fireworks. She drew a deep breath, then slowly released it and opened her eyes. "I've already lost *enough* people who are close to me."

Xavier reached out to pat the back of her hand. "Elisabeth, if we fail, if we can't prevent the Cube from destroying the protective barriers around our dimension, there will be no place to hide from the destruction, no place to call a safe haven. It will be the beginning of the end, not just for our world, but for *every* world across the countless dimensions. And if that were to happen, we *both* know I'd be in as much danger here on the citadel as I would on Earth." He shook his head. "No, I'd much rather go out fighting, doing my best to end this perverted dream of Magneto's once and for all, as I've tried to do for so long." He smiled. "Besides, if Erik runs true-to-form, as most of his fellow would-be conquerors do, he won't kill me . . . not right away, at least. After all, where would the glory of the moment be if he didn't have someone to gloat to about his victory over mankind—*especially* if that someone happens to be his greatest foe?"

Betsy returned the smile, her brush with death at von Doom's hand now cast in a new light. She slowly shook her head in amusement. "You'd think, with all those James Bond movies available on video and DVD, they would have picked up on the flaw of talking the ear off your enemy instead of killing him outright." Her smile widened. "Not that I'm not grateful for their little egomaniacal rants, of course. Letting someone like Doom or Magneto prattle on about how insignificant we all are in relation to their vast intellects *does* give one more than enough time to think of an escape plan." The smile faltered. "But, seriously, Professor..."

"Your objection has been duly noted, Elisabeth," Xavier replied evenly, "but this discussion has reached its conclusion. We could debate the issue all day long, with arguments and counterarguments about the dangers involved in this mission, but I *have* made up my mind." His chair slowed, then came to a soundless halt; Betsy stopped as well. The Professor pointed ahead of them. "And now, it is time to inform Roma."

Betsy turned in the direction Xavier indicated. With a start, she saw that they had arrived at the entrance to the Supreme Guardian's throneroom.

Three white marble steps, each ten feet wide, lay in front of them, leading to a set of ornate doors twenty feet high, made of solid gold; both were decorated with the image of a blazing sun, rays of light streaming out to all the edges of the panels. In front of the doors stood a quintet of male guards—the first line of defense between Roma and anyone foolish enough to attempt seeing her without permission. All were garbed in golden armor, white, ankle-length capes, and sky-blue tunics, the latter bearing the Guardian's symbol: three golden, interlocked ovals surrounded by a white circle. It always reminded Betsy of a "Hazardous Materials" symbol. In addition to the uniforms, the men shared a common background: all had been members of the Captain Britain Corps, promoted to their current stations by Roma for services above and beyond the call of duty.

One of the guards—a man with a lantern jaw, and shoulder-length red hair tied in a ponytail—stepped forward. "Good morrow, Professor," he said pleasantly, then glanced at Betsy. The smile he had shown Xavier flowed off his handsome features like ice melting under extreme heat. "Miss Braddock."

"Good *morning,* Alecto," Betsy replied, being overly polite. "*Always* nice to see you." She grinned devilishly, well aware of how much he disliked members of her family. "How's your hip? Still aching from the last time my brother came past here unannounced?"

The Captain of the Guard looked at her in disgust, then turned to the Professor. "Her Majesty is expecting you." He glanced over his shoulder and nodded to his men. They responded immediately, pushing on the massive doors, which opened soundlessly, and with surprising ease.

Betsy and Xavier mounted the steps, the guards moving aside to let them pass.

"I'll tell Brian you said 'hello,' the next time I see him," she said softly, just loud enough for Alecto to hear. She turned and blew him a kiss as she followed the Professor across the threshold.

If she hadn't been a hardened warrior, a woman trained in the ways of the ninja, and a powerful telepath who had been inside the minds of some of the world's deadliest villains and survived to tell the tale, the choice invectives that filled the captain's thoughts might have made her blush.

Inside, Betsy came to a sudden halt, mouth dropping open as she gazed in wonder at the throneroom. It had changed a great deal since the last time she had visited—when Brian had finally gotten around to marrying his shapeshifting girlfriend, Meggan—and she couldn't help but be impressed by the sheer size of the place. Clearly, Roma had picked up a sense of the dramatic from

Merlyn, what with the massive design, cathedral-like atmosphere, and a ceiling that was lost in shadow. It gave the impression that you were about to have an audience with God.

She certainly is *her father's daughter . . . at least in tastes . . .* Betsy thought dryly, willing her feet to start moving again. She trailed along behind Xavier, stealing glances at the shadows around them. If she looked out of the corners of her eyes, she could just make out the faint movements of creatures that lurked in the darkness—a second line of defense against the uninvited, it appeared. It seemed that Roma had upgraded, not just her private area, but her personal security, as well. A smile played at the corners of Betsy's lips. *I wonder if* Saturnyne *knows about this . . . ?*

Xavier stopped his chair at a respectful distance from the Supreme Guardian, who was standing at the darkened scrying glass, her back to them. It was the set of her shoulders that suddenly made Betsy feel uneasy—they hung loosely, as though slumped in defeat.

At Roma's side was Saturnyne, whose scarlet lips seemed chiseled into a permanent frown. She turned to face teacher and student, and grunted—a *very* un-Saturnyne-like response.

An inexplicable chill ran up Betsy's spine. Instantly, she created a telepathic link with Xavier. *Something's wrong, Professor . . .*

I surmised as much, Xavier replied. *But I don't think it's the right moment to press for answers. We'll just have to wait until—*

"It's all gone to hell!" Saturnyne said loudly, her words reverberating around the chamber.

"I beg your pardon?" the Professor asked; Betsy could tell he was surprised by her comment through the link. She quickly disconnected it, not wishing to intrude on his thoughts.

"I *knew* this was going to happen!" Her Whyness replied, ignoring his question. She snarled, and pointed an accusatory finger at Xavier. "I *knew* it would happen, but you *refused* to listen! You'd rather sacrifice all of Creation rather than destroy your precious world, *wouldn't* you? And *now* see where your selfish actions have—"

A hand lightly touched her shoulder. Saturnyne turned, eyes flashing with anger, only to see it was Roma who gently held her arm. Although Betsy couldn't see the expression on the Guardian's face, it seemed to quell the fire that raged within Her Whyness' breast. The Majestrix fell silent.

"Saturnyne, what are you talking about?" Betsy asked.

The white-haired lieutenant glanced at her superior; Roma nodded her approval, but said nothing. Saturnyne stepped forward, boot heels clicking loudly as she made her way across the transept to join the X-Man and her leader.

"See for yourself," Her Whyness said icily, gesturing toward the podium containing the omniversal crystals. Betsy and Xavier exchanged confused glances, then followed the Majestrix as she walked over to it, quickly mounting the short flight of steps right behind her.

As she reached the top step, Betsy saw Xavier's eyes widen in shock. His skin took on a sickly-white hue as she watched the blood drain from his face.

"A *very* bad day, indeed," he whispered hoarsely.

Seeing him like this made Betsy shiver; in all her time with the X-Men she couldn't remember ever seeing him act in such a manner.

"Professor . . . ?" she asked haltingly. When he didn't respond, she followed the direction of his unblinking gaze, to the collection of crystals that, as Brian had once explained to her, contained the life-forces of every dimension in the omniverse. These, too, she had last seen on his wedding day, and she had marveled at the purity of the quartz pieces.

But something was wrong with them now. A large number of the crystals—normally a brilliant white in color—were dotted with inky black spots.

"That doesn't look right . . ." Betsy said.

"Of *course* it's not right!" Saturnyne roared. "The Cube has infected a hundred realities already, and the taint is spreading to others!"

Now the reason for Saturnyne's hostile behavior, for Roma's solemn attitude, for Xavier's shocked expression, became clear to Betsy—and it terrified her. Back on Earth, Jean and Scott had told her of the threat the Cube posed to the omniverse, of how Roma might be forced to destroy their universe to save others, but the impact of that statement hadn't really struck her until now.

She began nervously chewing on her bottom lip as she gazed at the crystals. It was almost impossible to believe: a device no bigger than a child's toy, capable of wiping out whole dimensions? It was like something out of *Star Trek*, or *Doctor Who.*

And yet, she had seen for herself what the Cube could do in von Doom's hands, had fallen under the spell it had cast without even knowing it had happened. Was it so hard to believe, then, that the same wishbox that had so effortlessly made the villain's dreamworld a reality could just as easily tear apart other continuums, exterminate billions upon billions of innocent souls as its cancerous influence penetrated dimension after dimension, until the omniverse was thoroughly consumed?

Unfortunately, no, it wasn't.

The stains continued to spread across the infected crystals, further marring their once-pure facets. "Which is the one representing *our* dimension?" Betsy asked. She suddenly felt unable to breathe.

Saturnyne snorted. "Does it really matter? At the rate the reality-cancer is spreading . . ." The Majestrix slowly shook her head. "There's no point in destroying 616's crystal now. The damage is done. We've lost." She gazed coldly at Xavier. "Are you happy now, Professor? *Your* world has been spared, for the moment . . . but millions *more* are now suffering because of our hesitation."

"Saturnyne, please believe me—this is *not* what I had in mind when I asked for the opportunity to send the X-Men back to Earth," Xavier replied. "All I wanted was a chance to put things right. If I had known what might occur—"

"You *still* would have fought for the continued existence of your dimension," the Majestrix interjected. She turned away from

Xavier, head bowed. "I don't fault your intent, Professor," she said in a lower tone. "I have nothing against your world. I wasn't looking to punish it for some perceived slight against the cosmos, and I took no pleasure in petitioning the Supreme Guardian for the eradication of your dimension. But it is my duty as Omniversal Majestrix to maintain order throughout the length and breadth of time and space. *Your* universe was a threat to that order, and it should have been dealt with immediately, instead of being turned over to a bunch of costumed do-gooders whose intentions were well-meant, but inadequate to the task." She sighed. "I *wanted* your students to succeed, Professor. Unfortunately, they did not, and now we must pay the ultimate price for their failure."

Betsy stared at the crystals, her mind still reeling from the realization of what the Cube was capable of doing to the fabric of reality. "But . . . how can this be possible? Doom said the flaw in the Cube only affected its possessor."

"I thought you said you didn't believe that," Her Whyness responded, her back still turned to her and Xavier.

"I said I didn't believe he couldn't fix it," Betsy shot back. "But the mind-scan proved me wrong." She turned to Xavier. "Is it true, Professor? *Are* we too late?"

"*No,*" said Roma, mounting the steps to join them. A look of fierce determination was etched on her exquisite features. "There *is* still time, my friends, but we must move quickly . . ."

He was alive; he knew that much. And for Victor von Doom, living meant there was still time. Time enough to learn all he could about this place to which he'd been brought; to learn about his captors, and how they had become involved in his affairs.

Time enough to plan his next strike.

The mutant telepath *had* come close to killing him, however; far too close for his liking. He hadn't felt death's gentle touch, coaxing him toward oblivion, in quite some time—not since his final battle with the Mandarin. What a glorious day *that* had been! The two longtime foes, soaring high above the Great Wall of

China, unleashing the full power of their weapons upon one another: von Doom, with his armor's death beams and concussive
blasts; the Mandarin with his ten alien rings, each jewel-encrusted
bauble capable of laying waste to an entire city. The war had gone
on for days, neither combatant willing to concede defeat, neither
side giving quarter, for both knew that only one man could rule
the world. And in the end, that man had been Victor von—

But wait. That conflict had never actually happened. Von Doom
knew this to be true—after all, it had been part of the history of
the world he had formed with the Cube; a tiny bit of detailing
added to fill a spot on the canvas on which he had created his
masterpiece.

Why, then, should he be recalling some minor fantasy as if it
were a true memory, when he already had a lifetime's worth of
them from which to draw? Why did it seem so . . . so *real* . . . ?

"And how are we today?" asked a lilting male voice close by.

Von Doom slowly opened his eyes. A physician was standing
over him, a broad smile lighting his elfin features; the tyrant surmised it was meant to be comforting.

He took an immediate dislike to the man.

"Doom lives," he said, his throat thick with phlegm, "despite
the best efforts of his enemies to alter that situation."

"Excellent," purred the physician. "I must admit, it was a bit
touch-and-go there for a while, when you were first brought in—"
his smile broadened "—but from what I've been told, you're an
extremely difficult man to kill."

"Where is the mutant?" von Doom demanded.

"The mu—? Oh, you mean the young lady who caused your
mental seizure." The Chief Physician shrugged. "I imagine she's
with the Supreme Guardian." His voice lowered to a friendly, con-
spiratorial murmur. "I understand there's some sort of omniversal
crisis going on that requires Roma's undivided attention."

"Doom is aware of that, you fool," the monarch replied testily.

The physician stared at him thoughtfully for a few moments.
"Hmm . . . I wonder if Doom is aware of *other* things . . ." he said

mysteriously, then flashed a bright smile. "Tell me, would you mind chatting with one of our specialists? We had some . . . unusual readings pop up during our examination of you, and we're hoping you might be able to shed a little light on the matter."

The elderly despot glared at the man. "I will tell you nothing."

"I . . . see," the physician said slowly. "Perhaps later in the day?"

"*Leave me,*" his patient said with a sneer. "And do not return unless I have summoned you."

The physician's eyebrows rose dramatically. "Ah. I see. I'm being dismissed, is that it?" He chuckled softly. "You humans—your heightened sense of self-importance never ceases to amaze me." He winked slyly at his patient. "I'll check in with you in a bit, after you've had a spot of breakfast." A wicked smile crawled across his features. "I'll ask the nurse to increase your dosage of bran—considering your advanced age and increasingly overbearing demeanor, you could probably use a—"

"*GET OUT!*" the tyrant bellowed.

Laughing softly, the physician turned on his heel and hurried off, presumably to continue his rounds.

"Cretin," von Doom muttered. He closed his eyes and rolled onto his right side, groaning softly at the momentary pain that flared up in his hip.

He was growing tired of this body, of its frustrating limitations—the slower speed, the blurring vision, the aches and pains in every joint. His mind was still active, still capable of orchestrating grand schemes, but the Cube had robbed him of his youth, his vigor. At the time, it had seemed a fair exchange—world domination for advanced aging—but that was before Lensherr and Xavier's meddlesome students had disrupted what would have been his last order for the Cube in the coming days: to destroy the world the moment after he had drawn his last breath. After all, why allow the dream to die, to let others tear down what he had worked so hard to build, just because the dreamer had departed on his final journey?

The chance had been stolen from him, though, and he had been forced to withdraw because he could not defend himself—yet another damnable limitation of this withering husk in which his mind was trapped. Had he been at full strength, von Doom would never have left the field of battle; he would have fought Magneto for possession of the Cube . . . and won. Instead, he had been struck across the face, cast aside like a piece of refuse, at the hands of a genetic inferior. The former emperor growled softly and pounded his fist once on the edge of his bed, more angry with himself for letting the Cube slip from his grasp than from any pain Magneto had been able to inflict upon him.

Patience, Victor, a voice suddenly whispered in his mind. *You should not exert yourself so—not when there is still so much left to do.*

Von Doom's eyes flew open. He raised his head and looked around, but the physicians—including that Scottish-voiced buffoon—and nurses were quite a distance away, at a monitoring station, and the beds around him were empty.

"Braddock?" he rumbled softly. "Is that you, mutant, picking up where you left off? Invading my mind once more, seeking answers I do not have?" He closed his eyes, focusing his energies on erecting a mental barrier. "You will not find Doom unprepared this time."

Listen to me, Victor, the voice insisted; on closer examination, much to his surprise, it sounded exactly like his own. *Conserve your—our—strength; such actions will only weaken us further.*

Who are you? von Doom demanded.

Were I to tell you, the voice responded, *you would say I am lying. I am quite familiar with the workings of your mind, you see. But heed my words,* it said sternly, *or all will be lost. I am no creation of the Cosmic Cube, no figment of your imagination. It is only now, as this body slowly heals, with pain dulling your senses, that I have been able to pierce the layers of your mind and succeed in contacting you.*

The despot grunted. *And now that you have, phantom, of what use is a disembodied voice to me?*

A soft chuckle echoed through the depths of the former emperor's subconscious. *A great deal, when that voice can relate information concerning a certain palace that floats at the center of time and space, and the Guardian who resides there—a god-like being whose powers give her complete mastery over the forces of Creation itself . . .*

A sinister smile split the reed-thin lips of the elderly despot. *Continue, then, phantom. I am listening . . .*

"Pardon my ignorance, m'lady," Saturnyne asked, "but if the Cube has already begun ravaging the omniverse, *how* can you say there still may be time to combat its influence?" She glanced at the crystals, the one eye that was visible beneath her mountainous white hair widening in fear. "Unless you mean to destroy *all* the infected realities . . ." she whispered.

"Not at all, Saturnyne," Roma replied. "But my plan, you see, requires the use of the flawed Cosmic Cube." She turned to Xavier and Betsy. "I will need one or both of you to return to Earth and retrieve it for me."

"No, m'lady!" Saturnyne interjected. "You'd only be worsening the dilemma! By bringing the source of the reality-cancer here, to the very heart of time and space, you run the risk of complete omniversal destruction!"

"I am all *too* aware of the possible repercussions, Saturnyne," the Guardian replied. "Unfortunately, if I am to have any chance of excising this cancer, it must be done here, where my powers are greatest, where I will be able to draw upon the energies generated by the countless dimensions and, hopefully, use them to destroy the Cube."

"And if you're *not* able to destroy the Cube?" Betsy asked, though she really didn't want to hear the answer.

"It will be the end of everything," Roma said. "The omniverse will collapse in upon itself, and in its place shall be . . . nothing."

"Un-space," Saturnyne said cryptically.

Betsy nodded morosely. It suddenly felt like some massive weight had settled in the pit of her stomach. "I . . . thought as much . . . " she murmured.

Roma turned to the Professor. "Are you ready to begin the journey, Charles Xavier?"

Betsy noticed that the color had returned to the Professor's cheeks—a welcome sign in this troubling time. "You have merely to open the portal, Your Majesty," he replied, "and Psylocke and I shall do as you ask."

Roma nodded, a gentle smile bowing her lips; clearly, she was pleased by his enthusiastic response. "Then, my friends, let us begin . . ."

6

ONE HOUR later, they were ready to go.

Clad in black, bootcut leather pants, black Doc Martens, a white silk blouse, and round-lensed sunglasses, Betsy looked more like a resident of Manhattan's trendy Upper West Side than a member of the X-Men. That was the idea, of course—the last thing she and Xavier wanted to do was draw attention to themselves by having Betsy walk around Magneto's dreamworld in her eye-catching costume. Stealth was required for this mission, so plain clothes were the order of the day.

"Plain clothes." Betsy smiled. She'd been watching *Law & Order* reruns once too often, it seemed. If she wasn't careful, she'd soon be referring to super-villains as "perps" and "skells."

She'd thought about washing out the lavender dye in her hair as part of the disguise, going with her natural dark color, but found she didn't have the heart to do it. After having worn it that way for so long—a curious affectation she'd acquired during her brief career as a model—it was now as much a part of her identity as the crimson tattoo splashed across her left cheek—and *that* wasn't about to wash off. Besides, she still had four or five bottles of the hard-to-find dye under the bathroom sink, back in the apartment she shared with—

Betsy paused.

Say it, she told herself. *With* Warren. *The apartment you shared with Warren.* She exhaled sharply. *There. That wasn't so hard to do, now was it?*

Actually, no, it wasn't—which surprised her. She'd expected the ache that had torn at her heart to flare up again and send her spiraling once more into depression . . . but it hadn't happened. Maybe she was starting to heal, after all. Or maybe it was the mission; focusing on it, as she had surmised, was deadening the pain . . . at least for a while.

Or maybe she was just holding back her emotions, waiting for the right moment to release them—like when she'd have her hands clasped around Magneto's throat, finally able to make him pay for his crimes . . .

"You look marvelous," Xavier said, gliding up to join her.

Betsy shook her head to clear her thoughts, and smiled. "Thank you." She noticed that he wore the same suit he had put on a short time earlier. "And *you* cut quite the dashing figure."

"What? In this old thing?" Xavier asked, feigning modesty. He smiled warmly. "Thank you."

The sharp sound of boot heels ringing on the tile floor caught their attention. They turned to see Saturnyne approaching. In one hand, she held a metal box no larger than a pack of cigarettes, its surface dotted with small lights, and one very large red button. She handed the box to Xavier.

"It's a recall device," she explained. "The temporal engineers at the Dimensional Development Court assure me it will work, even in the heart of the anomaly. Press the button, and a portal will open, bringing you back here."

"Simple enough to operate," Xavier said pleasantly.

The Majestrix snorted. "Only at my insistence. I know how little boys are with their toys, and this mission is delicate enough without some giddy technician adding unnecessarily complicated bits to it, like racing stripes, or a death ray generator, or a mini-toaster oven. It's a recall device, after all, not a Swiss army knife."

Betsy eyed her suspiciously. "I'm waiting for the other shoe to drop," she commented. "Simple the device may be, but what trouble might we be getting into once we use it?"

"Oh. Well, it's only good for one jaunt," Her Whyness said. "So try to refrain from activating it until you've got the Cube."

"And you don't consider *that* a complication?" Betsy asked.

The Majestrix shrugged.

Xavier cast a warning glance at Betsy; he obviously didn't want her to pursue the issue. "Thank you, Saturnyne—for both the device *and* the word of caution."

"Seeing that you have returned to the citadel, successful in your mission, will be thanks enough, Charles Xavier," Roma said as she joined the trio. "And now, it is time."

She raised her arms, then closed her eyes in concentration. A pinpoint of light appeared just beyond the tips of her fingers. As Betsy watched, the point became a swirling, kaleidoscopic vortex that grew progressively larger until it was approximately the same size as the set of double doors leading into the throne room.

"Now, as I explained to your comrades when they embarked upon their mission," Roma said, "I will be able to return you to your world, but the energies of the Cosmic Cube have created a great deal of interference—it prevents me from controlling the entry point of the portal. You might emerge right beside the Cube when you step from the vortex ... or find yourself on the wrong side of the planet."

Behind the dark lenses of her glasses, Betsy rolled her eyes. *Marvelous,* she thought.

"Regardless of where we make our arrival, Your Majesty," Xavier said, sounding cheerfully optimistic, "Psylocke and I *will* find the Cube. We *will* end this madness."

The Supreme Guardian nodded appreciatively, and waved a hand toward the blindingly-bright vortex. "Then step through the portal, my friends ... and good hunting."

Xavier glanced at Betsy and smiled. "Are you ready to step through the looking glass, Alice?"

Betsy reached down to grab hold of the black carryall by her feet; it contained a few changes of clothes for them both, as well as a few choice weapons she had "borrowed" from an armory located near the citadel guards' barracks. She had insisted on bringing them, despite Xavier's protests about violence begetting violence; he was hoping to accomplish this mission through peaceful means. Betsy saw his point—really, she did—but, as she explained, she would have felt naked racing into battle without a razor-edged *katana* in her hand and a pair of *sai* hanging from her belt.

Of course, the Professor hadn't understood—he was a man. The importance of properly accessorizing one's outfits was lost on him.

Betsy's eyes narrowed, and her jaw set in fierce determination. "Let's finish this."

Together, they entered the portal. An instant later, it closed behind them, and the throne room was once more plunged into semi-darkness.

"I sincerely hope you know what you're doing, m'lady," the Omniversal Majestrix remarked.

"As do I, Saturnyne," Roma said softly. "As do I . . ."

"If *this* is as close to the Cube as she could get us," Betsy snarled through gritted teeth, "then we're in very big trouble . . ."

"*I* think you should be grateful the portal did not open above the Atlantic Ocean," the Professor replied. "After all, Roma *did* warn us of her inability to control it."

Betsy grunted, not really satisfied with that answer. While it was true the portal hadn't placed them in any danger, they'd stepped into a situation that was just as bad . . . in her opinion, at least. She snarled, and gazed in disgust at their surroundings. The vortex had deposited them on the deck of a barge that was being pulled down the East River by a tugboat.

A garbage barge, to be specific—one filled to capacity.

In the middle of a hot, humid, summer day in New York.

"I'd wager this type of thing wouldn't happen to one of the

Avengers," Betsy muttered, doing her best to breathe through her mouth. She sighed. "We'll never get the smell out of these clothes."

Xavier wrinkled his nose in disgust. "Indeed. But we have much greater concerns at the moment than the odor of rancid fried chicken settling into our wardrobe."

Betsy nodded. "The Cube." An inquisitive eyebrow rose above the frames of her glasses. "Well, since you're mission leader, Professor, how do you think we should begin our search?"

"Well, I think the first order of business is to get off this barge—" Xavier grimaced as a gust of thick, hot air blew a moldy scrap of toilet paper past his nose "—as soon as possible. Then we'll need lodgings, so we can set up a base of operation from which to work."

"What about the mansion?" Betsy asked.

Xavier shook his head. "It may not exist in this reality, and we can't spare the time to find out. But even if it does, I'm certain Erik has taken steps to pervert its use in some way, if only to spite me." His lips drew together in a thin, bloodless line. "I . . . don't really want to find out."

Betsy saw the haunted look in Charles' eyes. The Westchester mansion—and the school for mutants that it housed—meant a great deal to him; probably more than she could imagine. It was the center of his universe—the place where he felt most secure; the launching pad from which his dreams of mutant equality had first taken flight. Having already lost his students to his greatest enemy, just the very *idea* that the school might have become a mockery of that dream seemed to have the Professor poised on the brink of a severe depression.

She loudly clapped her hands together, just once, to get his attention.

"*Right,* then," she said. "Time we were on our way."

Placing her hands on the Professor's hoverchair, she mentally summoned forth one of the powers she'd acquired from her exposure to the Crimson Dawn: the gift of teleportation. Tendrils of dark energy flowed from her pores, seeping through her clothing

to pool at her feet. The substance spread outward, forming a perfect circle around her and the Professor as it pushed aside the foul-
smelling trash that surrounded the duo. Betsy noticed, with some
amusement, Xavier's mildly concerned expression as he watched
a midnight-black portal open beneath his chair. It was impossible
to tell where it might lead—or what might lurk within its depths.

"Don't worry, Professor," Betsy said with a smile. "You won't
feel a thing."

Xavier gazed at her suspiciously from the corner of his eye;
clearly, he didn't believe her. "You know, that's exactly what my
dentist said the time I went in for a root canal. I didn't believe
him, either—and I was right, unfortunately."

They were moving downward now, sinking into the chilly darkness, Betsy glanced around at the garbage piled around them once
last time, then turned back to the Professor. "Fried chicken, eh? I
wondered what that was." She grimaced. "Now I know why I had
that sudden urge for mashed potatoes and gravy. . . ."

Saturnyne's stomach growled.

Having left the Supreme Guardian in the throne room—per
Roma's request for privacy—Her Whyness was on her way to her
quarters when the rumbling had started. She looked around to see
if any of the staff or visitors passing her in the corridor had heard
the sound; if they had, they were apparently wise enough not to
comment on it. That lack of reaction—caused, more than likely, by
the fear she generated among them—pleased Saturnyne. It
wouldn't do for an Omniversal Majestrix to have the citadel buzz-
ing with talk about how, though she could command legions of
soldiers in battle, she had no control over the noises made by her
internal organs. It might make her seem fallible. Commonplace.
Mindnumbingly ordinary. Like she was one of *them*. And that
would *never* do . . .

"Special Executive?" called out a voice laced with more than a
touch of the Scottish Highlands. "May I have a moment of your
time?"

Saturnyne turned. Hurrying down the corridor after her was an odd little man in a surgical blouse and checkered pants. She recognized him as the Chief Physician from the medical wing, but couldn't remember his name—she had far more important things to do than try to remember the names of everyone who worked for the Supreme Guardian.

"I haven't gone by the title 'Special Executive' since I left the DDC, Doctor," she said, drawing herself up to her full height and looking down her nose at him. "You must address me as 'Your Whyness' now."

"Ah!" The physician smiled broadly, grabbed her right hand, and began vigorously pumping it up and down. "Congratulations! It couldn't have happened to a nicer Majestrix." As Saturnyne pulled her hand free, he bowed his head slightly. "I apologize for my *faux pas*. It's just that it takes so long for news of anything to trickle down to the medical wing these days . . . I must never have received a copy of the notification."

Saturnyne frowned. "What did you wish to speak with me about?" she asked, hoping to move the conversation along before her stomach made another demand for food.

The Chief Physician unclipped a small, hand-held computer from the belt he wore under the green scrubs. "Now, I realize you don't have a full understanding of medical procedures, beyond whatever unnecessary bits of information the lads at DDC might have filled your head with when you worked with them . . ." He grinned broadly, seemingly unaffected by the icy stare he was receiving. ". . . but I'd like you to take a look at these readings, before I bring them to the Supreme Guardian's attention, and tell me what you see."

Saturnyne took the device from him and scanned the Information displayed on the small screen. "Who's the patient?"

"That *charming* elderly gentleman Roma sent down to me for treatment," the doctor replied sarcastically.

The Majestrix's visible eye widened in surprise. "*Doom?* These are *Doom's* readings?"

"Yes." The doctor smiled slyly. "Quite interesting, wouldn't you say?"

"You have a gift for understatement, Doctor," Saturnyne replied dryly. She pointed to one finding in particular. "Have you ever seen anything like this before?"

"I really can't say that I have, Your Whyness," he replied. "But then, I've never met a man with *two sets* of thought patterns." He pointed to the computer screen. "And if I'm right—which I am invariably am—then, based upon these readings, which, before you ask, my staff has already checked and rechecked a number of times, it would appear we have a case of *two* versions of the same man sharing *one* body." He raised an inquisitive eyebrow. "Do you think the Supreme Guardian might be interested in this rather intriguing situation?"

The only response to the doctor's question came, unexpectedly and decidedly unwanted, from the Majestrix's burbling digestive tract.

"Well, *this* is something I never expected to see," Betsy commented.

From their vantage point on the observation deck of the Empire State Building, she and Xavier could see most of the island of Manhattan stretched out before them in the bright, noonday sun. The city didn't look all that different from how it normally appeared in the "real world"—its streets congested with far too many vehicles, its sidewalks jammed with tourists, bike messengers, and food vendors—but there *were* changes, if you knew where to look for them. About the biggest that came to mind, once Betsy had focused on it, was the absence of superpowered beings. During the day, the skies were usually full of them—heroic men and women soaring high above the streets as they raced off to answer a call for help, or power-hungry villains recklessly zooming toward a confrontation with their most hated enemies. Now, though, the only occupants of the air were an assortment of birds and a number of traffic helicopters, the latter emblazoned with the logos of the television stations for which their crews were reporting.

The people were different, as well. Having lived in the city for a while now, Betsy had always been struck by the blasé attitude of New Yorkers toward the unusual; not even the first arrival of Galactus years ago had closed down Wall Street. But now, it seemed, even the *tourists* were taking everything in stride—those gathered on the observation deck hadn't reacted at all to the unexpected appearance of two mutants emerging from a pool of oily darkness right within their midst.

It was almost unnerving.

"I have to tell you, Professor," Betsy said, "that, after all the clashes the X-Men have had with Magneto over the years, after hearing his endless diatribes about how *Homo superior* should be the dominant species on the planet, I was expecting concentration camps and armed stormtroopers, not clean streets and a harmonious society." She glanced at her companion, and chuckled softly. "If I didn't know better, I'd think we were standing in the middle of *your* dream."

"It *is* strange," Xavier agreed. "Erik has been set in his ways for as long as I have known him. Based on our discussions, I never would have thought him capable of creating such a world." He paused, and scratched his jaw, obviously deep in concentration. "However," he said slowly, "now that I stop to think about it, there *was* a brief period, long before you joined us, when his views about dominating the world began to change. I had asked him to run the school during an extended leave of absence I was forced to take for health reasons."

Betsy was nonplussed. "Just a moment. You put *Magneto* in charge of the school?"

Xavier nodded. "And he did an admirable job, from what the others told me ... although it *did* take him quite some time to begin earning their trust."

"No surprise there," Betsy commented sarcastically. "It's amazing, though, that Wolverine didn't try to kill him, considering his intense hatred for the man."

The Professor grunted. "Nevertheless, despite his initial set-backs, Erik was eventually able to work alongside Cyclops and the others. It seemed to have a beneficial effect on him—he changed. His obsession with punishing humanity for its harsh treatment of our kind began to dwindle, and, with the help of the X-Men, he focused his energies on finding ways to bring about peace between the races." A wisp of a smile played at the corners of his mouth. "I imagine it had a great deal to do with having to interact with the students on a daily basis, with coming to better understand the very men and women he had been trying to destroy for so many years, and the dream in which they so strongly believed." The smile quickly faded. "Unfortunately, it was not meant to last." He sighed deeply, and gazed off into the distance.

Looking at his pained expression, it was obvious to Betsy that he somehow felt responsible for Magneto's return to his old ways. That, maybe if he'd tried harder, his former friend wouldn't have abandoned the slow, difficult path toward universal harmony that he'd started walking in favor of a far easier shortcut that led him back to violence as the best solution for eradicating prejudice to-ward mutantkind. She'd heard the Professor express similar thoughts over the years—absolute rubbish, in her opinion. Some people just couldn't help being what they were, including super-villains. If subjugating humanity was the only way the mutant overlord believed that peace could be achieved, then that would forever remain his focus until he reached his goal, no matter how many times Charles Xavier tried to convince him otherwise.

"And yet, Professor," she said, gesturing toward the city around them, "it's clear your arguments about trying to find a peaceful solution to the man-versus-mutant problem *didn't* fall on deaf ears." She shrugged. "Maybe all it took was some time for him to eventually realize that you had been right all along. Maybe, once he had the Cube in hand, he realized he didn't need to take out his aggressions on mankind; that he could do better than that. Maybe he just grew tired of all the fighting. The bottom line, though, is that he actually used the Cube's powers to do some good. Magneto might be the one in charge, but this is the closest realization of *your* dream that I've ever seen."

Xavier sighed. "Yes. And now, here I am, ready to tear down that dream because it presents a far greater danger than anyone could ever have imagined." He glanced at his lavender-haired companion. "There's a certain irony to the situation, don't you think?"

"It's not the *dream* that's dangerous, Professor," Betsy said, gently placing a hand on his shoulder. "It's the *dreamer*. And this isn't *your* dream, remember, no matter how close to it this world might appear; good, bad, or indifferent, it's all *his.* And *that's* what's endangering the omniverse—not anything *you've* done."

The Professor reached up to pat the back of her hand. "I suppose you're right." He looked up at her, and smiled. "Thank you, Elisabeth."

She grinned. "Better you hear an encouraging speech from *me* than, say, from Wolverine. Logan would just tell you to 'get over it.' "

Xavier chuckled. "Indeed."

"Now, let's see about setting up that base of operations, shall we?" Betsy said. She dramatically waved a hand at the metropolis below them. "Somewhere down there is a hotel room waiting to be booked, and a hot shower guaranteed to wash away both our troubles *and* the nauseating stench of rotted food that has worked its way into our pores." She pointed to the crowd of tourists gathered around them. Both humans *and* mutants had drawn back as the hot summer sun warmed the X-Men's clothing, increasing the eye-watering odor that wafted up from the garbage-stained material by a factor of ten.

Xavier nodded. "We appear to have overstayed our welcome."

"Then, we're off," Betsy said. Instantly, another portal began to form beneath their feet.

The Professor grimaced. "If you don't mind my saying so, Elisabeth," he said uneasily, "perhaps a taxi cab might be an easier mode of transpor—"

Any further words of mild protest that he might have been about to utter were quickly lost as the duo plunged into darkness.

The Stuyvesant Arms was not the type of hotel one would find listed in a visitor's guide to New York. Located on East Houston Street on Manhattan's Lower East Side, it had not yet benefited from the sweeping changes of gentrification that were slowly transforming its surrounding neighborhood. Once known for its high crime rate and drug trafficking, the area had become a mecca for trendy coffee shops, exclusive nightclubs, and chic, hole-in-the-wall art galleries. But the Stuyvesant—named after Peter Stuyvesant, the first mayor of New York, though no one on the hotel's staff was aware of that fact, or even cared about the man's place in history—was a throwback to an earlier time, when the city was a tad less civilized, and it wasn't out of the ordinary to hear gunshots ringing in the hotel's hallways, or hear of guests awakening in the middle of the night to find a rat the size of a mountain lion sitting on the edge of their beds, watching them with hungry eyes.

But that, of course, was back in the days when New York was nicknamed "Fun City." Times were different now . . . or so the city's administration often said. And yet, the more things change . . .

Sitting behind the registration desk in the hotel's dimly lit lobby, safely protected by a wire cage that kept some of the more . . . colorful denizens of the neighborhood from getting too close to him, Marty Keeler was a man who liked to dream of a better life—one where he dined in the finest restaurants, owned three or four mansions around the world, and traveled in style wherever he went. And women—there were always plenty of beautiful women populating his dreams, and each and every one of them thought he was the hottest guy on the planet. It was all a big joke, of course; he never really expected to see those visions become a reality. But for someone who used to be a lowly Morlock—a mutant who once lived with others of his kind in the abandoned subway and maintenance tunnels that ran beneath the city—dreams of power and wealth were all he had had in the years before Magneto's ascendancy to world leader.

Not that things had improved all that much for him *since* then.

That was another joke, that whole "equal partners" thing that Magneto and his followers espoused. The world might have become a much better place to live in, but that really only applied to the "beautiful people." Morlocks like Marty Keeler—with his pustule-covered face, sallow skin tone, and grotesque lack of dental hygiene—were still struggling to eke out a living, taking whatever jobs were available. After all, what kind of high-paying gigs were out there for someone whose genetic "gift" was spewing forth a corrosive acid from the boils that rose like tiny volcanoes above his unhealthy-looking complexion? It wasn't exactly the sort of power that got you a lot of dates; actually, Marty couldn't even remember the last time a woman—human or mutant—had even just gone to dinner with him.

But he could always dream . . .

"Excuse me," said a male voice from the other side of the cage.

Marty looked up from the tiny black-and-white television secreted under the desk . . . and found himself looking at the type of woman that, until this very moment, he thought only existed in the more creative recesses of his mind. He didn't care much for the purple dye in her hair, but, suprisingly enough, the unusual coloration didn't detract from her beauty; in an odd way, it actually enhanced it. There was something familiar about her; he could swear he'd seen her someplace before, but couldn't remember exactly where or when. A men's magazine cover, perhaps? Or maybe on an MTV awards show? She was a looker, though, whoever she was—long legs, supermodel face (he wondered what color her eyes were, behind those dark glasses), and a *great* body. If only she didn't smell like she'd been sleeping in a dumpster for a week . . .

"Can I help you?" he asked, leaping to his feet, his attention completely focused on her. *Where* had he seen her? Not knowing was starting to bother him, but he didn't think it'd look cool to come right out and ask. Besides, from the way she kept glancing over her shoulder, checking the front entrance as though she expected someone she didn't want to see to walk through the door, it was pretty clear she didn't want anyone to know she was here.

Had she been on a TV show? Yes, maybe that was it. But which one . . . ?

"We'd like a pair of adjoining rooms, if they're available," her male companion said.

Marty continued to stare at the woman, to the point where she began to appear uncomfortable. He couldn't help himself, though—he knew he was close to figuring out her identity, if he had a few more seconds . . .

"Sir?" the man said, a bit more pronounced.

Reluctantly, Marty forced himself to glance toward the guy. He was bald and middle-aged, with piercing eyes and sharp features. The suit he wore looked as expensive as the woman's outfit, and he was seated in some kind of wheelchair; the thing looked like it was actually floating a foot or so above the threadbare carpeting. Marty figured some women might consider the guy handsome; his sister, Estelle, certainly would want to have his baby if she met him. Still, he was nowhere as pleasing to the eye as the woman standing beside him.

"Huh?" Marty grunted.

"He said we'd like adjoining rooms," the woman replied, her voice low and throaty. She removed her glasses and smiled. "Can you help us?"

"Uh . . ." Marty said, suddenly at a loss for words. She had the most incredible lavender eyes—he could almost feel himself getting lost in their depths . . .

"The rooms?" the woman asked sweetly.

Marty shook his head to clear his addled thoughts. "Umm . . . sure, I can give you two together," he finally managed to say. Actually, after the last sweep the police had made on the hotel, clearing out the few remaining drug dealers in the area, he could have given them half a *floor* to run around in, but why bring that up? As Jerry Mardeck, the surly manager/owner of the Stuyvesant often pointed out, telling guests about the hotel's less than sterling reputation didn't do anything good for business—it just sent them heading for the nearest Salvation Army shelter as quickly as possible. "Will that be for an hour, or do you plan on staying longer?"

The man blushed slightly, which looked even more amusing to Marty because the entirety of his bare head turned a light shade of crimson. "We'll be staying overnight, at least."

"Cool," Marty said. He pushed a well-worn book through the slot on the cage. "If you'll just sign the register . . ."

The man did the honors while Marty treated himself to another eyeful of the Asian beauty. She'd slipped her glasses back on, and returned to her door-watching duties. Now that he really thought about it, he was sure she was some kind of actress on an action series—he'd seen it at least once . . .

"You *do* have running water, correct?" she asked without turning around.

Marty nodded, then realized she couldn't see his response. "Yeah."

"Wonderful." The woman turned to face him, sliding the glasses to the end of her nose with one shapely finger. "I'm absolutely *dying* to toss off these clothes and climb into a nice, *hot* shower." She smiled wickedly. "I'm feeling *ever* so dirty."

Marty felt his knees go weak. He *just* managed to grab hold of the edge of the desk to keep from collapsing.

"Elisabeth . . ." her companion said in a warning tone.

Elisabeth? With a start, Marty suddenly knew where he'd seen the woman before. The hair color should have been a dead giveaway, but he hadn't been able to put two and two together until now—after all, why would a woman of *her* caliber be lurking around a skanky flop house just a few short blocks from The Bowery? But now it all made sense: the nervous glances at the front door; the sunglasses worn even in the semi-darkness of the lobby;

the male "friend" who signed the register instead of her.

She was having an affair.

He didn't know who the man was—her manager, maybe?—and he didn't really care about his identity. What he *did* care about was the woman—now that he knew who *she* was, her presence here was *definitely* big news. Maybe It was even worth a few dollars to someone . . .

Flashing a shark's-tooth smile, Marty unhooked a pair of keys from a set of hooks mounted on the wall behind him, and slid them across the desk. "Here you go. Rooms 524 and 526. That'll be forty-five bucks."

The man, of course, was the one who paid and took the keys. "Thank you."

"Enjoy your stay," Marty said brightly.

The man nodded pleasantly and turned to his companion. Together, they crossed the lobby and entered the dingy elevator— there was just enough space in the car to accommodate the bald guy's wheelchair, or whatever the contraption was supposed to be. With an ear-piercing grinding of gears, the door closed, and the car began its ascent to the fifth floor.

As soon as the new arrivals were on their way, Marty reached for the phone and quickly dialed a number.

"Thank you for calling WSLP," said a prerecorded female voice, "home of *Viewpoints* and the hard-hitting WSLP News Team. If you know the extension of the party you wish to contact, please dial it now. If not, stay on the line, and an operator will answer your call as soon as possible. And please be sure to watch *Viewpoints* with host Archer Finckley this Friday night at 9 P.M. on the East Coast, 6 P.M. on the West Coast, when his guest will be—"

"WSLP, how may I direct your call?" another female voice cut in; this one was live.

Marty looked over his shoulder, half expecting to find the woman standing on the other side of the cage. Thankfully, she wasn't. "Yeah, I'd like to talk to somebody in the newsroom," he said to the operator. "I think they might be interested in a story

I've got to tell. It's all about a major TV actress—who's *married*—who's doin' the nasty with a guy—who's *not* her husband—in the hotel where I work *right now*." He grinned broadly. "I'll hold, if you want—I don't think the lovebirds are goin' anywhere anytime soon. . . ."

7

SHE FELT almost like a new person.

The shower had been an absolute godsend after that unexpected visit to the garbage scow; she hadn't even been bothered by the brown-colored water that spewed from the showerhead when she first turned the faucet. Now squeaky clean, lightly perfumed, and with a fresh shade of lavender applied to her hair, Betsy was ready to face the world once more . . . even if it wasn't really *her* world. Tucking a new silk blouse into the leather miniskirt she now wore, Betsy slipped into a pair of black leather high heels and headed for the door, grabbing her sunglasses along the way. She didn't really want to leave her belongings in a room with a lock on it that a child with a safety pin could open, but carrying around a bagful of weapons all day had become a burden—the muscles in her back had already started to protest, and her hands were reddened and tender from the straps cutting into her palms. She could do with some time off. Besides, she and the Professor would only be gone for a few hours while they did their research—the bag should be safe enough under the bed until she got back. And if anyone *really* wanted to steal from her, she *had* been nice enough to leave her previous outfit draped across a weatherbeaten armchair in a corner of the room—*that* should fetch a few dollars. She doubted anyone would *want* something that odorous, but then, this *was* New York...

She stepped into the hallway to find Xavier also exiting his room. His skin was still a little rosy from the heat of the shower, and he had changed into a light gray linen suit, white shirt, and dark blue silk tie.

"Ah," he said. "I was just coming over to see if you were ready."

"As ready as one can be, considering the conditions of this place." Betsy waved a hand toward the worn carpeting—it may have been burgundy in color when it was laid down, but it was hard to tell from the decades of dirt and food ground into its fibers—and the faded, peeling wallpaper. "*Really,* Professor—I know you wanted to avoid the more expensive hotels that would have required credit cards, and I know you want to avoid running into a situation that might make Magneto aware of our presence ...but I think *this* is going too far."

"Oh, it's not so bad," Xavier replied, "once you get past the cracked plaster and roach droppings. I've stayed in far worse surroundings. Remind me sometime to tell you about my lodging experience in Marrakech—you may wind up thinking this place is a paradise by comparison."

Betsy wrinkled her nose in disgust. "No thanks—*this* experience is quite enough for me." She looked up and down the corridor. "So, now that we've showered and changed our clothes, what's the *next* plan of action?"

"Intelligence gathering," the Professor replied. "We need to know how this world functions, where Erik is keeping himself, and how we might be able to get to him."

"Well, I doubt this cozy little hostel has Internet access," Betsy said, "so our best bet is a library or some sort of cyber-café. And given the neighborhood we're in, there are probably a half-dozen of the latter within walking distance."

"Excellent," Xavier said. "I'm in the mood for a latté and a bit of web-browsing."

They walked to the elevator, and Betsy pressed the DOWN

button. A few moments later, they were rewarded with the familiar sound of gnashing gears that heralded the car's arrival. Thankfully, no one was inside, so Betsy was able to squeeze into the tiny space left unoccupied by the bulky hoverchair. She pushed the button for the lobby, and the car began its slow descent.

"I hope that desk clerk has gone off-duty," Betsy commented. "Did you *see* the way he was staring at me?" She shivered. "I was beginning to feel like a prize mare on the auction block. I'm amazed he didn't ask to see the condition of my teeth!"

"I would imagine the notion of a woman of your obvious beauty coming into such a disreputable place such as this is unheard of," Xavier said. "And, given the poor man's physical condition, having such a woman carelessly throw double-entendres his way must have been a shock." He frowned and shook his head. " 'I feel *ever* so dirty.' It's a wonder you didn't send him into cardiac arrest."

Betsy flashed that wicked smile of hers again, and chuckled in a *most* sinister fashion.

Xavier sighed. "It seems I can't take you anywhere . . ."

With a jolt, the elevator came to a halt at the first floor. Poorly greased rollers moved along their tracks, opening the door—and plunging the two X-Men into madness.

Lights flashed. People screamed. Momentarily blinded by the explosion of a strobe close to her face, Betsy staggered back, shielding her eyes with one hand while she fumbled in the breast pocket of her blouse with the other to grab her sunglasses.

"W-what's going on?" she stammered as she bumped into the back wall of the elevator.

"It appears we've been discovered," Xavier said morosely.

Blinking rapidly to clear her vision, Betsy began to make out a group of hazy shapes huddled in the lobby, all pushing and pulling and straining against one another. It reminded her of the strange creatures she had glimpsed lurking in the shadows of Roma's throne room. As her eyesight slowly returned to normal, she realized these shapes were actually dozens of people holding photographic and television cameras—and they were all calling her by name.

"Reporters . . . ?" Betsy muttered.

Beyond the legions of press and paparazzi, out on the sidewalk, was what seemed to be a street full of people. Like the news folk, they pushed and fought for the best position that would allow an unobstructed view of the hotel interior. Someone pressed up against a picture window pointed in Betsy's direction, and the crowd cheered.

Close the door! Xavier told Betsy through the mind-link.

She stabbed at the button, and the door started moving. But before it could separate them from the howling mob, a dozen arms slipped between the frame and the padded emergency panel that prevented the door from trapping passengers halfway in or out. The door opened wide, and the press corps poured in, pinning the two X-Men against the wall.

"Betsy! What brings you to New York?" asked a man with thinning hair sculpted into a hideous comb-over—a vain attempt to hide his increasing baldness.

"Aren't you supposed to be in New Zealand right now, working on your series?" a woman with collagen-injected lips demanded, shoving a microphone in Betsy's face.

Another man pointed an accusatory finger at the Professor. "Is it true that *this* is the man you're sleeping with?"

The question was like a slap in the face. Startled, Betsy looked to Xavier—*he* seemed to be in as much a state of shock as she.

"Does your *husband* know you're having an affair?" the reporter asked, following up his first unexpected question.

Betsy started. "*Husband?*"

"Get back, all of you!" Xavier roared. Much to Betsy's surprise, the mob complied, moving back a couple of steps. *Elisabeth, get us out of here!*

But what about—

If Erik doesn't know we're here by now, he will *soon enough,* Xavier interjected. *Now, do as I say.*

All right, Betsy replied, and triggered her 'porting ability. This *should make for some interesting headlines . . .*

It also made for interesting television, especially when the broadcast was seen by members of the teaching staff at the Lensherr Institute for the Genetically Gifted.

Unlike Charles Xavier's Westchester-based facility, this school was not only public knowledge, but after Jean Grey and Scott Summers' appearance on *Viewpoints* only a few days past, its web site and toll-free number had been flooded with an astonishing number of requests for more information from parents of mutant children. The institute was located on Ellis Island, near the New Jersey shore at the entrance to New York Harbor, and the buildings now housing its classrooms and dormitories had originally been used—from 1892 to 1954—for processing newly-arrived immigrants who had come to America in search of a new life. Erik Magnus Lensherr, his wife, Magda, and their daughter, Anya, had been among those "huddled masses, yearning to breathe free," as Emma Lazarus' 1883 poem "The New Colossus"—inscribed on a plaque on the nearby Statue of Liberty—had described these travelers arriving on a foreign shore. And when Lensherr eventually became the world's leader, he had commanded his "subjects" to transform the island into a learning center for his kind, partly from a sense of nostalgia, but mostly to send the message that the institute was a gateway, as Ellis Island had once been, to an amazing and wondrous new life; *this* entry point, however, would be used solely for ushering the genetically gifted into a wondrous new *world.*

A world controlled by the one mutant who had made it all possible.

Classes ranged from the basics—reading, writing, and arithmetic—to advanced Physical Education and science levels, all of which were designed to help the students understand what they were and how they could best reach their potentials in using their new powers. Based on their individual abilities, students were taught to fly, or run faster than the speed of sound, or teleport short distances with just a thought, or even read minds.

And then there was the final test. Ten levels below the Main Building was an area called the "Danger Room," where the most advanced students were expected to show how well they had learned to control their abilities during their time at the institute. It was a two-hour session in the Danger Room at the end of four years that separated the graduates from those who would be left back. An inexperienced mutant, the faculty often pointed out, was a danger not only to the mutant, but to the rest of society as well, and a student who didn't learn that lesson the first time would not be allowed to graduate until it had fully sunk into their minds.

Dozens of powers to work with; thousands of young minds to mold. It was a terrifying responsibility, but Lensherr knew *just* the mutants for the job. He had personally selected the staff members— *why* he had chosen the people he had was a topic he refused to discuss—and was pleased to see how well they responded to his orders, and how successful they were in keeping the spirit of his dream alive.

Cyclops. Phoenix. Nightcrawler. Rogue. Storm. In the past, they had all sided against him as members of the X-Men, causing him no small amount of trouble over the years. But now, their code-names forgotten, their identities reconstructed, their minds reconditioned, they worked for Magneto—their greatest enemy—and followed his instructions with blind obedience ... because he willed it to be so. And the Cube had made it all possible.

Ah, he often wondered, what would Charles think of his most trusted followers now ... ?

The answer would not be long in coming.

It was just after four o'clock that the day became *really* interesting. Classes had ended. And as the students filed back to their dorm rooms to eat and begin their homework assignments, some of their teachers headed for the staff lounge to unwind, catch up on small talk with their peers, and watch a little television before heading for their apartments on the other side of the island, or traveling to Manhattan for a quick dip in the nightlife.

Acrobatics instructor Kurt Wagner was one of those teachers. In his mid-twenties, dressed in a skintight uniform—consisting of a red bodysuit, over which were worn purple gloves, boots, and trunks—he was one of the more unusual members of the staff, and it had nothing to do with his clothing, since all the teachers wore the same type of outfit. It did, however, have everything to do with the fact that his hair and the short, fuzzy fur covering his body were colored a deep blue, his hands and feet only had three digits each, and he possessed a three-foot-long, prehensile tail, which had grown from a spot just above his buttocks. Combined with bright yellow eyes and sharp, white fangs, his overall appearance was less like that of an educator, and more like that of a demon set free from hell.

Oddly enough, it was a look that made him incredibly appealing to women—something about "good" girls being attracted to "bad" boys, he'd once been told. He'd never understood that particular psychological aspect of dating, but he *did* know that his sinister appearance seemed to fill all the requirements. And, even though he was really the epitome of an old-fashioned gentleman— well, who was he to disappoint a lady and her expectations?

He was a rare catch, indeed: suave, well-mannered, highly romantic, he had an adorable German accent, and, most importantly, he was single. What woman *didn't* want to bed him?

Well, for one, there was the woman he found sitting on the leather couch in the lounge. Boot heels resting comfortably on the teak coffee table in front of her, a bag of barbecue-flavored potato chips in her lap, Rogue—no one had ever been able to find out if that was her real name—thought Kurt was cute, maybe even sexy, but she just wasn't attracted to him; and he, being a gentleman, never pressed the point.

Like her blue-furred peer, Rogue wore a red-and-purple uniform, but hers was complemented by a worn, brown leather aviator's jacket, befitting her title as "Flight Instructor" for those students capable of defying the laws of gravity, but still getting used to their powers. Her waist-length mane of dark-brown hair— its color offset by a large patch of white that started just above her forehead and ran down the center—was in a state of disarray, which was to be expected, considering the amount of time she spent during the course of the day zooming through the skies above the island with her classes.

Shoveling another handful of chips into her mouth, Rogue chewed noisily, her attention focused on the flatscreen television mounted on the wall across from her. There was some sort of courtroom scene being played out in the broadcast she was watching, the cameras focused on a female judge who was yelling at one of the two litigants standing before her.

"*Hey!*" the judge barked. "You think I was born yesterday?" She pointed to her forehead. "Does it *say* 'STUPID' here?"

"Catching up on the latest adventures in jurisprudence, *meine freunde?*" Kurt asked with amusement.

Rogue turned from the set and smiled wearily. "Hey, Kurt— how'd it go today?" she asked, her normally throaty Southern drawl sounding unusually flat. Picking up the remote from the cushion next to her, she lowered the volume on the television. As he drew closer, Kurt could see her features were strained, a dull light shining in her eyes. She looked exhausted.

"Better than it did for *you*, it seems," Kurt replied. He sat down beside her. "What happened?"

Rogue brushed broken pieces of chips off her uniform and, groaning softly, shifted position to face him. "Well, a couple'a the kids decided to have a race t'see who was faster when my back was turned. I didn't even notice they were gone 'til they were almost halfway t'Manhattan, an' then I had t'go an' chase 'em all the way to Battery Park." She reached up to rub the area between her shoulder blades; the pain was apparently severe enough to make her bite down on her bottom lip and grunt. "Got so focused on gettin' my hands 'round their scrawny little necks I didn't even see that freighter comin' down the Hudson 'til it was too late."

Kurt raised an eyebrow in surprise. "I would not think something as large as a *ship* would be difficult to miss."

Rogue glared at him. "I *told* you I wasn't payin' attention."

"So you did," Kurt said hastily. He knew all too well that flight was not the only mutant power his friend possessed: she was also virtually indestructible, and had enough strength that, if she became angry with him, could easily result in him being thrown through a wall—and into the harbor. "Are you in much pain?"

"It only flares up when I'm movin' around," Rogue said through gritted teeth. "Or breathin'."

Kurt smiled warmly, and waved his hands at her, indicating she should turn around. "May I?"

Rogue grinned and nodded gratefully, then moved to turn her back to him. Kurt began easing the walnut-sized knots out of her back with the skill of a trained masseur. She moaned softly in appreciation.

"So, what did your hellraisers say when you finally caught up with them?" Kurt asked.

" 'We're so *sorry*, Mistress Rogue,' " she said in a whiny, nasally voice. " 'We'll never do it again.' " She snorted. "Like I'd believe the little polecats after this."

Kurt's eyebrows rose in surprise. " 'Mistress Rogue'?"

"Yeah," she said wearily. "It's somethin' the boys started callin' me, an', y'know, I'm gettin' kinda tired of that crap. Makes me sound like a dominatrix or somethin'."

Kurt playfully hung his head over Rogue's right shoulder to gaze down at the latex-like uniform she wore, and the way it hugged her considerable curves. "I do not know where they'd *ever* get *that* idea."

Rogue laughed. "*You're* one t'talk, Kurt Wagner. I've *seen* the way the girls in your classes look at you when you're hoppin' all over the gymnasium." She reached back to poke his knee with her thumb. "That outfit don't leave a whole lot t'the imagination, either."

"Yes, I know." Kurt sighed dramatically. "But if I am to be

objectified by young women, then it is a burden I am willing to bear for the good of the school." Still working on her shoulders, he shifted his gaze to the flatscreen television. "What exactly are you watching now?"

Rogue turned her head in the direction of the set. "Hey, that ain't *Judge Judy*."

A ruggedly handsome, sandy-haired man sitting at a news desk had replaced the courtroom scene. In the upper right-hand corner of the screen, near the reporter's head, was a publicity photograph of a woman with light purple hair and a jagged, J-shaped mark across the left side of her face, dressed in what looked like a blue swimsuit, and holding a pair of samurai swords, the blades crossed in front of her chest to form a razor-edged "X."

Kurt leaned forward, his attention focused on the story. "Could you raise the sound, please?" Rogue pushed the volume control on the remote.

"—we'll have a story about television star Elisabeth Braddock's unexpected appearance in a Lower East Side hotel this afternoon, and her mysterious disappearing act before a roomful of reporters," the broadcaster was saying. The newsroom shot cut to a video-taped replay of a bald-headed man and the same, lavender-tressed woman in an elevator; they were trying to conceal their faces from the camera, but there was nowhere for them to hide in the cramped space.

Rogue pointed at the screen. "Hey, it's that girl from that..." She paused, waving a hand as though encouraging a memory to come to the front of her brain. After a couple of seconds, she snapped her fingers. "Yeah, I know—that *Kwannon, Bushido Mistress* TV show! The kids are always talkin' about it."

"*Freeze that picture!*" Kurt yelled, gesturing wildly at the television.

Rogue punched another button on the remote, and the jumpy image recorded by the hand-held camera providing the shot came to an abrupt, slightly unfocused halt. "What's the matter?"

Kurt slowly rose from the couch and moved toward the

television, staring hard at the screen. "That man . . ." he said quietly. Eyes widening in surprise, he pointed to the grainy image of the man in the hi-tech wheelchair. "It *is* him!"

"Him who?" Rogue asked.

Kurt turned to face her. "Don't you remember the man Erik warned us about? The mutant terrorist he said would try to tear down everything Erik has spent a lifetime building? The one who'd send us plunging back into the old days of prejudice and hatred?"

"Xavier . . ." Rogue whispered.

Kurt nodded. "We'd better inform Scott and Jean of this. If Xavier *is* here, in New York, then it must mean he's getting ready to strike." His jaw set in determination. "*We'll* have to strike first. . . ."

8

"KWANNON, BUSHIDO Mistress? What sort of nonsense is this?"

Betsy stared in annoyance at the computer screen at the station in which she sat beside the Professor. After escaping the madness in the Stuyvesant Arms lobby, she'd directed the exit point of their spatial jaunt to the rear of the main branch of the New York Public Library, on Fifth Avenue, deciding to forego any cyber-café appearance that might result in another riot. A quick trip to the ladies' room after their arrival, and Betsy had concealed her attention-getting crimson tattoo beneath a layer of makeup, tied her hair back in a severe ponytail so the strands would look a little darker grouped together, and slipped on her sunglasses. Minor changes, but hopefully they'd be enough to conceal her identity.

Maybe I should *have washed out the dye* . . . she'd thought glumly.

A short time later, they'd gotten access to a computer with Internet capabilities and started researching the world of Magneto. They'd been quite surprised when they'd discovered the reason for the wild scene at the hotel.

"Well, it *does* explain why all those people were camped out in the lobby and the street—you're a television star with a highly successful syndicated series, and legions of fans across the globe," Xavier replied.

Betsy sighed. "So much for traveling incognito . . ."

Xavier nodded. "Indeed. Our pictures must have been broadcast via television and the Internet three times around the world by now." He frowned, and pinched the tip of his chin between thumb and forefinger. "However, it *doesn't* explain why you should have a duplicate on this world. Based on what you've told me, you departed with von Doom *before* the Cosmic Cube had an opportunity to restructure you to fit within the scope of Erik's plans. Therefore, there shouldn't *be* another Elisabeth Braddock in existence, beyond the possibility that another woman would have the same name . . ."

"But it certainly doesn't explain *this.*" Betsy gestured toward the screen, and the picture displayed on it. The full-color, digital photograph had been taken, according to its accompanying caption, at a party in Santa Barbara, California, just two months ago. There were a number of celebrities in the shot, mingling with politicians and their families. A bright red banner, strung across the back of the hotel ballroom in which they were all gathered, read HAPPY 40TH, HENRY! in canary-yellow letters.

And standing in the center of the picture, an arm comfortably wrapped around the waist of TV star Elisabeth Braddock, was a ruggedly handsome, blond-haired man in his twenties. He cut an elegant figure in his dark-gray Armani suit, but he looked more like an angel than the multi-millionaire that he actually was, his smile bright and boyish, his wings a brilliant white, spread wide like a feathered backdrop against which he and the *Kwannon* star stood.

His name was Warren Worthington III, and he was—as evidenced by the golden bands encircling the third fingers on the couple's left hands—Elisabeth's husband.

He was also, it appeared, very much alive.

"That sick monster," Betsy said through gritted teeth. Her eyes flashed with unbridled anger. "Not only does he *kill* the only man who ever really meant anything to me, but then he goes so far as to *resurrect* him—and for what? So he can have the chance to do it all over again?" She fell silent, then, and just sat there for a while, staring at the photograph. Slowly, her expression softened. "I remember this party—it was for Senator Gyrich's fortieth birthday, and it happened last year, not two months ago. Warren asked me to sing a couple of numbers to get the party going. . . and then Gyrich pinched my bottom as I headed for the stage." She snorted derisively. "The little toerag."

"Elisabeth."

Betsy turned from the monitor to face the Professor. "Yes?"

"That's the second time now you've mentioned an event at which I *know* you were never present," Xavier replied. "Or, to be more accurate, an event I know never happened at all."

Confused, Betsy stared at him for a moment. "What are you talking about?" she finally said.

The Professor pointed to the picture on the monitor. "This party you remember. Henry Gyrich isn't a United States senator—he's a government liaison who, as much as he likes to remind people that he despises superpowered beings, usually works with the Avengers from a Washington, D.C. office. I'm certain the man has political aspirations—what person living there *doesn't* have them?—but right now he's nothing more than a glorified pencil-pusher."

An inquisitive eyebrow rose above the frames of Betsy's sunglasses. "Are you sure about that?"

"Absolutely," Xavier replied. "And these singing engagements you keep mentioning—I know you've performed once or twice at Warren's nightclub in Manhattan, but you've never made a *career* out of it. You've been far too busy with your duties as an X-Man."

Betsy's mind was reeling. "But, then . . . why do I remember them so clearly?" She shook her head. "No—you're wrong. I *know* that they happened—"

"*On von Doom's world,*" Xavier interjected. "Don't you see, Elisabeth? You're recalling events that were essentially works of fiction—minor details among millions of others that helped to flesh-out von Doom's fantasy realm. Your love for Warren was real—everything else was fabricated by the Cube as it reached into your subconscious and brought forth a personality that would be more in line with the world it was creating. An Elisabeth Braddock with no psychic abilities, no memory of being an X-Man, no knowledge of the depths of evil to which von Doom is capable of sinking in order to have his way."

"But *Jean* was the one who restored all my memories," Betsy insisted. "Are you saying she didn't do a complete job of it?"

Xavier shook his head. "No, but I *am* saying that these false recollections may be a sign that you're still under the Cube's influence." He frowned. "Perhaps you shouldn't have come . . ."

Betsy glared at him. "You were *not* leaving me behind. Your 'friend' has done quite enough damage to all our lives—it's time he's stopped once and for all."

"This is *not* a mission of *vengeance,* Psylocke," Xavier said sternly, "but one of *mercy.* The dimensions the Cube has infected need our help—and *I* need *you* to focus solely on the task set for us." His eyes narrowed, and he leaned in close. "You may have been able to attack von Doom by catching me with my guard down—my error, for expecting *better* of you, even under such trying circumstances—" Betsy flinched; the heated comment had struck her like a slap to the face "—but do not think that I will allow it to happen a second time when we confront Magnus." He paused.

"I loved Warren like a son, Elisabeth," he said softly. "I *know* the pain you're suffering; there's a heaviness in *my* heart, as well. But the chances of failure here are too great for us to allow vendettas to distract us from our goal. I realize you're angry, and you're hurt, and you'd like nothing better than to lash out at Erik and make him pay for the atrocities he's committed . . . but you *know* that's *not* how we do things in the X-Men." He gently placed a hand over one of hers. "And it's not how *Warren* would want you to act."

Betsy slowly nodded, unable to look him in the eye. "You're right, of course. It's just that . . . it's just so damn hard to . . ." She inhaled sharply, then slowly exhaled through her nostrils, forcing herself to remain in control. "I apologize."

"As do I," Xavier said. "I didn't mean to take such a cheap shot at you. I *know* what to expect of you, Elisabeth—and you've *never* disappointed me."

"Thank you," Betsy said softly. Slowly, she raised her head. "Shall we continue?"

Xavier nodded, and smiled. "By all means. However, the source of these strange memories, and any reasons Erik may have for creating twins of you and Warren, will have to be examined later—right now, we still have a great deal of work to do." Fingers skipping across the keyboard, he entered the LOCATE field of the search engine they were using and typed in a request for information on the mutant overlord. "Let's see what *else* we can learn about this world . . ."

It was certainly an education. The end of wars, famine, racial intolerance. Mutants and humans living side-by-side in harmony. The building of a worldwide community dedicated to the sanctity of peace and understanding for one another.

"Incredible," Xavier muttered, hours later. He rubbed his tired, red-rimmed eyes. "He's accomplished so much with the Cube, changed so many lives for the better." He shook his head in astonishment. "It's absolutely amazing."

"But let's not forget, Professor," Betsy pointed out, "that, in order to bring about such peace and harmony, he's *also* used the Cube to take control of everyone on the planet . . . *including* our friends." She pointed to an article from *Time* magazine that glowed brightly on the computer screen. "This shared, worldwide dream mentioned in everything we've read is obviously Magneto's explanation for how he started manipulating their minds. It's easy to think of him as a great peacemaker when he's eliminated hatred towards mutants by rewiring everyone's brains." She sneered.

"*We're* the only ones who know what a monstrous, murdering creature he truly is."

Xavier nodded slowly, but it was clear he was saddened by having to agree with that description of his once-friend. He exhaled sharply. "And yet, if there was only some way to preserve part of what he's done. To lose so much, after we've seen what heights the people of the world are capable of achieving, once they've come to understand our kind . . ."

Betsy gently placed a hand on his arm. "Professor . . ." she said quietly.

Xavier fell silent, then slowly smiled. "Yes, I know—now, *I'm* the one who's lost focus on the mission." He sighed.

"It happens to us all, you know," Betsy said, and grinned broadly.

Xavier chuckled. "I suppose."

"All right, so we know Magneto is living in Paris with his family," Betsy said. "Now, all we need to do is force him to give us the Cube, and take it to Roma so she can sort out this whole bloody mess."

Xavier nodded in agreement.

"But first we'll need to recover my gear from the hotel."

The Professor frowned. "That might not be possible. Knowing how the media works, I would imagine the hotel is literally crawling with representatives of the Fourth Estate by now."

"It will only take a minute," she politely insisted. "Come on, Professor—I didn't load up that carryall with the tools of my trade and drag it around the city so I could leave it behind now." She grinned broadly, like a child excited about what she found in her Christmas stocking. "Besides, I was just getting used to the *katana*—it's got an incredibly delicate balance. I've never held one like it. I'd hate to lose it before I got a chance to try it out."

Xavier shook his head. "I really don't think it's wi—"

An elderly man in the next booth leaned back. "Hey! Pipe down over there!" he whispered hoarsely. "This is a library, not a bar—ya wanna yak it up, go outside!"

Betsy leaned over to speak with him. "Sorry," she said quietly, and smiled. "We didn't mean to disturb you."

The man stared at her for a moment, then his gaze began a slow descent, taking in her tight-fitting clothes and the hourglass shape of her body, finally lingering a bit on her legs. Slowly, he looked up and grinned. " 'Sall right," he whispered.

Betsy gently patted the man on the shoulder. "Thank you."

He nodded, then turned back to his computer. As she moved to rejoin the Professor, Betsy caught a glimpse of the man out of the corner of her eye—he was leaning back to get another appreciative look.

She chuckled softly. *What's that saying the Americans have? "Take a picture—it'll last longer?" Bet he wished he'd brought along his Nikon . . .*

"Very well, Elisabeth," Xavier said. "We'll recover your 'gear.' But we can't stay too long—there's a far greater chance now that Erik may have dispatched his minions to capture us. I'd rather we meet him on *our* terms."

"I'll be quick about it," Betsy replied. "In and out before anyone even knows we've been there." She looked over her shoulders in both directions—no one was paying them any mind, and the old man had gone back to surfing the Web, or whatever it was he'd been doing before he became involved in their conversation. "Let's go."

And with that, they plunged into darkness.

Somewhere beyond the boundaries of time and space, another darkness of sorts was forming.

In the medical wing of the Starlight Citadel, for the first time since Merlyn had created the facility hundreds of years ago, the staff received an unusual—and most welcome—visitor: Roma, Supreme Guardian of the Omniverse. She was accompanied by a retinue of guards and the always tension-creating presence of Saturnyne. It wasn't some kind of surprise inspection, or any sort of annual physical Roma needed to undertake. She was here to examine the facility's lone patient, and to learn the meaning of the strange test results gathered by the physicians.

She was grateful for the distraction. Anything that could pull her away from the throne room and the constantly depressing sight of the reality-cancer spreading unchecked throughout the dimensions she was no longer able to protect was most welcome, indeed. A medical mystery was as good a diversion as anything else that might pop up while she waited in agony for Professor Xavier and Elisabeth Braddock to complete their mission.

The odd little man with the checkered slacks and the wide, friendly grin bowed dramatically as Roma and her party approached. "It is an honor and a rare privilege, indeed, Your Majesty, to have you visit our humble facility."

Saturnyne rolled her eyes in disgust and snorted.

"I understand you are in need of my assistance, Doctor," Roma said pleasantly. "And so, here I am." She glanced at von Doom, who was propped up in his bed, arms folded across his chest, staring at her with as much open contempt as she was staring at him. There were straps binding his arms and legs to the sides of the bed—obviously, he'd tried to escape. "Saturnyne has shown me your findings, and you were correct—they *are* quite intriguing."

"I thought you might agree." The little man sidled closer. "And since you do, Your Majesty, I was hoping to obtain your permission for a small experiment. It might aid in our quest for answers to this most puzzling situation."

"It would depend upon how 'small' your experiment is, Doctor," the Guardian replied. "I am not of a mind to allow you to do anything that might jeopardize the well-being of the citadel and its citizens."

The doctor shook his head. "Oh, no—nothing quite that grand, Your Majesty. No, what I have in mind involves our patient, Mr. von Doom—"

"*Lord* Doom, you nattering jackanapes," the elderly dictator snapped.

The doctor nodded obligingly. "Yeess . . . *Lord* Doom, and a multiphasic crystal accelerator."

Saturnyne raised an inquisitive eyebrow. "Planning on a bit of vivisection, Doctor? Shouldn't you have permission from your patient before you go slicing him up like a loaf of bread?"

"Believe me, Your Whyness," the doctor replied testily, "I *have* tried to get it. But if what I suspect is true, we won't need it. The accelerator should provide the answers we need, while still leaving the patient unharmed."

"And your patient was less than willing to comply with your initial request for his participation?" Roma commented. She smirked. "I find that sort of response hard to believe, coming from a man so dedicated to science as he."

The doctor rolled his eyes dramatically. "The patient, Your Majesty, has been less than willing to do *anything* more than bark orders at my staff, and the only *dedication* he's shown has been toward tapping into the depths of his mental thesaurus to come up with new and increasingly complex combinations of invectives to hurl at me. I dare say some of them might even make a *sailor* blush."

"I see," Roma said. She gazed at von Doom, and a wicked smile turned up the corners of her lips. "Well, Doctor, we would not be assembled here this day, wondering if the omniverse can survive one more hour, were it not for the unmitigated *arrogance* of our guest in thinking that he can play at being a god." She turned back to the physician. "Therefore, I am *more* than willing to give you permission to conduct whatever experiments you think are necessary. Please proceed."

"*Spawn of the devil!*" von Doom roared, pulling at his restraints. He pointed a bony finger at her. "Listen well, daughter of Merlyn: Doom *will* have his revenge upon you, *and* that white-haired lackey of yours! Before this day is done, *all* of you shall be begging for your worthless lives!"

"Dear me, m'lady," Saturnyne quipped. "You seem to have gone and upset him."

Roma smiled maliciously. "A pity." She glanced at the physician. "Doctor?"

The doctor bowed once more. "Thank you, Your Majesty. We'll begin shortly."

"And *I* shall be there to watch," Roma said. "*Every* moment of it." Her smile broadened. "After all, we would not want anything to happen to our guest before we learn the truth . . . would we?"

The ominous tone in which she made that statement caused even Saturnyne to feel a chill race up her spine.

The multiphasic crystal accelerator was another invention of Merlyn's. As a multidimensional being who traveled from one continuum to the next, he had been surprised to discover that there were forces in existence that could harm even *him,* in those centuries before he learned to control all his god-like powers. Using the crystalline technology developed by his father to contain the life-forces of the different dimensions, Merlyn constructed the accelerator as a means to repair the various injuries he receiving during some of his early adventures. Essentially, the energy released by the device would open a minor ripple in the space/time continuum, which would then be directed at the wound in need of repair. The rift separated the damaged tissue from Merlyn's body and shunted it elsewhere, leaving behind healthy tissue. It had worked wonders for him over the course of millennia.

However, it had never been used on a *human* before . . .

A short time after the conference in the infirmary, the players involved reconvened in one of the medical wing's larger laboratories—larger, in this case, meaning it was roughly the size of a warehouse. Roma and Saturnyne sat in an observation booth one floor above the work area. They were joined by the doctor, who was there to monitor the patient's vital signs, and to make certain nothing went wrong with the powerful device they were about to activate.

Down on the floor, the other med-staff members were busy finalizing preparations, lining up the pressure tube of the accelerator and consulting its pre-ignition checklist. In the center of this hive of activity, an angry von Doom stomped back and forth across the glass chamber into which his guards had placed him—none too gently. His lips were moving, but at this height, it was impossible to hear what he was saying; more colorful phrases about his captors, no doubt.

"Now, then, Your Majesty," said the doctor, "everything has been made ready. The procedure won't take all that long—by its conclusion, we'll hopefully have an answer to our intriguing little mystery of the twin brain patterns."

"Splendid, Doctor," Roma said. "You may begin."

At a cue from the physician, the medical technicians below activated the device. Switches were thrown, buttons pushed, and the room filled with the sound of the accelerator cycling up to full power. As the Supreme Guardian and her entourage watched, a series of emerald-hued lightbeams shot from the pressure tube and began playing across von Doom's body, head to toe, first vertically, then horizontally. He was being scanned.

"All right," the doctor said, checking the readings from the accelerator, "everything looks normal . . . given the circumstances. I think we're ready for Phase Two." He nodded to the technicians.

Further calibrations were made to the controls. The roar of the accelerator increased in volume.

The chamber in which von Doom stood filled with light. The former emperor stiffened, his head snapping back as the energy of the crystals poured through him, building in intensity until the bright green illumination not only surrounded him, it also poured from his open mouth and eyes.

And then von Doom split in two.

It wasn't that his body fell in twain; it was that a *second version* of the tyrant—a more powerful-looking version, whose face was obscured by a metal faceplate—separated from the old man. With a shared groan, both Doctors Doom tumbled to the floor.

Immediately, the technicians shut down the accelerator. At the direction of Dr. Stanton, his fellow physicians rushed over to help the men from the chamber and onto stretchers, where they began monitoring their vital signs.

"By the blackened soul of my father," Roma whispered, eyes wide with shock. "Now it all becomes so clear..."

"M'lady?" Saturnyne asked, clearly worried by her superior's attitude.

Roma turned to face her. "Do you not understand, Saturnyne?" She gestured to the semi-conscious figures. "*Two* Victor von Dooms—one contained within the body of the other. One in his prime, one long since past."

"I can see that, m'lady," Her Whyness replied. "Obviously, one of them is the *real* von Doom, but whi—"

"*No!*" Roma shouted. "*Both* are real, Saturnyne!" She pointed to the new arrival. "*This* is the Victor von Doom of Earth 616, as he has always been, unaffected by the power of the Cube." She gazed at the older version of the despot. "And *this* man is an alternate von Doom, whose body has been ravaged by the cosmic energies he tried to control."

It took a few moments for the realization to sink in, but, slowly, the Majestrix began to understand what Roma was talking about. "Mitras wept..." she muttered in astonishment. "But then, that would mean..."

"Yes," Roma said. "It would mean that we have uncovered the *true* flaw in the Cosmic Cube, and it is more than a minor mathematical error." She stamped her foot in a very unregal manner. "Merlyn take me for a fool! I should have realized what was taking place sooner!" She turned on her heel, and began pacing up and down the room, deep in thought.

Standing beside Saturnyne, the doctor quietly cleared his throat, in an obvious attempt to get her attention. "Pardon me for asking, Your Whyness, but what exactly *is* this flaw you're talking about?"

"Are you familiar with the concept of a search engine on a computer, Doctor?" Saturnyne asked. "It seeks out the type of information you've requested, and then presents the appropriate files

for you to download onto the computer's hard drive. It may take a while for it to compile that information because it will essentially 'flip' through hundreds, even thousands, of files before it gathers everything together for your use."

The doctor pinched his bottom lip between thumb and fore-finger, and gazed thoughtfully at the floor for a few moments. "So, what you mean is that this Cube you keep mentioning is acting as a search engine of sorts."

"Exactly," Roma said, joining the conversation. "However, a normal, fully-functional Cosmic Cube does *not* work in that man-ner. Once its possessor has activated its powers, the Cube's energies physically restructure everyone and everything on the planet, all the way down to the molecular level." She glanced at the twin dictators. "Von Doom's Cube, though, was formed incorrectly. And because the device is flawed, it did not transform Earth 616 when he activated it. Instead, it scanned the worlds of the omniverse, located the version that closest resembled von Doom's vision, *and pulled it across time and space to layer it on top of the original.*"

"That, I take it, would be the equivalent of downloading a cor-rupted file," the doctor commented.

"Indeed," Roma concurred. "When the Cube's work was done, every being on Earth 616 had been absorbed into the bodies of their otherworldly counterparts, their identities lost, their psyches forced into the subconscious of their 'hosts.' " The Guardian frowned. "But that is not the reason the omniverse faces its greatest hour of peril; given enough time, I would have been able to correct that situation, with no ill effects to either world. But by plunging in and out of realities as it searched for the right world, the Cube's energies infected an untold number of dimensions with a reality-cancer. The device has caused the protective barriers to weaken, and soon, worlds that occupy the same space, yet lie in separate dimensions, will collide as they phase into existence in one spot."

"And now Magneto has exacerbated the situation," Saturnyne

added. "By creating his own world, he's caused the Cube's taint to spread even further."

The physician turned to Roma. "Is there anything that can be done to stop it, Your Majesty?"

"There is nothing that *we* can do, Doctor," the Supreme Guardian replied. "Unless the two remaining X-Men are able to retrieve the Cube before the damage to reality becomes irreparable, the only function we will still be able to perform is to act as observers. To watch as the omniverse collapses in upon itself—just before we die. . . ."

9

THE SUN was just rising in the northeast when Betsy and Xavier stepped from the jump portal, and into her room.

"Now, as soon as you collect your belongings," Xavier said, "our next stop is Paris. We can't lose anymore time getting to Erik—we'll have to confront him directly." He looked around the room, peering into the darkness. "Where's the light switch?"

"Lemme get it," said a slightly raspy, but all-too-familiar voice from the shadows.

The ceiling light snapped on. Betsy and Xavier turned. Standing by the door was Rogue, clad in her trademark leather bomber jacket. The green-and-gold bodysuit she would normally wear under it, though, had changed—now, it was red and purple, and its style was similar to that of Magneto's costume. One gloved hand rested comfortably on her hip; the other held the carryall.

"Y'all lookin' fer this?" she asked, holding it up. "Y'know, it's kinda heavy for an overnight bag, but I guess that's t'be expected . . . what with those weapons an' all." Taking her other hand off her hip, she gestured for them to approach, and smiled malevolently. "Why don't y'all come on over here an' get it?"

Betsy groaned softly. "Well, *this* day could have gone better . . ." she muttered.

The hairs on the back of her neck suddenly stood on end—someone was behind her. She glanced over her shoulder. On the other side of the room, Nightcrawler clung to the wall, barring access to the windows. He, too, was dressed in a Magneto-like outfit.

"Much, *much* better ..." Betsy murmured. She stepped away from Xavier, flowing easily into a combat-ready pose, her attention shifting from Rogue to Nightcrawler and back again, waiting for one of them to make the first move. "Professor, I think it's time we were going. *Now.*"

"Just a moment." Xavier tried what appeared to be his most comforting smile. "Now, Rogue, Kurt—I'm certain Erik must have told you a wild tale or two about Elisabeth and me, but I can assure you they're not true. We're your friends, not your enemies. We only want to help."

"Y'know, you're *right*, Baldy," Rogue said, and dropped the carryall. The small room reverberated with the sound of heavy metal objects crashing to the floor. "Erik *did* tell us some pretty incredible stories 'bout you, an' the stuff you can do." She stepped away from the door, balling her hands into fists. "An' y'know what?" Her smile faded. "*I believe 'em.*"

That was enough for Betsy. Focusing her incredible mental powers, she concentrated on a weapon—a very *special* weapon. Her right hand began to glow with rose-colored energy, the light solidifying and elongating until it extended a foot in length from her fist.

It was called a psychic dagger, and it was Betsy's most devastating armament—greater than her martial arts skills and sword-wielding capabilities combined. By plunging the blade into an opponent's skull, she was able to "shut down" their mind, overloading their synapses with pure psychic energy. And it was accomplished without inflicting any physical damage. The effects it had on the person on the receiving end were temporary, but memorable—once they had felt the blade's power, they were never quite the same.

"Come on, then, you two," Betsy said, kicking off her shoes. "The Professor and I have places to be, and no time for your silly posturing." She tensed, preparing to spring at Rogue—

And then psychic claws tore into her mind, sending her reeling in agony. The dagger quickly dissipated as she lost control of her powers; the room's lighting returned to its normal, dull coloration.

"It's . . . Jean . . ." Betsy gasped, fighting to remain conscious. The room was spinning wildly, and she felt her knees weaken. She looked to Xavier. His hands were clasped to his head, his mouth moving in a scream she was unable to hear.

The bathroom door opened, and Jean and Scott emerged. Betsy threw herself to one side, barely managing to avoid the blast of Scott's optic beams that struck the spot where she'd been standing—it left a hole in the floor a foot wide. Her jump to safety, however, brought her right in line with Kurt's fist. A three-fingered hand smashed against her jaw, and she crashed to the floor, her head glancing off the edge of the coils of a large metal radiator standing in a corner. Blood trickled down from a cut just above her left temple—if she didn't staunch the flow soon, it was going to make seeing out of that eye impossible.

She rolled to the left, hearing the whistle of air that streamed around Rogue's fist as it rocketed toward her head. The punch connected with the radiator, shattering the rusted metal and sending shrapnel flying through the air. Betsy gasped as a half-dozen pieces plunged into her right thigh like miniature harpoons.

This fight was not going well *at all*.

And *still* Jean continued her psychic attack, though the pain in Betsy's head had lessened a bit—it meant the red-haired woman was concentrating the assault on Xavier, who was trying, in turn, to overpower her *and* her husband. Betsy caught a glimpse of Scott being thrown against a wall as the Professor struck him full-force with his hoverchair. The former leader of the X-Men slumped to the floor in a daze.

An azure-hued tail suddenly wrapped around her neck, cutting off her air as it pulled the lavender-tressed mutant to her feet. Kurt wasn't giving her time to collect her scattered thoughts. Just the opposite, in fact—he was trying to choke her into unconsciousness before she could think of escaping.

"Hang onto her, Kurt!" Rogue said. "I'll finish this!"

Lightheaded and off-balance, Betsy managed to grab hold of Kurt's tail and pull with her remaining strength. Caught by surprise, the blue-furred mutant was torn from the cheap plaster wall, to collide with Rogue as she charged at Betsy. Both teachers struck the floor, their faces lightly brushing against one another on the rebound.

It was enough of an accident to create chaos.

Rogue, Betsy knew, was a mutant with an unusual—and unwanted—power: she was an energy leech of sorts. Anyone who made contact with her bare skin would momentarily be robbed of strength, of consciousness, of memories—they would all flow into Rogue. She would absorb their talents, their mannerisms, their personalities; in essence, for a brief period of time, she would *become* the other person, while her unintended victim lapsed into a short-term coma. And she had *no* control over this ability.

Such encounters tended to leave her an emotional wreck.

And that's *exactly* what Betsy had been counting on when she hurled Nightcrawler into her friend. As cruel an action as she knew it to be, she'd had no other option—winning a battle meant relying on your enemies' weaknesses . . . even if the enemies, in this case, were normally your friends. Had their positions been reversed, and Betsy been the one under Magneto's control, she had no doubt that the X-Men would have done the same to her.

Rubbing her sore throat and wheezing for air, Betsy slumped against the wall behind her and watched Rogue. The brief contact had had a startling effect on the Southern powerhouse: her skin was now the same deep-blue shade as Nightcrawler's, her eyes fairly ablaze with the same golden glow.

"Oh, God," Rogue gasped, her attention now focused on her fallen teammate. "Kurt, I'm sorry!"

"Elisabeth . . ." Xavier croaked. Betsy turned to him. His head slick with sweat, shoulders hunched, eyes screwed shut, he was doing his best to push back Jean's psychic attack, but the effort was taking its toll on him. "You must . . . escape . . ."

"*No!*" Betsy cried. "I won't leave you!" She leapt across the room and frantically grabbed her carryall, reaching inside the canvas bag for her *katana*.

"You *must* . . ." Xavier gasped. "If this mission . . . is to succeed, you *must* get to . . . Erik . . . stop this madness . . . before it is . . . too late . . ."

A loud groan from the floor near the Professor alerted Betsy that Scott was beginning to stir. With his remaining strength, Xavier reached into a compartment in his chair and pulled out the recall device. He tossed it to her.

"Remember what we discussed . . . about the Bond films," the Professor said. "I'll . . . be all right . . ."

Gritting his teeth, Xavier suddenly cried out, as though in terrible pain. Jean staggered back, clutching the sides of her head, and dropped to her knees. The Professor slumped in his chair—he'd obviously put all his remaining psychic strength into that countermove, and now he was both physically and mentally exhausted. For him, the fight was over.

"Go . . ." he said weakly. "*Now* . . ."

Betsy knew he was right—she *couldn't* remain. With the Professor incapacitated, she couldn't even *consider* the possibility that she might be able to hold her own against four of her teammates—between psi-powers and sheer physical strength, she was hopelessly outmatched and outnumbered. Add to that the fact she was cut and punctured in a dozen spots and growing weaker from blood loss with each passing second; her head was still aching from the combination of Jean's psychic assault, the blow from Kurt's fist, *and* the collision with the radiator; and her windpipe was now swollen and inflamed from Kurt's attempt to throttle her with his tail, making it difficult to breathe properly, and it wouldn't take all that much for the group to finally overpower her—or kill her, if that was their goal.

"Damn it all . . ." she muttered.

Pushing herself to the limit, Betsy moved as quickly as her injuries would allow. She leapt over Rogue and the comatose Nightcrawler, shoved the recall device into the carryall, and bolted for the door . . . only to stop short as, in a burst of brimstone-laced smoke, Rogue suddenly appeared in her path.

Kurt, as Betsy well knew, *also* possessed the ability to teleport. Now that she had momentarily inherited his powers, Rogue could, too.

"I never *did* like your stupid TV show," Rogue said, flashing her newly-acquired fangs.

Betsy leapt away from the leather-jacketed mutant, executing an impressive but slightly off-balance backflip that caused her to land on one instead of both feet halfway across the room. Fire seemed to shoot up her left leg—she'd twisted her ankle. Ignoring the pain, Betsy turned and dove for the window, just as another of Scott's power-blasts blew apart the wall behind her. Glass and termite-weakened wood shattered as she catapulted herself through the window.

Luckily, there was a lower-constructed roof on the building next door that broke her fall . . . and almost her neck, if she hadn't dropped the bag and concentrated on landing safely. Considering the alternative, scraping off the top layer of skin on her hands and knees as she rolled across the rough concrete didn't seem like such a bad trade-off. Unfortunately, her expensive clothing hadn't survived as well as she—the blouse was tattered and torn, and the leather skirt had split along one seam.

"She's down there!" she heard Scott yell. Betsy looked up to see him pointing at her. "Rogue—"

Before he could finish giving the order, the skunk-haired Flight Instructor soared through the broken window frame and took to the air. Her skin color was now a pale blue, which made it to clear to Betsy why she hadn't simply teleported to the roof—the powers she'd "borrowed" from Nightcrawler were fading.

Retrieving the carryall, Betsy hobbled her way across the roof, ignoring the whistle of air that grew louder behind her as Rogue started her attack run. She needed to concentrate on escape, getting as far from here as possible.

Paris, she told herself. *Think about Paris. About getting to Magneto.*

The scream of rushing air filled her ears.

She dropped down quickly, her chin bouncing off the concrete roofing; it caused her to bite the tip of her tongue. Betsy groaned, annoyed at herself for adding another to her growing list of injuries. And yet, although it seemed to her that she was doing more damage to herself than the X-Men had tried to do, she *had* managed to avoid having her skull smashed open by Rogue's granite-like fists. Based on the speed at which the Southern powerhouse had borne down on her, it was all too clear to Betsy that, under Magneto's Cube-powered influence, her former teammate was set on killing her.

Looking skyward, Betsy spotted Rogue turning sharply, like some sort of red-and-purple-hued heat-seeking missile. She wouldn't miss her target twice—unless . . .

Betsy closed her eyes—it was now or never. *ParisParisParis,* she thought quickly, and was rewarded with the icy sensation that always crept through her bones when her teleportation power was starting to kick in. She felt herself sinking into the concrete as the darkness flowed over her and pulled her into its murky depths.

Rogue crashed into the roof a half-second later, her momentum carrying her all the way down to the building's second floor.

Of her intended target, there was no sign.

He was lost in darkness.

Unable to move, the Victor von Doom of Earth 616 struggled against the infinite blackness that surrounded him, that held him immobile. How that could be possible, he did not know; it was more than likely the work of those two infuriating women and that insufferable little physician. What he *did* know, however, was that he needed to escape from it, so that he would be able to enact his revenge upon them. There was no doubt in his mind that he would—he *was* Doom, after all, and he *had* vowed to punish his captors for their lack of respect. In the end, their deaths were as certain as his escape. It was merely a question of time—time, and opportunity . . .

Forcing himself to cease his struggles, he tried to recall how he might have ended up in this situation. The last thing he remembered was a brilliant green light flowing over him, *through* him, the voice that had spoken to him from the depths of his subconscious suddenly crying out in pain, and then . . .

And then, nothing. He had found himself here, alone with his thoughts, the other voice silenced, perhaps forever.

It had served its purposes, though. From it, he had heard the stories of the Starlight Citadel and its master, Merlyn; of the cosmic schemer's daughter, Roma—the dark-haired woman who would be the first to bow before von Doom and acknowledge his superiority; and of Saturnyne, the white-haired cow who had shown the greatest disrespect for the man who would have her put to death soon enough. All this information, the voice had explained, came directly from the mouths of Roma's own servants—members of an organization called the Dimensional Development Court, who had been captured while visiting another Earth in order to initiate a process called "The Push."

The agents, once the depths of their knowledge had been fully plumbed, had not lived beyond their last moment of usefulness.

What interested von Doom the most, of course, was the power contained in both the citadel and its mistress—power, according to the voice, over the forces of time and space themselves. Power that made the world-transforming energies of the Cosmic Cube pale by far in comparison . . .

To von Doom's surprise, the darkness began to fade, its limitless depths giving way to a spot of light that grew brighter as the former emperor watched. An image began to form before his eyes—hazy, at first, devoid of color, but it quickly solidified into a familiar white shape:

A laboratory coat.

"Awake at last, I see," said a terse voice. "Excellent."

The former emperor opened his eyes fully. He was still in the medical ward, lying once more in bed, his battle armor removed—for security purposes, no doubt. But the man standing above him was not the annoying little fop who always seemed to be hovering around him. This person—another physician, from the looks of him—was taller, balding, and perpetually scowling.

Von Doom opened his mouth to speak; his tongue felt bloated and extremely heavy.

"If you plan to launch some colorful stream of invectives my way, I'll be more than happy to sedate you," the physician said sternly. "Unlike the Chief Physician, I'm not nearly as patient of verbal abuse as he is, and I've already had my fill of such language from your counterpart."

Counterpart? Von Doom turned his head to the right, though the sudden movement caused his temples to ache. Lying on the bed next to his was an older version of himself—a face with which he was intimately familiar, since it had stared back at him every time he looked in a mirror during the time he controlled the Earth with the Cosmic Cube. It was the face that had constantly reminded him of how quickly the flawed device was killing him, minute by minute.

How, then, could he be staring at that face, when it was his?

Wasn't it?

"What is the meaning of this?" he mumbled around his leaden tongue.

The physician gestured from one tyrant to the other. "Victor von Doom of Earth 616, meet—" he leaned forward to consult the old man's chart, which appeared on the monitor above the bed "—the Victor von Doom of Earth 892." He grunted. "It took the DDC some time to track down his point of origin—since *you* moved it."

The former emperor forced himself to speak—he had to know more. "What are you talking about, you fool?" he rumbled.

The doctor folded his arms across his chest and frowned. "I'll thank you to address me as 'Dr. Stanton,' not 'you fool.' And from what the Supreme Guardian has *deigned* to tell those of us she sees as 'lesser beings'—not counting the Chief Physician, of course," he added bitterly, "it would appear that, in the course of whatever experiment you were running, you succeeded not only in abducting one of your counterparts from an alternate reality and taking control of his body, but you brought along *his entire world* and layered it on top of your own." He snorted. "Not exactly what I'd call a well-thought-out scientific endeavor."

The news was a genuine surprise for von Doom. If what this smug cretin was telling him was true, then it would explain a great deal, from his advanced aging to the false memories he'd been experiencing—like the one involving his conflict with the Mandarin—to the "voice" in his head. The memories weren't false, they were the recollections of his alternate, and the voice had been that of his counterpart, providing information about Roma while fighting to regain control of the body von Doom had taken over when the Cube was activated. It would also explain the reality in which he had lived as emperor: not a physical reconstruction of the world, as he had commanded the Cube to perform, but a transfer of the closest approximation of the world he desired, shifted from one dimension to another.

It was beyond belief. It also meant that the device he had held in his hands not so long ago was probably the most powerful reality-influencer ever created—and he had allowed it to slip from his grasp. Now, the Cube was in the hands of that mutant dog, Magneto, and he was powerless to stop him.

Or was he? If the withered body and sagging face actually belonged to the Doctor Doom of another Earth, if it was *that* von Doom whose body had been ravaged by the Cube's life-absorbing flaw, then—

"A mirror," he ordered.

Stanton clearly didn't seem to understand why the request had been made, but he did as he was told, and handed von Doom a small mirror from a portable equipment cabinet that stood nearby.

The scars, the mottled flesh, the ghastly complexion—they were all there, but on a face that, though severely disfigured, still bore the features of a man in his early forties, not late eighties.

The face of Doom.

The Latverian dictator was pleased. He reveled in what he saw in the reflection, no longer bothered by his grotesque appearance as he had been in his youth, when a scientific experiment gone horribly wrong had forever scarred the face of a teenaged Victor von Doom. Now, he saw only the power, the majesty, the nobility that were carved into the visage of this man, this conqueror, this intellectual giant known far and wide as "The Lion of Latveria." True, while holding the Cube, he had allowed his vanity to get the best of him, causing him to place part of his consciousness in the electronic brain of a Doombot—an android replica of the emperor, but one with the handsome features of that younger Victor—so that he could travel across the length and breadth of his brave, new world at the side of his wife, Ororo—the white-haired, African, elemental-controlling mutant known as Storm ... or, had she actually been the wife of his counterpart?

It didn't matter anymore—that was another time, another dream, lived through the eyes of the decrepit old man lying in the next bed. And through those eyes, von Doom had ruled the world; now, though, he wanted so much more ...

He looked at the straps binding his limbs, then to the physician. "Release me."

Stanton shook his head. "I can't do that. Beyond the fact that you've just undergone a traumatic, multiphasic transformation from which your body is still recovering, you're ..." He paused. "Well ... you're a very dangerous man ... or so I'm told."

"Dangerous only to my enemies, physician," von Doom replied. "Do you wish to be counted among them ... or among my allies?"

"I'd rather not be counted at all," Stanton said.

Muscles twitched in von Doom's face, approximating a smile. "Ahh, I see. You would prefer anonymity."

Stanton nodded. "Something like that."

Von Doom chuckled softly. "You surprise me, Stanton—I would have thought a man of your station would desire more from your life."

"How so?"

"I have seen the way in which you look at your superiors, Stanton," von Doom replied. "You stand in the shadows, your skills unappreciated, your opinions ignored, while that buffoon you call a 'Chief Physician' orders you about and makes infuriating asides to your peers about your apparent lack of medical abilities. Were I in your position, I would take steps to show the Supreme Guardian my true value—and prove to her the poor administrative choice she made in passing you by for the position that should have been yours, and not that prancing clown's." He paused, then shrugged. "But perhaps you are right, Stanton—perhaps it *is* far better to remain in the shadows, rather than to be ridiculed in the light."

The former emperor fell silent, waiting for a response. He had played this sort of game before—many times—and he knew when it was time to speak . . . and when it was time to let the other player make the next move.

Stanton stared at him, his face slowly reddening, his teeth pulling back in a feral snarl—and with that, von Doom knew that he had won. With just a few well-chosen words, he had shattered the physician's thin veneer of detached professionalism, and reached the enraged, insecure, easily manipulated egotist lurking beneath the surface.

"I can end all that, Stanton," von Doom purred. "The anonymity, the disrespect . . . I—*we*—can make it right. Together." His eyes blazed with a cold, hypnotic fire. "All you need do . . . is join me."

The moments passed slowly, and von Doom waited—*tried* to wait—patiently. Push too soon, too hard, he knew from experience, and Stanton might back down, the heat of anger raging in his heart replaced with a mindnumbingly cold fear—of Roma, of Saturnyne, of losing his job. And then all would be lost . . . at least, until the *next* opportunity presented itself. The Lion of Latveria, however, had never been known for having *that* much patience ...

"What ... *kind* of steps would you take?" Stanton asked haltingly.

Scarred lips pulled back in a Cheshire Cat-like grin. "Free me from this bed, provide me with my armor, and I will show you ..."

"How many guards are on-duty?" von Doom asked one hour later, fitting his mask into place. The seals along its edges closed with a satisfying click. Clad once more in his armor, he at last felt complete—and ready to set his plans into motion.

"Two members of the Captain Britain Corps are stationed right outside the door at all times," Stanton replied. "But if they suspect anything is wrong, they'll be able to summon reinforcements within seconds."

"Then they must be rendered incapable of raising such an alarm," von Doom stated. "*You* will call them in—then *I* shall deal with them." He glared at Stanton. "Do not fail me, physician—or Doom shall make certain it is your *last* mistake."

Stanton swallowed, hard. "I ... understand."

"Very good. But first ..." Von Doom turned to face the other bed. His counterpart slept soundly, deep in the throes of a drug-induced coma. It appeared Stanton had been quite serious about his intense dislike for being the target of verbal abuse ... and his ability to put a swift end to it.

"Umm ... what are you doing?" the physician asked as von Doom moved to stand near the top of the bed.

The Latverian dictator raised a gauntleted fist above his head. "In the chessgame of power, there is only room for *one* king."

The sound of metal smashing through bone and brain was quickly swallowed by the vastness of the infirmary.

Von Doom wiped his gore-slickened hand on the bedsheet, then turned wordlessly and walked across the infirmary to stand at one side of the entry portal. He looked around for something with which to attack the guards; after a few seconds of searching, he found it. He nodded to Stanton.

"Um . . . guards?" the physician called out. "Could you please lend a hand? I'm having some . . . trouble with the patients."

The door irised open.

Projectile or energy weapons were useless on the citadel, as Saturnyne had explained when von Doom had attempted to use his armaments. "A state of temporal grace," she had called it, which prevented them from firing. That security system, however, had no effect on the syringes he plunged into the bases of the guards' brains as they stepped through the door—syringes filled with nothing but air.

He rammed the plungers home as the guards, panicked, reached back to pull out the needles.

They were dead before they hit the floor.

Stanton looked ill. "Is all this killing really necessary, von Doom?"

A gauntleted hand shot forward, to grasp the doctor by the throat. "Doom does as he pleases, lackey—and it *pleases* him to eliminate *all* who stand in his way." His grip tightened, cutting off Stanton's air. "Are *you* at Doom's side, physician—or have you chosen to stand in his way as well?" He opened his hand, and Stanton staggered back, rubbing his reddened throat.

"At . . . your . . . side . . ." the doctor gasped.

"You show a glimmer of intelligence, worm," von Doom commented. He relaxed his grip, and Stanton staggered back a few steps, rubbing his tender throat. "My counterpart told me of a 'stasis chamber' that may prove useful to my needs," the dictator continued. "You will take me to it."

"There's only *one* prisoner being held there right now," Stanton said, finally able to breathe normally. "Someone who's supposed to have been no end of trouble for Roma, and her father before that. I've heard it said that just her *presence* in the citadel makes

Roma nervous—even though she's been sealed away since her arrest."

Behind the gleaming mask of Doctor Doom, an eyebrow rose in an inquisitive fashion. "How . . . interesting. And what is the *name* of this individual whom the Supreme Guardian fears so greatly?"

"Opul Lun Sat-yr-nin," Stanton replied. "She's the Majestrix's counterpart from Earth 794. The X-Men of your Earth aided in her capture not too long ago."

"Indeed?" A malevolent, electronic chuckle burbled out from the mask's mouthpiece. "Then, I should like to *meet* this extraordinary woman. It would appear we share similar tastes in enemies. . . ."

Interlude III

'IS PARIS burning?' No, but soon enough it *will* be—when I am in control of the Cube..."

In the light of early morning, two figures stood at the railing on the observation deck of the Eiffel Tower, and gazed down upon the quaint homes and magnificent palaces that comprised the centerpiece of Magneto's world. To the east, the sun was just beginning to climb above the horizon, painting the landscape in soft pinks and yellows. On the streets below, a lone jogger—it was impossible to tell whether the person was a human or a mutant from this altitude, or even if it was a man or a woman—hurried along on what must have been their daily regimen. And from the girders somewhere high above the watchers, the sound of doves cooing softly could be heard.

The start of a new day, on a new world.

The Controller sneered. "I think I liked this place better in von Doom's version, where it was nothing more than a smoking pit devoid of life. A killing ground that stood as testament to the destructive abilities of a sub-human allowed to run free, when he and all his genetically-inferior brethren should have been long dead."

"Have you ever been here before, sir?" Leonard asked. "I mean, before Magneto destroyed it and then rebuilt it?"

The Controller nodded. "Oh, yes. Many times. And each time I have been reminded of better days, when the people of the world trembled in fear at the might of the empire that was taking form then. Awestricken by the sheer power of the dedication we had to the dream of a great man, of the lengths we would go to make that dream come true." He sneered. "But that was before the dream began to fade. Before the dreamer was murdered by an inhuman creature that dared to think of itself as a man." His teeth ground together noisily. "Before I was swallowed by the mists of oblivion and trapped there for decades, lost within the trackless depths of my *own* dreams."

"Like what they say happened to Captain Ame—"

"I have *heard* the story," the Controller snapped. He grunted. "Fanciful, overly romanticized *lies* told to impress a gullible pub-lic—" he gazed coolly at his young assistant "—and children."

Leonard's cheeks turned a deep crimson shade, but he declined to respond to the insult. Clearly, he understood how foolish it would be to talk back to his superior—especially when they were so very high up . . .

"I remember a night in June," the Controller murmured, his voice surprisingly soft, "when the air was filled with the sounds of merriment. I stood beside the leader at the top of the Eiffel Tower, as we do now. There was a cool breeze gently blowing from the east—from the homeland. A good sign. We stood there, that night, and watched our men celebrate their recent victory over the once-mighty French forces. There was song, and laughter, and a sense of fulfillment. We realized then that the world truly *was* ours for the taking. We felt—no, we *knew* we were . . . invincible." An approximation of a smile cracked his grotesque features. "It was an . . . inspiring moment."

"So, what happened?" Leonard asked.

The Controller snarled and lashed out with a gloved fist, sav-agely backhanding the young man across the mouth. Leonard fell back onto the platform, his head rebounding against the metal flooring.

"*Dumbkopf!*" the Controller roared. "Has your entire generation become so lost in decadence that you now take some sort of perverse *pride* in your ignorance? Do you know *nothing* of history?"

Leonard slowly sat up, rubbing the back of his head. He spat out a wad of bloody phlegm; sunlight glinted off the enamel coating of a premolar that floated in the crimson-hued mucous. "I know your side *lost*," he said sullenly.

The Controller flashed his death's-head grin and chuckled. "Ah. Then you are *not* the imbecile I feared you might be." Arms folded across his chest, he watched as his assistant struggled to regain his feet. "Pay more attention to history, Leonard," he said sternly. "A wise man once remarked, 'Those who cannot remember the past are condemned to repeat it.' *I* am *always* aware of my past, though I see no need to dwell on unpleasant memories. It is the *future* that holds the greatest promise; the future . . . and the Cube."

The Controller looked at the rising sun, a half smile twisting a corner of his mouth. "Yes . . . the Cube . . ." he said quietly, as though he had lapsed into a trance. He closed his eyes, inhaled deeply, then slowly released the breath through his nostrils. "I feel it. It calls to me as a lover would, caresses me with tendrils of the purest energy, entices me with dreams of ultimate power. Dreams of godhood." He chuckled. "It promises nothing I have not already experienced." His eyes suddenly opened, and his relaxed expression flowed into one of confusion. "But there is something wrong . . ."

"Is it Magneto?" Leonard asked. A handkerchief was clumsily stuffed into one corner of his mouth, to staunch the bleeding of the empty socket from where his broken tooth had originated.

"No. It is the Cube." The Controller looked to the lightening skies. High across the stratosphere, stretching off in all directions to disappear beyond the horizon line, multihued bands of energy flowed and sputtered, draping the world in colors that only the Controller could see with the naked eye. "The wave patterns are different. They are not in keeping with those normally associated with a Cosmic Cube." He casually waved a hand, as though to dismiss the topic. "It is an unforeseen complication, but one that will not delay my appropriation of the device."

"You can *see* the Cube's energy?" There was a tone of astonishment in Leonard's voice.

"Of course, I can," his master replied testily. "Just as I was able to redirect that same energy so that you and I were not transformed when it struck the command center." He poked a thick finger into Leonard's chest. "Remember, lackey, you speak to a *superior being*—a man who has been as one with the universe itself through the power of the Cube; who once walked the Earth as a god; who has slipped free of death's cold embrace time and again to take revenge upon his enemies. And once the Cube is mine, there will be *nothing* I cannot do. Nothing."

The Controller glanced over the railing. Far below, Paris was beginning to awaken, as a few early risers appeared on the sidewalks, and the first signs of vehicular traffic took to the roads. "We must go. I do not wish to tip my hand yet and, given my . . . *striking* appearance—" he gestured toward his hideous face "—it would not be long before Lensherr received word of my presence in his precious city." His eyes glimmered with the fires of intense hatred. "But we *will* return later, when the city sleeps once more, to set my plans in motion. And *then* Magneto will know I am here, as his dream begins to die around him. . . ."

10

BETSY HAD always had a fondness for Paris.

She'd visited it often during her short modeling career, when she'd been in demand for spring runway shows, fought over by practically every fashion designer in the world. The charming cafés, the cozy little streets, the museums and galleries . . . If she hadn't been on the run from people who had once been her friends, and on her way to confront a man who could turn her into a glistening, gore-drenched paperweight of shattered bone and tattered sinew, either with or without the aid of the glowing little box of cosmic energy that had caused all this trouble, she might have been able to enjoy the trip. As it was, she was more than willing to sacrifice the lure of sightseeing just for an opportunity to survive this adventure in one piece.

After her narrow escape from the ex-X-Men, Betsy had awakened the following morning to find herself draped across a wooden bench in Place Jean XXIII, near the Cathedral of Notre-Dame. She'd felt stiff and sore and woolly-brained, and the curious stares she'd received from the couple sitting across the path from her made her all too aware of the sad state of her appearance, even if she hadn't detected those particular thoughts when she scanned their minds to find out if they were working for Magneto. Bruised, bloodied, tattered and torn, with nowhere to go and no one to call upon for assistance, she'd left the square as quickly as possible, hobbling off into the early morning sunlight on her injured ankle before anyone had a chance to ask questions.

After that, matters had definitely worsened. She'd tried to enter a streetside pay toilet to clean her cuts, assess her situation, and change clothes, only to realize she wasn't carrying any money—having escaped von Doom's crumbling world with only the clothes on her back, she hadn't even thought about needing cash when her focus had been on getting to Magneto. It was the reason why Xavier had been the one to pay for their rooms at that nasty little flophouse in New York. Much to her distaste, it meant that the only way she was getting inside the lavatory was by using her teleportational power for a short jaunt.

Why is it I can't see the Scarlet Witch or Warbird finding themselves in this type of situation . . . ? she'd thought darkly.

Once inside, she'd gazed at her reflection in the mirror above the small sink, and immediately wished she hadn't. She literally looked like bloody hell: her eyes were puffy and red; chin and hands caked with dried blood; the left side of her face horribly bruised from where Kurt's fist had struck; a bright red ring around her neck, created by Kurt's tail; arms cut in a dozen or so places from her encounter with the hotel window. The bottom half of her was no better—both knees scraped raw, a thick patch of dried blood running along her right leg from thigh to calf, left ankle swollen and stiff.

"Was this the face that launched a thousand clothing lines?" she quipped bitterly, disgusted and depressed by the haggard face that stared back at her. "And climbed the topless towers of Lagerfeld?" She sighed. "What would Gianni Versace think of me now, God rest his soul?"

Cleaning up had been a slow, deliberate process. Since she couldn't go to an emergency room for treatment (again, too many questions would be asked), she had to do the best she could with the first-aid kit she'd remembered to pack—an essential item in her line of work. So, in lieu of sterile pads and yards of gauze, it was cotton balls and *Flintstones*-decorated Band-Aids (courtesy of the Chief Physician); instead of tetanus shots and witch hazel, iodine and Bactine. She'd used a pair of tweezers to remove the shards of metal from her right leg, and the glass from her arms, and then, pleased with her adequate field dressings, set her sights on tackling the clothing issue. Unfortunately, beyond the first-aid kit, all that remained in the carryall were her dark-blue X-Men uniform, a *katana*, a pair of *sai*, a small makeup bag, and the recall device. No other clothes, no money, no credit cards . . . and no food.

Her stomach rumbled.

"This *proves* I was right," Betsy had muttered sullenly. "This *never* would have happened to the Avengers . . ."

Now, hours later, as a brilliant, noonday sun blazed overhead, she wandered the streets of Paris, waiting for night to fall so she could begin her siege on Palace Lensherr. Her body didn't feel quite so much like she'd been run over by a train, and her head was much clearer than it had been earlier in the morning. The acetaminophen capsules in the first-aid kit had helped her aches and pains, but it was the baguettes, diet sodas, and chocolate-covered marzipan fruits she had "appropriated" from a closed market during the wee hours that had gone the longest way toward helping her organize her thoughts.

Such are the amazing restorative powers of caffeine and sugar, she thought happily.

As she strolled along the bustling sidewalks of Rue Saint Jacques, contentedly munching on the small confections, she glanced at the people around her. Much to her surprise, no one had paid the slightest attention to her unusual appearance, with her oddly-colored hair and provocative clothing and children's bandages. Perhaps, in this "enlightened" society created by Magneto, super hero uniforms didn't seem all that unusual. Or perhaps she was on the cutting edge of fashion, with her latex clothing and purple hair—this *was* Paris, after all; styles might have changed to reflect the New World Order. Or perhaps the Parisians were just more tolerant of strangely-dressed young women who hummed Cole Porter songs while their mouths were full of bread.

Of course, it just might have to do with the possibility that *Kwannon, Bushido Mistress* wasn't broadcast here. In America, based on the reactions from the press and her "fans" in New York, taking a stroll in an outfit that looked exactly like the one worn by her television counterpart would have probably started a riot.

More than likely, though, the reason for the apparent disinterest of passersby was due to Magneto's control over their minds—if the tourists at the Empire State Building hadn't reacted to her arrival with Charles from the dark portal, why should the citizens *here* pay her any mind?

Gazing up at the brilliant blue sky, Betsy stepped to one side to get out of the flow of pedestrian traffic and stopped in front of an antiques shop, reveling in the sunlight that warmed her face. Maybe, she thought, there was a *little* time for sightseeing—perhaps a walk in the tree-lined lanes of the Jardins des Plantes to help ease the tension in her body. After all, it was *such* a beautiful day—who knew if she might live to see another after tonight . . . ?

Slowly opening her eyes, a winsome smile pulled at the corners of her mouth. *I just wish Warren could be hear to enjoy it with m—*

She froze.

That face on the man who had just passed her. The boyish smile and sparkling blue eyes. The shoulder-length blond hair. The powerful build that not even a dark business suit could conceal. She knew them as well as she knew the contours of her own body—they could belong to only one person.

It was Warren.

Well, it was, and it wasn't. The man certainly *looked* like Warren, *walked* like Warren, was humming a Brian Wilson tune off-key like Warren, even wore the same cologne, but it wasn't *really* Warren.

Not *her* Warren, that is. The one who had fought beside her as

a fellow X-Man against the toughest odds. The one who had won her heart with an unbeatable combination of charm, humility, and irresistible sexuality. The one who had sacrificed part of his soul in order to bring her back from death's door, after her particularly fatal encounter with the sociopathic mutant assassin called Sabretooth.

The one who had died in her arms on a storm-swept grassy field in Washington, D.C.

This man was an impostor; she knew that. His skin wasn't blue, as Warren's had become as a result of a run-in with the creature called Apocalypse, who was one of the X-Men's deadliest enemies.

And his thoughts must have been focused a million miles away, because he had brushed past her without even noticing—something Warren never would have done. He'd always been too much the lady-killer to miss the opportunity of spotting a pretty girl on a crowded street. And considering the fact that Betsy was a) standing in the middle of the sidewalk in a formfitting, latex swimsuit, and b) supposed to be this man's wife in this reality, being so completely ignored by her faux-husband was saying a lot.

Not that it really mattered, of course. She wasn't in the mood to play "Twenty Questions" with a doppleganger of her dead lover, try to explain what she was doing in Paris, or find out why he was here, for this one-in-a-million chance encounter. Seeing this man only reminded her of the beast who had so callously shattered her world, and of her resolve to make him pay for it, no matter what Xavier had said. The Professor wasn't here now—*she* was, and this mission would be accomplished on *her* terms, hero's code of ethics be damned.

And yet . . .

And yet, despite the fact it couldn't be him, no matter how hard she might wish it were so; despite the fact that Warren had died right in front of her only days before; despite her initial anger at Magneto for creating a duplicate of that same man, she found herself unable to resist the impulse to follow him.

Just to be certain, of course, that it *wasn't* him . . .

Somewhere on the edge of Creation, a different sort of quest was coming to an end—a journey along the road to ultimate power, traveled by two men. One was a ruthless dictator whose machinations had resulted in nothing less than the weakening of the entire space/time continuum. The other was a physician who was just now beginning to think that allying himself with an armored tyrant had *not* been such a good idea after all . . .

Located at the bottom-most level of the Starlight Citadel, the stasis chamber—constructed for the incarceration of only the most dangerous criminals in the omniverse—was contained within a high-security area manned even when there were no prisoners to guard. Access to this level was restricted to a select few: Roma and her personal guard, Saturnyne, certain high-ranking officials of the Captain Britain Corps . . . and medical technicians charged with monitoring the vital signs of the inmates.

The Chief Physician was counted among the last group. So was Dr. Stanton.

He stood beside von Doom at the entrance to the innermost room, trying to ignore the broken, lifeless bodies on the floor behind them—med-techs and guards caught unawares and quickly dispatched by the villain before they could call for help.

"Proceed, physician," the tyrant snapped. It seemed his patience had finally come to an end, annoyed as he had been with the constant delays they'd encountered along the way—traveling along rarely used access tunnels to throw off any pursuers, hiding in shadows whenever a member of the Corps headed in their direction. So far, they'd been fortunate enough to remain undetected for this long, and it appeared that the corpses in the medical wing hadn't been discovered—yet. Soon enough, though, Stanton knew, the entire citadel would be ringing with the sound of alarms, alerting the staff to von Doom's disappearance.

Right now, however . . .

Stanton stepped in front of an electronic eye; it lit up immediately.

"Identify," demanded a synthesized voice. It sounded very much like Saturnyne's.

"Stanton, Henry P.," the physician replied. "World of origin: Earth 1629. Starlight Citadel Xenobiology Division, Level 817. Access Code 5-1-9-8-2-6. Password: Einstein."

A light flashed from the eye, bathing Stanton in a pale green aura. The beam faded after a few seconds, the computer's scan of his DNA structure completed.

"Identity confirmed," the computer stated flatly. "Stanton,

Henry P. World of origin: Earth 1629. Starlight Citadel Xenobiology Division, Level 817. Access Code accepted. Password accepted. Please state the nature of your visit."

"Medical examination of prisoner Opul Lun Sat-yr-nin."

The computer paused, obviously running a check on the infirmary's medical records. "Examination performed at 2930 hours, Citadel Standard Time. Next examination not scheduled until—"

An armored fist shattered the electronic eye.

Stanton raised an eyebrow and turned to the glowering despot beside him. "I *would* have found a way around that problem."

"Silence!" the former emperor barked. "Doom has no use for time-consuming protocols—not when there are worlds to be won!"

Roughly pushing past Stanton, the tyrant stepped over to the door leading to the heart of the chamber. Gripping the section of the circular portal where the two halves met, he used the full strength of his incredible armor to force the door open. He stepped inside the next room, not bothering to see if Stanton was following.

There were no furnishings here, no cots or chairs or tables—merely row upon row of medical equipment and monitoring stations.

And one very special occupant.

There, in the center of the room, was the object of von Doom's quest, and the cornerstone of his plan:

Opul Lun Sat-yr-nin.

She floated serenely in a large tube—a crystalline structure filled with an azure liquid that glowed faintly—her shoulder-length white hair drifting lazily around her stunning features. Features that perfectly matched those of the woman who was second-in-command to the Supreme Guardian.

To see her at rest like this, sleeping so peacefully, one would never know she was completely insane.

As Mastrex of Earth 794, Sat-yr-nin had ruled her world with an iron fist. But she had always desired more than a mere planetary empire, when she knew there were countless other planes of reality out there in the omniverse, all waiting to be conquered. She might have succeeded in attaining her goals, someday, if it hadn't been for the intervention of Brian Braddock, the Captain Britain of Earth 616 who, it turned out, was an alternate version of her royal konsort, Byron Brah-dok—her world's Kaptain Briton.

Sat-yr-nin eventually escaped the prison into which her people placed her, and journeyed to Brian's world seeking revenge. Unfortunately, he'd joined up with a group of England-based heroes called Excalibur by then, and it had been his shapeshifting girlfriend, Megan, who ultimately upset her plans and forced the Mastrex to flee back to her homeworld. Of course, things had worked out for the best, anyway—she'd still had followers on 794 and, with their aid, she was soon back in power, gleefully staging public executions and constantly reminding her subjects that she was here to stay.

Or *had* been there to stay, that is, until the combined might of the X-Men and the Captain Britain Corps changed the situation . . .

"Release her," von Doom commanded.

Stanton didn't comment this time. He simply stepped over to the tube's controls and began the extraction process.

A pump at the bottom of the crystal began siphoning out the suspension fluid, revealing the flawless contours of her body. Once the liquid had been drained, the crystalline glass slid upward. Stanton crossed over to the opened tube and quickly removed the monitoring devices attached to Sat-yr-nin's skin. With a soft groan, the Mastrex slowly started to revive.

The physician turned to von Doom. "It may take a few minutes for—"

Before Stanton could grab her, Sat-yr-nin suddenly pitched forward, her body heaving uncontrollably. Dropping to her knees, fingers splayed to keep her head from crashing down onto the cold metal beneath her, she opened her mouth wide, and spewed onto the floor a fair amount of the azure liquid. She gasped for air as, for the next minute, her lungs continued to pump out the dark fluid that filled them in order to make room for oxygen. When that was finally accomplished, she fell into a severe coughing fit that made her double-over, clutching her sides in obvious pain.

And all the while, von Doom watched in silence, arms folded across his chest.

Eventually, the Mastrex's breathing problems ceased, and she eased into a steady rhythm of inhalations and exhalations. Wiping away the traces of spit and blue-tinged snot that hung from her lips and nostrils with the back of one hand, she slowly looked up at the armored figure towering above her.

"Welcome back to the land of the living, Opul Lun Sat-yr-nin," the monarch said. "I am Doom—and I bring you an offer you would do well to accept. . . ."

11

THE DRUGS were beginning to wear off.

Moaning softly, Charles Xavier tried to open his eyes, but each lid felt as though it weighed a hundred pounds. He attempted to raise his arms so he could rub at the ponderous folds of skin with the edges of his hands, but his limbs were just as heavy. Whatever the dosage he'd been given, it had obviously been meant to keep him unconscious for quite a long time.

"Scott, I think he is waking up," said a voice in a clipped German accent. The Professor immediately recognized the speaker: Kurt Wagner. It sounded as though Kurt was standing a mile away, but Xavier knew that, as dazed as he was by the sedative, his student could be right beside him and still sound distant.

Though as yet unable to focus his thoughts, he was aware of a dull roar that filled the air around him, and felt pressure building in his ears. Were they on a plane? A sealed aircraft cabin *would* account for his limited hearing. But where were they heading? Even through the drug-induced fog, one possible answer came to mind: He was being taken to Magneto for interrogation—and, more than likely, a round or two of gloating about how he'd finally won. If the Professor had been able to coax his facial muscles into forming a smile, he would have done so.

Good old Magnus, he thought fuzzily. *I can always count on his predictability . . .*

There was the sound of footsteps approaching—more than one set.

"Already?" That was Scott Summer's voice; he sounded angry. "I thought you said he'd be unconscious for the entire travel time."

"I'm a *gymnast,* not a doctor," Kurt snapped. "I was only repeating what Dr. MacTaggert told me before we left. How was *I* to know his constitution might be strong enough to shake it off?"

"Boys, boys, calm down." Xavier recognized the soothing tones of Jean Grey as she entered the conversation. "Getting huffy with one another is just going to make this trip seem twice as long. I realize we're all a bit on edge, having this killer in our midst, but Erik will take care of everything once we get to the palace. Now . . . just relax."

The two men muttered in agreement. Xavier felt the cool touch of Jean's delicate fingers on his face, felt her hands tilting back his head, and then light blazed into his exposed left eye as she pulled up the lid. He groaned in mild discomfort. The pupil instinctively rolled upward, and he found himself blearily staring at some sort of metal ceiling. Jean released the lid, and it snapped shut, plunging him back into darkness.

"He's still out of it," Jean said. "Between the phenobarbital in his system and the neural inhibitor shutting down his psi-talents, I *really* don't think we're going to have any problems with him."

Xavier felt a brief wave of panic surge through his body. They'd robbed him of his telepathic abilities? He concentrated as best he could, attempted to sweep the room with his mind, to see if he could detect the thoughts of his former students.

Nothing. Even the soft buzz of voices that normally crackled in the back of his mind—not even a telepath as powerful as the Professor could block out *every* thought being broadcast by six billion people around the globe—was gone. The inhibitor he'd been fitted with had taken away his most powerful weapon, and he suddenly felt . . . ordinary. And very helpless.

"But, if *you* think he's still a danger to us, Scott," Jean continued, "then I could always put him under again with a psi-bolt."

Xavier started. He *couldn't* let them knock him out again—he needed a chance to talk, to convince them to help him find the Cube. If he lost consciousness now, he knew he wouldn't reawaken until he had been brought before Magneto. He tried to move his slackened jaw, tried to open his mouth to speak, but his tongue felt as heavy as his arms. He grunted, attempting to create the guttural sound closest to the word "no."

It came out as "goo."

"Did you hear that?" Scott asked. "I think he's trying to say something."

"Not very well . . ." Kurt commented.

"Oh, stop that!" Jean chided. "*You* get shot up with enough sedatives to slow a bull elephant and see how well *you're* able to form words." Xavier felt a ticklish senation as strands of hair drifted across his face; his nostrils filled with the fragrance of perfume and apple-scented shampoo. She was leaning down close to him, only inches from his left ear. "Would you like to tell us something, Professor?" she asked in a low, breathy tone.

"Yes" was a tad easier to pronounce, since the "ess" sound only required him to blow air through his cheeks.

"Then, let's find out what it is, shall we?" she said. Fingertips settled against the sides of his temples. "Contact."

It was like having a SWAT team kick down to the door to his mind.

In an instant, Jean was in his thoughts, forcing her way into his subconscious, effortlessly crashing through the few minor psychic defenses that the neural inhibitor hadn't managed to disrupt. The pain created by her violent entry sizzled across his synapses, and almost caused him to black out.

When she finally burst through the final layer of consciousness, she found him waiting for her, seated behind the desk in his study. Well, not *really* his study, but rather a mental reconstruction of his inner sanctum, back at the Xavier Institute for Higher Learning in the pre-Cube world. In pop psychology terms, this was his "happy place"—the refuge that existed deep in his subconscious, to which his tired mind would go to seek some measure of relief whenever the pressing burdens of his responsibilities became too taxing. There was mahogany furniture and plush red carpeting. Framed paintings hung on the walls. A pair of high-backed lounging chairs with big, fluffy cushions were positioned to face a large, brick fireplace. Logs burned in the hearth, warming the room and providing most of the lighting. It all felt incredibly . . . cozy.

The room itself was immense—oak-paneled walls that seemed to stretch into infinity, lined with bookshelves filled with volumes. Between the cases stood sets of double doors, each portal leading to a different memory. At one end of the room, the main doors leading to the study lay in large, jagged pieces on the carpet. Standing just inside the entrance, hands resting on her hips, Jean turned her head from side-to-side, then up and down. She looked impressed by her surroundings. *I like what you've done with the place, Professor.*

Thank you, Xavier replied. *But you've been here before.* Many *times, in fact.*

Jean frowned, and tapped a finger against her chin, as though searching her memories. *Have I? I think I'd remember being here if I had. It's so . . . different from all the other minds I've traveled through. So well-organized.*

The Professor smiled. *It makes it easier to find things when I need to.*

No doubt. Jean's eyes widened as she turned in a slow circle, gazing at all the portals. *That's a lot of memories you have here, Professor—and a lot of* secrets, *as well. I'd very much like to see what lies behind them . . .*

Her bright green eyes flashed, and Xavier suddenly found the arms of his chair closing around him, pinning him to the seat. He squirmed mightily, but the wooden and leather restraints only tightened even more, forcing the air from his lungs. He gasped as the unyielding arms scraped against his rib cage.

Don't get up, the fiery-tressed telepath said, smiling wickedly. *I can find my way around.*

Jean—no! You don't have to do this— Xavier tried to push up in the seat to free his arms, his face turning beet red with the effort, but it was no use. He was held fast.

His former student concentrated, and, one by one in rapid succession, the doors of his mind began opening, revealing memories both joyous and haunting, and all seen from the Professor's point of view:

—the smiling face of a twentysomething Moira MacTaggert (who looked exactly like the physician who worked at the Lensherr Institute with Jean and the others), lying in the grass beside Xavier, staring up at the puffy white clouds high above, head resting comfortably on his chest. The feel of warm sunshine on Jean's/ Charles' face. The smell of honeysuckle and freshly cut grass wafting through the cool spring air, mingling with the scent of jasmine in Moira's flame-red hair.

"D'ye *have* t'go, Charles?" she asks, her lilting voice echoing with the sounds of the Scottish Highlands.

"It's not as though I've been given a *choice,* Moira," Xavier replies. "Once that letter arrived in the mail, the decision had already been made *for* me. I've been *drafted,* and there's nothing I can do about it. My unit is being shipped off to Korea in the morning."

"But, what about yer doctorate? Ye're still in school—shouldn't that give ye some sort o' special dispensation t'keep ye from goin'?"

Xavier chuckles. "Well, I *did* try giving the Draft Board a note from my mother, asking to excuse me from combat, but they recognized my handwriting from the forms I had to fill out."

Moira turns her head to face him; her dark expression shows

she's not amused by his attempt at humor. "Tis nae somethin' t'be jokin' about, Charles," she says sternly. "Ye could be killed."

A hesitation. "Yes," he says softly. "I know." He reaches out to stroke her cheek, then quietly clears his throat. "Moira..." Another hesitation. "Moira, there's something I've been meaning to ask you—something I've been putting off for far too long. But now, with my departure in the morning, never knowing when I'll see you again... it can't wait any more."

"An' what would that be, dear heart?" she replies sharply, her beautiful features drawn taut with concern. "Would ye like me t'take notes fer ye at yer classes while ye're away, so ye can continue workin' on yer doctorate while ye're crouched in some muddy foxhole, wi' bullets whizzin' past yer head?"

"No, nothing like that." A pause. Nervous energy runs through him; his heart beats wildly, pounding against the wall of his chest. Sharp intake of breath as he tries to steady his nerves, then:

"Moira MacTaggert... will you marry me?"

Her eyes open wide in shock. She blushes, and places a hand to her cheek as though she's trying to hide it. Slowly, surprise gives way to a warm, dimpled smile.

"Aye," she says simply.

A surge of adrenaline races through the Professor's body. It's the happiest day of his life.

Sitting up, Moira reaches out to pull him towards her. The sun is blotted out by her fiery tresses as she draws near, and there's the warm sensation of her lips pressing against his...

—a disgustingly obese man dressed in an ill-fitting white suit, a maroon fez perched haphazardly on the top of his bald head. Beautiful, but extremely sad, Mid-Eastern women in expensive jewelry and low-cut gowns fearfully hover around him—they're his slaves. The man introduces himself as Amahl Farouk, and he runs the Thieves' Quarter in Cairo, Egypt. Like Xavier, he is a telepath. Unlike the Professor, he only uses his powers for personal gain, destroying the lives—and minds—of anyone who has ever dared oppose him. He is the first telepath, and the first evil mutant, Charles has ever faced.

Xavier eyes his opponent across the length of the bar in which they sit, the air foul with the stench of sweat and stale tobacco and human misery. "I swear I will not rest until you're brought to justice for your crimes!" the Professor declares, though he knows he's out of his league.

A sinister smile ripples the cheeks of the fat man. "So be it."

And then the psychic battle is joined . . .

—Erik Magnus Lensherr floats high in the air above the Professor, years before the world will come to fear him as the mutant overlord called Magneto. It is this defining moment in the two friends' relationship that will affect the lives of every mutant on the planet.

"You are far too trusting, Charles—too naive," Magnus says, his voice laden with sadness. "You have faith in the essential goodness of man. In time, you will learn what I have learned—that even those you love will turn from you in horror when they discover what you truly are." The morose expression flows quickly from his face, replaced with one of fierce determination. "Mutants will *not* go meekly to the gas chambers. We will *fight* . . . and we will *win!*"

—a younger Jean, dressed in a black sweater and matching beret, white kid gloves, and knee-length blue skirt, standing before a wheelchair-bound Xavier. Four men enter the room; one of them is a teenaged Scott Summers, wearing a ridiculous pair of green checkered slacks and a dark green pullover. She recognizes one of the others as Warren Worthington III, the multi-millionaire gen-active who's now married to that TV star, Elisabeth Braddock.

Worthington steps forward to shake her hand. "Welcome to the X-Men, Miss Grey. . . ."

—Jean, Scott, Worthington, and one of their teammates (the *Beast?!*), all wearing costumes of bright yellow and dark blue materials. They're trapped inside the gondola of a weather balloon, rising toward the upper layers of the stratosphere as their oxygen supply dwindles. Hands in front of her face—they actually belong to Xavier. He reaches up to touch the sides of his temples. A moment of concentration, then—

"It's the Angel's parents!" Xavier blurts out. "Magneto has captured them!"

Jean! Stop! Please! the Professor cried out. He lurched in his seat, pushing against the restraints. *You're hurting me!*

Just looking for any hidden booby traps, Professor, Jean replied, throwing wide another door. There was a momentary flash of another memory—

—a bedroom in the Israeli port city of Haifa, ceiling fans slowly turning to dispel the heat of the day, a beautiful, dark-haired woman named Gabrielle Haller lying beside him—

—then the door slammed shut, and Jean moved on to the next. *Neural inhibitors only affect* active *powers, after all, not latent abilities. And after seeing what you could do back at that transients' hotel, I wouldn't be surprised to find out you've got a psychic land mine or three hidden in the back of your mind, squirreled away on the off-chance that someone might go poking around your thoughts without permission. It's what I would do.*

There are *no "land mines," I assure you,* Xavier said, gritting his teeth. *Now, if you would* please *stop doing this . . .*

I hope you'll pardon me for not taking your word for it, Jean said wryly. *After all, a girl can't be too careful when she's dealing with her mentor's greatest enemy . . .*

The search continued for another ten agonizing minutes—at least it felt like minutes, though it might have only been seconds, time being relative in the dreamscape—before Jean finally closed the last door, and Xavier was able to relax.

Are you finished? he asked, breathing hard.

Jean shrugged. *I suppose so.* She stepped across the office, and gracefully lowered herself into a seat across from him. Then she plopped both feet on the edge of his desk, and crossed her ankles. *Now, what did you want to talk about?*

Pulling himself together, Xavier decided to ignore her discourteous action—*and* the chair arms still crushing against the sides of his body—and concentrate on more important matters. *First off, I was hoping we might be able to discuss finding a way to free you and the others from Magneto's mind control.*

The corners of Jean's mouth curled up in a half smile. *And here I'd always thought Erik was pulling my leg when he told us that that would more than likely be your opening line.*

Did he, now? Xavier smiled politely. *Well, Erik and I have quite a bit of history between us. If anyone could be said to know my methods intimately, he would be the obvious choice. But that doesn't change a thing—you and I still need to talk about it.*

Jean stretched, arms above her head, and stifled a yawn. *Of* course *we will. Eventually. And your* second *topic of discussion?*

The smile faded from the Professor's lips. *I need your help.*

Jean looked amused. *Shouldn't you ask for that after* you've *freed us from being*—she held up both hands, using her index and middle fingers to form quotation mark symbols—*the "mindless thralls" of the "villainous" Magneto?*

This is no laughing matter, Jean, Xavier insisted. *What I am about to tell you affects the lives of everyone—including Magnus's.*

The redheaded telepath grinned. *Then, by all means,* do continue . . .

It was an arduous task, as Xavier did his best to explain the full scope of the situation, giving the smallest details—including highlights of their entire history as members of the X-Men—and speaking almost nonstop, allowing her no opportunity to make some snide comment and attempt to change the subject. He talked about Magneto's background, which greatly deviated from what Jean knew when he reached the part about the mutant overlord dedicating his life to crushing humanity and making *Homo superior* its masters. She chuckled when the Professor mentioned the death of Lensherr's daughter, Anya, and how revealing his magnetically-based powers had resulted in Magda fleeing in terror, horrified by the knowledge that she had been married to some kind of monster.

Undeterred, he pressed on, and was soon bringing her up to speed about the Cosmic Cube and the disastrous effects it was having on the onmiverse. And when he had finished, his face red from the effort, he slumped back in his chair and waited for her response.

She laughed.

Oh, my God—this is the best *example of a raging psychosis I think I've ever seen,* Jean said, grinning broadly. *Cyclops? Nightcrawler? Phoenix?* She chuckled. *Well, at least* Rogue *gets to use her own name.* She shook her head. *Really, Professor—I think you've been reading too many comic books. "The Cosmic Cube?" Wasn't that in an old* Space Ghost *cartoon? And come on—no one in their right mind would go around talking in codenames, or strut about in public dressed like you've described—* She caught his annoyed expression, as he gazed at her form-fitting outfit, with its ornate collar and three-inch boot heels. This *is a* school uniform, *designed to honor a man we greatly admire, not some crimebusting "super hero" costume, if you must know. I'm dressed for* teaching, *not marching around in a Halloween parade.* She paused. *I must admit, though—I do like the green-and-gold one I saw in one of your "memories." It would go so well with my hair . . .*

Jean—please, Xavier said. *I know this all seems highly amusing to you, but I am* quite *serious. You and Scott, Kurt and Rogue— you are* all *my students. We have worked together, fought together, faced death side-by-side countless times. You and I have been the closest of friends. Search your feelings—you'll know that I am right.*

Jean arched a delicate eyebrow. *You're not going to tell me next that you're my* father, *are you?* Xavier blankly stared at her, confused by the question. She waved a hand dismissively. *Never mind. Pop culture reference.*

The red-haired telepath rose from her chair, smoothing the wrinkles in her clothes with the palms of her hands. A bright spot appeared in the center of her forehead; as the Professor watched, it began to grow, blazing with a pale yellow light. She was preparing to unleash a psi-bolt. *It's time for me to leave, Professor; I think I've learned everything I needed to know. Thanks for the chat—it's been . . . interesting. We'll have to do it again soon—after you've had time to fully recover, that is.*

Xavier struggled against his bonds, trying to break free, but Jean had made them much too tight. He cursed, the veins prominently standing out on his neck, wishing he could draw upon his telepathic powers for strength, but the drugs and the neural inhibitor made that impossible. All he could do was wait for the inevitable to happen.

The psi-bolt lanced forward. It flared brightly in his mind, painting the walls of the study with harsh shadows—and then darkness descended.

"So, did you learn anything?" Scott asked.

"Well, he's certainly got a vivid imagination," Jean replied, taking her hands away from Xavier's head. His head lolled onto his chest; a thin line of drool seeped out from his slackened mouth, soaking into his dark blue tie. "He's convinced himself that *Erik* is the real menace, and that we're actually *his* followers." She shook her head in amazement. "You should have *seen* the outfits he dreamed up for us. And *then* there were all the colorful little codenames he had for each for us!" She snorted. "I don't know *why* Erik would want us to bring him to the palace. This man is *permanently* out to lunch."

"And yet, he considers Xavier the greatest criminal mastermind in the world," Kurt said.

"Well, y'all know what they say 'bout his type, Kurt," Rogue called back from the cockpit. "It's always the ones who seem t'make the most sense who turn out t'be the craziest."

Jean suddenly rubbed her temples and winced. "*Ow,*" she muttered.

Scott looked at her, clearly concerned. "You okay, hon?"

His wife nodded. "A little psychic feedback, I think. Guess I shouldn't have stayed inside his head as long as I did, but I—" she smiled "—just couldn't pull myself away. I'll be right as rain after I've had a little nap. Do we have the time?"

Scott walked up through the cabin of the Blackbird transport jet to join Rogue, who was seated in the pilot's chair. Just beyond the cockpit windshield, the waters of the Atlantic Ocean flashed beneath the plane, the water sparkling with flecks of golden sunlight. "What's our ETA?"

Rogue checked a series of gauges and dials. "At present speed, we oughtta be over France in another couple hours or so."

"Great!" said Jean. "I'm going to stretch out in the back, all right?" She turned and headed for the rear of the Blackbird. "I'll see you guys in a bit . . ."

And deep within the mind of Jean Grey, a tiny voice screamed in frustration.

No, damn it! I almost had *her! Almost got her attention! Damn it, I was so* close!

Locked away in the darkest corner of her subconscious, held fast by psychic chains that bound her from neck to ankle, the owner of that voice struggled to break free, but was unable to find the strength. Garbed in a form-fitting, green spandex bodystocking and gold opera-length gloves and thigh-high boots, bright red hair framing a face that contained the exact same features as those possessed by the co-director of the Lensherr Institute, the X-Man the Professor had referred to as "Phoenix" during his discussion with Jean shouted as loud as she could, trying to penetrate the layers of the telepath's consciousness. She tried to let her know that Xavier *had* been telling the truth, tried to make her aware of the threat to countless dimensions posed by Magneto and the Cube, tried to convince her that she had to help put an end to the mutant overlord's reign. None of her words, though, traveled very far.

Jean Grey—the Jean Grey of Earth 616, this is—didn't know how long she'd been trapped here in the darkness. What she *did* know was that she'd only started to regain her senses as soon as she'd heard the familiar voice of Charles Xavier ringing in her duplicate's head.

Yes, she remembered. Her duplicate. The woman who'd taken over her body, forced her consciousness into the deepest recesses of her own mind so that the doppleganger could become the dominant personality.

But, how had that happened? She vaguely remembered a room somewhere, and costumed men and women fighting. Now that she thought about it, *she* had been one of those combatants—until there had been an explosion of pain in her mind, and then she hadn't known anything else before she awoke here.

And now I'm a prisoner in my own head, she thought angrily. *I'd almost consider this a telepathic cliché, except I've never had another me try slipping into my skin before.* She struggled to a sitting position, grunting in discomfit as the chains bit into her arms and chest. *All right, Jeannie—one more time. You've got a lot of psychic barriers to pierce—you should know, you put them there—so just bear down and push through. If the Professor is in any kind of danger, you've got to convince the bodysnatcher to let you out of the dungeon.*

Phoenix took a deep breath, held it, slowly released it through her nostrils. Then, screwing her eyes shut and gritting her teeth, she concentrated as hard as she could.

Jean—please! she cried out. Listen *to me! You've* got *to listen to me. . . .*

12

MY DEAR child, I hope you will not take offense at this question, but . . . are you trying to kill us all?"

Eyes widened in mild panic, Erik Magnus Lensherr gripped the limousine's dashboard with both hands and held on for dear life, fingernails dug deeply into the rich Corinthian leather. To his right, in the driver's seat, was a beautiful young woman in her late teens; *her* fingers were wrapped around the steering wheel. Her clothing choices were as wild as her driving skills: She was dressed in a short, white T-shirt that exposed her abdomen, baggy green pants that hung low on her waist, and short black boots with inch-thick soles. The window beside her was rolled down all the way, and the blast of cool air generated by the vehicle's slipstream was whipping her shoulder-length, dark brown hair around her high-cheekboned face. Beyond the window, Lensherr noted with some concern, the vineyards of the Loire River Valley looked like nothing more than one big, never-ending, green-and-brown blur.

"Anya—please! Slow down!" Lensherr cried in exasperation. "This is a limousine, not a Formula-1 racer!"

"Father, you have spent *much* too much time flitting about the skies with your magnetic powers!" his daughter chided. "You know *nothing* of defensive driving!" She slapped the horn with the palm of her hand, and stuck her head out the window. "*Get out of the way, you moron!*" she yelled at the driver of the car in front of them.

Lensherr sighed. "I should *never* have agreed to letting you take your driving lessons in New York . . ."

Anya giggled, and pressed harder on the accelerator with her foot. The limousine jumped forward in response.

For a moment, Lensherr considered taking control of the situation, either by demanding that she stop the car *this instant,* or by using his gen-active abilities to lift it from the road and fly it toward their destination—at least that way, the chances of them getting in an accident would be greatly reduced. But when he looked at her joyful smile, heard her light, bubbling laugh, he saw in her all the unfettered, pure joy of life that had never been his. How could he deny her *any* pleasures, so soon after the Cube had enabled him to reunite them?

The glass partition behind them slid down with a soft whir of gears. Seated in the back of the vehicle were Magda Lensherr—who, based on what Erik saw reflected in the rear-view mirror, clearly did not share her daughter's enthusiasm for the methods of the LeMans School of Driving—and Anya's two older siblings: Wanda and Pietro. Like her mother and younger sister, Wanda possessed the striking beauty and chestnut-brown hair of all Lensherr women, though her tresses were curly, and hung past her shoulders. Pietro, on the other hand, was the spitting image of his father, right down to the silvered hair and sharp features—and brooding personality.

Both children had inherited their father's mutated genetic structure—a trait not shared by Anya. Exactly why that was, Lensherr didn't know; he hadn't ordered the Cube to create that imperfection. Wanda possessed an almost supernatural ability to affect probabilities; with a wave of her hand, she could change the odds that a certain building might collapse during an earthquake, or that a rain of fish might pour from the skies on a sunny day.

Magda had once commented that her daughter should use her talents to affect the odds that she might finally find a man good enough to marry; so far, it hadn't worked.

Pietro was a speedster, capable of running fast enough to break the sound barrier. At the moment, he looked extremely annoyed by the family's predicament. But that, Lensherr knew, was more likely due to the fact that, despite the car's high rate of acceleration, to Pietro's eyes, it appeared to be moving in slow motion. On his own, he could have outraced the limousine to its destination—the family's castle on the river Cher—eaten lunch, run five laps around the whole of the Loire River Valley, and jogged back to the car, all before his family had traveled another two miles. To sit here quietly, growing increasingly impatient with this excruciatingly long trip from Orly airport that *never seemed to end,* must have been maddening for him.

Sitting beside Pietro was his beautiful wife, Crystal. She was tall and blond-haired, with a rounded face and sparkling blue eyes, and was also a mutant of sorts—a member of the House of Attilan, a royal family that benevolently ruled over a race of uniquely mutated men and women known as Inhumans. Her powers were derived from the four elements: with but a thought, earth, air, fire, and water were hers to command. She and Pietro had married some years ago, and had gifted his parents with a granddaughter: Luna. Considering the wild ride they were currently experiencing aboard the "rocket sled" that normally functioned as a 1999 Mercedes Benz limousine, it seemed that Crystal had made a wise choice in leaving the child with the servants at the Lensherrs' country home.

Noticing her husband's dour expression, Crystal gently patted him on the arm, clearly attempting to console him. He grunted.

Crouched in the farthest corner of the rear was the final member of the party: the family's personal chauffeur—a grotesque little man known only as "The Toad," who was wearing an ill-fitting black suit, a black velvet Greek sailor's cap perched ridiculously on the back of his football-shaped head. The blood drained from his face, the corners of his mouth were pulled down in a lipless scream.

"I'm sorry, Master!" The Toad screeched. "I *know* I shouldn't have let Miss Anya drive the car back from the airport, but she *insisted!* And now we're all going to *die!*"

"*Silence, you sniveling worm!*" Lensherr roared. "We are *not* going to die, but I *am* tempted to throw you from this vehicle, if only to put an end to your incessant whining!"

"Oh, for heaven's sake, Erik!" Magda shouted. "Don't yell at The Toad—tell your daughter to stop driving like a lunatic!"

Taking a moment to glare at his cowardly lackey, Lensherr turned back to address his youngest child. "Anya, my sweet..." he said gently.

His youngest child sighed. "Very well, Father," she muttered. Her foot eased back on the accelerator, and the limousine began slowing to traffic speed.

"Thank you," Lensherr said. He decided to ignore the joyous whimpering of the terrified chauffeur that drifted up from the back seat. "Now, then, do you think you could get us home without causing your mother any further worries?"

He couldn't help but smile when Magda's indignant snort reached his ears.

The remainder of the trip passed uneventfully. Once she had gotten past her initial urge to navigate the limousine like a New York City cabbie, and her short period of brooding had ended, Anya turned out to be quite the skillful driver. An hour after their perilous journey along D751, the limousine was pulling through the ornate, iron gates that led to the grounds of Castle Lensherr.

It was a magnificent sight, this towering, two-hundred-room, white-and-silver edifice built over the Cher River, its grounds extending across ten thousand acres of vineyards, grassy fields, woodlands, and Japanese gardens. The castle had been constructed under Lensherr's supervision, the gardens under Magda's. The accommodations were so grand that, if they wished, each member of the family could have, not their own room, but their own apartment. That never happened, of course—the family preferred staying in close proximity to one another—so the balance of rooms were either left unoccupied, or were used by the occasional guest. Most of the time, though, since Erik and his family preferred the comforts of Paris, the only people living in the fortress were a skeleton staff of servants who maintained the upkeep on the numerous rooms and sprawling landscape. But every now and then, the Lensherrs liked to get away from the pressures of a metropolitan lifestyle, and retreat to the country—and *that* was when the castle truly came to life.

Anya brought the limousine to a halt before the towering white oak doors that led to the gallery. As she turned off the engine, the doors of the fortress opened, and a coterie of servants filed out to greet the family. At the head of the line was a dark-haired, forty-year-old human named Batroc, whose powerful legs could propel him incredible distances; he served as the Lensherrs' butler and the head of the household staff. Behind him trailed Slither, a green-skinned, humanoid lizard with a long neck and snake-like head—he was the gardener; Lifter, the handyman—a bear of a mutant in his thirties, with a powerful build and a small head covered with deep-brown hair and a coarse beard; Shocker, his fortysomething assistant, whose arms and legs ended, not with hands or feet, but with pincer-like extremities capable of delivering strong blasts of electrical current—a handy power, on those stormy nights when the castle's generator failed; Burner, the other chauffeur, who was in his mid-thirties, and possessed the ability to cause fires with just a thought; and Jeanne-Marie Beaubier, the Lensherrs' beautiful, white-haired maid, who could fly as fast as Pietro could run—and who, at the moment, was holding Pietro and Crystal's daughter, Luna. Following Jeanne-Marie were a number of other servants, totaling a staff of thirty in all.

At the end of the line was Peeper, a diminutive, bald man with unusually large eyes—so large, in fact, they actually protruded beyond the sockets in his skull. His job was ... well, no one knew exactly *what* his job was, other than apparently trying to get under everyone's feet while they carried out their own duties. The family liked him, though, so the other servants—except for The Toad, of course, whom no one really liked—were willing to put up with his annoying behavior.

"Welcome home, Miss Anya!" Peeper said in a high-pitched, Peter Lorre-esque voice. "I saw you coming from fifty miles away!" He put his hands to his face. "Oh, you were driving so fast, I was worried for your safety!"

"*Quiet,* you fool," Batroc said heatedly, and turned to the new arrival. "Miss Anya, it is *so* good to 'ave you 'ome a-gain." He spoke pleasantly to her in English, in a broad French accent that was reminiscent of the late Peter Sellers' Inspector Clouseau character in the *Pink Panther* movies. A gentle breeze from the east made the ends of his pencil-thin, waxed mustache quiver slightly.

Anya grinned, clearly amused by the comical antics of the two servants. "Thank you, Batroc. It's good to be home again." She glanced at his much shorter sidekick. "And thank *you* for your concern, Peeper. It's nice to know that someone is looking out for my safety—literally."

Peeper blushed and, giggling nervously, hid behind Jeanne-Marie.

The other members of the family stepped from the car, with The Toad bringing up the rear. He cringed and shook visibly as he realized that Lensherr was standing next to him. The mutant over-lord glared down at him.

"Get the bags, you cowering oaf," Lensherr muttered, his voice just audible enough for only The Toad's serving platter-sized ears to detect. The chauffeur literally jumped to carry out the order.

While The Toad started unpacking Anya's bags from the limousine's trunk, Lensherr led his family into the narrow, three-story, white walled gallery that stretched across the river to the castle proper. The first floor of the gallery was just over three hundred feet long, with a dozen windows on each side that looked out over the gentle waters of the Cher, toward the north and south; the two upper floors of the building were used as servants' quarters. The floor was covered with alternating gray and white ceramic tiles. The walls were bare of decorations, though small alcoves had been built into them at regular distances, each recess containing a statue or bust—some, traditional works of art; others, representations of the Master of the World and his family. Low, marble benches stood in front of the alcoves, so that admirers could sit and enjoy the pieces at their leisure.

"You know, Father," Anya said, "you didn't have to go to the trouble of bringing us all the way out here. I would have been more than happy to stay at your apartments in Paris. That's where all my friends are, after all . . ." She smiled. ". . . and the clubs."

"I believe you've led *enough* of a wild life away from here, Daughter," Lensherr replied, gently tapping the end of her nose with a stern index finger. "Now is the time for you to spend a few days with your family." He smiled, and draped an arm around her shoulders. "Once you've settled in, I want to hear all about your adventures in the United States over dinner this evening."

"Better put Story Hour on hold fer a while, bub," said a gruff male voice from behind a bust of Pallas that rested on a pedestal just ahead. "You an' me, we got more *important* things t'discuss."

The Lensherrs turned to face the speaker as he stepped out to meet them. He stood just over five feet tall and appeared to be in his mid-forties—although, based on the weather-beaten features he possessed, it was very possible he was much older. Just how *much* older, no one knew, and he wasn't about to say. He also seemed to take perverse pleasure in being at odds with his surroundings. Unlike the Lensherrs, who dressed in the finest European fashions, the man wore clothing more suitable for a farm worker—or a back-woods hunter: a bulky, brown leather jacket, red plaid shirt, black jeans, and black hiking boots. He clasped a battered, black Stetson cowboy hat in hands covered by thick, brown gloves. His hair was shaped in a highly unusual style, beginning as a widow's peak just above his forehead, then expanding outward to form a pair of tufts that protruded from the sides of his head, each tuft tapering to a fine point. The tufts, in turn, were joined to a thick set of sideburns that ran down the sides of his face and past his ears, ending at the jawline. Seen at a glance, a casual observer might mistake this exceedingly hairy individual for some sort of humanoid lion.

Or a wolverine.

Anya's face lit up with sheer delight the moment she spotted him.

"Logan!" she cried, and rushed forward to throw her arms around his neck. He responded with a gentle, affectionate hug. "Father didn't tell me you were here."

"Father did not know he *was,*" Lensherr commented evenly, "although he *did* expect him to arrive sooner or later." He nodded pleasantly to his guest. "It's always a surprise to see you, Logan."

"That's the *idea,* bub," Logan replied. "Then, they never see ya comin' . . .'til it's too late." Disengaging himself from Anya's warm embrace, he stepped forward and extended his hand to Lensherr in a show of comradeship.

Lensherr watched this action with more than a touch of amusement. Here, standing before him, was a man who had tried innumerable times to kill him over the years. Yet now they greeted each other as though they were old friends. It was all he could do to keep from laughing in the diminutive Canadian's pug-ugly face.

Tried? Lensherr knew better than that. As a member of the X-Men, the feral little mutant codenamed "Wolverine" had come damn near close to *succeeding* on one or two occasions. His last near attempt, in fact, hadn't been all that long ago—for Lensherr, only days had passed since the events that unfolded on von Doom's World . . .

He had just brought together his closest followers—his acolytes Mystique, Forge, Fabian Cortez, Amanda Voight, Scanner, Vindaloo, Mellancamp, Unuscione, and his son, Pietro—and dispatched them to von Doom's Psi Division Headquarters in Langley, Virginia, to rescue the X-Men, who had blundered in from some other dimension. The mission had *almost* gone according to plan— until somebody tripped an alarm. As von Doom's troops bore down on the mutants, left with no other options, the X-Man called Gambit sacrificed his life to save his teammates.

Rogue never quite recovered from the shock of losing the only man she had ever loved.

A short time later, when the two groups sat down to organize a plan of attack against von Doom, Logan had tried to eliminate the Master of Magnetism, rather than allow his friends to ally themselves with Magneto and his acolytes. His intended actions, however doomed to fail they might have been, were cut short by an order from the team's leader: Scott Summers, who, in his costumed identity, was known as "Cyclops" because of the visor he wore over his eyes to harness the destructive power of his eyebeams. Despite the checkered history between the heroic mutants and their longtime enemy, Summers had agreed to the alliance, if only because von Doom and the Cosmic Cube presented the greater threat to the continued stability of the omniverse. Wolverine hadn't been pleased with Summers' decision, and made it clear that, once the mission was completed, the alliance would come to a quick—and bloody—dissolution . . .

But now, though, things were different; the Cube had changed all that. A simple command given to the device, and Logan was as loyally committed to the mutant overlord as his once-bothersome teammates. In fact, his former would-be executioner was so ensorcelled by the Cube's power that he might even lay down his life for his new master, if Lensherr so desired.

It's all so deliciously . . . ironic, Magneto thought. He reached out to clasp Logan's hands in both of his. "Thank you for making the trip. I imagine it was a long flight from Canada."

Logan shrugged. "Hopped on a plane from Québec soon's I got Jeannie's call. Yer just lucky I was done huntin'—a week earlier, an' I would'na been anywhere near a phone."

"Where are the others?" Lensherr asked.

"Still in-flight. I talked to 'em a little while ago." A savage snarl split Logan's lips. "The dirtbag's with 'em, but he ain't givin' 'em no trouble . . . yet. Jeannie mentioned somethin' 'bout an accomplice o' his givin' 'em the slip: Asian girl, 'bout twenty-five, pretty good scrapper, 'cordin' t'Rogue. Purple hair, if ya can believe it."

Lensherr started. That sounded suspiciously like Psylocke, if he wasn't mistaken, but he was *certain* he'd dealt with her—and von Doom—when he unleashed the chaos storm back in the White House. In fact, wasn't she the star of some television program in this world? If that were true, then she should have had no knowledge of Xavier's existence, or even a desire to join him on whatever quixotic journey he'd been planning before his capture.

The mutant overlord frowned. Something was definitely out of sorts here . . .

"Is something wrong, Father?" Wanda asked, concern evident in her voice. "For Logan to travel all this way . . ."

"Is merely in response to a courtesy I extended him," Lensherr replied, turning to face her. He smiled. "I simply thought he might wish to be present when our guests from the institute arrive with . . . an old acquaintance."

"And who might this 'old acquaintance' be, Erik, since you've neglected to mention him until now?" There was an edge to Magda's tone that made it clear she was far from pleased with her husband's subterfuge. "Might he have anything to do with these 'important matters' Logan mentioned?"

"He does," Lensherr replied. "And his name is Charles Xavier."

His wife's eyes widened in shock, and her jaw dropped. "*Here?* You'd bring that murderer *here,* to our *home,* with your *family* present? Have you lost your mind?"

Lensherr smiled disarmingly. "I assure, you, Magda, you and the children have nothing to fear. Charles has been outfitted with a neural inhibitor, so there will be no psychic trickery on his part. He's also being accompanied by some of my most powerful followers, including Jean Grey, who is more than capable of dealing with any remaining telepathic abilities he might possess." He clapped a hand on Wolverine's shoulder. "And, with our Chief of

Security present, even *Charles* would know how foolish it would be to upset his hosts by causing us any difficulties."

Beside him, Logan grunted in agreement. "But if he *does* try makin' any trouble—" a half-dozen, foot-long metal spikes suddenly protruded from the backs of his hands, the sharpened tips slicing through his leather gloves as though they were made of paper "—I'll convince him how bad an idea that is, real quick."

"Down, boy," Anya said, clearly trying to break the tension that had suddenly filled the air. "We're all friends here."

Logan gazed at her for a moment, the heat of anger quite evident on his fuzzy cheeks, then sheathed his claws. "Sorry, darlin'— got a little worked-up there." His attempt at a smile was well-intentioned, but a tad on the grotesque side. "Thanks fer the reality check."

"My pleasure," she replied, and slipped an arm around one of his. "Now, let's forget about Father's guests until they get here, all right? We're supposed to be here to *enjoy* ourselves."

Lensherr chuckled. "As ever, my child, you are the voice of reason."

Anya took hold of Lensherr's arm with her free hand. "Not true, Father—that's *Mama's* job. *Mine* is the voice of reckless youth." She grinned broadly. "And the voice of reckless youth says it's time we stopped standing around a drafty old gallery and got ready to receive our guests. If Kurt Wagner is one of them, I want to look my best."

"I'd stay clear o' the fuzzy elf if I were you, darlin'," Logan said. "That kinda guy'll break yer heart in the longrun."

Anya chuckled. "I'm certain you've done a fair amount of heart-breaking yourself, Logan." She nodded toward his rough-and-tumble appearance. "Women go for that rugged look—it says so in *Cosmopolitan*."

Logan's soft laugh sounded like the growl of a hungry lion stalking its prey. "Can't argue with facts like that, I guess."

Pulling the two men along the gallery, her mother and siblings close behind, Anya guided the family toward the castle proper.

"Come along, now, everyone," she said. "I can't *wait* to tell you about the wonderful tattoos Paige Guthrie and I got in Greenwich Village . . ."

As he allowed his daughter to pull him down the tiled corridor, Erik Magnus Lensherr couldn't help but openly stare at her, marveling at the brightness of her smile, the life that shone in her eyes. Here, at last, was the daughter he hadn't been able to save on that horrific night, decades past, in the Soviet city of Vinnitsa. *That* Anya had only been ten years old then, and completely unaware of the blinding hatred humans felt toward mutants, of the fear they showed toward anything that was different.

Fear that had cost her her young life.

He still remembered it all vividly: Magda and he going to the market, leaving Anya to play with her dolls; the unexplained fire that trapped her in the small, third-floor apartment they called home; his public display of his mutant talents in order to protect Magda and himself from burning debris; the mob's vicious attack—hands pulling at his clothes, his hair. Fists pummeling his body and face; cries of "freak" and "monster" ringing in his ears.

Cries of a child as the fire consumed her.

A body falling from the window, arms and legs pinwheeling in slow motion—a fiery, human-sized comet, blazing crimson and gold against a black velvet sky.

And all the way down, the screams.

Screams of agony; of hellish torture.

Screams for her mother and father to save her.

Screams cut short by a sickening impact . . .

Lensherr started, his nostrils suddenly filled with the sickening odor of burning wood and plaster—and flesh. A phantom smell, culled from the deepest recesses of his darkest memories—ones that had haunted him for a lifetime . . .

"Father?" Anya asked, eyes wide with concern. "Are you all right?"

"I'm *fine,* child," Lensherr replied sharply, then winced, angry with himself for acting so brusquely. All she had done was ask about his well-being; he shouldn't be so upset. If only it wasn't always the most painful memories that refused to fade away...

"I'm fine, Anya," he said gently, and stroked her chestnut hair. "My mind was just wandering."

He smiled brightly—and why not? Thanks to the Cube, he had her back now—her *and* her mother. There *was* no fire; there never *had been* a fire. It was all nothing more than a nightmare—a disturbing figment of his imagination; "an undigested bit of beef, a blob of mustard, a crumb of cheese, a fragment of an underdone potato," as Charles Dickens put it so eloquently in *A Christmas Carol.*

Erik Lensherr's nightmares were ended, the weight on his soul finally removed. His wife and daughter were here, the two people who had always mattered more to him than life itself, as vibrant and young and beautiful as he wished them to be, in a world where they would never know the true meaning of fear... or terror... or death...

The Cosmic Cube had been his savior... and the means of his redemption. And having found redemption, Lensherr silently vowed that nothing—not even the sudden, but expected, reappearance of Professor Charles Xavier—would ever take away that sense of wholeness, or deny his daughter the peace and love he had at last been able to give her....

13

WHAT DO you mean, 'he's missing'?"

The Omniversal Majestrix was *not* in the best of moods. It seemed like she had just put her head down on her pillow, after retiring to her quarters for the "evening," only to be rudely awakened by the shrill tone of the comm-set she'd forgotten to remove from her right ear. Being told that the von Doom of Earth 616 had escaped from the infirmary, *and* that he had killed two guards and his elderly alternate along the way, had only made her normally acerbic tone that much harsher.

Saturnyne ordered a full alert, then glanced at the chronometer near her bed—according to its readout, she'd only been asleep for roughly twenty-five minutes. She unclipped the comm-set and tossed it on the bed, savagely threw back the sheets, and stepped onto the carpeted floor.

"Lights!" she snapped. Responding instantly to her command, the computer activated every bulb in the suite, filling the darkened bedroom with brilliant illumination. Momentarily blinded, Saturnyne stumbled into a chair, barking her shin against its legs; it elicited a heated growl from her slender throat.

"Oh, I *knew* that tin foil-coated worm was going to be trouble, the moment I laid eyes on him," she muttered, now hobbling toward her closet. "Should have had him thrown from the highest tower and into the vortex as soon as Braddock told us about the Cube . . . "

Selecting her wardrobe choices—white satin floor-length gown, white cape with fur trimming, white leather belt bearing the large, rose-colored jewel that denoted her station as Omniversal Majestrix—Saturnyne laid them across the bed, then stepped into the shower, letting the cold water shake the last vestiges of sleep from her tired body.

A few minutes later, now fully awake, powdered and perfumed, she exited the bathroom—and came to an abrupt halt.

Standing before her was Doctor Doom, arms folded across his broad, armored chest. Dark-brown eyes stared evenly at the Majestrix from behind the emotionless metal mask he wore. His gaze flickered briefly over her body, taking in her state of undress, then moved back up to lock on her cool blue eyes. For a moment, Her Whyness wondered if she should be insulted by his lack of response.

But, as strange and unnerving as that completely unexpected sight was for Saturnyne, it wasn't von Doom who had truly surprised her—Mitras knew it wasn't the first time a man had been in her quarters—but rather the woman standing next to him. *The woman who was wearing her clothes.*

She had the same features as Saturnyne. Wore the same choice of blue eye shadow and matching lipstick. Possessed the same shoulder-length white hair parted above the left side of her face, to cascade down in a snowy wave that concealed the right eye. But unlike Her Whyness, the one visible eye of her doppelganger shone brightly with the fires of hate—and madness.

"Hello, 'sister,' " her duplicate said, lips pulled back in a malevolent sneer. "I'm certain you never thought you'd see *me* again."

The Majestrix's pale blue eyes went wide in shock. "Sat-yr-nin . . ." she gasped.

Before she could say more, a hand clamped tightly over her mouth, and Saturnyne felt the sharp pinch of a needle as it pierced the base of her neck. Her limbs suddenly grew heavy, her thoughts becoming clouded, as the drug she'd been injected with took immediate effect. An arm circled her waist to keep her from falling to the floor.

"What are you doing, Stanton?" von Doom asked ominously.

Stanton? One of the physicians from the medical wing? Saturnyne tried to pull away from him, but it was taking all her remaining strength just to stay conscious. Her hands fluttered uselessly at her sides as the doctor pulled her toward the bed.

"There's been enough killing, Lord Doom," Stanton replied. "I'd like to avoid raising the death toll any higher than it's already become." Gently, he lowered Saturnyne onto the thick mattress, removing his hand from her mouth as he did so. She moaned softly, eyelids growing heavier; oblivion wasn't too far away. "The sedative I've given her will keep her unconscious long enough."

"Long enough for what?" the Mastrex asked, glaring at him.

"For us to transport her down to the stasis chamber," Stanton replied, "where she'll take your place." When Sat-yr-nin didn't respond, he continued, as though lecturing a student. "At this point, citadel security is focused on locating Lord Doom and, therefore, is more than likely unaware of your . . . early release from their good graces." He gestured toward Saturnyne. "If Her Whyness is secured in the suspension tube before they realize what's occurred, then the guards will never suspect that you've switched places with her. Thus, you'll have free reign to roam the citadel unmolested—" he glanced at von Doom "—and there will be no need to kill her. *That's* why I suggested we come *here* once the Mastrex had recovered from the stasis effects, rather than attempt an open confrontation with the Supreme Guardian."

"How deceptively clever." The monarch chuckled. "Congratulations, Dr. Stanton—you have at last proven your worth to Doom . . . for one more day."

"I'm so glad you approve," Stanton muttered sarcastically.

Sat-yr-nin sat on the edge of the bed and playfully stroked her double's hair. "And once dear old Opal Luna here has been tucked in for the night, we can turn our attention to more important matters—like removing that witch, Roma, from power." She sneered. "I owe her a *great* deal of suffering for having me shoved into that claustrophobic little tube and left to pickle—" she snorted "—simply because she disagrees with the way I run my world." A wicked smile slowly split her lips. "As Roma will discover, much to her dismay, I have *always* believed in repaying my debts . . . *in full.*"

As if on cue, the comm-set lying on the bed near the semi-conscious Majestrix chirped loudly.

"I think that's for me," Sat-yr-nin commented cheerfully, and picked it up, clipping it to her right ear. "Yes?" She sat quietly for a few moments, nodding her head as though in agreement, the person on the other end of the communication doing all the talking. "Of course, Supreme Guardian—I shall be there shortly."

Sat-yr-nin rose from the bed and turned to her partners. "If you'll excuse me, gentlemen, I have been summoned to the throne room. It appears that some armor-clad dictator from another Earth is running about the citadel without a proper escort, and Roma has asked for my assistance in tracking him down." Eyes glittering with unbridled hatred, she gazed down at her helpless duplicate. "And it wouldn't do to keep m'lady waiting, my first day on the job."

"M-Mitras, no . . ." Saturnyne said weakly. She tried to rise, but she couldn't even turn her head. Or open her eyes. Or—

And then the drug finally overwhelmed her senses, and she was falling into darkness.

She'd lost track of him somewhere along Boulevard Saint Germain. And considering that, as a warrior, she had been trained in the arts of Ninjitsu, and should have been able to track him from one side of Paris to the other without being detected, even *she* had to admit that it was an incredible—and highly annoying—feat on his part.

As the late afternoon sun shone brightly above the streets of the Left Bank, Betsy stood at the intersection of Rue de l'Université and Rue des Saints Peres, hands on hips, tapping her foot in mild annoyance as she mentally scolded herself for being so incredibly stupid. For someone with an interest in American police television programs, it seemed she hadn't learned a great deal about the finer points of tailing a suspect.

So much for the educational power of television . . . she thought.

For a moment, she considered psi-scanning the area—the faux Worthington couldn't have gone that far on foot—but the prospect of tapping into a mind that might so closely mirror that of her lost love's set her nerves on edge. She was afraid—of what she might find there, of what she might not, of what touching on familiar, shared memories might do to disrupt the tight control she'd been able to maintain over her emotions since returning to Earth. Still, despite her reluctance, she couldn't deny the fact that she wanted to learn the reasons for Magneto's decision in recreating Warren and her as part of this Cube-fashioned world. And the answers, quite possibly, might be contained within the mind of this doppelganger.

Not for the first time, she began to wonder what she'd do when she finally caught up to him . . . and why she'd want to put herself through such a traumatic experience.

Around her, the citizens of Paris streamed by, still oblivious to her unusual appearance—but more than aware that she was standing in the middle of the sidewalk. She flinched as yet another shoulder slammed into her side, this time courtesy of a sour-faced, white-haired old man with hawk-like features—*actual* hawk-like features, right down to the layer of small, light brown feathers that framed his face—who clearly wanted her out of his way. As he passed, Betsy heard him mutter a few choice words in his native tongue—something about her parentage, if she wasn't mistaken.

Betsy growled.

"Excuse me, Miss," a pleasant male voice suddenly called out, "but has anyone ever told you you look *just* like my wife?"

Startled, Betsy looked around, turning quickly in a tight circle. The voice had come from somewhere close by, but she couldn't see any sign of the speaker. So, if he wasn't standing on the side-walk . . .

She looked up.

Warren Worthington III—the *other* Warren, she quickly re-minded herself—was standing on a small balcony three stories above the street. Behind him were an open set of doors leading to an apartment; the sweet notes of a jazz recording could just be heard above the sounds of the bustling city. Worthington had taken off his jacket and shirt, revealing a chiseled body and lithe, powerful arms; with his square jaw, shoulder-length blond hair, and bare chest, he looked more like a male model posing for the cover of a romance novel than a millionaire playboy. Then again, with his brilliant white wings folded around him, and the way in which the sun outlined them in a dazzling golden glow, she could almost believe she was looking at an angel.

At Warren.

But, this isn't *Warren, you stupid cow,* she scolded herself. *He's just Magneto's blasted carbon copy.*

"You saw me following you," she said flatly.

Worthington shrugged. "Well, babe, you *are* talking to a guy who doesn't only fly like an eagle—he's got its eyesight, too." He gestured toward her dark-blue outfit. "Besides, you *do* tend to stand out in a crowd—not that that's a *bad* thing." He smiled, and gestured toward a street-level door on Rue de l'Université. "Come on up—the door's open."

Betsy smiled in return; she couldn't help herself. Just seeing that boyish grin again—even on another man's face—made her heart beat a little faster.

She mentally kicked herself.

What's wrong *with you, Braddock? You've seen duplicates of your friends before—it wasn't all that long ago the Skrulls tried that very trick. Why, then, can't you get it through your* stupid, *thick skull that you're getting all weak in the knees over a cheap imitation?*

She knew why. Because she wasn't ready to admit to herself that this man wasn't really her lost love; wasn't yet ready to give up hope.

Wasn't yet ready to let go.

The pain in her heart was still too fresh, the wound still too raw. She would heal, in time, she knew, but right now . . .

With a start, Betsy suddenly realized that she had already entered the apartment building.

You see? she thought. *You see what happens when you let your mind wander? Nothing but trouble!*

She couldn't argue with that—but then, if she'd been thinking clearly from the start, she never would have followed Worthington through the streets of the Left Bank; she would have ignored his presence entirely and focused on her mission. But it was her heart that had been directing her body for the past few hours, not her head; all she could do was hold on and hope that things would turn out for the best.

The strains of Dave Brubeck's classic composition "Take Five" drifted down along the stairwell from the third floor. Ignoring the insistent warnings of her inner voice, Betsy began mounting the steps. On the second floor landing, she flashed a weak smile at an elderly woman who was coming down the stairs. The woman gave her a stern looking over, and sniffed loudly—apparently, she didn't care much for Betsy's choice of clothing.

I'd like to see you *look this good in it, Grandmother,* Betsy thought. The image of what that might look like flashed across her mind's eye, and she laughed. The old woman huffed as though insulted, and continued on her way.

Reaching the third floor, Betsy followed the music to its source. The door to the apartment had been left open—an invitation from a hungry spider to a lovelorn fly, perhaps? Taking hesitant steps, she pushed the door wide open and entered, half wishing some kind of deathtrap would be sprung so she could be faced with a problem she knew how to handle.

But there were no traps, no villains seated comfortably in the living room, waiting to attack—just an immense apartment in a fashionable Paris neighborhood. It was almost a disappointment. Worthington was nowhere to be found; presumably, he was in another room, doing whatever he felt was necessary to prepare for her arrival. The high, crystalline note of glasses clinking from a room off to the left confirmed that suspicion—it sounded like he was making drinks. *How positively domestic,* she thought with a slight sneer. Setting her carryall on a fluted mahogany pedestal near the door, Betsy paused to take in her surroundings.

For someone living in a city as rich in tastes as Paris, Worthington's sense of décor seemed to come straight from the pages of a furniture catalog—there were Seville chairs and leather Tacoma sofas and Indio-Tibetan area rugs and teak trays and mahogany tables. There were expensively framed paintings scattered about the place, offset by a framed, six-foot-tall poster that hung in one corner of what she assumed was the living room. It was an advertisement for *Kwannon, Bushido Mistress*—the kind of large format poster normally found hanging behind large glass panels in Urban American bus stops. The full-color image on the poster was of her duplicate, teeth bared, *katana* raised high above her head—a warrior charging forward in the heat of bloodlust. The background was filled with a ghostly representation of the Crimson Dawn tattoo both Betsy and her double sported; the X-Man was willing to bet good money that the other woman's mark was nothing more than makeup. Across from the poster, one wall was occupied by an immense home entertainment system—the source of the slick musical tones that filled the air. All in all, it certainly didn't strike Betsy as the sort of place in which one would find a multi-millionaire and an international television star living together; perhaps it was Worthington's private apartment. That made sense, in an odd sort of way, given his taste in furniture; if it wasn't for the gold wedding band she'd spotted on his left ring finger from the street, she might have mistaken him for a bachelor.

As he entered the room carrying a pair of fluted champagne glasses in one hand, Worthington used the remote control in his other hand to lower the volume on his stereo system. Coming to a halt before Betsy, he held out one of the glasses, and she obligingly took it.

"Welcome home, Madame," he said in a broad French accent that was pure John Cleese in *Monty Python and the Holy Grail.* "It is always a pleasure to have your beauteous form besmirching this 'umble abode."

"*Merci,*" Betsy replied pleasantly.

Worthington looked her up and down, but there was not even a trace of sensuality to his gaze; he acted more like a man examining a prize mare at an equestrian auction. "You look good, hon," he said. There was a tone in his voice when he said it, however, that made it sound as though he was leading up to something more than a casual compliment.

"Thank you," she said.

Worthington nodded. "Yeah, real good," he muttered, then turned to walk over to one of the couches. Not bothering to sample the wine, Betsy set the glass down on a magazine table beside the entertainment center. She remained standing, waiting to see where the conversation would lead.

"You're turning out to be quite the world traveler, aren't you, hon?" Worthington asked, settling down on the soft leather cushions. "Two days ago, you were in New Zealand. Then, you were in New York yesterday, and now, suddenly, you're here in Paris." He smiled, and raised an inquisitive eyebrow. "Trying to cash in all your Frequent Flyer miles before the week is over?"

Betsy flashed a brief smile. "Something like that."

"Well, I think that's great." He sipped at the wine, then placed the glass on a coffee table in front of him. "I just wish you'd told me you were coming—I would've made plans."

She shrugged. "That's all right. I've plans of my own for the evening."

Worthington sneered. "With a certain baldheaded cripple, right?" The change of expression that came over him, going from boyish charm to seething anger in an instant, was a startling one.

" *'Cripple'?*" Betsy frowned—now *there* was a word the real Warren never would have uttered; she doubted it was even in his vocabulary.

"Come on, babe, I saw the pictures on *E! News Daily* this afternoon. Once the story broke, I spoke with your producer. *He* said you were down with him in New Zealand, working on the show, but *I* think he was just covering for you—and doing a lousy job of it, based on the amount of press coverage you've been getting. And then this afternoon, my office was flooded with calls asking about our impending divorce." Worthington eyed her suspiciously. "*Is* there an impending divorce? Because if there is, I would've thought you'd have the class to at least e-mail me before you started posing for photo ops with your new lover."

Betsy grimaced. *There* was a mental image she'd never needed to have floating around in her head. "Oh, good Lord. He's *not* my lover, he's—"

"What, a stopover between flights?" Worthington snapped. He rose to his feet and thumped his bare chest. "Are you trying to tell me *this* isn't good enough for you—you have to go looking elsewhere to have your fun?"

"This is ridiculous," Betsy said. It was more than that, she had to admit—it had been an utter mistake to come here. She'd known that even before she walked through the door, but, romantic masochist that she was, she'd ignored the voice of reason that echoed in her thoughts and found herself walking right into a scene from an Aaron Spelling soap opera. And she absolutely *loathed* soap operas.

"I've got to go." She turned on her heel and headed for the front door, grabbing her carryall along the way.

"Damn it . . ." she heard him mutter. There was a soft flutter of wings beating, and a gentle breeze tousled her hair.

He reached the door ahead of her, wings spread wide to bar her exit.

"Get out of my way," Betsy said. If the warning tone in her voice wasn't clear enough, she was willing to give him another five seconds to think it over before she snapped one of his arms.

"Elisabeth, come on," he said softly. "I apologize. I shouldn't have mouthed off like that, and I'm sorry. I *really* don't want to fight."

Two seconds.

He flashed that boyish grin again, and brushed aside a lock of lavender hair that had draped across her right cheek with his fingertips, and she stopped the countdown. Damn him, why couldn't he have an overbite, or bad teeth, or a missing incisor—*something* that would distinguish his smile from the one she knew so well, so she could hate him?

She quickly lowered her gaze so she wouldn't have to look at it. *Let him speak his mind, and then leave, you stupid git—get out before something happens. Something you'll regret.*

"Look, Elisabeth," he said, "I know this long-distance relationship has been hard on both of us, what with you spending half the year in New Zealand and me shuttling between our places here and in the States, but I thought we could always work things out. If there's a problem, if there's something I've done that makes you think you need somebody else in your life, then tell me what it is. I don't want us to break up—I just want to make it right."

He gently placed a hand under her chin and tilted it up, then moved forward to kiss her. For a second—just for a second—she wavered in her resolve . . . but it was enough time for her to finally give in to the temptation.

His lips brushed against hers, and a pleasant surge of electricity raced through her body, prickling her skin. She shivered slightly, feeling her defenses start to crumble . . . yet she did nothing to stop it from happening.

A fake . . . he's just a fake . . . her mind called out, but she wasn't listening anymore. She dropped the bag, wrapped her arms around him, and pulled him close, losing herself in the smell of his skin, thrilling to the touch of his hands as he ran his fingertips down the length of her spine. It all felt so right, and she just wanted—so desperately needed—the pain to end.

But then the memory

wings fluttering helplessly, his handsome features stretched tight as searing pain wracked his body, the odor of burnt flesh in her nostrils

flashed brightly across her mind's eye, and she pulled back.

"N-no, this is wrong..." she whispered. She pushed him away, roughly, and he fell back, staggering for a moment before he regained his balance.

"What are you talking about, Elisabeth?" Worthington demanded. "*What's* wrong?" His eyes flashed with anger. "You're my *wife,* damn it—"

"*I'm not your wife!*" Betsy roared. "And *you're* just a lie!"

She was angry now—more at her own actions than by anything he had done—and hurt, and wanted to do nothing more than blindly lash out at the monster who had compounded her suffering, who had used his damnable wishbox to trivialize the death of the only man she had ever truly loved. Unfortunately, that monster wasn't available... but she was willing to settle for the next best thing.

Unbidden, her right hand suddenly began to glow with rose-colored energy—instinctively, she'd called forth her psi-blade. Her eyes seemed to blaze with the same energy as she menacingly closed on her prey.

Worthington backed away; *his* eyes sparkled with the growing light of fear. Maybe he was coming to the realization that the woman advancing on him really *wasn't* his wife.

"What the hell is *that?*" he asked, his voice a few octaves higher, and pointed to the foot-long dagger.

"*My wrath,*" she said coldly—and plunged the blade into his skull.

* * *

She found herself standing on a beach on a hot summer day.

The sky was ablaze with color as the sun set in the west; looking toward the east, Betsy could see stars twinkling brightly against a midnight blue curtain. Judging by the fact that the constellations were different here than those she normally saw above the lights of New York, she came to the conclusion that she was in the Southern Hemisphere.

She remembered this place, but not as a psychic construct floating around in someone's mind. It was an actual island, owned by Warren, that was located in the Bismarck Sea, about one hundred miles off the coast of New Guinea. She'd been here with her beau, a year or so past, along with Bobby Drake and his non-mutant girlfriend of the moment—a pretty, blond-haired artist named Cindy Appleton. The quartet had traveled there to unwind after a particularly grueling battle the X-Men had fought against one of the group's oldest enemies: Kukulcan, an ancient Mayan deity. Warren was bruised and battered from taking the brunt of one of the sun god's solar bolts—at one point, he'd commented that he ached so badly that even his *hair* hurt. Betsy's soothing ministrations, however, made him soon forget all about his pains . . .

A low moan caught her attention, and she looked down to find the "other" Worthington lying face-down in the golden sand. Planting a stockinged foot firmly against his rib cage, she pushed hard, rolling him onto his back so he could breathe. It wouldn't do to have him suffocate while she was inside his mind. The last thing she needed after the horrors she'd recently experienced was to be trapped inside the subconscious of a dead man.

Betsy gazed at her surroundings. Out on the ocean, a pair of dolphins leapt from the water, playing tag in the turquoise waters. Behind her, palm trees swayed in the gentle Pacific breezes, the broad leaves rattling softly with a sound like sails unfurling. Beyond the trees, rising majestically above the island, was Mt. Pindalayo, a dormant volcano she had tried to climb a number of times during the brief vacation. She'd given up after twisting her right knee on the third attempt, and had grudgingly settled for a quick trip to the top courtesy of Air Worthington.

Everything here was just as she remembered it—except that Warren wasn't with her now to enjoy the view.

Forcing herself to ignore the prostrate form spread out by her feet, Betsy started walking toward the jungle, knowing that any answers she sought would be found there, in the depths of Worthington's subconscious.

The path through the jungle wasn't a real path, of course—it was merely a representation of a psychic conduit that allowed her easy access to Worthington's memories; the further she traveled along it, the more information she'd be able to gather. If she wanted, she could even interact with those memories, and peel back their layers to discover what really lay at the heart of this creation that had been formed by Magneto's black sense of humor. For now, though, she settled for simply playing observer, glancing from side to side at a brief scene here, a childhood fantasy there, with all the mild interest of someone strolling through the Central Park Zoo on a pleasant Sunday afternoon.

As she continued her journey, however, mild interest quickly grew to open-mouthed astonishment. She was shocked—and a tad frightened, she had to admit—by how so many of Worthington's memories were the same as Warren's. The night he'd coaxed her into singing at the Starlight Room in New York. Their first moonlit flight above the city, arms wrapped around one another, chasing the stars as they flitted across the night sky. Vacations in Rio de Janeiro, in Switzerland, in Venice. That wild, passionate night in New Orleans when he'd finally admitted his love for her.

But how could this be possible? If Worthington and everyone else on the planet were just constructs of Magneto's mind, then how could this version of Warren possess memories that Lensherr would never have been privy to? Was the Cosmic Cube so powerful it could even reconstruct the thought patterns of a *dead man?*

Unfortunately, she couldn't find any answers to her questions—not in Worthington's mind, at least.

Betsy shook her head; this was getting her nowhere. It was obvious that Worthington didn't know anything else about Magneto beyond what the rest of the world had been duped into believing. As much as she hated to admit it, this detour from her mission had only succeeded in accomplishing one goal: killing a few hours before she had to face the mutant overlord. She'd been a fool to put herself through all this trouble—all this misery. It was time to move on.

But then, just as she prepared to withdraw from Worthington's subconscious and return to her own body, she felt the presence of *another* mind, and a familiar voice called out to her from the darkness:

Betts? Betsy? Is that you?

Her breath caught in her throat. No—it couldn't be, she told herself. He was gone, and no matter how much she wished otherwise, there was nothing she could do to bring him back. It had to be some part of Worthington's mind, another memory she'd stumbled across. It would be best to ignore it; better to go now, before she caused herself any more grief by poking around where she didn't belong. She'd be an utter fool to remain here a moment longer.

So why, then, did she find herself venturing further into the jungle, into the shadowy depths of Worthington's mind, hoping to find the source of that voice . . . ?

14

THE FIRST sensation Saturnyne had was of being cold and wet. Her feet were numb, for some inexplicable reason. The chill spread to her ankles, then up along her legs. It was around that moment that she also lost all feeling in her fingertips.

She struggled to open her eyes, but it turned out to be a difficult task—her body refused to respond to her mental commands. No real surprise there, she thought dimly—she'd been going nonstop almost from the moment the Cube-created anomaly began to warp reality in Dimension 616. If *she* were her body, she wouldn't want to get up, either...

But then why did she feel so blasted cold? And something else: hadn't she been in the process of responding to some sort of alert in the citadel?

The numbness continued to spread; she couldn't feel anything below her waist or elbows now. Cold this intense should have made her joints ache, but she couldn't feel those, either. Had she gotten out of bed in the middle of the night and passed out on the bathroom floor?

Slowly, the heavy eyelids began to rise, and she was able to catch brief, hazy glimpses of her surroundings through gummy, crust-covered lashes:

A dark area—a room of some sort?

Colored lights twinkling like stars.

A flash of white moving across the darkness.

Her mind fought hard to process the information provided by her eyes, but her thinking was all muzzy; if only she weren't so cold . . .

She vaguely remembered a hand over her mouth, the stab of something sharp penetrating her neck—then nothing.

No, there was more. A woman. There'd been a woman in her quarters—one with snow-white hair like hers; a face like hers. A mirror image. An evil twin.

Sat-yr-nin.

That psychopathic little git from Earth 794. *She* was the one who'd been in her quarters, wearing her clothes, her jewelry—

Her identity?

But, wait a moment. Wasn't Sat-yr-nin supposed to be locked away in the bowels of the citadel? Of *course,* she was—Her Whyness had seen to that herself, supervising her insane double's placement in the stasis chamber shortly after the X-Men had captured her. Roma had been uncomfortable with the idea of putting the Mastrex to death, no matter *how* severe her crimes against humanity might have been; all life was sacred to the Supreme Guardian.

There were days, Saturnyne had thought darkly at the time, when she missed having Merlyn in charge. A right buzzard he might be, a schemer, a liar, and a callous manipulator, but at least he understood the need for swift, decisive actions—like summary justice. If only Roma could be a little more cold-hearted, like her father . . .

Nevertheless, the Mastrex of Earth 794 had been sealed away, hopefully forever—or at least until Roma saw the light of reason, and had her atoms scattered across the length and breadth of the omniverse. But if Sat-yr-nin *had* been in Her Whyness' rooms just a short while ago, then obviously she had escaped. And if *she* was now wandering about the citadel, impersonating the Omniversal

Majestrix, then *where,* in turn was the *real* Majestrix . . . ?

Saturnyne's eyes snapped open, a sudden adrenaline surge providing her with the strength she needed to throw off the lingering effects of the sedative. She was in a crystalline tube, medical sensors attached to various points on her head and body. She went to touch the glass, but found herself unable to move her arms. Or her legs, for that matter.

Forcing her head to tilt downward, she saw a viscous, azure liquid filling the enclosure from a hole in the bottom of the tube. The level of fluid had already risen above chest level, and as it climbed higher, more and more of her body became numb. It took her a moment to realize what was happening.

Suspension fluid, her mind told her. *You're in the stasis chamber. Being cryo-sealed.*

"Mitras, no!" she cried. Panicked, she looked through the crystal wall, to find a sour-faced, balding man in a white laboratory coat watching her.

A doctor, she thought. *He's a doctor—but if he's a doctor, then why isn't he trying to* help *me? Doesn't he know who I am?*

Of course, he did, she realized with growing horror. Because he was the one who had drugged her; the one who had freed Sat-yrnin; the one who was working with von Doom.

Stanton, she thought hazily as the cold seized her around the collarbone, digging its wintry talons into her flesh. *His name . . . is . . . Stanton . . .*

It was getting harder to think clearly—her mind was closing down, her heart stopping, the flow of blood to her brain inching to a halt. All she could focus on was the chill that had seized her body—the icy fist that held her immobile in her crystal coffin, its grip tightening to such a degree that each remaining breath felt like shards of broken glass were being scraped against the back of her throat. She was cold . . . so very cold . . .

She opened her mouth wide, to scream one last time in defiance—

And then the thick, blue liquid was flowing down her throat, filling her lungs, and a numbing rime closed over her thoughts.

Stanton watched with a sense of relief as the suspension fluid reached the top of the tube, and Saturnyne's vital signs settled down to normal—well, normal for cryo-sleep, that is. It had been a close call, transporting her to the stasis chamber before the sedative wore off; the job might have gone easier, and much faster, if von Doom hadn't abandoned him to go off on his own.

"Doom is no man's lackey," he had said in that annoyingly imperious tone of his. "It is *your* plan, Stanton—see it through to its conclusion. I, meanwhile, have more important matters to which I must attend." Then, turning on his heel without waiting for a response, he'd exited Saturnyne's suite, leaving the dour physician to the task of dragging an unconscious Majestrix back through the service tunnels they'd used to gain access to her quarters.

The return trip to the stasis chamber had taken twice as long to travel, since Saturnyne was nothing but dead weight in his arms, and he'd had to hide from citadel security patrols at least a half-dozen times. Nevertheless, his supposition *had* been correct: no one had thought to check on Sat-yr-nin, so focused were they all on locating von Doom. The bodies, the broken doors—they were all still there when he arrived with his charge, all lying exactly as they had been when he, von Doom, and Sat-yr-nin had departed for the upper levels. He'd just managed to bundle the insensate Majestrix into the crystalline holding cylinder as the first soft moans of returning consciousness escaped her lips.

Stanton leaned back against the monitoring station, and used the sleeve of his coat to wipe away the perspiration that had accumulated on his bare scalp. He was a doctor, not a dock worker—he wasn't built for all this heavy lifting. His back ached, his head pounded, his arms felt like lead ingots; there were moments when it hurt just to breathe. As shapely as the Majestrix was, one hundred and fifteen pounds was still one hundred and fifteen pounds, whether on Earth or the citadel, and carrying all that weight up and down access ladders, through service tunnels, and across numerous corridors had certainly taken its toll on him. All he wanted to do right now was collapse into bed and sleep for a week. But then an image of von Doom floated before his bleary eyes, and Stanton was quickly reminded of the armored fist that had crushed the skull of the elderly counterpart from Earth 892; of the splash of blood and bone that had turned the white bedding a disturbing crimson hue; and of von Doom's ominous comment about the expendability of his pawns. Perhaps it might be better to stay awake and keep busy . . .

Still, Stanton's plan had worked to perfection . . . so far. Saturnyne was alive, her alternate was moving freely about the citadel, and no one was the wiser. And, as long as von Doom didn't tip their hand too soon, the masquerade could continue undetected.

Stanton smiled. Could the Chief Physician have done anything this masterful? Highly unlikely—the man could barely dress himself properly. Such precise planning could only have been accomplished by someone possessing a great mind—an intellect so vast it staggered the imaginations of lesser beings. An intellect like the one that resided in the mind of one Henry P. Stanton.

Now, he just had to put that intellect to use, and think of something to do with all the bodies outside, before anyone took notice . . .

With a heavy sigh, Stanton pushed off from the monitoring station, and headed for the outer chamber, his back already complaining. Behind him, Saturnyne floated in azure tranquillity, her beautiful features twisted grotesquely with fear, her mouth locked in a scream that would never be heard . . .

"How's the head, Professor?" Jean Grey asked. It was clear from her tone of voice that she didn't really care one way or the other about any ill effects he might be suffering from her psi-bolt.

"Oh, *much* better," Xavier replied politely. It was true—now that the phenobarbital had worn off, and Jean had taken to trusting the neural inhibitor to keep his mental powers in check, rather than continue rooting around in his memories, he almost felt like his normal self. "Thank you for asking. And yours?"

Jean started, then eyed him suspiciously. The Professor could almost hear the wheels turning in her head—was he using some telepathic ability he'd managed to hide from her scans? If so, another psi-bolt might be in order . . .

"I've noticed you've been wincing in pain a great deal since we landed in Orly, *and* you've taken to consuming aspirins as though they were after-dinner mints," he explained quickly, and smiled. "You don't have to be a telepath to recognize the signs of a headache."

Jean grunted, and turned her seat around to face the road.

Xavier sighed. It looked like nothing he could say or do would be able to break through Magneto's control. Jean had seemed to be the obvious choice among the X-Men for him to try and bond with, given their closeness in the past, but that had turned out to be the wrong assumption—if anything, she was probably the one *most* able to resist his attempts at rekindling their friendship, since she already knew his true intentions. Scott was even more difficult to reach—his devotion to Magneto bordered on fanaticism. As for Kurt and Rogue, while their personalities were essentially the same as always, they tended to remain silent in his presence, preferring instead to simply glare at him with undisguised hatred and loathing.

How complete was the Cube's effect of them? he wondered.

Through the windows of the mini-van that his former students had requisitioned at the airport, Xavier could see the sun setting in the west, its rays painting the Loire Valley landscape in brilliant hues of blue and gold, crimson and purple. It was peaceful here, positively serene, much like it was in the rest of the world, as he'd learned while he and Betsy were doing their research back in New York. Mankind and mutants living in harmony—thanks to Magneto. Again, Xavier felt a pang of jealousy stab at his heart—

But it wasn't *just* jealousy, though. He felt sadness, as well.

Yes, he knew that the people of the world had been transformed into living puppets, with Magneto pulling the strings. Yes, he knew this world was nothing but an illusion, the creation of a—what had Psylocke called it? A "Monkey's Paw." A device that would give its owner whatever their heart desired, only to savagely turn that wish against the dreamer at the last moment, and plunge them into the midst of a nightmare from which there might be no escape. Yes, the Cube was all that and more, capable even of tearing apart the fabric of reality if its power wasn't shut down, or its flaw corrected.

But still . . .

Did he really have the right to destroy *everything* Magneto had created? *Could* he destroy it all, given the opportunity?

What if Roma could repair the Cube so that it would return to its original function of physically restructuring reality? What if the damage to the omniverse could be repaired, with no ill effects to any dimension? What if the Cube's powers were then used for good, by the right person, with the right vision?

Was it wrong to want to live in a world where there was no more fear, no more hatred, no more war? Was it wrong to finally have man and mutant living in harmony, not under a dictatorship, but freely, walking hand-in-hand towards a brighter future?

Then again, was it wrong for *only* Charles Xavier's dreams to be the foundation upon which that world was built?

These, and many other questions, continued to swirl about his mind, all the way to the front gates of Castle Lensherr.

Unfortunately, he couldn't come up with a single answer.

Minutes later, escorted by his "honor guard"—comprised of Scott, Jean, Kurt, Rogue, and a few mutants who obviously lived here as servants—Xavier directed his hoverchair through the labyrinthine corridors of Magneto's fortress. The Professor was mildly surprised by both its rural location, and its design; again, as with the manner in which he ruled the world, here was a gentler side of Erik Lensherr he had never seen before. Maybe Psylocke *had* been right—

finally taking control of the world may very well have mellowed the most notorious of super-villains . . .

Xavier glanced at the people around him—these talented, caring men and women whom he had trained, admired, considered his own family for so long. The same fierce dedication they had once shown him still burned in their eyes, but they were dedicated to Magneto's cause now, and he . . . what was *he* to them? Erik had turned them against him—he'd been expecting it, to be quite honest. As the X-Men's greatest foe, could he have passed up the opportunity to use the Cosmic Cube to control their minds, and convince them that their mentor was some kind of inhuman monster? Of course not; the temptation would have been too great.

That didn't mean, however, that the ache in the Professor's heart was any less painful . . .

A heavy, oaken door opened at the end of the hallway down which they traveled. The group moved through it, and Xavier found himself in a large, oak-paneled drawing room, its ceiling twenty feet above him, the floor covered in thick maroon carpeting. Bookcases lined the walls, their shelves holding collector's editions of some of the planet's greatest literature. To the left of the door, immense windows looked down upon the sprawling gardens that lay to the west side of the castle; to the right of the door, an immense stone fireplace took up the length of a wall.

He was startled to find Wolverine waiting for them, but it made sense, in a strange way. Who better to protect Magneto from his enemies than the man who had tried the most often to kill him? It was a Cube-derived example of the old saying about keeping your friends close, and your enemies closer.

Charles glanced around the room, but saw no sign of Gambit, the wily, dark-haired Cajun who had accompanied the other X-Men on their mission to locate the source of the reality-cancer infecting their home dimension. No doubt he was on some mission for his master, Xavier surmised.

"Welcome, Charles. I've been expecting you."

Erik Lensherr turned from the window at which he'd been standing. He was dressed in his familiar, red-and-purple Magneto uniform, complete with flowing cape and gladiator-style metal helmet. It looked extremely out of place in such an opulent setting—the armor of a space-age knight, worn amidst the genteel trappings of a sixteenth century-styled palace.

"If I had known formal wear was required," Xavier commented, eyeing the costume, "I would have chosen a more appropriate suit."

Lensherr smiled. "I wore it for old times' sake, my friend. After going to all the trouble of popping back into existence from wherever it is that you've been hiding, I thought the least I should do to honor your arrival here was to be attired in the sort of outfit you'd expect the Master of the World to be wearing."

Xavier's mouth twisted in a wry smile. "I'm flattered."

Logan stepped forward, moving with the grace of a panther. "So, *this* is the piece'a terrorist trash who's been givin' you so much trouble all these years, Erik?" He snorted. "Don't look like such a threat t'me."

The Professor smiled pleasantly. "Appearances, as the saying goes, *can* be deceiving, Logan." If the diminutive Canadian was surprised to discover that Xavier knew his name, he hid it well. Xavier turned to Lensherr. " 'Terrorist'? Wouldn't you say that's a case of the pot calling the kettle 'black'?"

Lensherr said nothing, but it was clear from his amused expression that he had enjoyed the opportunity to reverse roles with his former friend.

"Charles, I *know* why you are here," Lensherr finally replied. He reached up and removed his helmet. "I know all about your great mission of mercy, and the alleged threat the Cube poses to the multitude of alternate dimensions that exist beyond the pale." Handing the helmet to Wolverine, he leaned down close to the Professor's ear, so that only he could hear him. "Miss Grey was kind enough to telepathically bring me up to speed on von Doom's world."

"Then you also know why *your* vision of the world can't continue to exist, either," Xavier said.

Lensherr shook his head and stepped back. "I know why *you* say it cannot continue—that does not mean it is the *truth*." The

Professor glared at him, but the mutant overlord merely snorted in response. "Really, Charles, I *hate* it so when you play at being the outraged victim. You cannot tell me that this would be the first time you have not told your X-Men the complete truth about one of their missions, or that you have never manipulated their actions—used them as pawns in some grander design of which they knew nothing." His eyes narrowed. "If I remember correctly, you *did* once convince them you had died, solely for the purpose of furthering one of your plans."

Xavier quickly waved a hand through the air, dismissing the accusation. "I am not attempting to deceive or manipulate you, Erik. The Cube *is* a danger to us all—its influence over the world, over our universe, must be ended, and quickly."

"Even if it meant returning to the old days of hatred and mistrust and fear, Charles?" Lensherr asked. "Even if it meant the end of The Dream?"

Xavier shook his head. "The Dream will not die, Erik, simply because the Cube is deactivated and the world returns to normal—it will continue to live on, in our hearts and minds. Removing this 'shortcut' von Doom has created just means that we will have to work twice as hard—together—to make it a reality once more." He paused. "*Without* the self-centered fixations on world domination, of course."

Lensherr chuckled. "Of course."

A knock at the door suddenly interrupted their conversation.

"Enter!" Lensherr barked.

The door opened, and an attractive, dark-haired woman poked her head into the room. "Father, dinner is almost—" She stopped, realizing that Lensherr was not alone. Her eyes almost immediately settled on Wagner, who was standing near the Professor's hover-chair.

"Good evening, Anya," Kurt said. He flashed a winning smile.

The young woman blushed, and turned her gaze to a spot on the floor. She was clearly embarrassed, and Kurt seemed to find that amusing.

Wolverine growled, and stared heatedly at the blue-skinned mutant.

Xavier's eyebrows rose. Anya? That was the name of the daughter Magnus had lost decades ago—the one who died in the fire. The realization of what was going on here struck the Professor like a blow to the head: Magneto hadn't recreated the world solely to end the increasingly violent disputes between humanity and mutantkind; he'd recreated the world so that he could reunite the members of his shattered family—including his late daughter.

Suddenly, convincing his old friend to give up the Cube had become a *much* more complicated issue . . .

"Come in, child," Lensherr said, beckoning her forward. "You're among friends." She stepped inside, and walked over to join her father, trying not to make eye contact with Kurt. Smiling proudly, the mutant overlord turned to Xavier. "You've never met my daughter, Anya, have you, Charles?" There was a warning flash in his eyes that was all too clear: *Say nothing about the Cube, nothing that will upset my daughter, or you will not live long enough to regret your mistake.*

"I don't believe I've had the pleasure." Xavier smiled and nodded toward Anya. "How do you do, Miss Lensherr?"

Anya stared at him, eyes wide as saucers. "Father," she whispered, "is this the man you were telling us about today?"

"It's all right, child," Lensherr said gently. "He doesn't bite—at least, not in polite company." He chuckled at his own joke. "Now, what urgent matter requires my attention?"

"Dinner is just about ready," Anya replied, "and your presence is required."

"Ahh—a *most* important matter, then." Lensherr smiled, and kissed her softly on the forehead. "Tell your mother we shall be joining you soon enough." He slapped her playfully on the back-side. "Now, off with you—my associates and I still have business to attend to."

Anya kissed him lightly on the cheek. "Don't be too long,

Father—you know how Mama gets when you let your food get cold."

"Fifteen minutes—no more," Lensherr promised.

Anya nodded, accepting his terms. Then, sparing a moment to take a quick glance at Kurt, she turned on her heel and exited the room, closing the door behind her.

"She's a lovely young woman, Erik," the Professor commented.

"She is my light and my life, Charles," Lensherr replied, his voice surprisingly soft. "The part of my soul that had been lost for so very long. And now that I am whole once more, I find myself unable to even consider for a moment a world in which she does not exist." He gazed evenly at his old friend.

"I . . . understand," Xavier said simply.

"You always *were* highly perceptive, Charles," Lensherr said, a touch of sarcasm in his voice. He stared wistfully at the closed door for a moment, then shook his head as though to clear his thoughts. "Now, then—my acolytes have informed me about your traveling companion, and how she managed to evade their good graces. You would not happen to know where our dear Miss Braddock might have gone to ground since you were separated, would you?"

Xavier folded his hands on his lap, and smiled politely. "I'm sorry, Erik—were you actually expecting me to answer that question?"

Jean stepped forward, a sneer on her lips. "I *could* find out for you, Erik, if you'd like."

Lensherr gently waved her off. "There's no need for psychic torture, Miss Grey; Charles doesn't know. I'm certain, however, that she is not all that far away from her master." He glanced toward his former friend. "But even if you *did* know her location, you would not tell me—is that not so?"

Xavier's smile broadened. "As I mentioned to Miss Grey earlier today, you *do* know my methods quite well."

"Quite . . ." Lensherr chuckled. "And, as so often has occurred in the past, we find ourselves at another impasse." He shrugged.

"No matter—once you and I have finished our conversation, I will simply call upon the power of the Cube and have her appear before me."

"*Are* we going to converse, Erik?" Xavier asked. He couldn't keep a sly grin from lighting his features, as images from James Bond movies flitted across his mind's eye. Magneto *was* running true to form . . .

Lensherr nodded. "Oh, most definitely, Professor. I am not the sort of host who would be so callous as to invite you into his home, and then kill you immediately—that would be . . . uncivilized. But, rest assured, there *will* be more than enough time for such unpleasantries—for both you *and* Miss Braddock—later." He smiled disarmingly. "Tell me one thing, though, if you would be so kind, Charles: If Miss Braddock accompanied you on your mission, does that mean that von Doom is here, also? Or has that aging windbag finally been sent on his way to his final reward—in Hades?"

"*You* are not so far behind him, old friend, from what I can see," Xavier replied. He gestured toward the signs of advanced aging that were so clearly evident on Magnus's face. "The Cube's influence, I take it?"

The mutant overlord nodded somberly. "I did not think much of it when the process started—I attributed it to the strain of battle, when I led the attack against von Doom and his forces. But it appears I made a . . . misdiagnosis." A wisp of a smile curled the corners of his mouth. "I am no longer the man I once was, Charles—soon, I will have been alive for three-quarters of a century." The smile faded. "I did not need von Doom's help in reaching—and then passing—that milestone any faster."

"Erik, there still is time to reverse the process . . ." Xavier began.

"By handing you the Cube?" Lensherr smiled and shook his head. "I'm sorry to disappoint you, old friend, but I will have to decline your offer for assistance." He turned from the Professor to face his acolytes. "Leave us now, my friends. Charles and I have some . . . catching up to do, and I wish to do so in private."

"You sure about that, Erik?" Wolverine asked, eyeing Xavier.

"I am in no danger, Logan," the mutant overlord replied. "Although Charles may possess the greatest telepathic abilities on the planet, they pale in comparison to the powers *I* wield—as he well knows."

Logan shrugged. "Awright, you're the boss," he said, though it was all too apparent that he didn't like the idea of leaving the world's greatest peacemaker alone in a room with his deadliest adversary. "But watch the wheelchair. Scott tells me Baldy here drives it 'bout as well as Anya does when she gets behind the wheel o' the limo."

Lensherr winced dramatically. "I shall keep it in mind." He smiled. "When Charles and I have finished our discussion, I will ask you to rejoin us."

"Just give a holler." With a final, heated glare at Xavier, Wolverine spun on his heel and followed the other acolytes from the room.

Once the door had closed, Lensherr slowly turned to face the Professor.

"And now . . . ?" Xavier asked.

"And now, Charles, I think it is time you experienced the power of the very object you sought to destroy," Lensherr said in an ominous tone. A darkly sinister light burned in his gray eyes. "It should be an . . . enlightening experience for you. . . ."

15

IF HE hadn't been so focused on formulating his plans for revenge, he might have been impressed by the vast collection of medical technology around him ... though it was doubtful.

In a darkened supply room—one roughly the size of a parking lot—located some twenty levels below the infirmary, was Victor von Doom. The former emperor of the Earth sat at a workbench, disassembling the very device that had been used to free him from the atrophied body of his now-deceased counterpart. It hadn't taken him long to find the device—a layout of the citadel, obtained by tapping into its main computer systems, had led him unerringly to his destination ... eventually. He'd had to avoid a number of armed guards who were obviously searching for him along the way, and sift through the contents of two other vast supply rooms before he'd found the device. But once he had, taking apart the multiphasic crystal accelerator had been child's play—although he still wasn't quite certain of half the functions of the alien technology contained within its housing. It didn't really matter to him, however; the items he'd chosen were more than suitable for his needs.

Laid out across the table in front of him was a small collection of parts, alongside components he'd removed from his battle armor—including his gauntlets. Using an array of tools he carried in a pouch on his belt, von Doom opened a small panel in each metal glove, exposing the delicate circuitry of the energy discharge mixing chambers—the source of power for the charged particle projectors that were built into the palms. He ran a quick diagnostic on both, and was surprised to find them functioning perfectly. By all rights, then, the blasters should be able to fire. Yet some outside influence had succeeded in penetrating his armor's defenses and shutting down the plasma flow between the mixing chambers and the particle accelerators. It had to be the by-product of a forcefield of some kind, he surmised, one generated from deep within the citadel. He refused to believe Saturnyne's childish explanations about a "state of temporal grace" that prevented most weapons— mainly those that fired projectiles or plasma-beams—from being used. But whatever the reason for the limitations on his armor's offensive capabilities, whatever technology might be in use by Roma and her people, it hadn't taken long for von Doom to think of a solution to the problem.

Beneath the cold metal of his mask, the tyrant's scarred lips twisted into an approximation of a smug grin. Once again, he had been underestimated by his enemies, and now they were beginning to learn just how great a price they were to pay for their brashness. He had already fulfilled his promise to Saturnyne that she would be punished for her lack of respect, and Roma would soon follow. Of course, there *had* been one minor deviation from his plans—if it hadn't been for Stanton's intervention, he would have snapped the Majestrix's neck and ended her life, rather than settle for simply tucking her away in a darkened alcove at the bottom of the citadel. Still, the doctor's suggestion had been a sound one—though the proud monarch would never admit it to the man's face—and one better suited for the current situation. Giving Sat-yr-nin a chance to get close to Roma, and perhaps even divert the witch's attention away from the hunt, would provide him with the time he needed to properly prepare for his confrontation with the Guardian—so long as his scheming ally didn't do anything foolish . . . like attempt to seize control herself.

But allowing an enemy to live—even one trapped in a state of suspended animation, like Saturnyne—was not a wise move, in the long run. Von Doom had lost count of all the times he'd left a battlefield, wrongly presuming that Reed Richards and the rest of his Fantastic Four were dead, only to have them rise up once more and strike him down in his moment of triumph. In *this* circumstance, however, there was a simple solution to the problem: Once Roma had been removed from power, and von Doom sat upon the throne, he would order her lieutenant's death, and eliminate any chance that the Majestrix might eventually find a way out of her liquid prison.

And then, perhaps, he would do the same with her wild-eyed counterpart . . .

"Ah. *There* you are," said a soft, Scottish voice from behind him.

Von Doom turned. The Chief Physician stood just inside the doorway, leaning against a tall metal cabinet. He did not look at all happy to see the monarch.

"I must say, you're looking rather fit," the doctor commented icily. "Kill any other helpless old men while you've been wandering the corridors unsupervised?"

Von Doom glared at him. "Not yet . . ." he said ominously.

Surprisingly, the doctor didn't seem taken aback by the threat. He merely frowned, and sniffed derisively in response, showing more backbone than Stanton had ever displayed in von Doom's presence. There had to be some reason for his courage . . .

"Tell me, physician," the former emperor inquired, "how many of Roma's lapdogs are on the other side of that door, waiting for your signal to attack?"

Now the doctor looked uneasy. He nervously cleared his throat, as though stalling for time until he could think of a suitable answer. "Ummm . . . none, actually," he finally admitted.

Behind the ion-implanted titanium facemask of the dictator, a single eyebrow rose in an inquisitive manner. "Really?" von Doom said. "So, am I to understand, then, that you took it upon yourself to track me to my lair, and offer your terms for my peaceful surrender?"

"Nothing of the sort," the Chief Physician replied, "although I wouldn't be adverse to the idea. It's just that, from time to time, I like to check on the equipment I have stored here—make certain it's still functioning properly. *You* just happened to pick the very same supply room for your hideout."

"And you expect me to believe that?"

The doctor shrugged. "Coincidence *is* one of the guiding forces in the omniverse."

"Bah," von Doom spat. "More metaphysical tripe. Must *everyone* in this accursed place speak in ridiculous axioms?"

"Only those with the proper understanding of the forces of order and chaos," the Chief Physician replied haughtily. "It's not a subject for everyone, though."

"*Bah,*" the tyrant repeated. He turned his back on the little man. If the physician wasn't going to attack, or run off screaming to notify Roma's dogs of his location, then the monarch no longer felt the need to acknowledge his presence. There were far more important matters to occupy his time.

"Hmmm . . . Judging from the way you've taken apart one of the multiphasic crystal accelerators, I see you have some experience with electronics," the Chief Physician commented. "I wonder what sort of project you might be working on . . ."

Von Doom ignored his attempt to draw him into a conversation and continued with the job at hand.

"You *were* made aware of the temporal state of grace that envelops the citadel, weren't you?" The doctor paused. "Yes, I'm sure you were. And yet you continue to tinker away with those parts you've . . . acquired from the accelerator."

Von Doom heard the soles of the physician's shoes scuffling across the floor. The wretch was actually moving closer—and without permission! The tyrant didn't know whether to admire the man's courage, or strike him down for his foolhardiness.

"So, if you already knew that any armaments built into your battlesuit wouldn't function in this setting," the doctor continued, "then you *couldn't* be constructing a weapon—at least not a *conventional* weapon."

Von Doom paused in his work, intrigued by the physician's line of reasoning. It was becoming clear to him that the little man might not be the imbecile he appeared to be . . .

It never ceased to amaze her just how incredibly *stupid* most people were.

In the time it had taken her to travel from the Majestrix's chambers in response to the Supreme Guardian's summons, Sat-yr-nin had passed hundreds of people in the corridors, spoken to at least a dozen citadel guards about von Doom's disappearance, had even barked orders at a couple of members of the Captain Britain Corps, and yet no one had caught on to her masquerade. But as she strode purposefully down one of the gleaming, white metal hallways that led to the throne room, it slowly dawned on the imposter why that might be—and exactly how much power Saturnyne had enjoyed. Passersby cast furtive glances at her, quickly averting their gazes when she looked their way. Staff members did their best to avoid her, flashing uneasy smiles as they speedily walked past, as though they were afraid she might address them. And then there was the manner in which anyone she *did* address would stiffen—backs ramrod-straight as they stood at attention, a sheen of sweat forming on their upper lips.

It all reminded her so much of the reactions she received from her subjects during her reign over Earth 794 that she actually felt a twinge of homesickness.

It was obvious what was going on, though. As Omniversal Majestrix, Saturnyne was not only respected by the occupants of the Starlight Citadel, she was *feared*. Saturnyne didn't have to order her people to carry out their duties—they accomplished them quickly and efficiently, if for no other reason than a simple desire to avoid the sort of reprisals her station allowed her to mete out if they failed.

The Supreme Guardian should have learned a lesson or two from that sort of iron rule, Sat-yr-nin thought, but she had never seen any evidence that Roma had even bothered to pay attention. The dark-haired technomage might be the one who controlled the tides of time, and commanded armies from her lofty multidimensional tower, but she was still the weak-willed and naive immortal child Sat-yr-nin had been battling for years; still the little girl who allowed her emotions to direct her actions. She wasn't a leader; a leader should be powerful, decisive, hard-edged—like the Mastrex. Or Saturnyne. Or Merlyn.

Merlyn. What would *he* think of his daughter these days, if he even still bothered to check on her progress? Roma hadn't been able to bring herself to order Sat-yr-nin's execution after her capture by the X-Men, preferring instead to indefinitely place her enemy in suspended animation. Sat-yr-nin knew all too well from her numerous conflicts with father and daughter that Roma had not been raised to be so . . . so . . . well, "pathetic" was about the best way to describe her.

She was also inexperienced in the ways of the worlds. Her father had walked the length and breadth of the omniverse, if the legends had any basis in fact, influencing lives, even whole civilizations, on a one-to-one basis. Roma, on the other hand, rarely left the protective coccoon of the citadel. She relied on Saturnyne far too much to keep her in the know, trusting her to help her reach the right decision in crucial matters.

Sat-yr-nin shook her head in disbelief. Why her counterpart had never tried to overthrow the child was something the Mastrex had never been able to fathom. It couldn't have anything to do with friendship—it was highly unlikely that the two power brokers were close; Roma was the Supreme Guardian, after all, and Saturnyne her subordinate. And when it came to relationships, Sat-yr-nin and her counterpart were very much alike in their beliefs:

people were tools, to be used as necessary and quickly discarded before you became attached to them—no more, no less.

So, if not friendship, then there could be only one reason for the Majestrix to postpone staging a coup: She was biding her time, waiting for the right moment to strike. Well, Sat-yr-nin thought happily, that decision was no longer up to her double. It was the Mastrex's to make now, and she wasn't about to wait all that long to seize the throne.

Of course, there *was* one obstacle that threatened to stand between her and the chance to realize her dreams of ultimate power: that armored cretin von Doom. She didn't fear the man and really didn't consider him much of a threat, no matter how much effort he put into his blustering. He was just another tool—one used to free her from her icy cell and who now provided a suitable distraction for Roma. Sat-yr-nin just had to find the right moment to dispose of him . . .

She came to a halt before the entrance to the throne room. Here, more than at any other location she had passed along her journey, security had been dramatically increased: a baker's dozen of guards stood rigidly in front of the doors, each man clad in full battle armor. If such a display of force had been deemed necessary because one man was running loose in the citadel, then Sat-yr-nin couldn't help but be impressed. Maybe von Doom was far more formidable than she'd believed; if so, he still might have his uses after she had taken possession of the throne.

Sat-yr-nin moved up the steps, head held high, mouth set in a firm line, ignoring the guards as they moved aside to allow her passage to the doors.

One guard, though, did *not* remove himself from her path. He towered over her by at least a foot, and possessed a jaw that seemed large enough to be used as a bludgeon; from the way he carried himself, he could be none other than the Captain of the Guard. Sat-yr-nin liked what she saw—on her world, she wouldn't have hesitated to consider him a candidate for the position of Royal Konsort. Nevertheless, good looks didn't count for much if the man lacked the sense to move out of the way of his betters—although any uses she might have for him in the near future certainly wouldn't require a great deal of intelligence . . .

"Stand aside," Sat-yr-nin ordered. "I have business with the Guardian."

Slowly, the man looked down at her. A few wisps of bright red hair drifting out from underneath the golden helmet he wore. "Her Majesty has asked that she not be disturbed."

Sat-yr-nin's eyes narrowed in suspicion. Were they on to her already? "But she just summoned me, no more than ten minutes ago."

"And now she is not yet ready to receive you." There was a tone in the man's voice that sounded almost condescending, as though he actually relished the opportunity to deny her entry to the throne room.

Sat-yr-nin opened her mouth to protest, then thought better of it. Her counterpart, more than likely, would not have argued the point, and doing so might serve to give her away. So, instead of snapping at the captain, she turned up her nose at him and snorted derisively. "Very well, then. I shall wait."

The soft groan of displeasure that issued from the guards brought a malicious smile to the Mastrex's lips.

Betsy groaned in disgust as she gazed at the immense structure that stood before her.

She couldn't help it, though. She'd never seen the Great Wall of China reconstructed in anyone's head before.

After what had felt like days of traveling through the jungles that grew so wildly in the depths of Worthington's subconscious, she had at last come to a clearing, and a welcome sight it had been. Although she might only be the psychic representation of a woman sitting on the floor of a Paris apartment, her fist closed around the hilt of the psi-blade that penetrated the forehead of a semi-conscious, alternate version of Warren Worthington III, to Betsy every bug bite, every palm frond that whipped across her face, every toe she stubbed as she tripped over rocks in the darkness felt just as real as they would in the real world. Finding an exit from the dense growth that pressed in around her had been a godsend. She just hadn't expected to be confronted by a wall that seemed to extend into infinity.

It wasn't going to stop her, though. She'd followed Warren's voice this far; a few tons of stone and mortar weren't about to put an end to her quest—not until she learned the truth. Now all she had to do was screw up her nerve enough to find out what that was...

Warren? she called out hesitantly. *Are you there?*

Betts! he cried out. *You made it!*

Well, you didn't think I was about to give up, did you? she asked.

Of course not, he replied. *But I hadn't heard from you in a while, and I'd started to get worried.*

It was true she hadn't spoken to him for some time after their initial contact, but that was because she needed to gather her wits. Discovering that you've suddenly made contact with your dead boyfriend's psyche in the body of his Cosmic Cube-spawned twin was unnerving, to say the least. She didn't remember Jean Grey or Charles Xavier ever mentioning anything like that happening to *them* during any of their adventures with the X-Men.

She had also wanted to be certain that this really was Warren she was talking to, and not some manifestation of the other Worthington's subconscious; it wouldn't be the *first* time she'd entered the mind of someone suffering from a Multiple Personality Disorder. From what she could tell, though, this wasn't the case. Warren—*her* Warren—was here, somehow, trapped in the mind of his duplicate, and nothing was going to keep her from him. Now she just had to find a way to get past this last barrier...

Can you fly over the wall? she asked. *After all, you* are *the one with the wings.*

Good plan, hon, but I've already tried that. She could almost see him shaking his head, his wavy, golden hair sweeping back and forth across his shoulders. *Everytime I got close to the top, I'd hear a voice telling me to turn back, and I couldn't stop myself from obeying it.*

Telepathic suggestion, Betsy surmised.

You're the expert, Warren said. *Well . . . one of them, anyway, next to the Professor and Jean, of course.*

Of course. Betsy pinched her bottom lip between thumb and forefinger, considering her options. *All right. Hang on, luv. I'll think of something.*

For the next minute or so, Betsy paced the ground in front of the wall, trying to come up with a plan. The obstacle couldn't be walked around because it was too wide, and it couldn't be climbed, because it was too high and there weren't enough places on its surface that could be used for handholds. That left her with one choice: She would have to go *through* it.

And how do you plan on doing that, *Braddock?* she asked herself. *I think you left your high explosives in your other costume.*

You wouldn't be carrying a spoon, *would you?* Warren suddenly asked. *You could use it to tunnel your way to this side. It used to work in all those World War II prison movies.*

Betsy winced. One of the dangers of being on the psychic plane was that anyone connected to you psionically could overhear your thoughts if you concentrated too hard. She'd have to be more careful; she didn't want to run the risk of dashing his hopes for freedom.

Sorry, luv. I usually don't pack eating utensils in my kit when I'm off adventuring out of my body. But thanks for the suggestion.

With a sigh, Betsy looked once more at the Great Wall—and it suddenly dawned on her what it actually represented.

From the accounts she had read of the "Morning of Unity," during the visit she had made with the Professor to the New York Public Library, it had been painfully obvious to a trained telepath like Betsy that Magneto had used the Cosmic Cube to rewire the minds of every man, woman, and child on the planet and impose his will on them. And there *had* been times during his battles with the X-Men, she remembered, when the mutant overlord exhibited limited psionic powers. He'd certainly been able to shake off the effects of her psi-blade without a great deal of difficulty, on the two occasions when she'd managed to get close enough to him to ram it through his thick skull. So, with the aid of the Cube, he had obviously been able to boost his psi-powers, and use them to subjugate the populace.

The wall, then, was the permanent barrier that Magneto had placed around the minds of his subjects to ensure their continued cooperation. It limited their freedom of choice, directed their thoughts in such a way that it had seemed quite logical to make the super-villain Master of the World.

But none of that concerned her for the moment. Right now, the only thing she was focused on was that *this* particular wall was keeping her from reaching the man she loved. *Not for much longer, though,* she thought with a smile. Magnus might be all-powerful because he held the Cube, but he was still out of his league when it came to matters of the mind.

And the heart.

Lips set in a firm line, Betsy called forth her psi-blade; the weapon immediately formed around her right hand. Focusing her powers, she refashioned it into a more formidable weapon: a *katana*. It was hard work—she'd never really tried to do this before—but she knew that only a strong enough tool would work against the psychic barrier enclosing Worthington's mind. And when she was done, she held a sword that was as fine as any blade she had ever used in the real world.

Raising the *katana* high above her head, she let loose a scream of utter fury and struck at the wall. The rose-tinted energy bit deep into the stone, gouging out a large section of the masonry.

And then a hand poked through the hole she'd made.

In a Paris apartment currently occupied by two silent figures, the body of Warren Worthington III suddenly stiffened, and a look of intense pain twisted his handsome features.

No one in the neighboring flats heard the high-pitched whine that escaped his lips.

Warren? Betsy cried. She leapt forward, grasping his hand as though fearing it might suddenly disappear. He gently squeezed her hand.

None other, honey, he replied. *What kept you?*

Betsy smiled. *I had to go to the front desk to get a spare key. But don't worry—I'll have you out of there in a few seconds.*

Great. And maybe once I'm out, you can tell me what the hell is going on. Feels like I've been locked away in someone's basement for ages.

Betsy laughed tremulously and patted the back of his hand. *As soon as I figure it all out myself, luv, you'll be the first to know.*

That's my girl, Warren replied sarcastically. *Always trying to cheer me up . . .*

She giggled at the comment, then had to fight to regain her composure. *Focus, you git,* she scolded herself. *You won't be any bloody use to Warren if you go carrying on like a giddy, purple-haired simp.*

Still, she couldn't stop a nervous spasm from running through her body; her legs were like jelly, knees threatening to buckle at any moment and send her tumbling to the ground. Her heart was beating so fast, it felt as though it was about to burst from her chest, and she suddenly found that she had trouble breathing properly.

Releasing his hand, she gripped the hilt of the *katana* and mouthed a silent prayer that this would work.

All right—stand back! she ordered. The hand immediately withdrew, and Betsy swung the psychic sword one last time.

The wall exploded, much to her surprise. And before Betsy could move out of the way, she suddenly found herself in the center of a deadly hail of masonry. One piece the size of a microwave oven caught her across the back of the head. The psi-blade dissipated immediately, her concentration savagely broken, and she dropped to her knees, legs suddenly unable to support her weight. She did her best to try and remain conscious, to at least find out if she'd been successful in freeing Warren, but she could already feel thick, black tendrils closing over her mind, pulling her down into darkness.

And then she felt nothing further.

Matters were about to become even worse than a psychic bump on the head, though.

In an apartment on the Left Bank of Paris, Warren Worthington III, jet-setting multimillionaire, winged mutant, and husband of Elisabeth Braddock—the international star of *Kwannon, Bushido Mistress*—shrieked in agony as every synapse in his brain short-circuited. His hands flew to the sides of his head, palms pressing against the temples as though to prevent his skull from exploding. His body spasmed, jerking his head away from the psi-blade that formed the bridge between his subconscious and Betsy's, and breaking the connection. Then he collapsed onto his expensively carpeted floor.

And died.

Countless dimensions away from the eerily silent Parisian apart-ment, *other* minds were also about to lock in a life and death struggle.

"I don't believe it," the Chief Physician said in astonishment. "It's a dimensional destabilizer." He looked from the small, cigar-shaped device attached to the circuits of von Doom's gauntlets, to stare at its armored creator. "I take it, then, that you figured out that the state of grace prevents weapons from firing—but *not* the particle accelerators used in medical technology. And by hard-wiring components from the MCA into your armor, you're hoping that the citadel's sensors will think you're conducting a procedure, and not a coup."

"Fascinating," von Doom said, closing the access panel on the remaining gauntlet. "You have shown far more intelligence in the past twenty minutes than your feckless colleague has in the six hours I have come to know and detest him."

"You idiot!" the doctor shouted. He pointed to the gauntlets. "Don't you know what might happen if you go around shooting those things in here? You'll destabilize the citadel's integrity, and send everyone hurtling into the vortex!"

"The path to ultimate power cannot be walked unless risks are taken," von Doom replied. "And they are risks I am willing for others to take on my behalf."

"Can't make an omelette without breaking a few eggs, is that it?" the Chief Physician shot back. He snorted. "Ridiculous. I've heard enough—I'm certain the Supreme Guardian will want to know what you've been up to, *before* you start destroying her home." And with that, much to von Doom's surprise, he turned on his heel and headed for the door.

The monarch grabbed him by the collar and lifted him off his feet. "*Now* who is the 'idiot,' physician?" von Doom asked. "Did you think Doom would allow you to just walk out of here so you could raise an alarm?"

"Then why don't you kill me and be done with it?" the doctor demanded. "Once you start firing that destabilizer, I'll be just as dead, anyway."

"Because I see potential in you, physician," the tyrant replied. "More so than in that imbecile Stanton."

The doctor started, eyes widening in surprise. "*Stanton?* He's working for *you?*" He growled softly. "Captain England was right—I should have watched him closely."

"Why bother yourself with that worm, physician," von Doom asked in silky tones, "when *you* could take his place by my side?"

The doctor shook his head. "Sorry. I've never been very good at taking orders from dictators." He wrinkled his nose in distaste. "Too much bowing and scraping involved in the process for my liking. Tends to wear out the knees of my trousers."

"Then you are a fool," the former emperor stated.

The Chief Physician smiled. "I've been called *worse* things in my time, Doctor . . . and by far greater megalomanics than you."

The tyrant snorted derisively and released the bothersome gnat; the doctor tumbled to the floor. As the little man picked himself up, von Doom reached back to the workbench and picked up one of his gauntlets. He slid it over his left hand, pointed it toward the physician—and activated the firing mechanism.

A burst of green-tinged energy lanced forward from the palm of von Doom's gauntlet, catching the Chief Physician square in the chest before he could leap aside. He screamed in agony as the power released by the Crystal Accelerator circuits opened a space/time rift *in the center of his chest,* splitting him in two from head to pelvis. The rift widened, and von Doom could actually see the swirling forces of Creation through the hole in reality, just before the suction pulled both halves of the doctor's body into the vortex. His dying screams echoed throughout the cavernous room, then quickly fell silent.

With a soft rumble like the first signs of an approaching storm, the rift closed, and von Doom was alone once more.

Interlude IV

The Cube was close now. Its siren call filled his mind, blotting out all thoughts but those related to seizing the device from his long-time enemy.

The Controller quickened his pace through the night-shrouded streets of the Left Bank, paying no attention to the direction in which he was being pulled, or the startled gasps of passersby who stared in horror at his grotesque features. Close behind him trailed Leonard, who was doing his best to keep up with his master's frenetic steps.

It had taken all of the Controller's strength of will to force himself to wait for nightfall, after he'd made that initial contact with the Cube's energies from the top of the Eiffel Tower. Since then, he had been unable to sleep, or eat, or sit still for a moment, constantly pacing back and forth through the small set of rooms he and Leonard shared, in a hotel located just off Rue de Babylone. He had cursed the daylight a hundred times or more, impatiently waiting for the sun to set so he could venture forth, yet receiving no satisfaction for his efforts. Eventually, realizing the universe refused to obey his commands and the day would pass no faster than normal, he had sat in a corner and settled into a meditative state. He knew that his success would depend entirely upon his ability to reign in his emotions.

But now that night had finally come, he was unwilling to wait a second longer to claim his prize. When Leonard had asked if his master intended to hide his unnerving features in order to avoid drawing unwanted attention, the Controller had scoffed at the notion.

"*Let* these sheep stare all they want, until they have had their fill," he had said. "Once the Cube is mine, I shall make certain that my face is the last thing they will have ever seen—before I wish them out of existence."

They strode past the Hôtel des Invalides now, with its ornate, golden dome, then across the Quai d'Orsay and onto Pont Alexandre III, the magnificent bridge that spanned the Seine, ending just before the Grand Palais, the glass-roofed, stately building that had been constructed for the Universal Exposition of 1900. Never breaking stride, the Controller hurried across the bridge, ignoring the late-nineteenth century blown-glass lamps and spectacular statuary that decorated the length of the structure. He continued on, stomping west along the Cours Albert 1er, in the direction of the Palais de Chaillot, then came to an abrupt halt at the corner of Avenue Montaigne.

As on most nights, the avenue was filled with people out for an evening of pleasure. On one side of the street, patrons of the arts were filing into the Théâtre des Champs-Elysées, while passersby on the other admired the displays in the windows of trendy *haute couture* shops.

But it was the entrance to a small courtyard just off the avenue that captured the Controller's attention. A dozen or so feet high and about eight feet wide, flanked on both sides by guardstones that once prevented drivers from attempting to squeeze their horse-drawn carriages through the small space, the entrance led to a cobblestoned courtyard that seemed no wider than twenty feet. On the far side of the courtyard were the front doors of two apartment buildings, their red brick walls draped with ivy.

It was from one of those buildings that the siren song of the Cube emanated.

The Controller was stunned by what he saw—or, rather, didn't see—as he stared at the courtyard. There were no guards posted, no colorfully-garbed freaks lounging about, no security measures of any sort that he could see. Was Magneto *that* certain of his power over the lowly creatures he ruled that he felt safe enough to leave the Cube unattended—or was he arrogant enough to think there was no one to oppose him? Whatever the reason, he was about to learn how costly such inattention could be . . .

Slowly, the Controller stepped into the entrance, expecting some hidden trap to be sprung at any moment, but pleasantly surprised when nothing happened. He reached the courtyard un-molested and then, closing his eyes, began to tune out the background noises of the city, opening his senses to the cosmic energies flowing around him.

There. It was coming from the building on the right. The Controller opened his eyes and smiled. Had defeating his enemies *ever* been this simple? With colorful dreams of a New World Order flashing across his mind's eye, he stepped toward the front door—

—and then the song was cut short.

"No . . ." the Controller whispered. "No!"

He threw himself at the front door, shattering its lock with a savage kick, and ran into the building. It was dark inside, but he didn't bother looking for a light switch—not when he could still feel the Cube's energy around him, leading him onward. He vaulted up a marble staircase, taking three steps at a time, until he reached the uppermost floor and burst into a drawing room, the windows of which provided a magnificent view of the Seine River and the Eiffel Tower.

Here. The song had come from this very room . . . but its remnants were already fading, the final notes echoing in the recesses of his mind.

And then he couldn't hear it any more.

The Cube was gone.

* * *

He staggered from the building, body trembling with rage.

Cheated. He'd been cheated out of his prize once more. Denied the opportunity to take what rightfully belonged to him. Robbed of his moment of triumph. And it was all the fault of Magneto.

Throwing his head back, he roared in anger at the heavens. *"Damn your soul to hell, you mutant swine! You play games with the wrong man!"* He lashed out with a booted foot, shattering a large flower pot that stood to one side of the building's entrance.

And then, as quickly as it had begun, the storm passed. The Controller inhaled deeply, slowly released the breath through his nostrils, and forced himself to regain his composure. Throwing childish tantrums was a waste of energy, he told himself, and a man who exhibited such behavior could never truly be a leader—a truism his mentor had come to learn, in the dark days when his world had started falling apart. His protégé, though, as the Controller proudly reminded himself quite often, was made of stronger stuff.

Leonard politely cleared his throat to get his attention. Apparently, the youth had followed him inside with a stealth the Controller had never known he'd possessed. "Sir . . . perhaps we should leave," he said quietly.

The Controller whirled to face his assistant, prepared to either verbally or physically vent some of his frustrations on the blond-haired youth. But he stopped short when he realized that Leonard was not looking at him, but *past* him. Curious as to why his follower was acting in such a manner, the Controller looked back over his shoulder, toward the entrance to the courtyard.

A small crowd had gathered out on the street, drawn to the scene by his histrionics. From the dark expressions on their faces, and the comments that were being uttered, it was clear they were angered by the use of the word "mutant" as part of his hate-filled diatribe.

"Umm . . . sir?" Leonard asked, his voice just above a whisper. "You *did* say you wanted to maintain a low profile until you were ready to strike, didn't you? Perhaps we should go now, before the crowd gets any bigger."

The Controller glared at the bystanders, his contempt for them growing with each passing second as his gaze flicked from one face to the next. Gathered before him were the pride and joy of the Master of Magnetism—shining examples of a world that had at last found peace. Men and women of various nationalities and races, young and old, human and mutant. They felt no animosity toward one another, saw no need to judge their neighbors solely on physical appearance or philosophical differences. In the world of Magneto, they were all beautiful.

Flawless.

Perfect.

The Controller sneered in disgust. How he longed for the opportunity to crush this saccharine-sweet world; to watch those beautiful faces contort with pain as he lashed out with his mighty fists, delivering unto them exquisite suffering, the likes of which only he could imagine; to thrill in the vacant looks that would come over their eyes as they drew their last breaths.

But now was not the time to indulge in fantasies; that would come soon enough, when his work was done and he could savor his victory.

"Yes," he finally said to his assistant. "It *is* time to leave. But we will keep watch over this place. Sooner or later, the Cube—and its master—will return, and then the moment shall be at hand. The moment when I fulfill the destiny for which I was trained, when I take my rightful place as the Earth's master. And then, how these sheep shall tremble with fear. . . ."

16

THE CUBE appeared in the palm of Magneto's hand as if by magic. It wasn't really magic, of course—merely a case of the villain summoning it with just a thought.

Erik Lensherr smiled, clearly pleased with the look of mild astonishment that appeared on the face of his old friend. "Impressed with my mastery over this little wishbox, Charles? Perhaps if von Doom had taken the time to experiment with it, he might also have discovered that it's unnecessary to carry this upon your person in order to make it work." He sneered. "Then again, that tin-plated egomaniac has never been known for his patience."

"I wouldn't say that I'm impressed, Erik," Xavier said, "given the fact that the Cube is stealing away your life with each passing second, and there is obviously nothing you can do to retard the process. *I'd* be more inclined to think it is the *Cube* that masters *you*."

Lensherr sighed and waved a hand in a dismissive gesture. "Have it *your* way, Charles. It has *always* been your nature to focus on the negative."

"Not always," the Professor gently countered. A trace of a smile curled the corners of his mouth.

Lensherr paused; then he, too, smiled. "No, not always, my

friend," he agreed. There was a melancholy tone to his voice—a feeling of regret, perhaps, for days long past, when their relationship hadn't been as strained, their meetings not so confrontational. They *had* been friends—a lifetime ago, it seemed—but the barriers that had come between them over the years had ended the closeness they once shared.

It was a loss that had always troubled Xavier, too. The dreams they had for the future of their race were not all that different. Both believed that their people shouldn't have to live in the shadows; both believed in creating a better world in which those mutants could exist in peace. But while Charles knew that humans tended to learn from their mistakes, and hoped that one day they would see beyond the "tunnel vision" of prejudice and come to accept mutantkind, Lensherr's experiences at the hands of the Nazis had only shown him the worst aspects of *Homo sapiens*, had permanently scarred him, both physically and emotionally. For the frightened child who had grown into the vengeful adult, there had only been one course of action to take in order to prevent his race from suffering the same kind of horrific treatment that led to the extermination of six million Jews: he had to use his powers to bring about the total subjugation of humanity.

That obsession created an irreparable rift between Charles and Erik—the two good friends became the greatest of enemies. It had been that way for years and, despite Xavier's best efforts, it seemed it would always be that way.

Until, that is, the Cosmic Cube somehow created a mid-ground that reflected *both* their dreams . . .

Xavier gestured toward the Cube. "I take it you did not summon this infernal device merely to impress me with parlor tricks." An inquisitive eyebrow rose. "Perhaps you've come to your senses, and you're just going to hand it over to me without a fight?"

The mutant overlord chuckled. "Nothing of the sort, Charles."

Now it was Xavier's turn to sigh melodramatically. "I expected as much." His mouth set in a firm, straight line as, eyes narrowed to slits, he glared at his captor. "So, where does that leave us? Am

I expected to make some sort of half-hearted attempt to battle you for possession of the Cube, deprived of my telepathic abilities as I am by the device your followers attached to my spinal column . . . or do you plan on using it to brainwash me, as you've done with my students?"

Lensherr snorted derisively. "For an intelligent man, Charles, you *stagger* me with your foolish assumptions. Even were you not crippled, I would not expect you to go leaping from your seat and attempt to wrestle the Cube from my hand—physical solutions to problems have always been beneath men of intellect such as you and I." He sneered. "That is why you have come to depend so greatly on smaller-brained creatures like Wolverine—using brawn instead of brains is the stock-in-trade of such buffoons. I came to that same conclusion years ago, first with the Brotherhood, and then the Acolytes. I'm pleased to see you agree with that approach." He seemed amused by Xavier's stern expression. "And insofar as 'brainwashing' goes, had I so desired, I could have ordered the Cube to tear your mind apart the moment you came out of hiding, then sew it back together . . . with some alterations made, of course."

"Of course," Xavier agreed.

Lensherr pointed an index finger into the air to emphasize his point. "*If* that had occurred, you would have arrived here as my most devoted acolyte, and not merely as a guest."

"And yet that did *not* come to pass," the Professor said.

Lensherr smiled. "Ahh. Now, at last, we arrive at the moment of demonstration."

With that, the Cube flared brightly, and both men disappeared in a flash of light.

They materialized on the crest of a grassy hill at dawn. It took a few moments for Xavier to realize they were no longer in France.

He tilted his head back and inhaled deeply. The air was different here, heavy with the smells of wild animals and the fragrances of plant life, all mingling in the warm, comfortably humid breeze that blew across the land. From somewhere off in the distance, the rush of water could be heard—a stream or river, coursing mightily through the valley below them.

"Africa?" he asked.

"Very good, Charles," Lensherr replied. "The West African state of Mali, to be precise."

"I passed through the region once, during my travels across the continent," the Professor said, "although I do not remember ever hearing of a river valley being located in such an inhospitable place. I take it this was your doing?"

"Indeed."

"And I imagine there was a purpose in bringing me here?"

"Of course." The hand that held the Cube swept dramatically across the mist-covered land. "What do you think of my greenhouse, Charles?" Lensherr asked. In the early morning sunlight, it was difficult to see his face clearly, but there was no mistaking the prideful tone in his voice.

"It's lovely—what I can see of it," Xavier said. "I had no idea you possessed such a green thumb."

"I don't consider myself a gardener," the mutant overlord replied, "but rather an artist, challenged by a blank canvas." He gestured toward the landscape. "All this was desert—the sterile wastes of the Sahara. Mile upon mile of endless sands, with little protection from the blistering heat of the relentless sun. This was a place of death, of despair. I have changed all that."

The sun was higher now, the light of its corona cresting the horizon, decorating the valley below with streamers of yellow and red. Leaning forward in his hoverchair, the Professor's eyes narrowed as he peered down into the thinning shadows. The morning mists began to dissipate, and the blocky shapes of man-made constructs slowly appeared among the lush greenery. Rising majestically above the treeline was a brick-and-mortar tower on which a pair of balconies had been built; pink-hued sunlight shone through the half-dozen arched openings at the top of the edifice.

"Is that a village?" Xavier asked.

"It is called Araouane," Lensherr replied. "Forty years ago, it was a thriving oasis that served as a way station for the trans-Saharan trade routes. Then, just a decade later, drought struck the land, and the sands began creeping forward, reaching out with dead fingers toward this one bright spot in the midst of nothingness. Reaching out, then clutching in an unbreakable grip what little life existed here, refusing to let it go. Killing all it touched, then continuing onward, never satisfied until it had claimed everything in its path."

"You make it sound almost human," Xavier commented.

"Possessiveness? Destruction? Death?" Lensherr paused. "Yes, it *does* sound almost human, doesn't it?"

"That's not what I meant."

"I'm certain it wasn't," Lensherr said. "It still applies, though."

Xavier said nothing.

Down in the village, the first signs of activity were taking place. A silhouetted figure appeared on the topmost balcony of the minaret, and an ululating sound filled the air—the cry of a muezzin calling the Moslem faithful to morning prayers. Below the tower, doors opened, and the men of the village exited their modest homes and began walking toward the mosque.

Lensherr turned toward his companion. "Before you ask, *no*, they do not worship me. I have no aspirations for godhood, Charles, though I'm certain the Cube could provide me with that if I so chose."

"I'm relieved to hear you say that," Xavier said. "It tells me you haven't completely taken leave of your—"

"Being Master of the World is reward enough for my efforts," Lensherr interjected. He smiled.

The Professor groaned softly and shook his head despondently. The man could be so insufferably one-tracked in his thinking when he wanted . . .

Ignoring Lensherr's infuriating grin, Xavier turned his attention back to the village. The streets were full of people as Araouane came to life, its inhabitants dressed in brightly-colored robes and more modern clothing. Not all were answering the call to prayer, though—there were shopkeepers opening their stores.

And then his gaze settled on one villager in particular: a woman who was standing on a rooftop at the outskirts of the village. His eyes widened with surprise. Even from a distance, even though she was clad in an ankle-length gown dyed in hues of green and gold and not in form-fitting black leather, her regal bearing was unmistakable—that, and the flowing mane of white hair that cascaded down her back to her waist.

"Ororo," Xavier whispered.

As he watched, the African-born woman raised her hands above her head. Instantly, she was enveloped by a strong gust of wind that she had summoned by using her mutant ability to control the weather. It carried her high into the air, then toward the rising sun. It was an act that Xavier had seen her perform countless times at the school: she was going forth to privately greet the new day and give thanks for it to the Bright Lady, the African deity she worshipped. She would return in an hour or so, when her period of glorification had ended.

"She settled here shortly after I transformed the land," Lensherr commented. "At the time, she insisted that I'd done more harm than good—that I'd thrown the ecological balance of the planet slightly off-kilter . . . though I have yet to see any real proof of that to bolster her arguments."

"And what did she say once you had . . . changed her mind *for* her?" Xavier asked pointedly.

Lensherr sighed. "Charles, I wish you would at least make an *effort* to understand all I have done. While it is true that I . . . helped the world come to an understanding about the importance of my role in their lives, I didn't completely abolish free will. That includes your former students, as well." He waved a hand in the direction of the white-haired mutant, who was now no more than a dark speck against the rising sun. "Ororo *still* argues with me, *still* warns me of the 'irreparable damage' I may ultimately cause to the planet by correcting environmental changes wherever I see fit. The very fact that she has chosen to live here, keeping a watchful eye over the environment, rather than accept my offer to be a teacher at my New York school should be evidence enough that I am no longer the puppet-master you once knew. She has *always* been a strong-willed young woman, and will *continue* to be so—I would not wish her to be otherwise." The mutant overlord paused. "As for your other former students . . ." He shrugged. "Well, Summers has always been a tad sycophantic when it comes to following powerful leaders, wouldn't you agree?" He pressed on, not giving the Professor the opportunity to answer the question. "After all, considering the level of devotion he'd shown you in the past, given the fact that he hung on every syllable you uttered with the intensity of an acolyte—"

He stopped suddenly, a slow, easy smile coming to his lips. "No, not an acolyte. More like a son forever seeking approval from his father, risking all, even his very life, for just a few words of encouragement." He nodded, clearly pleased with the comparison. "I must admit, Charles, you broke him in quite well." The smile broadened. "You've broken *all* of them in quite well. Sons and daughters of the atom, trained to sacrifice themselves for the glory of their species, rather than allow the dreams of one man to die." An eyebrow rose in an inquisitive fashion. "Sounds familiar, does it not?" He snorted. "And you dare call *me* a villain. Wouldn't you say that's a case of the pot calling the kettle 'black'?"

"That's not true!" Xavier snapped, slamming his fists down on the canopy of his chair. He was surprised—and troubled—at the fury in his voice. This was not the time to allow Magneto to goad him into some senseless argument. There were more important matters.

Lensherr chuckled. "My, how quick we are to defend our actions, especially when we know we are in the wrong!" He reached out to consolingly pat Xavier on the shoulder. "Don't worry, Charles—I won't tell a soul."

The Professor glared at him.

"Now, then, Charles," Lensherr continued, "I'm quite certain you're burning with curiosity about why I brought you here, and what my plans for you might be. For the moment, all I will say is that there is a reason for everything I do—even something as simple as . . . *this.*"

The Cube flared again—a modest glow this time, rather than a full-bore burst of light—and a warm, tingling sensation ran through the Professor's body. The feeling of pins and needles pricking his flesh intensified along the base of his spinal cord; it felt as though a strong electrical current was being run through it. Xavier screwed his eyes tightly shut and gritted his teeth against the pain, forcing himself not to cry out. He couldn't help but wonder if his former friend had brought him all this way just to kill him after proudly showing off one of his accomplishments—such behavior would not be out of character for Magneto.

But then the big toe on his right foot suddenly twitched. Xavier gasped.

His legs. He could feel his legs.

Startled, he looked to his old friend. "Erik, what—"

The hood of the hoverchair swung upward as if on its own— another Cube effort. Xavier reached down to rub his legs, to ease the mild burning sensation running up and down the atrophied limbs as damaged nerves repaired themselves and weakened tissue strengthened. Tentatively, he tried raising his left leg, and couldn't help but smile as it responded to his mental command.

"Come, Charles—walk with me," Lensherr said. "There are some people here I would like you to meet. By the time we reach the village, we should be just in time for breakfast." Not waiting for a reply, the mutant overlord turned on his heel and began making his way down toward the village.

Slowly, the Professor eased out of the chair. His legs trembled slightly, the muscles taking their time becoming acclimated to receiving orders from the brain again. First one foot touched the rich soil; then the other. Gripping the edges of the chair, he pushed up with his arms, allowing them to handle the weight of his body until he felt that his restored limbs could support it. The chair suddenly shifted forward, and he *just* managed to keep himself from falling face-first onto the rich soil. He chuckled softly, reveling in every tremor that ran through his body as he took his first steps onto the surface of this new world.

It was a trick—he knew that the moment he realized what was happening. Tattered friendship aside, there had been no reason for Erik to repair his damaged nerves—unless he had an ulterior motive. The Professor had a feeling he knew what it was: to entice him into letting Lensherr retain ownership of the Cube. If Xavier couldn't be convinced to side with him through philosophical debates or threats, then what better temptation to win him over than by giving him back the use of his legs?

But *why* Magneto was going to all this trouble—*that* was the maddening question gnawing at Charles' thoughts. Why not simply destroy him with the Cube and be done with him, instead of trying to continually demonstrate what good it could do?

Taking small, hesitant steps, Xavier slowly made his way down the hillside, determined to obtain the answers he sought.

According to Lensherr, Araouane's population had dwindled to a mere handful of inhabitants following the long periods of drought; when he lived here, there had been no more than twenty-five or thirty families. Now, more than three thousand people called the village their home. What had once been a sand-covered ghost town was now a thriving—and growing—city on the edge of Paradise.

As they strolled through the busy streets, Lensherr would stop and point at some shop where he knew the owner, or a structure—like the mosque—that had originally been eaten away by the corrosive sands, until he had restored it to its former glory. For all the terrible powers at his command, the Master of the World carried on like a tourist on holiday, speaking loudly and quickly as something caught his attention, marveling at something the villagers clearly considered quite commonplace, before moving onto the next attraction.

"So, what is your opinion, Charles?" Lensherr finally asked.

"Of what?"

Lensherr waved his arms around, gesturing at their surroundings. "Of the village, of course!"

Xavier glanced at the smiling faces of the bustling crowds around them, at the fertile soil beneath their feet, at the clear sky above. "It's very nice."

Lensherr laughed—the first genuine laugh that Xavier had heard since being brought before him at the castle. "You have *always* been a master of understatement, Charles! I think that that is one of your most charming—and oftentimes frustrating—qualities. *Nothing* seems to faze you."

The Professor smiled, but remained silent as they continued their walk. After a few minutes, they came to an intersection. The mutant overlord paused a moment, then set off down a connecting street, the Professor close behind.

"Tell me something, Erik," Xavier finally said. "What was it that changed your views toward humanity? Why did you give up your grand scheme for making *Homo superior* the dominant species?"

"I never gave it up, Charles," Lensherr replied. "I simply came to the realization that perhaps that vision of the world was far too narrow in its scope."

Xavier's eyebrows rose. "Really."

"Surprised that I've actually shown signs of emotional growth, Charles? You shouldn't be—you've known me long enough." Lensherr smiled. "If I could find the wherewithal to run your school and lead your churlish students into battle without turning against them, then the notion of me controlling the world with a velvet glove instead of an iron fist shouldn't be *that* hard to believe."

Xavier frowned. "Still, it didn't take all that long for you to revert to your old ways, once you had left the school."

Lensherr shrugged. "We are who we are, Charles. At the time, lashing out in anger seemed like the best approach to dealing with the problem of hatred toward our kind."

"And yet, you eventually moved beyond that belief . . ." Xavier said, encouraging his old friend to explain his actions.

"It was this village," Lensherr began slowly, his voice once again taking on an uncharacteristic softness. "I lived here for a time, while von Doom held the Cube. A hellish place—I have already told you it used to be an oasis, thriving with life, but the sands eventually swept across it, killing almost everything . . . except the people." He smiled as a boy and girl no older than nine or ten years ran across their path, giggling merrily at the sight of the two strangely-garbed men. "There were no mutants among them; they'd never even heard the word before I arrived. They merely accepted me for what I was. I made friends with them, over time. They hid me from von Doom's superpowered bloodhounds, shared their food, taught me their language, and, for all their acts of kindness, they asked for nothing in return."

He suddenly stopped before one of the mud-brick buildings. On a grass-covered lawn fairly bursting with wild flowers, a little girl, three or four years old, sat playing with a hand-crafted doll, its dress as bright and colorful as the girl's. Eyes sparkling with glee, she talked to the doll as though it were her own child, gently brushing its hair with her hand while cooing into its ear.

From the corner of his eye, the Professor quietly observed Magneto's actions. The white-haired mutant was positively beaming, his attention completely focused on the youngster. It appeared he understood everything she was saying.

As the two men continued watching, a door on the side of the modest home opened, and a tall, stately woman in her thirties emerged. There was a slight bounce to her steps as she walked toward the child, calling out to her as she approached.

"Do you see that woman, Charles?" Lensherr asked. "And the little girl?" Xavier nodded. "The mother's name is Abena Metou; her daughter's is Jnanbarka. On von Doom's world, Abena was one of three 'sandwomen' whose livelihood was sweeping the sand that accumulated at the doors of the villagers' homes during the night. It was a foolish notion, that she could prevent the vast

Sahara from one day swallowing her village beneath its relentless silicon waves; a battle she was destined to lose, even before she first picked up a broom." A trace of a smile played at the corners of his mouth. "That knowledge did nothing to deter her, though—in fact, it made her more determined than ever to continue fighting. As she often explained to me, she was doing it not for herself, but for her daughter. A day battling the sands meant food on the table."

Lensherr paused. "It was the child's eyes that haunted me, even when I slept—those dull, lifeless eyes that had seen nothing but death and decay and starvation. I had seen eyes like those before—in Auschwitz, after my parents were murdered. They stared back at me every time I looked at my reflection in a puddle of muddy rainwater." For the briefest of moments, the fearful eyes of a child of the Holocaust glittered in the blue-gray depths of his pupils. The mutant overlord shuddered slightly. "Even now, I cannot rid my mind of that image."

He fell silent for a moment, his gaze fixed on a spot on the ground. "I once swore that no other living being would suffer the kind of atrocities I had endured at the hands of the Nazis. And after looking into that child's eyes, it was as though a caul had been lifted from my own. For so long, I had boasted of the superiority of my race, demanded that it should be recognized as the dominant species, looked down my nose at those who so often opposed my actions, as though they were beneath me." Lensherr slowly shook his head. "I was acting no better than the Nazis. And though, in my heart, I knew I was wrong, my blinding hatred toward humanity for all it had done to our kind kept me from facing the truth. Terror tactics; threats of nuclear Armageddon; warring against the nations of the world—there had to be *another* way, a far more humane way, for me to force mankind to improve this planet for all people. And once the Cube was in my hands, I knew what had to be done . . ."

Xavier shook his head. "You may have used the Cube to better the world, Erik, but it was only accomplished by tinkering with the minds of six billion people—including my students. Call it whatever you like, convince yourself that you have changed your ways, argue night and day that the 'dream' you placed in their minds was for their own good, but the bottom line is that you are *still* Magneto. And no matter how noble your intentions might be, in the back of your mind, you never stopped pursuing your *true* dream: the final, lasting defeat over my X-Men, and the subjugation of the human race." He sneered. "Well, congratulations, Erik—you've finally gotten your wish."

"No, Charles," Lensherr insisted. "Don't you see? By using the Cube, I have brought *peace* to the world. There are no children starving, no families living in poverty, no mutants who feel they must hide their marvelous gifts from the world to avoid being ridiculed. *This* is the Earth as we always dreamed it should be." He shook his head. "I'm sorry, Charles, but there is nothing you can say or do that will change my mind—what I've done here is *right,* and you know it."

"No, old friend—it is wrong, and *you* know it, though you refuse to acknowledge your mistakes. And mark my words, I *will* find a way to make you see the truth and end this madness," Xavier said, jaw set in determination. "God help me, Erik, I will do *whatever* it takes to set things right. I must, if countless universes are to be saved."

Lensherr raised an amused eyebrow. "Would you *kill* me, then, Charles, to complete your mission? *You,* who once defended me before the World Court for my alleged 'crimes against humanity'? Are you *that* set on destroying all the good I have done?"

Xavier lowered his gaze. "I . . . hope it will not come to that, Erik," he said softly. "But this falsehood, this fantasy world you have created, cannot be allowed to continue. I appreciate your efforts, my friend, but there is far more at risk here than a clash of philosophical differences between two visionaries." He raised his head, then, and stared heatedly at the mutant overlord. "Do not force me to choose between sacrificing billions of lives for a dream, and sacrificing *your* life so those billions can go on living. I assure you, you would not like my decision."

Lensherr pursed his lips. "Interesting. I must say, this is a side of you I don't think I've ever seen before. It's a refreshing change— over the years, I'd grown exceedingly tired of hearing the same soporific speeches from you about the abuses of power." He smiled, and gestured toward the mother and child. "Now, come—the time for empty threats and useless posturing is over; I want you to meet my friends. And once we have eaten, I think you'll be in a far more appreciative mood for the other wonders I wish to share with you ... before we get to the heart of the matter. "

And with that, he strode away, calling out what seemed to be a greeting to the woman in her native tongue.

Left standing in the street, Charles Xavier pondered what his old friend had meant by his last words. "The heart of the matter." Words that could mean just about anything, from a peaceful resolution to their Cube-related problems ... to the destruction of the world itself.

17

H E WAS surprised when they returned from their travels, not to the sprawling Loire Valley castle, but to an opulent apartment in the center of Paris.

In the space of a few hours, Charles Xavier and Erik Lensherr had traveled across the globe, each stopping point along the way used to illustrate how Magneto had used the Cube to better the world and its peoples. The trip had also been used to put the Professor's mind at ease about the well-being of the other members of the X-Men—the ones who were *not* guests staying at the mutant overlord's castle.

After Ororo had joined them for breakfast in Araouane, the two men had continued their journey. First they visited the Ust-Ordynski Collective Farm in Siberia, where they had been greeted by Piotr Rasputin. In the "real" world, he was the armored X-Man called Colossus; here, though, he was just a simple Russian farmer, as he had been before Xavier had recruited him. Then it was on to Seattle, Washington, the home of Hank McCoy—the blue-furred Beast—who worked for a Seattle-based genetics laboratory. The Cajun-born Gambit, mysterious as always, could not be found in New Orleans, though there were rumors he now ran the notorious Thieves Guild. Bobby Drake, who went by the codename "Iceman" because of his frigid powers, was the manager of a Miami hockey team. From Florida, they crossed up the East Coast to visit the Holocaust Museum in Washington, D.C., where the current Assistant Director was a young woman named Kathryn Pryde; as an X-Man, she had been called Shadowcat, possessing the ability to shift slightly out of sync with her surroundings, which allowed her body to phase through solid objects. Then it was on to the Lensherr Institute on Ellis Island, followed by a brief inspection of the grounds of what had been the Professor's school (now a summer camp for troubled teenage mutants) in Westchester County, to prove to Xavier that a generation of "genetically gifted" soldiers were not being trained to help Magneto. They moved on to Glenfiddich, Scotland, to have a chat with Sean Cassidy—formerly the mutant named Banshee, because of the sonic cry he could emit—and his wife. To Xavier's deep regret, that woman had turned out to be his former love, Moira MacTaggert. Finally, their exhausting session of globe-hopping had ended in Lensherr's Parisian apartment.

As much as Xavier hated to admit it, all his X-Men had appeared to be hale and hearty, content with their new lives, and much happier than the Professor could ever remember seeing them while they had been under his tutelage. Yet, knowing that Magneto had influenced their minds with the Cube, making them forget Xavier's part in their lives, it was difficult to gauge how much of their happiness was heartfelt—and how much had been forced upon them.

Now, resting his weary legs as he sat in his hoverchair, the Professor contemplated Magneto's next move.

The Cube had been put back into its protective adamantium casing, behind a highly expensive Matisse original. Xavier had been left alone in the salon, while Lensherr had gone into one of the other adjoining rooms. From the sounds of clattering dishes and running water, it appeared Erik was . . . making tea? Xavier raised an eyebrow in mild surprise and chuckled, amused by the thought of a domesticated Magneto bustling about the kitchen.

Family life apparently *had* had a calming effect on his life—one more wondrous change brought about by the Cosmic Cube, it seemed.

The door to the kitchen opened, and Lensherr exited, a silver tray containing a large silver tea pot, cups, saucers, and milk and sugar dispensers hovering before him. Using his magnetic powers, he set the tray down on a table in front of the wall-mounted flatscreen television.

"I apologize for the lack of biscuits," Lensherr said, "but since my family and I are supposed to be vacationing at the castle for the next few weeks, the house here was closed, so no shopping has been done." He poured tea into two China cups, handing one to the Professor. "Now, where were we?"

Xavier took the proffered beverage, and sniffed at the vapors rising from the heated brown liquid. Earl Grey—his favorite. "Well, *I* was asking you to come to your senses and surrender the Cube willingly, and *you* were about to explain the real purpose for our travels today. And why you decided to restore my legs."

"Why *not* restore your legs?" Lensherr countered. "You weren't always a paraplegic, Charles. Is it wrong to want to be able to face an old friend eye-to-eye, rather than constantly have to look down at him? I thought I was doing you a favor." He tried to look hurt by the Professor's suspicions, but he could only manage a deeply wrinkled scowl.

"Favors always come with a price," Xavier said, a dark tone to his voice. "Giving me back the use of my legs at the cost of countless lives is too high a price to pay, no matter *how* tempting the offer."

The mutant overlord smiled. "You have been and still are a difficult man to bargain with, Charles."

"And one not easily distracted from obtaining answers to his questions," Xavier replied, a bit forcefully. "Now, the reason you wanted to show me all you've done with the world, why it seemed so important to you for me to meet your daughter, is because..."

"Because I am dying, Charles," Lensherr said, matter-of-factly.

Xavier started. It suddenly felt as though all the air had been driven from his lungs. "Erik . . ." he began.

Lensherr motioned him to silence with a wave of his hand. "Please, Charles—no mawkish words of sympathy. You and I have seen our share of death over the years; mine is just one more among millions that pass each year. Besides, I was well advanced in my years *before* the Cube began stealing away what few years remained to me. Even now, I can feel the strength ebbing from my body—in a month, perhaps less, there would be nothing left of me to sustain this world, this dream. But from what you keep telling me, the planet does not even *have* a month left to live."

"Yes," the Professor replied.

Lensherr nodded. "And that is why I want you to take the Cube."

His vigilance had finally been rewarded.

Slumped in an armchair just one floor below the two men, the Controller suddenly snapped awake from a light slumber. He'd been sitting in this very chair, in this third floor parlor, since the wee hours of the morning, when he and Leonard had forced their way in through a garden entrance at the rear of the building. A careful search of all five floors and basement had confirmed the Cube's absence, but the Controller could still feel the lingering presence of its addictive power; it hung in the air, seeped into the walls, floors, furnishings.

It was different, though. He'd known something was wrong with this version of the device almost from the moment he and Leonard had arrived on Earth, but here, in the heart of Magneto's fantasy world, that feeling was even stronger.

Normally, the energy field generated by a Cube gave off a comfortable, even calming, buzz that tingled the skin and sent a pleasant chill up the spine. But the cosmic forces that pulsed from this particular device felt more like sharp pricks that jangled the nerves and caused his joints to ache. It was not a sensation that could be experienced by someone who had never held a Cosmic Cube; only a select few, like the Controller, had ever had the privilege.

And then there was the double vision. Again, it was something undetectable to the eyes of the uninitiated, but having been the possessor of quite a number of the devices over the years, the Controller knew what to look for in a restructured world. And when he closely examined his surroundings on *this* world, there seemed to be a soft focus to everything around him, except for Leonard. It was as though he were staring at a three-dimensional picture without the special glasses required to combine the two separate images in order to create the illusion of depth.

It gave him a mild headache.

Stiff joints, headaches, and blurred eyesight had been quickly forgotten, however, the instant he realized that the Cube had returned. Its song seemed to fill the air around him, and his pulse quickened, heart beating in time to the music only he could hear. He'd waited so long—too long—for this moment.

And now, at last, he could answer the Cube's siren call.

He slowly rose to his feet, tapping Leonard on the leg to rouse him from his sleep. The youth, who lay sprawled across a flower-patterned sofa nearby, started to mumble a response—only to come fully awake as the Controller gripped his throat with one gloved hand to cut off his air, while the other clamped down tightly over his mouth to silence him.

"Not a sound, my little mouse," the Controller hissed through gritted teeth, his face mere inches from his assistant's, "or it shall be the last you ever make. I will *not* be denied my prize because of some drowsy imbecile mistaking me for his mother. Do you understand?"

Leonard quickly nodded his understanding, and the Controller released his grip. The youth shakily rose to his feet, rubbing his sore throat as he tried to catch his breath. His master studied his movements for a few moments, making certain that his blond-haired follower wasn't going to stumble into the furniture, then moved on cat's feet across the room. He paused at the entrance to the third floor hallway, peering around the molding to steal a glance at the staircase just outside. The hall was empty, but he could hear the sound of voices drifting down from the next floor. One he immediately identified as Magneto's; the other he didn't recognize, but from the general tone of the conversation, the speaker appeared to be a friend of Lensherr's.

He turned to find Leonard standing beside him. Clearly, the youth understood the need for stealth; the Controller hadn't even heard him draw near. Leonard looked to his superior for instructions, but wisely remained silent. The Controller held up his hand, signaling for him to remain here. Leonard nodded, and stepped back into the shadows of the darkened room.

Reaching around to the back of the wide black belt he wore around the waist of his dark-green uniform, the Controller withdrew a six-inch-long blade attached to a handle made of hard, black plastic; it slid noiselessly from its leather sheath. The blade was of a special design, because it wasn't made of metal, but rather sharpened obsidian—when dealing with a man who called himself "The Master of Magnetism," the last thing a potential assassin needed was a metal-based weapon that could be turned against him.

Keeping close to the floor, the Controller stepped into the hallway, then quietly crossed to the staircase. He could hear one of the men moving about the room on the next floor, his booted footsteps muffled slightly by thick carpeting. As long as they kept talking, the Controller considered, it should be child's play to get within striking distance well before they ever became aware of his presence; and by then, of course, it would be too late for them to do anything—but die.

Dagger at the ready, the Controller began moving up the stairs. A malevolent smile twisting his mangled lips, he was already imaging the shocked expression that would be etched on Magneto's features in his last moments before death claimed him, as he gazed upon the face of the man who had killed him—and his dream.

* * *

Xavier cocked his head to one side, unable to believe what he had just heard. "Would you mind repeating that, Erik? I think the neural inhibitor your followers fitted me with is affecting my hearing." He rubbed the base of his spine, feeling the lumpy shape of the device that kept him from using his telepathic abilities.

Lensherr grunted. "You understood me quite well, Charles. It's your *telepathic abilities* that have been hampered, *not* your hearing."

Xavier raised an inquisitive eyebrow. "You're going to hand the Cosmic Cube to me."

Lensherr nodded.

"Without any histrionics? Without any fighting?"

"Yes."

"No death threats? No tricks? No booby traps designed to scatter my atoms across the cosmos once I touch it?"

"None whatsoever."

The Professor eyed the mutant overlord suspiciously. "You're going to give it to me—just like that?"

A wisp of a smile played at the corners of the mutant overlord's mouth. "Now, Charles, what sort of super-villain would I be if there wasn't *some* requirement for my assistance in helping you reach the end of your great and perilous quest? After all, you *did* say so yourself: Favors *always* come with a price."

The Professor nodded. "Yes. How silly of me to think otherwise. What did you have in mind?"

Lensherr shrugged. "A simple request—one I am *certain* you will not hesitate to accept, given your altruistic nature. *And* your word, as a man of honor, that you will carry it out. Do we have an agreement?"

A gentle smile came to Xavier's lips. "Now, Erik, what sort of leader would I be if I blindly agreed to offers made by a man who refers to himself as a 'super-vil—' "

"It's Anya," Lensherr interjected, an unmistakable trace of desperation in his voice. "I want her to live."

The Professor tilted his head to one side, confused by the statement. "I'm not certain I understand what you're asking of me."

"I want you to *promise me,* Charles," Lensherr insisted. "Give me your *word* that, no matter what may happen once I have turned the Cube over to you, you *will* preserve and protect my daughter's life."

Xavier's eyes widened in surprise. Out of all the favors he'd imagine Magneto would ask of him, *this* request had been the farthest from his mind.

"Erik, I . . ." he began slowly. "I'm not certain I can *make* such a promise. There's a risk that anything remaining from this world—even Anya—might exacerbate the situation, might cause irreparable damage to the omniverse—"

"*Damn you, Xavier!*" the mutant overlord bellowed. "Are you so dedicated to your view of what must be that you would destroy all I have done—the dream we *both* hold dear—that you would sacrifice the one thing that has finally healed my soul?"

The Professor's gaze lowered. It was hard enough saying words even *he* didn't want to say without having to look his old friend in the eye.

"Erik, you must believe me," he said softly. "I wish there *was* another way to restore the cosmic balance, some way to keep even a small portion of the wonders you've created . . . but there *isn't.*" Slowly, he raised his head. "I'm sorry," he whispered, "but *no* trace of this world can remain, if the omniverse is to survive."

Xavier steeled himself for the inevitable. He waited for his oldest friend—his oldest enemy—to lash out in anger, using either his magnetic powers or the cosmic energies of the Cube to wipe him from existence. Waited for the killing blow he knew would come—and prayed silently that his death would be a quick one.

But then, slowly, the lightning faded from Lensherr's eyes. His shoulders sagged, and the feral snarl into which his mouth had seemed permanently set just a moment ago faded into a deeply furrowed frown. The transformation was startling—gone was the Master of the World, the master of the Cosmic Cube, the terrifying mutant overlord called Magneto; in his place stood a tired, beaten old man.

Lensherr sighed, and his entire body shuddered from the effort. Wordlessly, he turned from the Professor, and walked over to a window. He stood there, silently watching the lights of the city, for a number of minutes. Xavier remained where he was, not sure what to do next. Magneto's sudden fit of depression had taken him by surprise, but he knew that, if he pushed too hard about the dangers posed by the Cube, the ennui that gripped the scarlet-clad villain could quickly become a murderous rage.

"I thought, perhaps, you would act differently about this, Charles," Lensherr finally said, his voice barely above a whisper. "Threatening me with harm, as you did last night—such words come as no surprise. You and I have had similar exchanges, far too many to count... although it has usually been *my* role in those little dramas to be the one who delivers such ominous declarations, and you and your students the ones facing extermination. Heaven knows I've come close enough to killing all of you on a number of occasions, so I can understand your reluctance to help me on *any* level.

"But Anya is... not like you or I. She... her life has never become a vicious circle of hatred and prejudice and despair. She's never experienced the horrors of a cruel, fearful world; never had her innocence savagely stripped away; never been torn from her mother's arms, knowing she will never see her parents alive again." He turned from the window, a haunted look darkening his blue-gray eyes. "You were my last hope, Charles—the last chance to preserve a part of my legacy. Anya was—*is*—the one truly *good* thing I've ever done in my life. Why should she be made to suffer for the sins of her father? "

"Please, Erik..." Xavier said quietly. "You're not making this decision any easier—"

"*It's not* supposed *to be easy, damn you!*" Lensherr roared. He pointed an accusatory finger at the Professor. "You keep talking of the lives of countless billions threatened by the Cube's power—

faceless billions you don't even know, who shall never know you, and to whom you owe nothing! But you've *met* Anya, you've *seen* how much she means to me. You *know* the guilt I've had to live with, the emptiness in my soul I've felt since the day she died."

Xavier nodded in agreement, but said nothing.

"Then, *why*, Charles?" Lensherr demanded, stepping toward him. "*Why* can't you make this one exception?" He gestured in the direction of the Cube, hidden behind the framed painting on the other side of the room. "I'm going to die soon—the dream will follow me into oblivion once I have drawn my last breath. I'm willing to accept that fact, willing to turn the Cube over to you now, *before* that happens, while there's still time to preserve a tiny piece of it. Why, then, can't you find it in your heart to do this one thing for me? For *us?* Can you only see Anya as some sort of example of the singleminded goals I once pursued, instead of the embodiment of all the good I have achieved?"

Lensherr sighed. "We were friends, you and I, long before our philosophical differences caused us to drift apart . . ." His voice trailed off, and he stood silently, eyes closed. His hands clenched into tight fists, and a slight tremor ran through his body. It looked as though he was fighting a battle with himself, forcing his next words through stiffened lips: "I have never been one to beg, Charles . . . "

"Erik, listen to me," Xavier replied. "It's not that I don't *want* to help you, but with the very fabric of reality unraveling around us, even a small piece of your fantasy-realm might prevent us from reversing the destruction caused by the Cube. If there *was* some way for me to protect Anya, I would not hesitate to take advantage of it." He shook his head sadly. "It's true that we've had our differences over the years, but I would *never* seek to cause you misery by striking at your family—you *know* that."

The mutant overlord opened his mouth, as though to argue the point, then stopped. He frowned, then gently nodded his head. "Yes. Yes, I do."

Lensherr inhaled deeply, slowly releasing the breath through his nostrils. "All right, Charles, all right," he said wearily. "You win. I have made my arguments, and you remain unmoved." He lowered himself onto a nearby sedan and closed his eyes, resting his head against the cushions. "Nevertheless, I gave you my word, and I shall honor that promise." He waved a hand at the large oil painting on the far side of the room, behind which the Cube lay hidden. "Take the damnable device—and may God have pity on your miserable soul for what you do with it."

The heated comment was like a physical slap to the Professor's face, and he flinched from the blow. Ignoring the Cube, he remained seated, staring at the colorfully-garbed man lying before him. It was a sobering sight for Charles—he couldn't remember the last time he'd seen Erik look so vulnerable. *Had* he ever seen him look this vulnerable? The man had been a powerhouse for as long as Xavier had known him—a force of nature that not even death itself had been able to stop. "Vulnerable" had never been a word the Professor would have ever used to describe his former friend. But now . . . now, though, he looked drained—of energy, of life, of the will to live. Fantasy though she might be, Anya's presence in Lensherr's life had greatly affected him, and having at last come to the realization that he could do nothing to save her . . .

The weight of his decision sat heavily upon Xavier's shoulders . . . and he hated himself for the choice he had been forced to make. Knowing that he was right, that there had been no other conclusion to reach given the severity of the situation, did nothing to ease the burden.

"Tell me, Charles," Lensherr suddenly asked, his eyes still closed, "are you familiar with the writings of Christopher Dawson?"

"Not as much as I would like," Xavier admitted.

The mutant overlord nodded, as though in understanding. "He was a British cultural historian and educational theorist, born at the turn of the twentieth century. A gifted, insightful man—you might even consider him a visionary. As Hitler's jackbooted animals marched across Europe, as my family and I were rotting away in that squalid hellhole called Auschwitz, Dawson saw the direction in which the world was heading. There is a line in his *Judgment of the Nations* that proves how well he understood the dark days ahead—a line that, based upon your responses this day, I consider all too appropriate for this occasion: 'As soon as men decide that all means are permitted to fight evil, then their good becomes indistinguishable from the evil that they set out to destroy.' "

Lensherr opened his eyes, and gazed evenly at his old friend. "How does it feel, Charles—being the *villain* this time?"

For perhaps the first time in his life, Charles Xavier could think of nothing to say.

18

I T WAS becoming a nightmare from which she seemed unable
to awaken.

As she gazed down at the chessboard that floated before
her, Roma felt a cold weight settle over her soul. In the center of
the black onyx and white ivory squares were two white pieces:
miniature representations of Charles Xavier and Elisabeth Braddock. The Professor—the king—sat in his hoverchair, his finely de-
tailed features set in an expression of fierce determination. Beside
him, the female warrior called Psylocke—one of the knights—was
garbed in her traditional costume; one gloved hand was tightly
gripping the hilt of a *katana*. Roma stared at them despondently,
for they were the *only* white pieces on the board. Surrounding
them were a collection of black pieces, posed menacingly as if to
strike: Magneto, Doctor Doom, and the X-Men who had traveled
to Earth, only to fall victim to the very madness they'd tried to
end: Phoenix. Cyclops. Nightcrawler. Rogue. Wolverine. For some
reason, she could not locate the piece representing the last member
of the team: Gambit. Its absence only served to increase the feelings of anxiety that plagued her thoughts.

Much to her surprise, however, there was one other black piece on the board—one she couldn't identify; one she hadn't placed. Its features were indistinct, half-formed, and it stood off to the side, as though waiting for . . . what?

Roma picked up the Psylocke piece and studied it in the dim, gloomy lighting of the throneroom. It had been this figurine that had given her the first inkling of serious trouble in the omniverse. While Elisabeth had been under the controlling influence of von Doom during the time he'd held the Cube, she had come to believe that she was not a mutant, or even a member of the X-Men, but rather a cabaret singer. As Roma now knew, that second life actually belonged to an alternate version of the lavender-tressed telepath, who lived on a von Doom-controlled alternate Earth. But the Cube's restructuring of Elisabeth's psyche had not just changed the X-Man; it had caused her chess piece to morph, from warrior to chanteuse and back again. That peculiar instability had repaired itself, it seemed, the moment Psylocke materialized within the walls of the citadel.

Frowning, Roma wished Merlyn had bothered to explain why the board and its pieces seemed to know more about what was going on in the omniverse than the Guardian who protected it. It could be most frustrating at times.

Behind her, the main doors to the chamber opened slightly, and a figure dressed in a flowing white gown slipped inside. From the outside corridor came the brief sounds of shouting and feet scuffling, but they were sharply cut off by the closing of the doors.

"Did you grow tired of waiting, Saturnyne?" Roma asked, putting just enough emphasis in the question to make it clear her lieutenant shouldn't make a habit of disobeying her orders.

"Forgive my impertinence, m'lady," the Majestrix said, "but you *did* summon me earlier, and—" she glanced over her shoulder "—I have had my fill of arrogant children for one day."

A faint smile crossed Roma's lips. "I do so wish that you and Captain Alecto would reconcile your differences, Saturnyne."

"If m'lady commands it . . ." Saturnyne replied, ". . . although I am certain you have more important things on your mind than how I interact with the staff."

Roma nodded and sighed. "Yes. After much soul-searching, I have made my final decision—the crystal must be destroyed *now*. Charles Xavier and Elisabeth Braddock have had more than enough time to reverse the Cosmic Cube's effects—" she gestured toward the darkened scrying glass "—and yet the situation remains unchanged."

Her Whyness shrugged. "If you think that's best, m'lady."

Roma paused, and glanced at her trusted aide. For someone who had so eagerly campaigned for her to end the threat posed by the Cube, Saturnyne seemed strangely unconcerned about so grave a matter. Perhaps she was just being polite, not wishing to appear disrespectful now that Roma had at last come over to her way of thinking. Perhaps she no longer cared. Perhaps—

The Guardian shook her head. There had been enough contemplation on her part; now was the time to take action.

"Come, Saturnyne," she said, and gestured toward the collection of life crystals. "Let us put an end to this madness." She moved across the transept, heading for the platform, with the heavy tread of someone being led to their execution.

And then the main doors burst open, and Captain Alecto came flying into the throneroom.

He crashed down onto the cold, stone floor and bounced twice before coming to rest in the center of the main aisle. A low moan escaped his lips, and he made a feeble attempt to rise, only to sink back down and lie still.

As the Supreme Guardian stared in disbelief at the sight of her finest warrior lying broken and bloodied, virtually at her feet, his attacker entered the throneroom. Candlelight gleamed off the parts of his armor that were not concealed beneath dark-green cloth. Behind a facemask of gleaming metal, dark-brown eyes glared at her in triumph.

"Von Doom!" Roma snapped angrily, lips pulled back in an uncharacteristic snarl. "You *dare* enter my chamber in so bold a manner, after all the chaos you have unleashed upon the omniverse?"

The dictator strode across the vast room, boot heels ringing sharply against the flagstones that lined the floor. "Doom dares much, woman, when the prize he seeks is within his grasp!"

"Prize?" Roma's eyebrows rose in an inquisitive fashion. Did that mean he had come to try and depose her? That he was challenging a Guardian of the Ominverse—a celestial being with limitless power—for possession of the throne? Could he truly be that arrogant, that foolish, as to think he stood a chance against her in battle?

It was utter nonsense, and she had no time to waste on a power-hungry madman suffering from delusions of grandeur—especially when she had far more important matters to attend to, like trying to repair all the damage he had caused to reality with his scientific blundering. But if it was power von Doom craved, Roma decided, then let him have his fill of it—at the center of the vortex. Let him experience the terrifying forces of Creation, and know what it means to anger the protectress of the omniverse—before the temporal and spatial currents tear him apart. She raised her hands, prepared to rid herself of him once and for all.

Her intended attack was cut short, however, as a sharp, unfamiliar sensation exploded across the back of her head. She staggered forward, surprised at having temporarily lost her sense of balance. It took her a moment to recognize what she was experiencing.

Physical pain. She couldn't remember the last time she had felt it, but she definitely recalled its unpleasantness. Was the dull ache at the base of her skull *supposed* to be this intense? Did it have any connection to the black spots that danced before her eyes, making it difficult to see?

She'd seen how the limitations of the flesh had affected Merlyn, when one of his cosmic chess matches had gone wrong—his hands had been burned while he protected a piece from harm. So she knew that, immortal though she might be, her unusual longevity did not guarantee protection from injury. But still . . .

Dazed, she turned to face her attacker, and was shocked to

discover it was her dearest friend and confidante. The Majestrix had unbuckled the heavy belt she always wore around her waist and now held it in two hands, wielding it like a club. Roma noticed the gleaming jewel in its center was speckled with drops of blood. Placing a hand on the back of her head, the Guardian was surprised to find her scalp was disturbingly moist and tacky.

"S-Saturnyne?" she stammered. "But, why . . . ?" Her voice suddenly trailed off, as she saw the mad gleam in the woman's visible eye—and then she *knew*. This wasn't her friend, but an imposter. Yet, the only alternate version of her trusted aide who could be so bold as to openly confront a Guardian of the Omniverse would be . . .

"No . . ." she whispered hoarsely.

Sat-yr-nin grinned broadly. "Oh, *yes* . . ."

Any other thoughts Roma might have been about to express were lost in a spasm of incredible pain, as a burst of charged particles struck her in the back, spinning her around before roughly slamming her to the floor.

"I-impossible . . ." the Guardian said through gritted teeth as the energy discharge continued to burn its way into her brain's pain centers, overwhelming them. "N-no w-weapon can function inside the c-citadel . . ." She struggled to regain her feet, but could only succeed in balancing on one knee.

"So I understand," von Doom replied coolly. "But then, this is *not* a weapon—it's one of the medical devices you used to separate me from my elderly doppelganger, modified for my armor." He fired again, and Roma stiffened, mouth agape, head snapped back, eyes wide as saucers. The pain this time was so intense she was unable to make a sound.

And then another Roma suddenly peeled away from her body, and dropped to the floor, unconscious.

Von Doom stepped forward, and gazed down at the prostrate Guardian and her insensate twin. The second woman looked exactly the same as her "sister," but this one's hair was cut short, the ends frosted a cool pink color, and her clothing consisted of leather pants and boots, and a cut-off T-shirt emblazoned with the word MEGADEATH, whatever that meant. Her left ear was punctured with a dozen or more metal studs; another two pierced her left nostril.

"Interesting," the dictator commented, like a scientist who's discovered a new species of bug. "The beam has a different effect on you than it did on that bothersome little man."

Roma found she didn't have the strength to ask who he was talking about. It was taking all she had just to remain conscious.

"I think our Guardian truly is only as good as the sum of her parts," Sat-yr-nin quipped. "And she's just lost one of them." She put a hand over her mouth and giggled, amused by her little joke.

Von Doom stared heatedly at the Mastrex, but then a look came over his eyes that seemed to indicate he was giving serious consideration to her passing comment. "That *does* make sense, if one considers the situation multidimensionally," he said slowly. "If the Guardian protects all realities, and there exists an alternate version of her in each of them, then it would stand to reason that her powers are derived, not from this citadel, but from the collection of all variations in one body." He glanced from one version to the other. "Fascinating. I wonder exactly how many there are . . ."

"You must . . . stop this . . . madness . . ." Roma weakly demanded of the tyrant. "You have . . . no idea . . . what harm you are . . . doing . . ."

Von Doom snorted, and pointed to her duplicate. "The only harm, woman, is to *you,* for you are all that stands between Doom and his ascendency to the throne. The X-Men are either prisoners of Magneto, or are dead. Your lieutenant has been sealed away until I have decided upon her execution date, and your guards have been . . . incapacitated. You have no allies here. And once *you* have fallen, there will be *no one* to stop Doom from taking up the mantle as the new Guardian of Reality." He adjusted a dial on his gauntlet, and the hum of the accelerator circuits increased to a teeth-rattling howl. "First, though, there is the matter of *finalizing* your removal from office." He raised his hands, palms forward, and pointed them in her direction.

Roma could see the build-up of energy in the gauntlets' projectors. She tried to use her powers to teleport herself to safety, but the strain placed on her body by the removal of one of her alternates kept her from focusing her thoughts.

The light from von Doom's hands flared brightly, and Roma was enveloped in a brilliant green haze that tore into her, disrupting every cell in her body. Another variation of the Guardian fell to the floor.

And for the first time in millennia, Roma screamed.

He sat there in the gathering darkness, suddenly uncertain of what he should do next.

Charles Xavier hadn't moved from his hoverchair for the past ten minutes, his mind continually replaying Magneto's last scathing remark. Was it true? he wondered. Could it really be possible that, in his zeal to carry out his mission, he had crossed some moral boundary—the one that had always separated him from the villainous members of the mutant community?

His reverie was shattered as he suddenly noticed that Magneto was heading for the door.

"Are—are you leaving?" Xavier asked.

"Yes," Lensherr replied brusquely. "I wish to be with my family . . . when the end comes. The Cube is yours, Charles—I have already ordered it to obey your commands. All you need do is take possession of it." He turned to go, then paused. "Farewell, Charles," he said quietly. "I fear that, when next we meet, it shall not be so civil a reunion."

"No," Xavier murmured. "I would imagine not."

Lensherr turned, then, and opened the door to the hallway— and suddenly cried out in pain.

Startled, Xavier leapt to his feet, in time to see Magnus stagger back into the room, clutching weakly at his chest. "Charles..." he gasped hoarsely, and turned to face him.

The hilt of a large, black stone dagger was protruding from Erik's chest.

The hallway door opened wide, and a man entered the drawing room, pushing his way past the dying mutant overlord. He was tall and powerfully built, clad in a slightly baggy, dark-green jumpsuit, and polished, green leather jackboots. To the men and women who had served under his command on a now lifeless moonbase, a quarter of a million miles from their homes and families, he had been known as The Controller. For the past fifty-plus years, though, he had been known by a far more sinister name—one that, even now, was still spoken only in the softest whispers. A name that had been given to him by none other than his cherished mentor, now long deceased—a mentor named Adolf Hitler.

He was the scourge of life itself. A monster who had sacrificed countless lives in the continuing pursuit of his mad dream of re-creating the glorious days of the Third Reich. The first man to not only possess a series of Cosmic Cubes over the years, but to become as one with their incredible energies—and, thus, the universe itself.

He was the devil given form. He was a perpetually-grinning angel of death.

He was the Red Skull.

And he had come for the Cube.

"No..." Xavier whispered.

The Skull crossed the salon, apparently unconcerned by Xavier's presence; either that, or he was so intent on what he was doing that he hadn't even realized the Professor was there. He came to a halt before the Matisse, staring at it with far more interest than one would normally have, even for a work of art.

He *knew*, Xavier realized with growing horror. Somehow, he knew the Cube was behind that painting. And once he possessed it, no one would be safe...

"Charles..."

Xavier turned. Erik was still alive, but it was obvious from the severity of his wound that he did not have much time left. He fumbled at the handle of the blade that had sliced through his costume to pierce his heart, but he was unable to remove it from his chest; his hands were too slick with blood. The Professor hurried to his side.

"*Promise me, Charles,*" Lensherr gasped. "Promise me you'll save her." He gestured toward the Skull. "Don't let that monster do to Anya what his kind did to my parents. *Please,* Charles."

Inwardly, the Professor cursed. Why did the man insist on doing this? There were more important matters involved in this Cube-created insanity than maintaining a small facet of Magneto's fantasy life—the Skull, for instance. If he wasn't stopped before he took possession of the device, *no one* would be safe. But he had to say *something* encouraging to his old friend before he died . . .

"I . . ." Xavier began, then slowly nodded. "All right, Erik."

Lensherr slowly reached up, and gently placed the palm of his hand against his friend's face. He smiled. "I knew I was not wrong about you, Charles. You have always been a good man—a hero. It was something I had aspired to become, a lifetime ago, but it was not meant to be." He patted Xavier's cheek. "Take good care of her, Charles."

"I will," he lied.

"Thank you . . . my friend . . ." Lensherr whispered.

And then he was gone.

On the other side of the room, the Red Skull ignored the death of his rival and concentrated on the matter at hand. His only thought was of obtaining the Cube, of claiming his prize, and now there was no one to stop him from doing so—he had swept his opposition from the chessboard with just his first move.

He swung the painting aside on its hinges—and found himself facing a smooth metal wall the size of a small safe. There was no door, no access panel, no traditional means of entry. A container that could only be opened by someone possessing magnetically-based powers.

"Ingenious," the Skull murmured. "I would not have expected a sub-human like Lensherr to have thought of such security measures." His lipless mouth stretched wide in a hideous approximation of a smile. "Still, opening it is no effort for one who has touched the face of eternity."

He closed his eyes and concentrated, sending out a mental command. Calling the Cube to *him*.

Slowly, the block of metal began to open. A brilliant, white light filled the drawing room.

And then the Cosmic Cube floated out of its prison, and toward the Skull's outstretched hand.

"*No!*" the Professor shouted.

He leapt toward the murderer, and actually succeeded in knocking him away from the Cube; both he and the Skull went staggering around the room, locked in a deadly embrace. But Charles Xavier had spent most of his time as a man of peace, pursuing intellectual solutions to the problems he ordinarily faced. The Red Skull, on the other hand, was a sadistic killer who reveled in the amount of pain he was able to inflict upon his victims.

A gloved fist shot out, catching Xavier across the jaw; it was followed by the sharp stab of an elbow connecting with his left temple. Knocked off-balance, the Professor staggered to the side, missing his target and stumbling into a table. Before he could focus his thoughts, the Skull lashed out with a booted foot, driving the steel toe into the Professor's right knee. The air was split by the sound of bones snapping, and Xavier screamed in agony. A savage chop to his carotid artery cut short his cries, and he crashed to the floor, unconscious, to lie beside the body of his friend.

The Skull, however, wasn't quite done punishing his foolish would-be assailant. He didn't conclude his brutal session for another five minutes.

The Cube, meanwhile, floated quietly in the center of the

room—as though patiently waiting for its next owner to come along. It didn't have long to wait.

Stepping over the bodies of his enemies, the Skull at last claimed his prize. The Cube's light grew brighter, as though responding to his touch—and welcoming it. And as he held the ultimate power in the omniverse, his eyes sparkling with the flames of madness, a quotation crept into the Skull's mind—a passage from a short story composed by an American writer named Edgar Allan Poe that seemed darkly appropriate for the occasion:

" 'And now was acknowledged the presence of the Red Death,' " he said, his death's-head grin growing wider still. " 'And one by one dropped the revelers in the blood-bedewed halls of their revel, and died each in the despairing posture of his fall. And the life of the ebony clock went out with that of the last of the gay. And the flames of the tripods expired. And Darkness and Decay and the Red Death held illimitable dominion over all ...' "

And, once more, the world was filled with a terrible, harsh light. . . .

TO BE CONCLUDED